INTO THE VOLCANO

A GRAPHIC NOVEL
BY CALDECOTT HONOR ARTIST

Don Wood

SCHOLASTIC INC.

New York Toronto London Auckland
Sydney Mexico City New Delhi Hong Kong

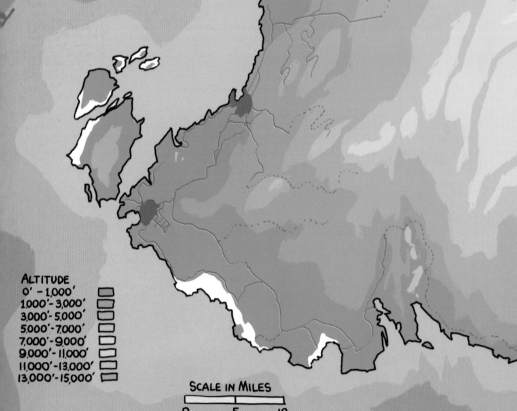

THE ISLAND NATION OF KOCALAHA

THE ISLAND OF KOCALAHA

"YOUNG" UNDERWATER VOLCANO POPIYA

ALTITUDE
0' – 1,000'
1,000' – 3,000'
3,000' – 5,000'
5,000' – 7,000'
7,000' – 9,000'
9,000' – 11,000'
11,000' – 13,000'
13,000' – 15,000'

SCALE IN MILES
0   5   10

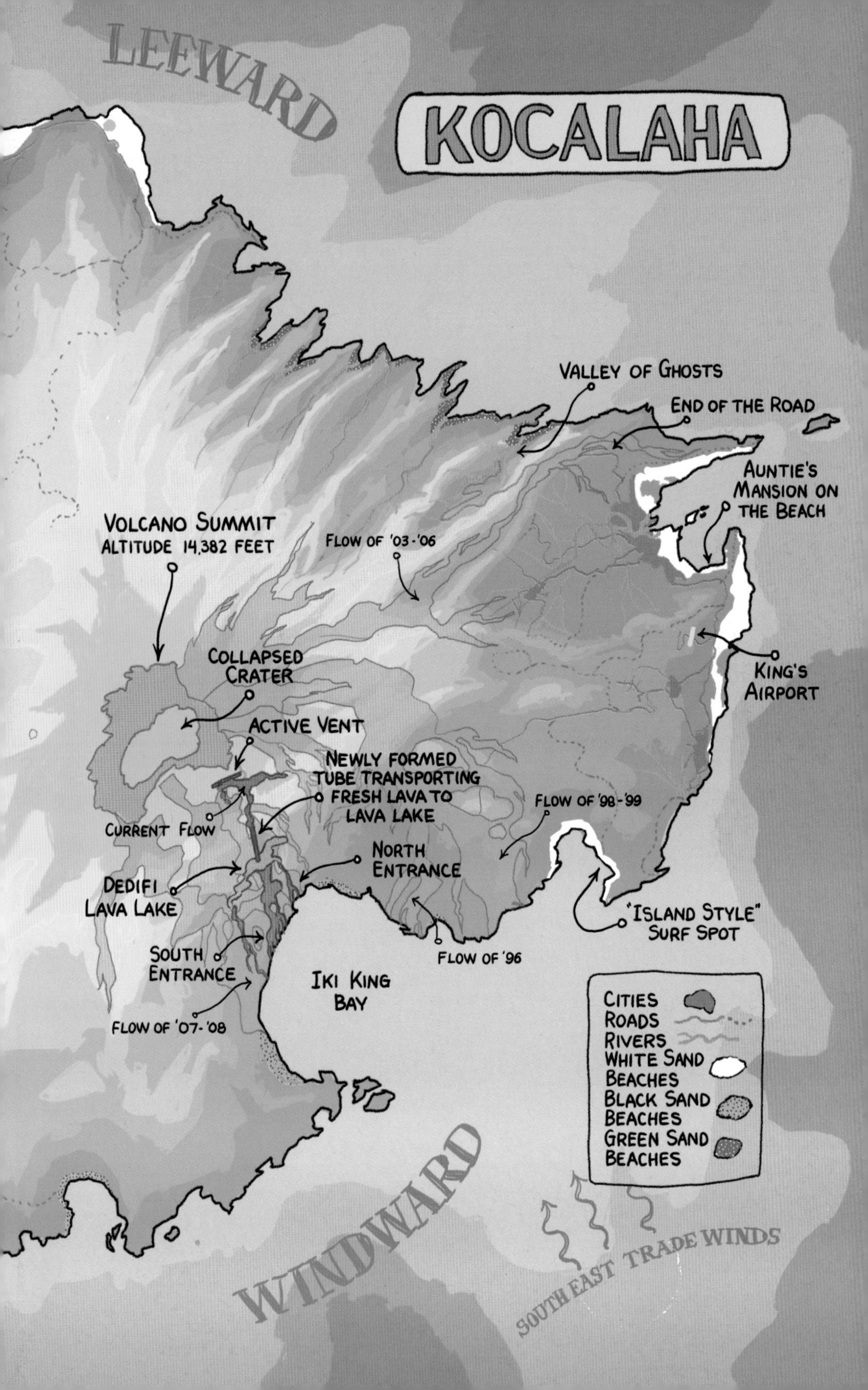
LEEWARD
KOCALAHA
VALLEY OF GHOSTS
END OF THE ROAD
AUNTIE'S MANSION ON THE BEACH
VOLCANO SUMMIT
ALTITUDE 14,382 FEET
FLOW OF '03-'06
KING'S AIRPORT
COLLAPSED CRATER
ACTIVE VENT
NEWLY FORMED TUBE TRANSPORTING FRESH LAVA TO LAVA LAKE
FLOW OF '98-'99
CURRENT FLOW
NORTH ENTRANCE
DEDIFI LAVA LAKE
"ISLAND STYLE" SURF SPOT
FLOW OF '96
SOUTH ENTRANCE
IKI KING BAY
FLOW OF '07-'08
CITIES
ROADS
RIVERS
WHITE SAND BEACHES
BLACK SAND BEACHES
GREEN SAND BEACHES
WINDWARD
SOUTH EAST TRADE WINDS

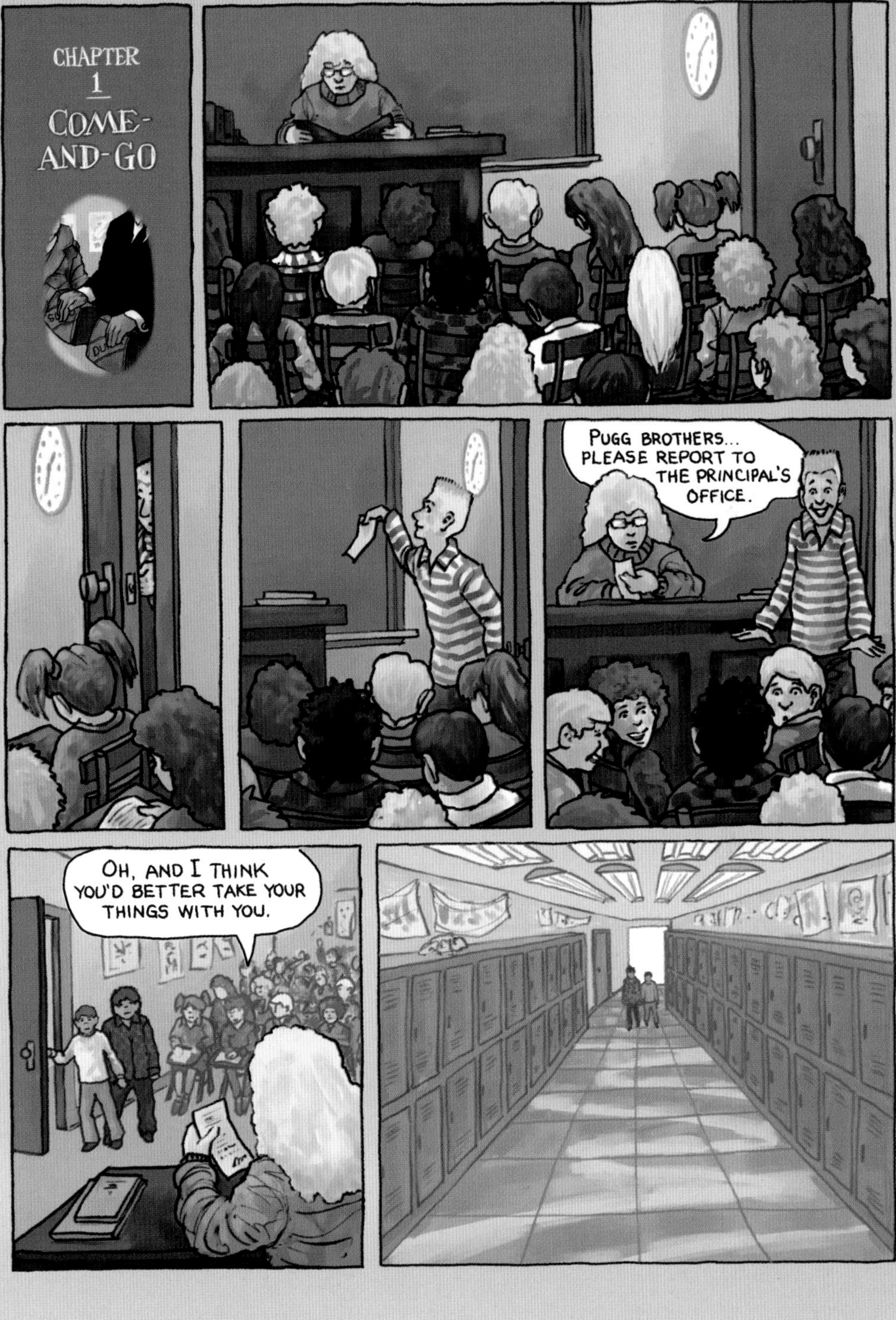
CHAPTER
1
COME-AND-GO
PUGG BROTHERS... PLEASE REPORT TO THE PRINCIPAL'S OFFICE.
OH, AND I THINK YOU'D BETTER TAKE YOUR THINGS WITH YOU.

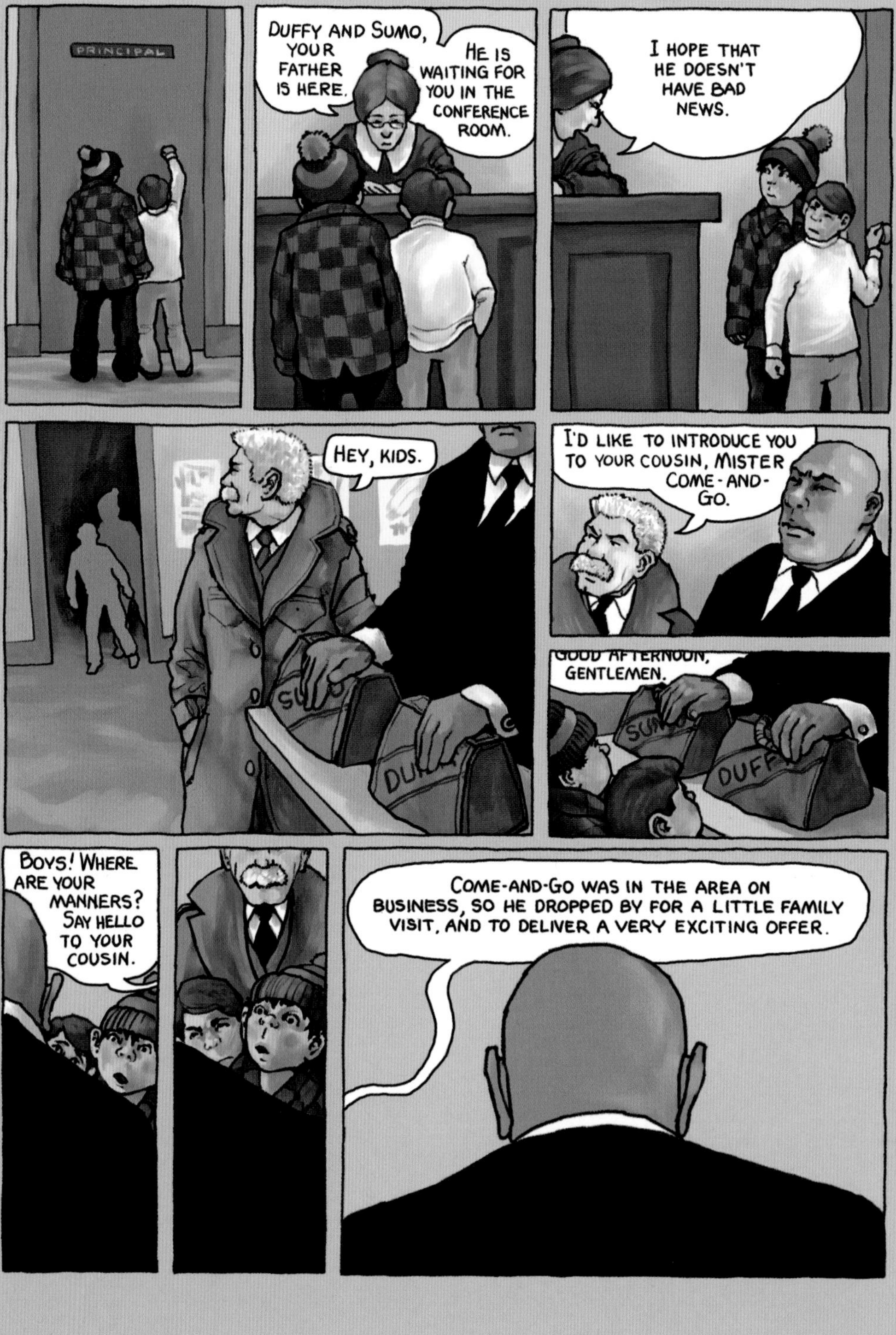
PRINCIPAL
DUFFY AND SUMO, YOUR FATHER IS HERE.
HE IS WAITING FOR YOU IN THE CONFERENCE ROOM.
I HOPE THAT HE DOESN'T HAVE BAD NEWS.
HEY, KIDS.
I'D LIKE TO INTRODUCE YOU TO YOUR COUSIN, MISTER COME-AND-GO.
GOOD AFTERNOON, GENTLEMEN.
BOYS! WHERE ARE YOUR MANNERS? SAY HELLO TO YOUR COUSIN.
COME-AND-GO WAS IN THE AREA ON BUSINESS, SO HE DROPPED BY FOR A LITTLE FAMILY VISIT, AND TO DELIVER A VERY EXCITING OFFER.

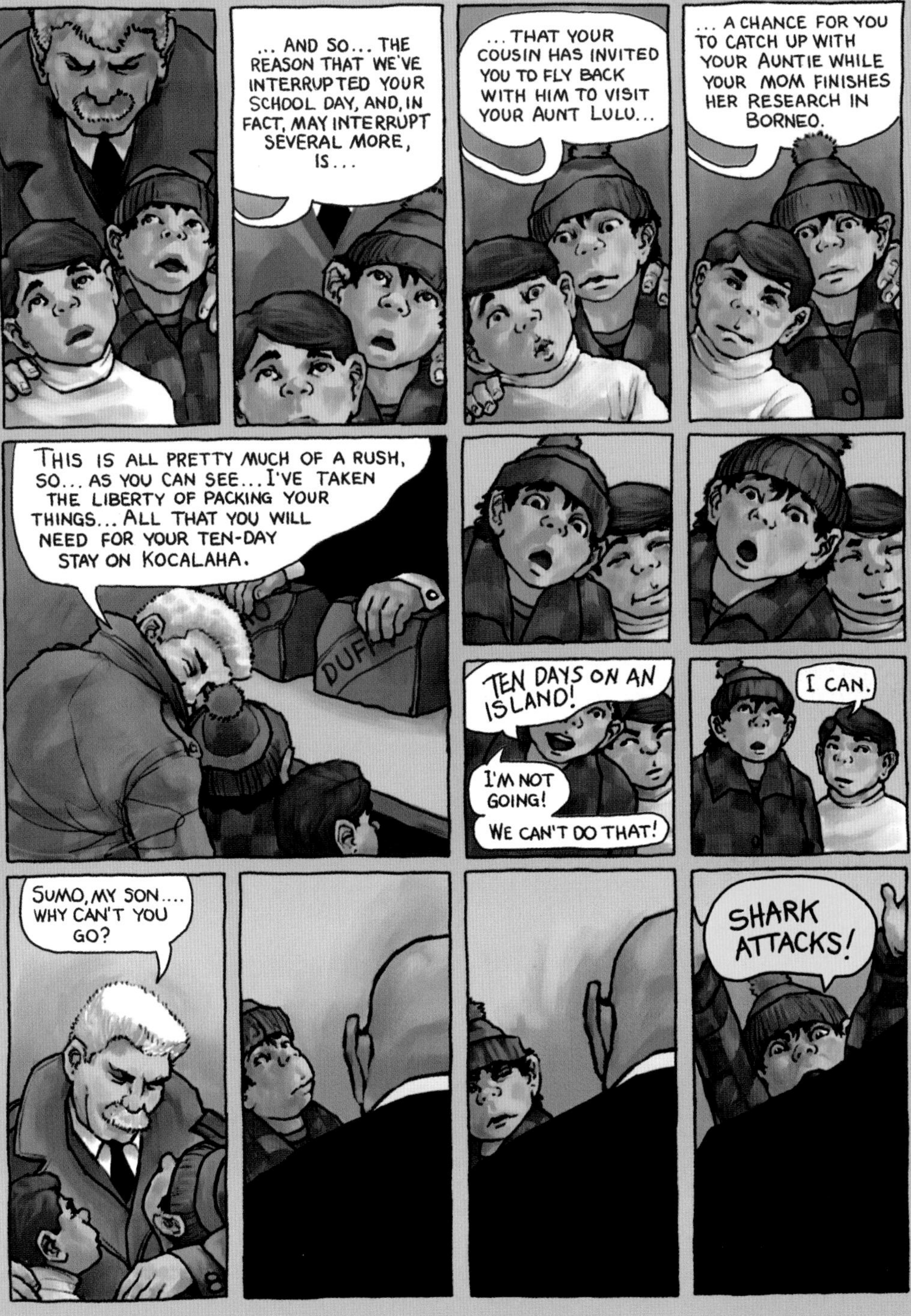
... AND SO... THE REASON THAT WE'VE INTERRUPTED YOUR SCHOOL DAY, AND, IN FACT, MAY INTERRUPT SEVERAL MORE, IS...
...THAT YOUR COUSIN HAS INVITED YOU TO FLY BACK WITH HIM TO VISIT YOUR AUNT LULU...
... A CHANCE FOR YOU TO CATCH UP WITH YOUR AUNTIE WHILE YOUR MOM FINISHES HER RESEARCH IN BORNEO.
THIS IS ALL PRETTY MUCH OF A RUSH, SO... AS YOU CAN SEE... I'VE TAKEN THE LIBERTY OF PACKING YOUR THINGS... ALL THAT YOU WILL NEED FOR YOUR TEN-DAY STAY ON KOCALAHA.
TEN DAYS ON AN ISLAND!
I'M NOT GOING!
WE CAN'T DO THAT!
I CAN.
SUMO, MY SON.... WHY CAN'T YOU GO?
SHARK ATTACKS!

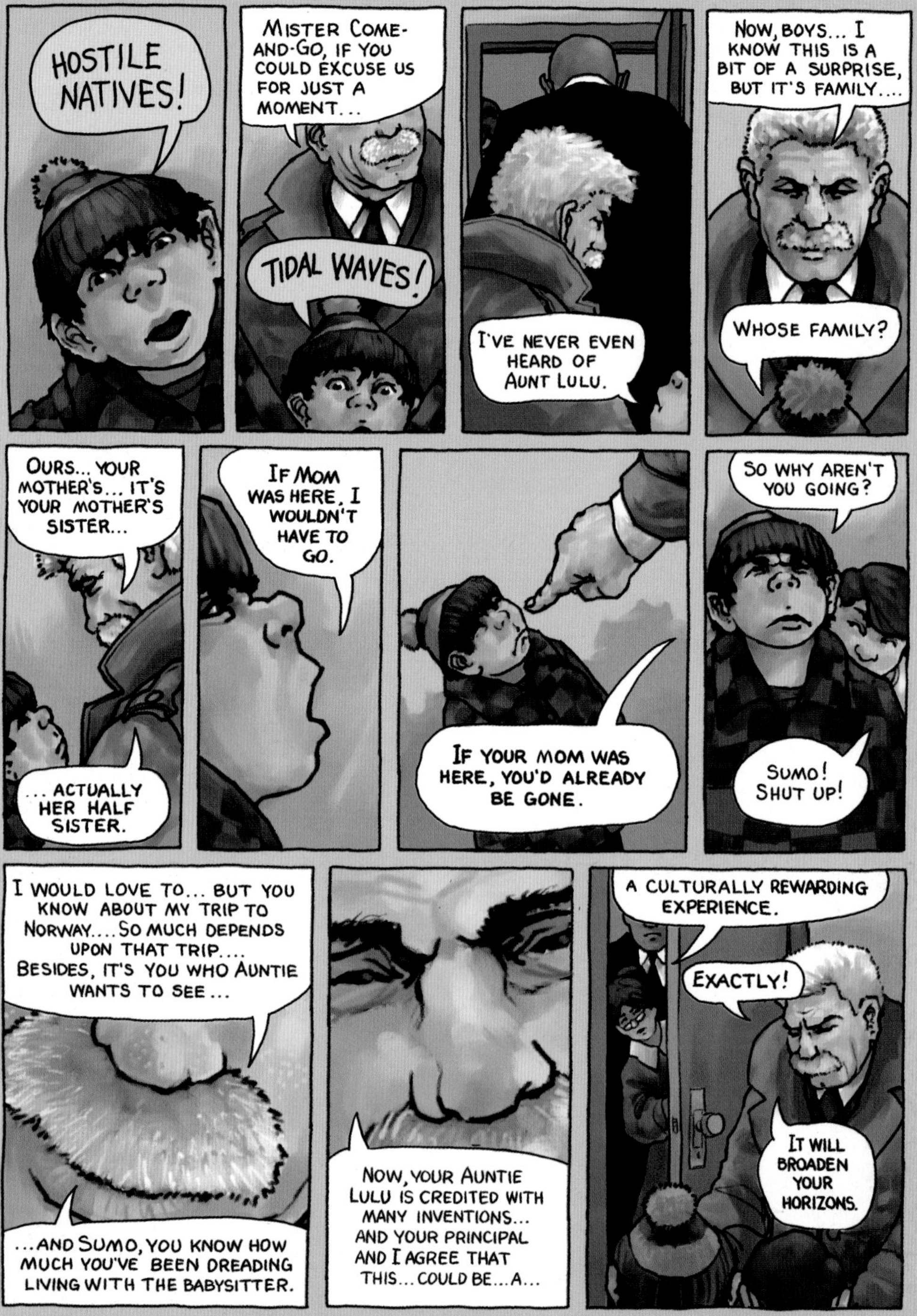
HOSTILE NATIVES!
MISTER COME-AND-GO, IF YOU COULD EXCUSE US FOR JUST A MOMENT...
TIDAL WAVES!
I'VE NEVER EVEN HEARD OF AUNT LULU.
NOW, BOYS... I KNOW THIS IS A BIT OF A SURPRISE, BUT IT'S FAMILY....
WHOSE FAMILY?
OURS... YOUR MOTHER'S... IT'S YOUR MOTHER'S SISTER...
... ACTUALLY HER HALF SISTER.
IF MOM WAS HERE, I WOULDN'T HAVE TO GO.
IF YOUR MOM WAS HERE, YOU'D ALREADY BE GONE.
SO WHY AREN'T YOU GOING?
SUMO! SHUT UP!
I WOULD LOVE TO... BUT YOU KNOW ABOUT MY TRIP TO NORWAY.... SO MUCH DEPENDS UPON THAT TRIP.... BESIDES, IT'S YOU WHO AUNTIE WANTS TO SEE...
...AND SUMO, YOU KNOW HOW MUCH YOU'VE BEEN DREADING LIVING WITH THE BABYSITTER.
NOW, YOUR AUNTIE LULU IS CREDITED WITH MANY INVENTIONS... AND YOUR PRINCIPAL AND I AGREE THAT THIS... COULD BE... A...
A CULTURALLY REWARDING EXPERIENCE.
EXACTLY!
IT WILL BROADEN YOUR HORIZONS.

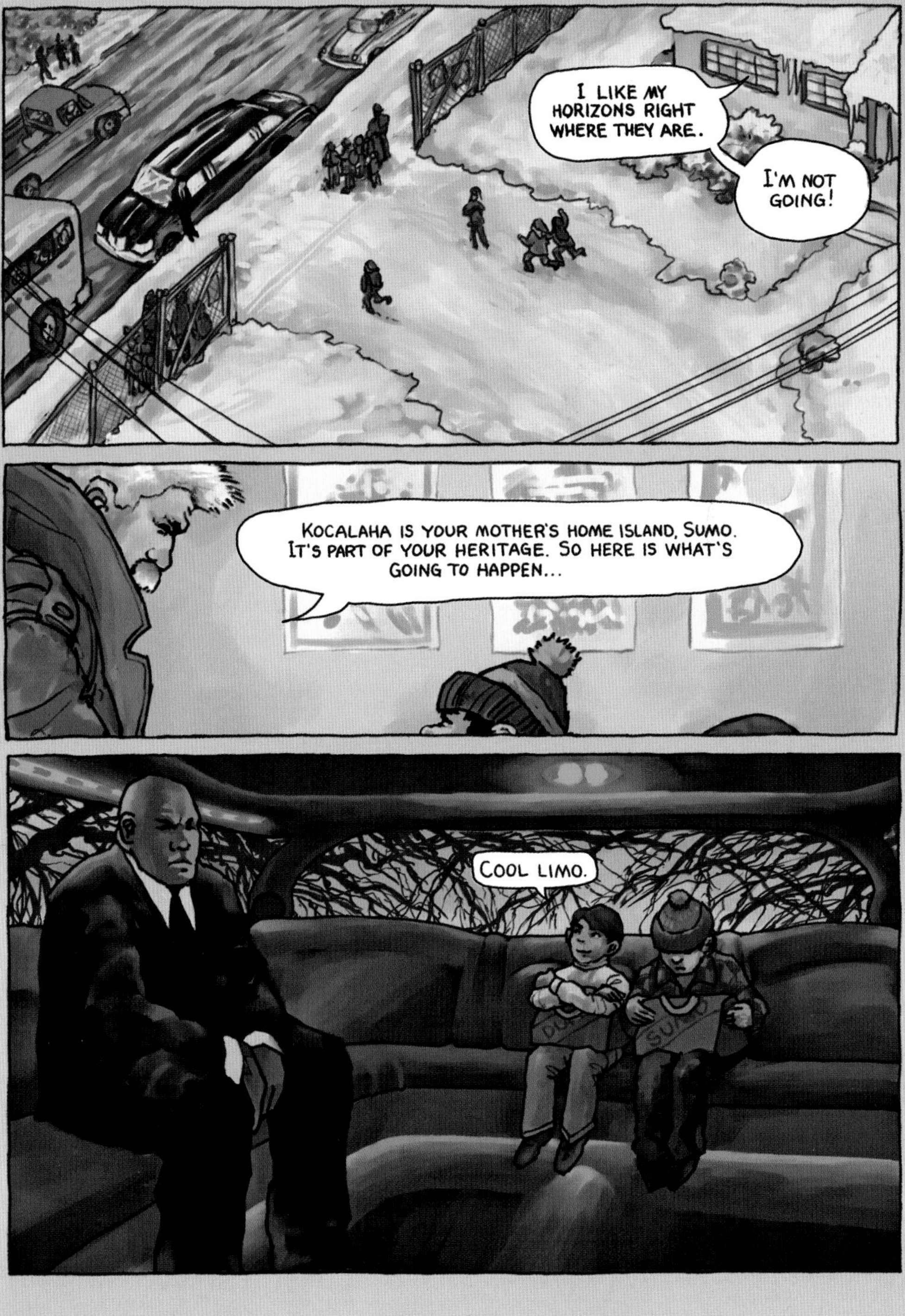
I LIKE MY HORIZONS RIGHT WHERE THEY ARE.
I'M NOT GOING!
KOCALAHA IS YOUR MOTHER'S HOME ISLAND, SUMO. IT'S PART OF YOUR HERITAGE. SO HERE IS WHAT'S GOING TO HAPPEN...
COOL LIMO.

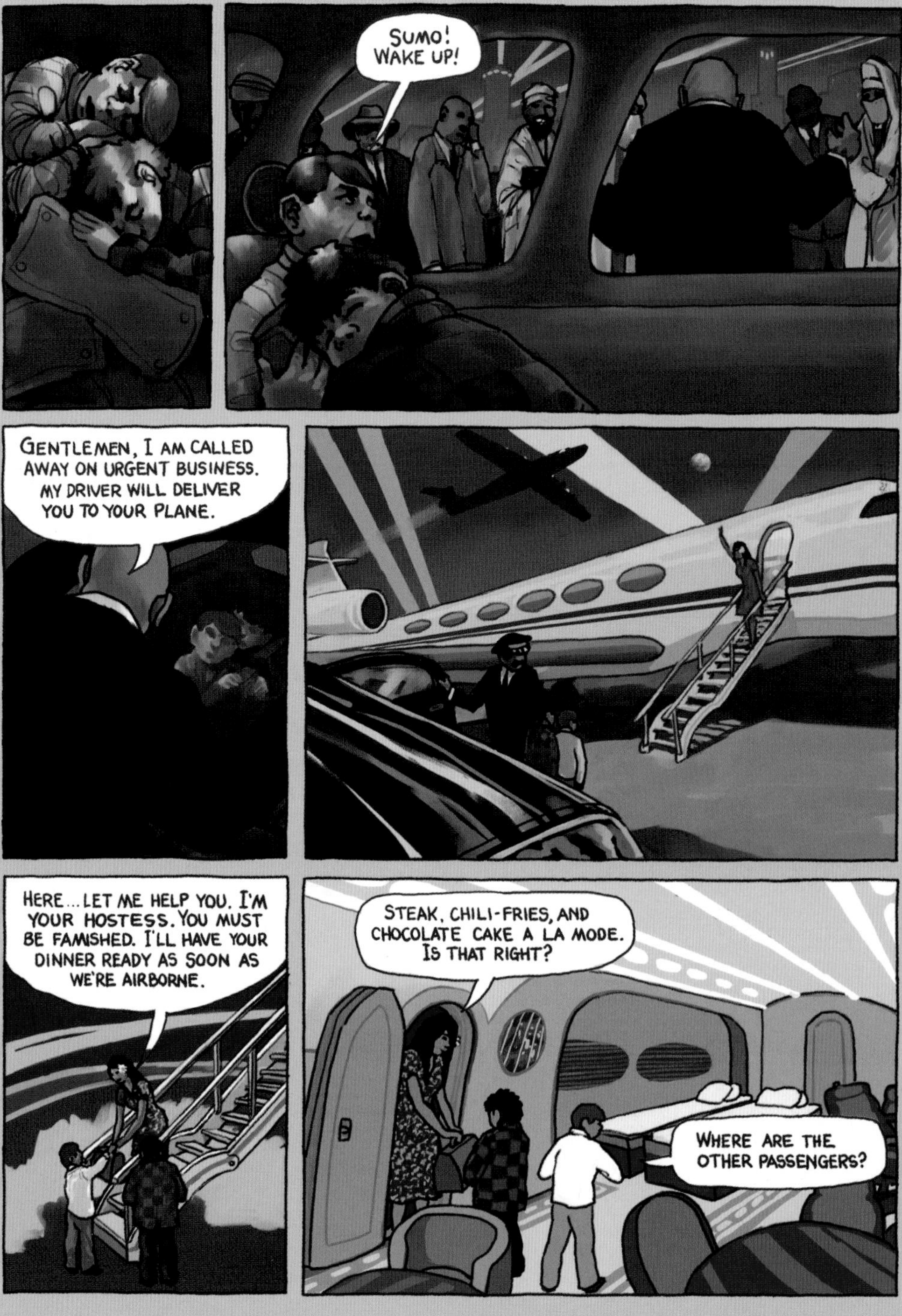
SUMO! WAKE UP!
GENTLEMEN, I AM CALLED AWAY ON URGENT BUSINESS. MY DRIVER WILL DELIVER YOU TO YOUR PLANE.
HERE... LET ME HELP YOU. I'M YOUR HOSTESS. YOU MUST BE FAMISHED. I'LL HAVE YOUR DINNER READY AS SOON AS WE'RE AIRBORNE.
STEAK, CHILI-FRIES, AND CHOCOLATE CAKE A LA MODE. IS THAT RIGHT?
WHERE ARE THE OTHER PASSENGERS?

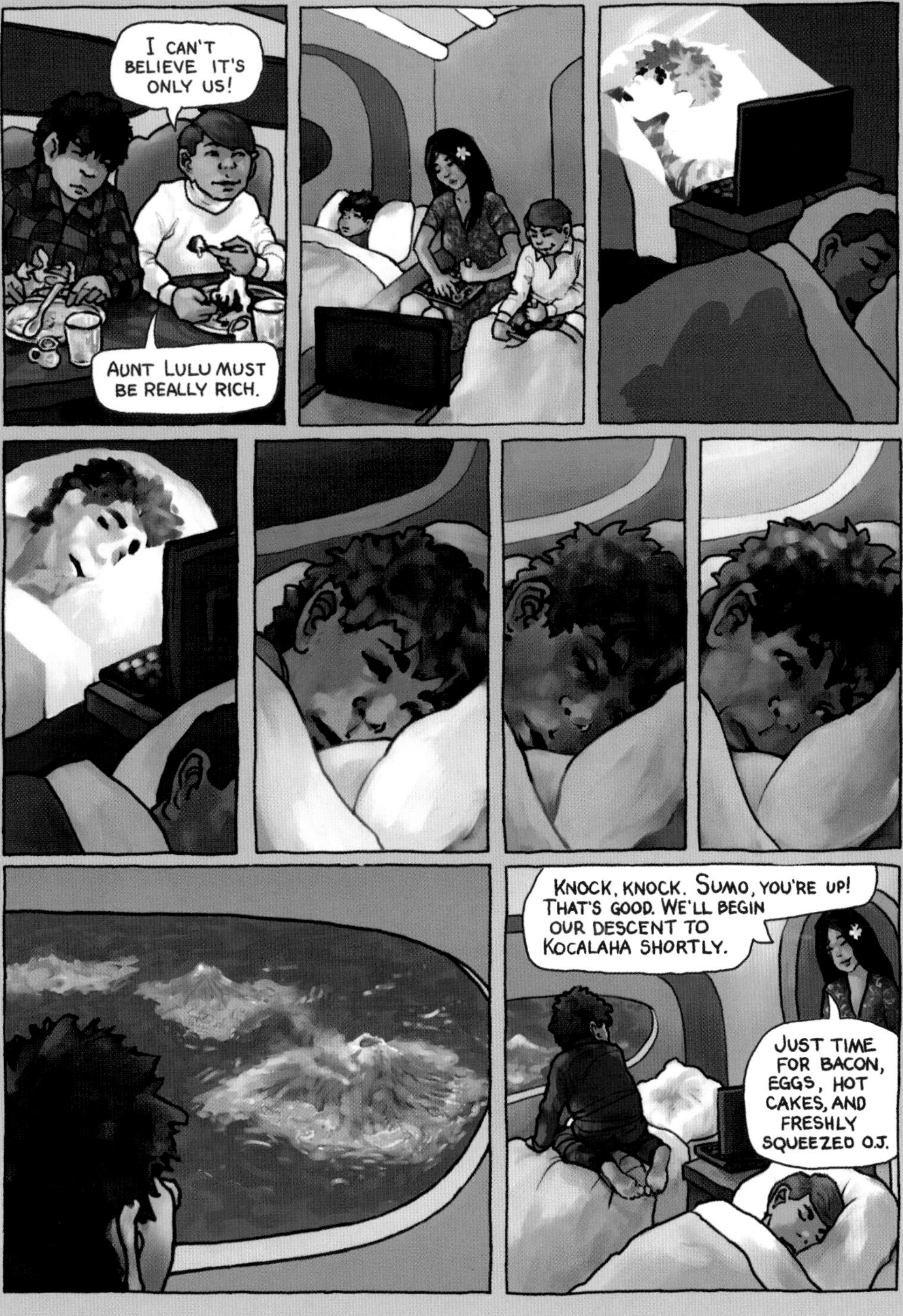
I CAN'T BELIEVE IT'S ONLY US!
AUNT LULU MUST BE REALLY RICH.
KNOCK, KNOCK. SUMO, YOU'RE UP! THAT'S GOOD. WE'LL BEGIN OUR DESCENT TO KOCALAHA SHORTLY.
JUST TIME FOR BACON, EGGS, HOT CAKES, AND FRESHLY SQUEEZED O.J.

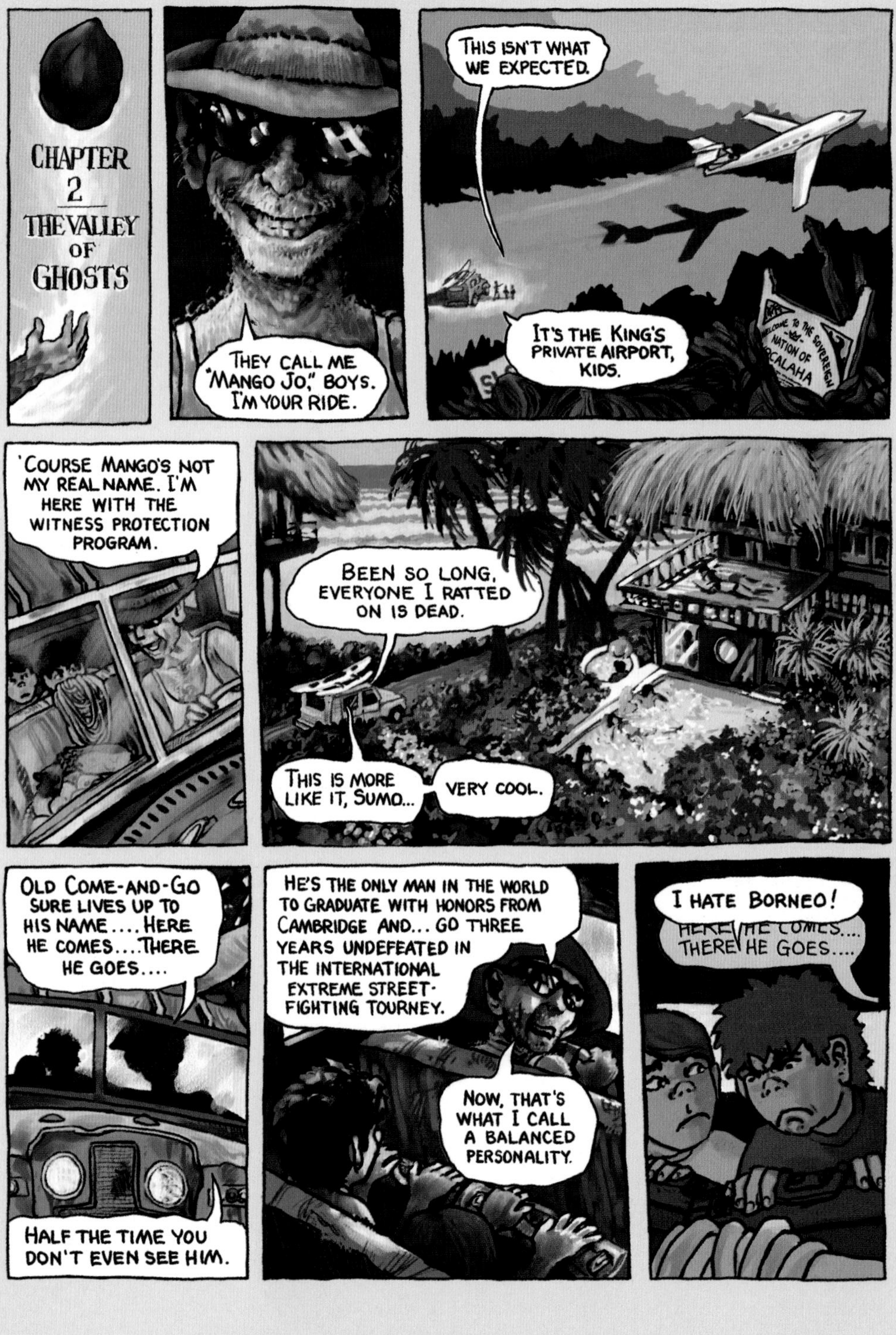
CHAPTER 2
THE VALLEY OF GHOSTS
THEY CALL ME "MANGO JO," BOYS. I'M YOUR RIDE.
THIS ISN'T WHAT WE EXPECTED.
IT'S THE KING'S PRIVATE AIRPORT, KIDS.
'COURSE MANGO'S NOT MY REAL NAME. I'M HERE WITH THE WITNESS PROTECTION PROGRAM.
BEEN SO LONG, EVERYONE I RATTED ON IS DEAD.
THIS IS MORE LIKE IT, SUMO...
VERY COOL.
OLD COME-AND-GO SURE LIVES UP TO HIS NAME.... HERE HE COMES.... THERE HE GOES....
HALF THE TIME YOU DON'T EVEN SEE HIM.
HE'S THE ONLY MAN IN THE WORLD TO GRADUATE WITH HONORS FROM CAMBRIDGE AND... GO THREE YEARS UNDEFEATED IN THE INTERNATIONAL EXTREME STREET-FIGHTING TOURNEY.
NOW, THAT'S WHAT I CALL A BALANCED PERSONALITY.
I HATE BORNEO!
HERE HE COMES.... THERE HE GOES....

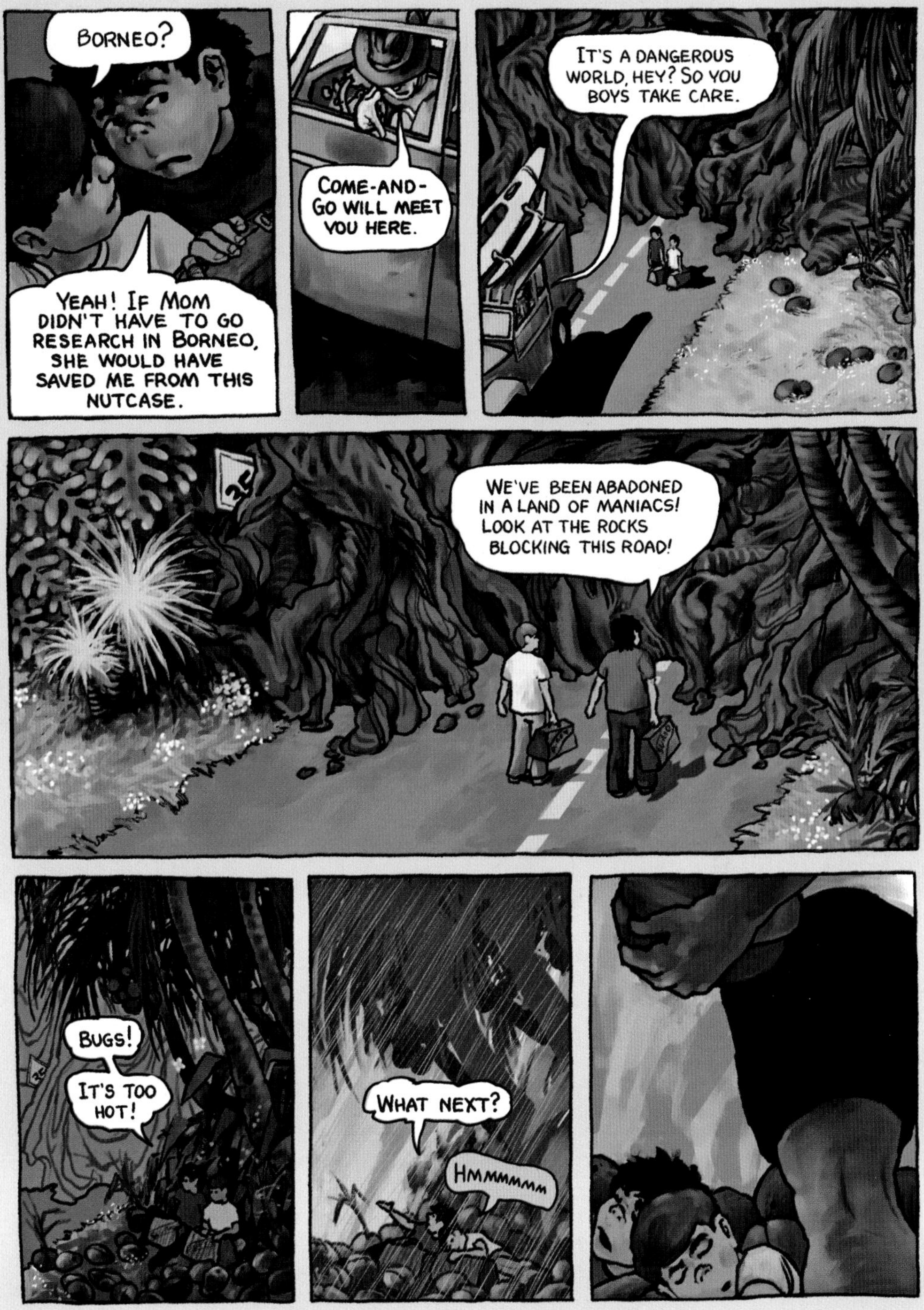
BORNEO?
YEAH! IF MOM DIDN'T HAVE TO GO RESEARCH IN BORNEO, SHE WOULD HAVE SAVED ME FROM THIS NUTCASE.
COME-AND-GO WILL MEET YOU HERE.
IT'S A DANGEROUS WORLD, HEY? SO YOU BOYS TAKE CARE.
WE'VE BEEN ABADONED IN A LAND OF MANIACS! LOOK AT THE ROCKS BLOCKING THIS ROAD!
BUGS!
IT'S TOO HOT!
WHAT NEXT?
HMMMMMM

CLONK
DO YOU GENTLEMEN WANT TO DIE ON THE FIRST DAY OF YOUR VISIT?
NEVER FALL ASLEEP UNDER A PALM LOADED WITH RIPE COCO-NUTS.
I WAS UNAVOIDABLY DETAINED. MY APOLOGIES FOR THE DELAY.

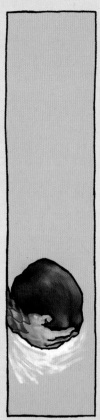

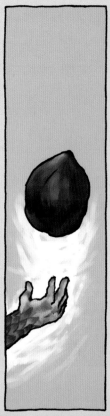

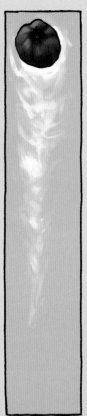

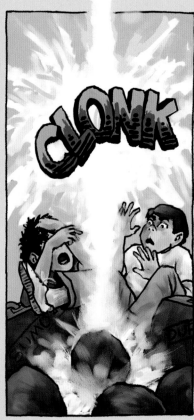

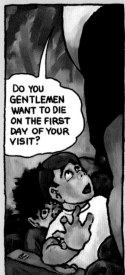

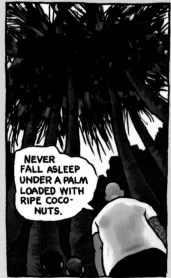

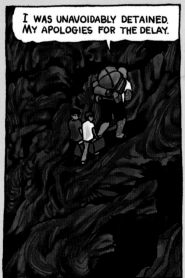

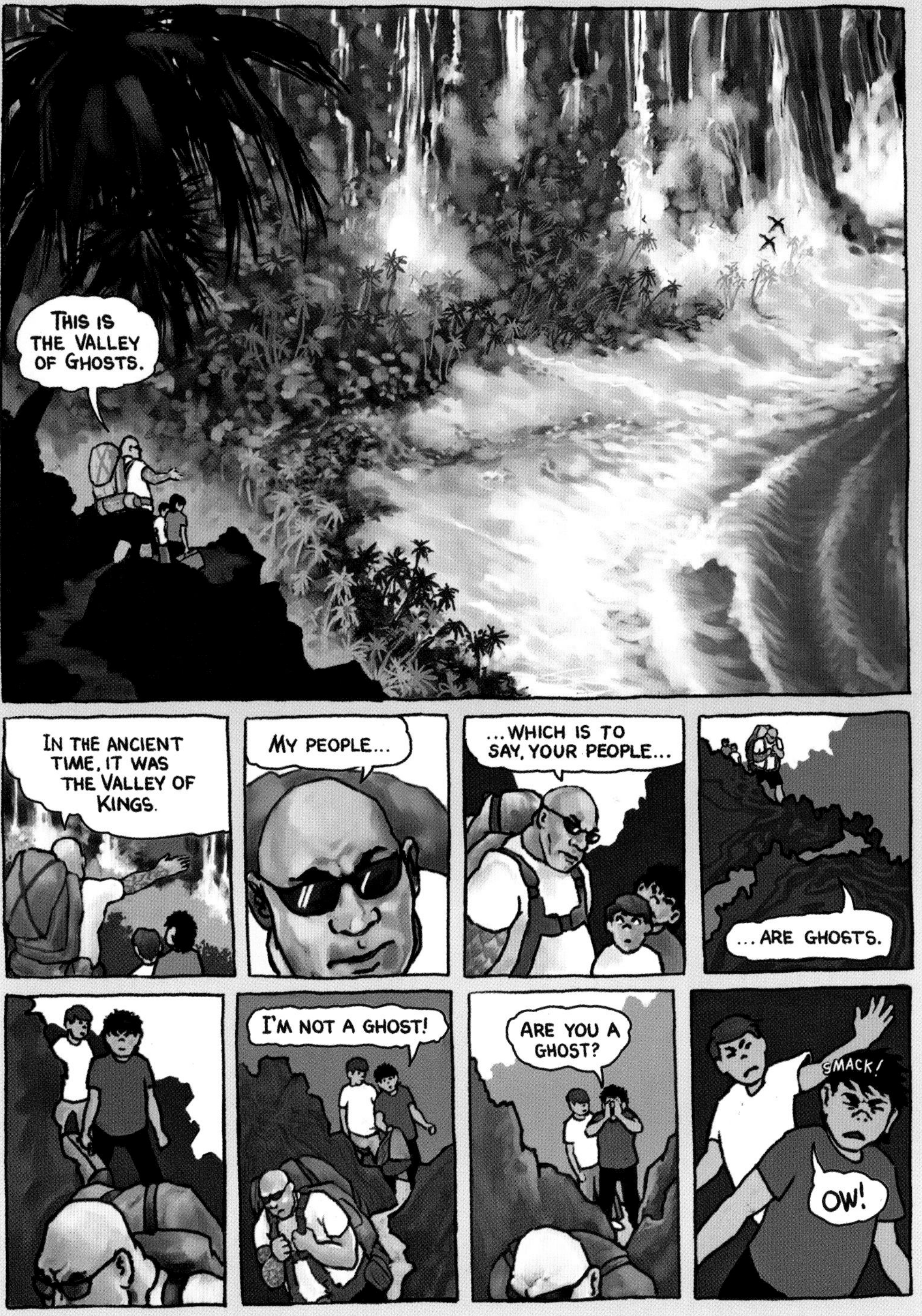
THIS IS THE VALLEY OF GHOSTS.
IN THE ANCIENT TIME, IT WAS THE VALLEY OF KINGS.
MY PEOPLE...
...WHICH IS TO SAY, YOUR PEOPLE...
...ARE GHOSTS.
I'M NOT A GHOST!
ARE YOU A GHOST?
SMACK!
OW!

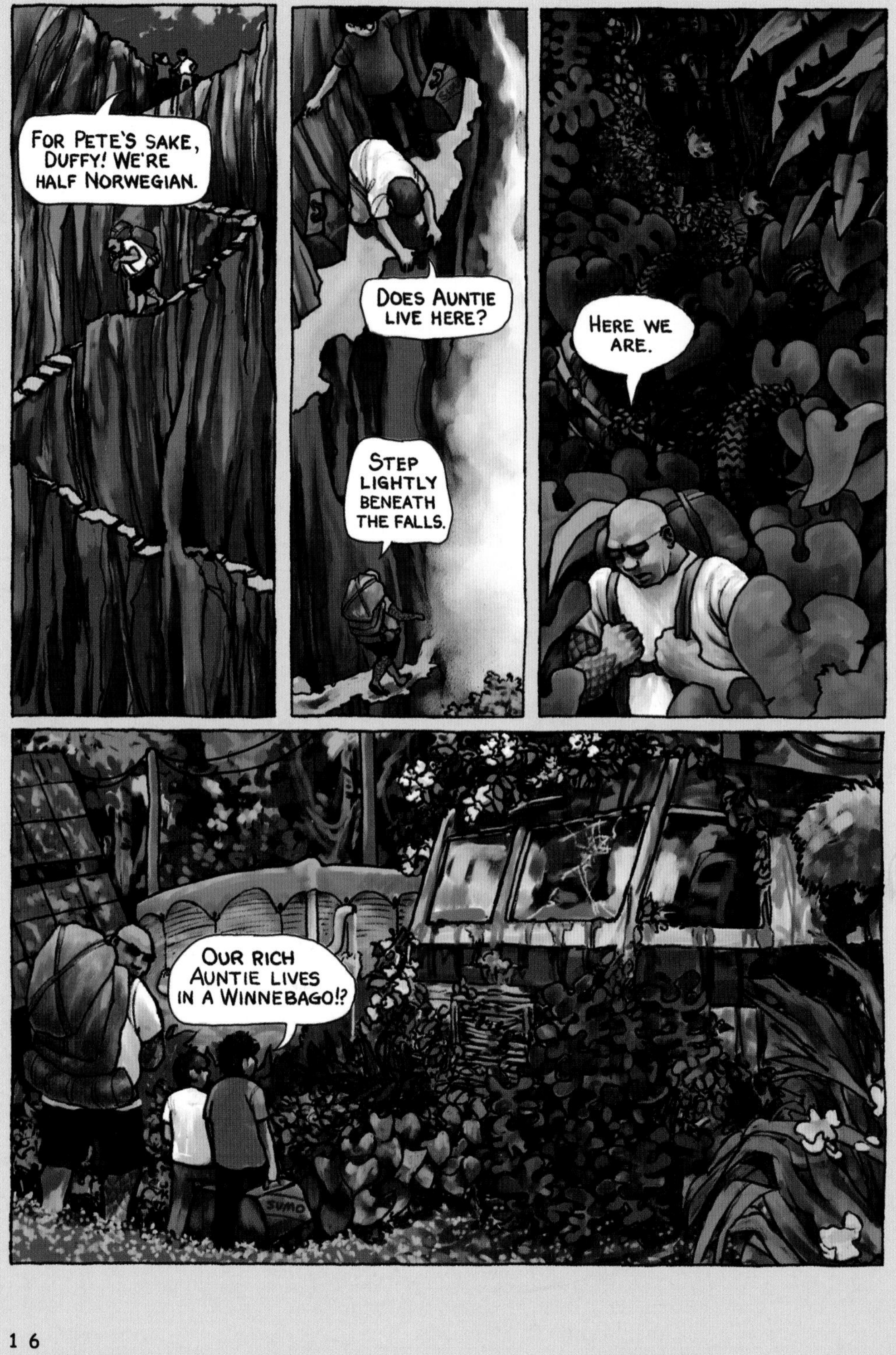
FOR PETE'S SAKE, DUFFY! WE'RE HALF NORWEGIAN.
DOES AUNTIE LIVE HERE?
STEP LIGHTLY BENEATH THE FALLS.
HERE WE ARE.
OUR RICH AUNTIE LIVES IN A WINNEBAGO!?
SUMO

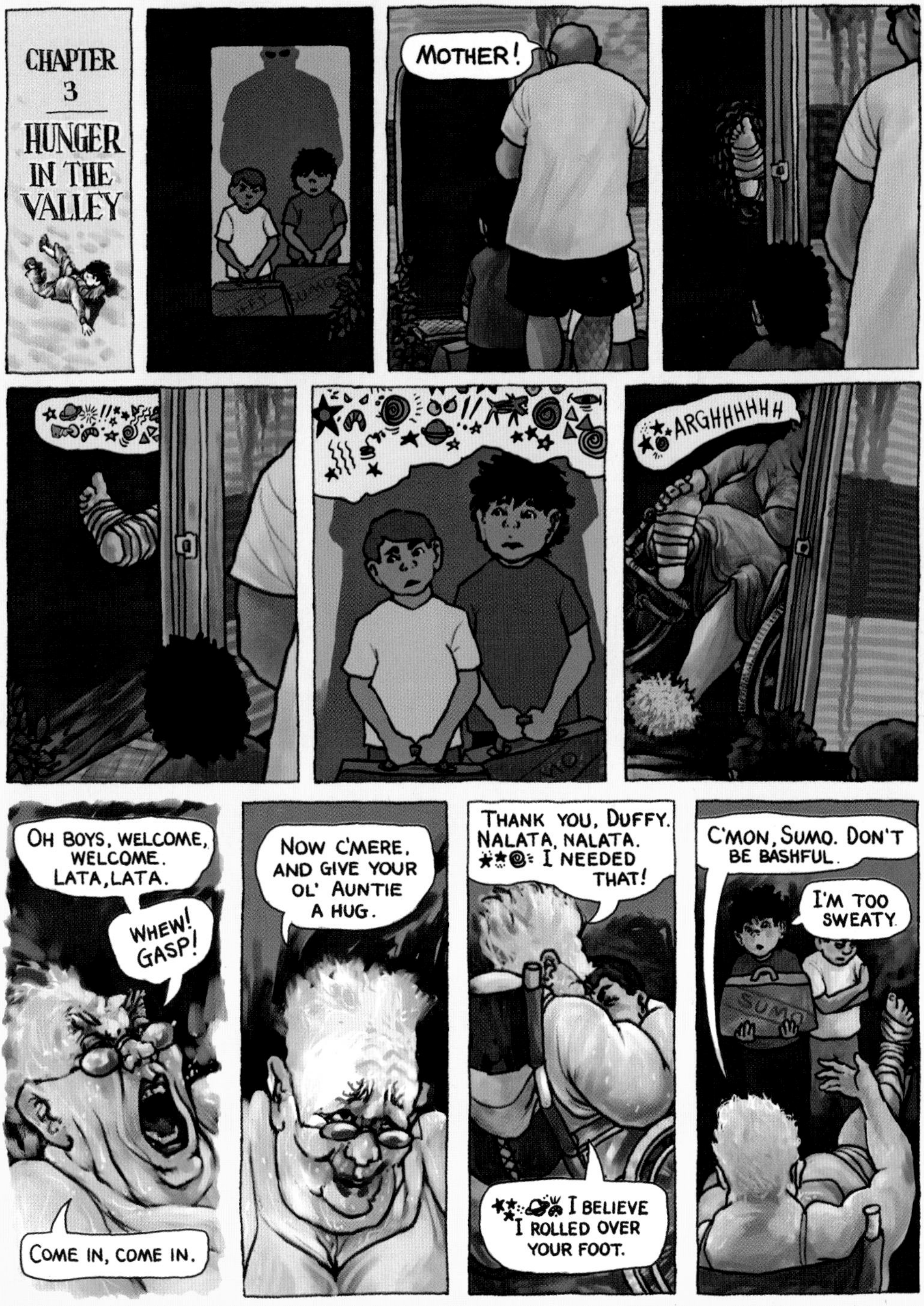
CHAPTER 3
HUNGER IN THE VALLEY
DUFFY
SUMO
MOTHER!
ARGHHHHHH
OH BOYS, WELCOME, WELCOME. LATA, LATA.
WHEW! GASP!
COME IN, COME IN.
NOW C'MERE, AND GIVE YOUR OL' AUNTIE A HUG.
THANK YOU, DUFFY. NALATA, NALATA. I NEEDED THAT!
I BELIEVE I ROLLED OVER YOUR FOOT.
C'MON, SUMO. DON'T BE BASHFUL.
I'M TOO SWEATY.
SUMO

AHAH! YOU COULDN'T BE ANY SWEATIER THAN ME! C'MON!

OK. I'LL TAKE A RAIN CHECK ON THAT HUG...

...BUT I ALWAYS CASH MY CHECKS.

NOW, WE'RE GOING TO MAKE SURE THAT YOU BOYS ARE VERY COMFORT-ABLE HERE, AND I'M SURE YOU'LL HA... YOU DA... TH... I... TO...

AND THANK YOU FOR ANSWERING THE REQUEST OF YOUR LONG-LOST AUNTIE. THE LOVE OF F... LY IS SO IMPO... A ESPECIALI... OU NOW W... WORLD CRAZY SOLID UNITY... ...EV... ...HT OF ...NT LL ...TY ...RE TRUE, ALL W... HAVE ARE EACH OTHER

AND SOOO... WHEN YOU FIND YOURSELF IN A SITUATION LIKE MINE IT CLARIFIES YOUR PRIORI...

...EEIIOOH

CLOSE THAT DOOR, MY SON... AND IF YOU EVER LET THE BREEZE BLOW ON MY FOOT AGAIN, I'LL...I'LL...

NOW, WE ALL KNOW WHO'S TO BLAME FOR THAT FOOT....

I WARNED YOU JUST LAST WEEK....

SORRY IF I STARTLED YOU BOYS. IT SEEMS THAT I'VE GOT A SLIGHT CASE OF THE GOUT.

COUGH! COUGH!

I'M SO WEAK. COME-AND-GO WILL SHOW YOU TO YOUR ROOMS....WE WILL TALK MORE TOMORROW.

THIS HAS GOT TO BE THE COOLEST TREE HOUSE IN THE WORLD.

DUFFY! THIS IS TOO WEIRD!

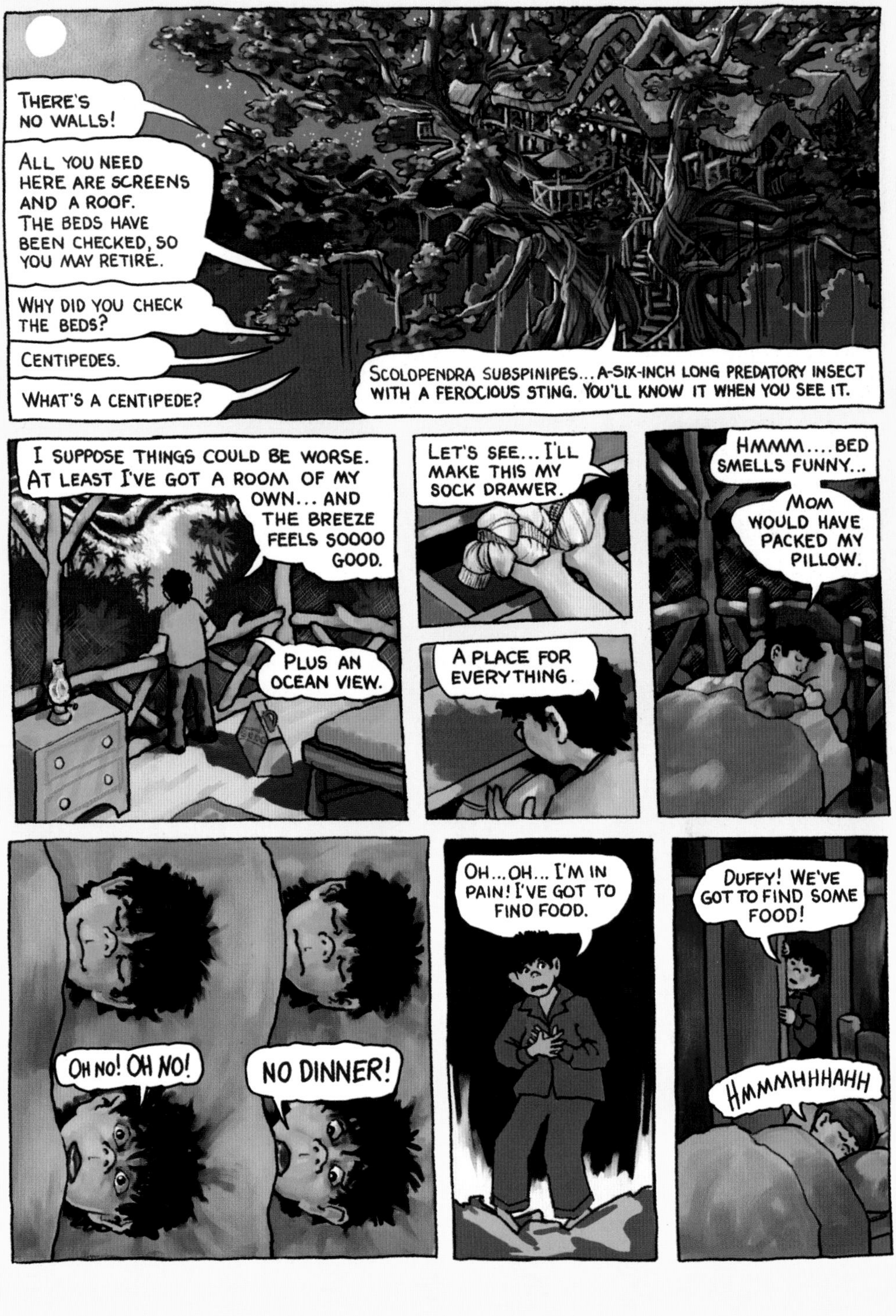
THERE'S NO WALLS!
ALL YOU NEED HERE ARE SCREENS AND A ROOF. THE BEDS HAVE BEEN CHECKED, SO YOU MAY RETIRE.
WHY DID YOU CHECK THE BEDS?
CENTIPEDES.
WHAT'S A CENTIPEDE?
SCOLOPENDRA SUBSPINIPES... A-SIX-INCH LONG PREDATORY INSECT WITH A FEROCIOUS STING. YOU'LL KNOW IT WHEN YOU SEE IT.
I SUPPOSE THINGS COULD BE WORSE. AT LEAST I'VE GOT A ROOM OF MY OWN... AND THE BREEZE FEELS SOOOO GOOD.
PLUS AN OCEAN VIEW.
LET'S SEE... I'LL MAKE THIS MY SOCK DRAWER.
A PLACE FOR EVERYTHING.
HMMM.... BED SMELLS FUNNY...
MOM WOULD HAVE PACKED MY PILLOW.
OH NO! OH NO!
NO DINNER!
OH... OH... I'M IN PAIN! I'VE GOT TO FIND FOOD.
DUFFY! WE'VE GOT TO FIND SOME FOOD!
HMMMHHHAHH

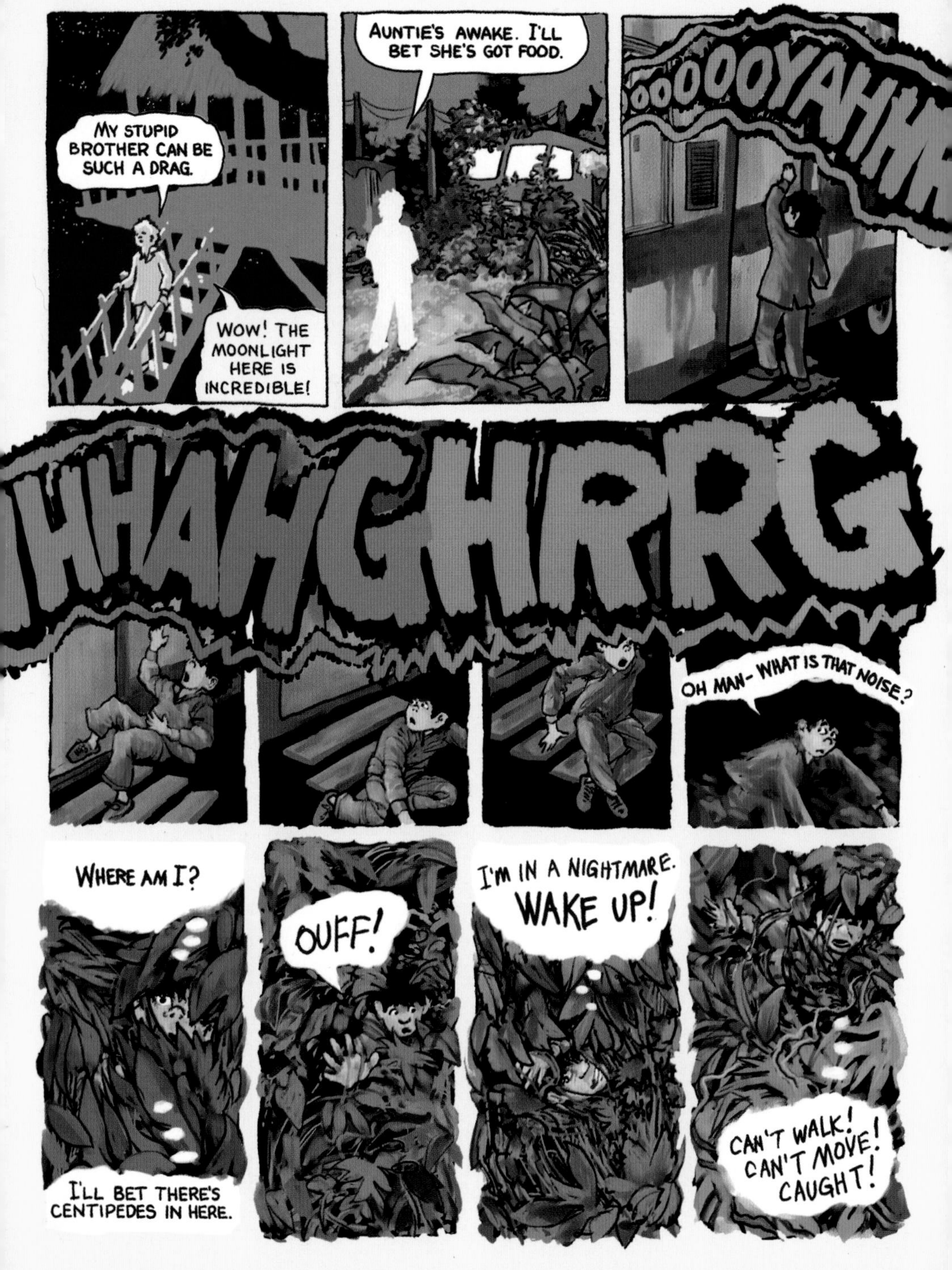
MY STUPID BROTHER CAN BE SUCH A DRAG.
WOW! THE MOONLIGHT HERE IS INCREDIBLE!
AUNTIE'S AWAKE. I'LL BET SHE'S GOT FOOD.
OOOOOOYAHH
HHAHGHRRG
OH MAN- WHAT IS THAT NOISE?
WHERE AM I?
I'LL BET THERE'S CENTIPEDES IN HERE.
OUFF!
I'M IN A NIGHTMARE.
WAKE UP!
CAN'T WALK! CAN'T MOVE! CAUGHT!

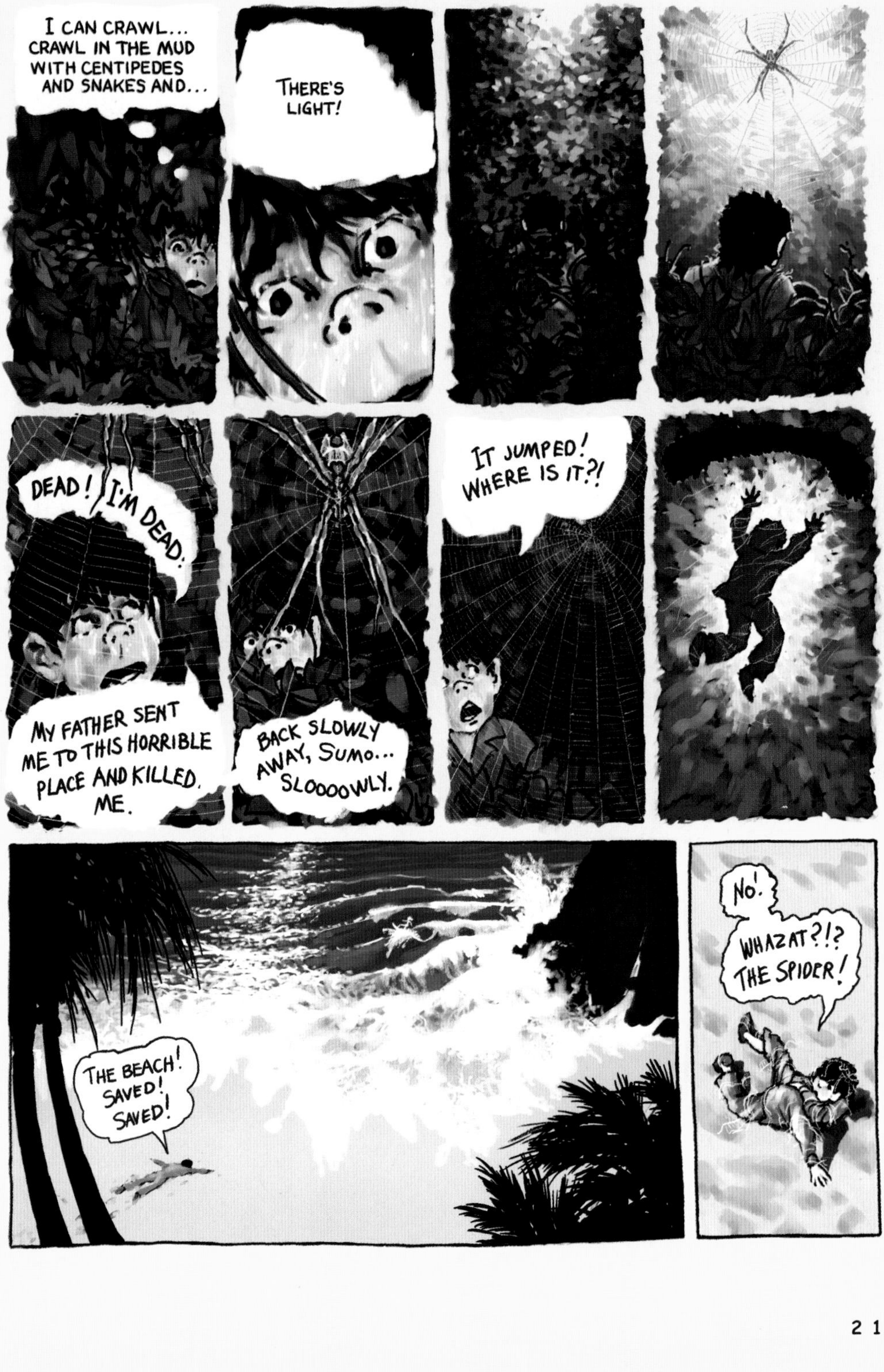
I CAN CRAWL... CRAWL IN THE MUD WITH CENTIPEDES AND SNAKES AND...
THERE'S LIGHT!
DEAD! I'M DEAD!
MY FATHER SENT ME TO THIS HORRIBLE PLACE AND KILLED ME.
BACK SLOWLY AWAY, SUMO... SLOOOOWLY.
IT JUMPED! WHERE IS IT?!
THE BEACH! SAVED! SAVED!
No!
WHAZAT?!? THE SPIDER!

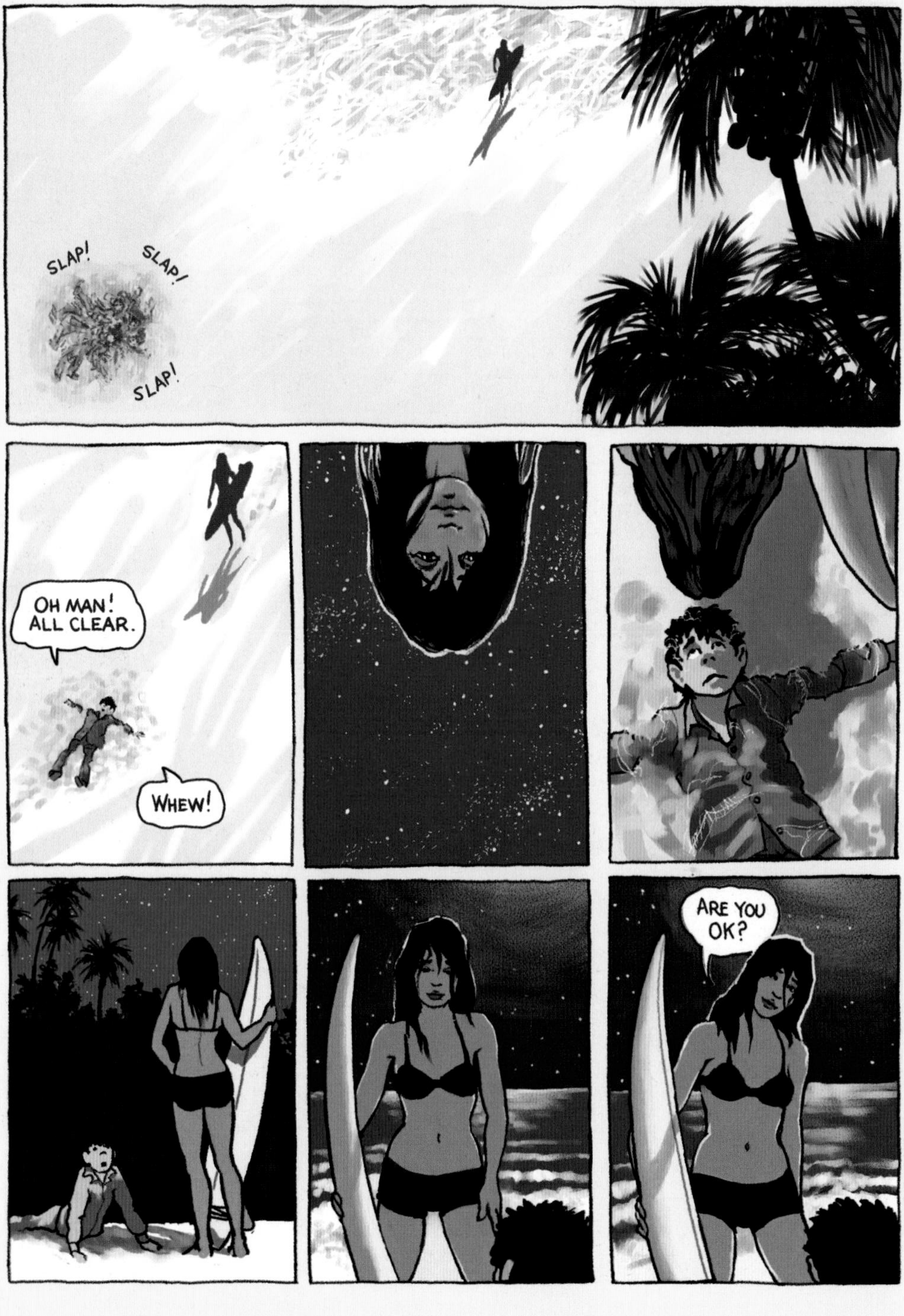
SLAP!
SLAP!
SLAP!
OH MAN! ALL CLEAR.
WHEW!
ARE YOU OK?

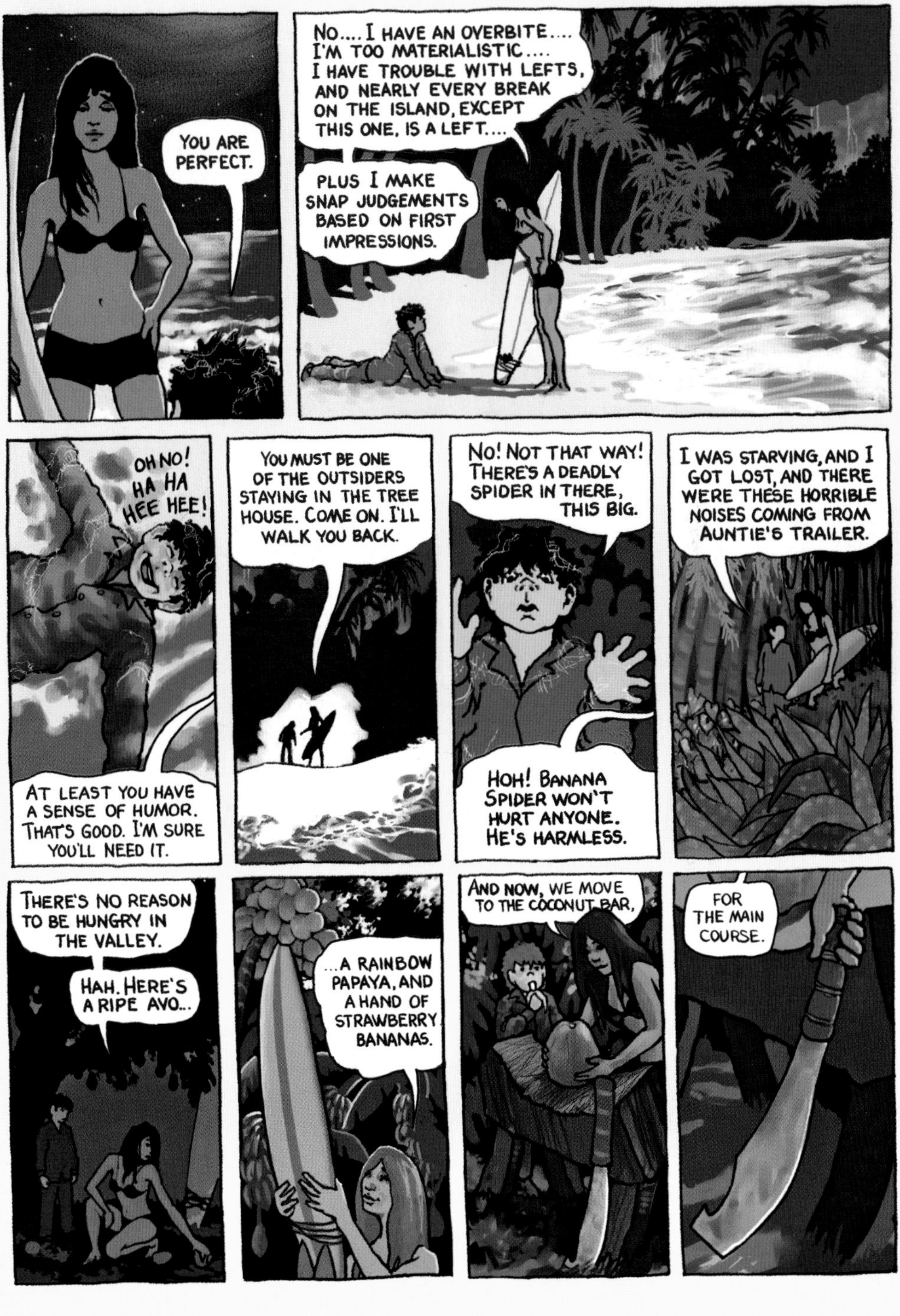
YOU ARE PERFECT.
NO.... I HAVE AN OVERBITE.... I'M TOO MATERIALISTIC.... I HAVE TROUBLE WITH LEFTS, AND NEARLY EVERY BREAK ON THE ISLAND, EXCEPT THIS ONE, IS A LEFT....
PLUS I MAKE SNAP JUDGEMENTS BASED ON FIRST IMPRESSIONS.
OH NO! HA HA HEE HEE!
AT LEAST YOU HAVE A SENSE OF HUMOR. THAT'S GOOD. I'M SURE YOU'LL NEED IT.
YOU MUST BE ONE OF THE OUTSIDERS STAYING IN THE TREE HOUSE. COME ON. I'LL WALK YOU BACK.
NO! NOT THAT WAY! THERE'S A DEADLY SPIDER IN THERE, THIS BIG.
HOH! BANANA SPIDER WON'T HURT ANYONE. HE'S HARMLESS.
I WAS STARVING, AND I GOT LOST, AND THERE WERE THESE HORRIBLE NOISES COMING FROM AUNTIE'S TRAILER.
THERE'S NO REASON TO BE HUNGRY IN THE VALLEY.
HAH. HERE'S A RIPE AVO...
...A RAINBOW PAPAYA, AND A HAND OF STRAWBERRY BANANAS.
AND NOW, WE MOVE TO THE COCONUT BAR,
FOR THE MAIN COURSE.

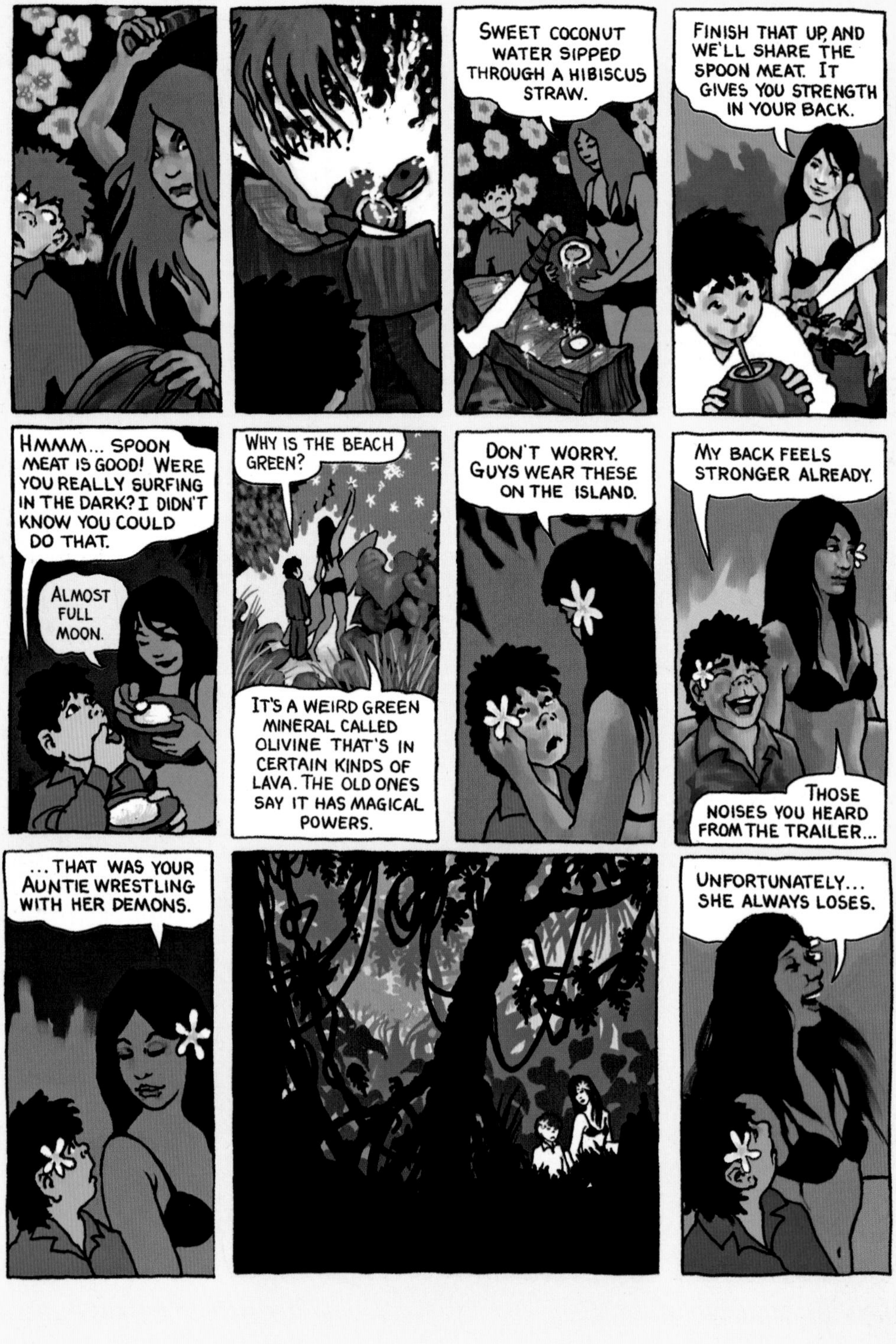
SWEET COCONUT WATER SIPPED THROUGH A HIBISCUS STRAW.
FINISH THAT UP, AND WE'LL SHARE THE SPOON MEAT. IT GIVES YOU STRENGTH IN YOUR BACK.
HMMM... SPOON MEAT IS GOOD! WERE YOU REALLY SURFING IN THE DARK? I DIDN'T KNOW YOU COULD DO THAT.
ALMOST FULL MOON.
WHY IS THE BEACH GREEN?
IT'S A WEIRD GREEN MINERAL CALLED OLIVINE THAT'S IN CERTAIN KINDS OF LAVA. THE OLD ONES SAY IT HAS MAGICAL POWERS.
DON'T WORRY. GUYS WEAR THESE ON THE ISLAND.
MY BACK FEELS STRONGER ALREADY.
THOSE NOISES YOU HEARD FROM THE TRAILER...
...THAT WAS YOUR AUNTIE WRESTLING WITH HER DEMONS.
UNFORTUNATELY... SHE ALWAYS LOSES.

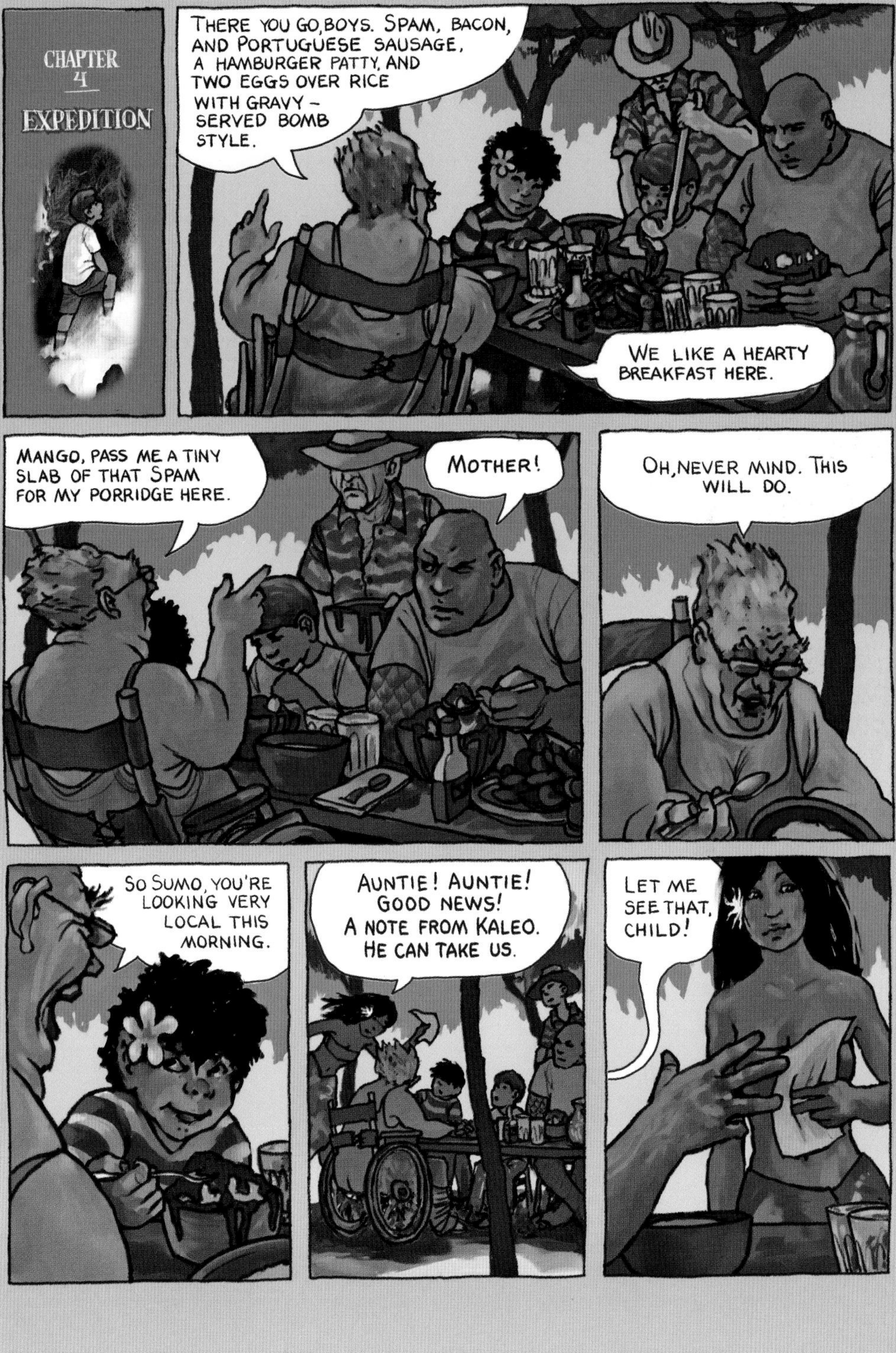
CHAPTER 4
EXPEDITION
THERE YOU GO, BOYS. SPAM, BACON, AND PORTUGUESE SAUSAGE, A HAMBURGER PATTY, AND TWO EGGS OVER RICE WITH GRAVY – SERVED BOMB STYLE.
WE LIKE A HEARTY BREAKFAST HERE.
MANGO, PASS ME A TINY SLAB OF THAT SPAM FOR MY PORRIDGE HERE.
MOTHER!
OH, NEVER MIND. THIS WILL DO.
SO SUMO, YOU'RE LOOKING VERY LOCAL THIS MORNING.
AUNTIE! AUNTIE! GOOD NEWS! A NOTE FROM KALEO. HE CAN TAKE US.
LET ME SEE THAT, CHILD!

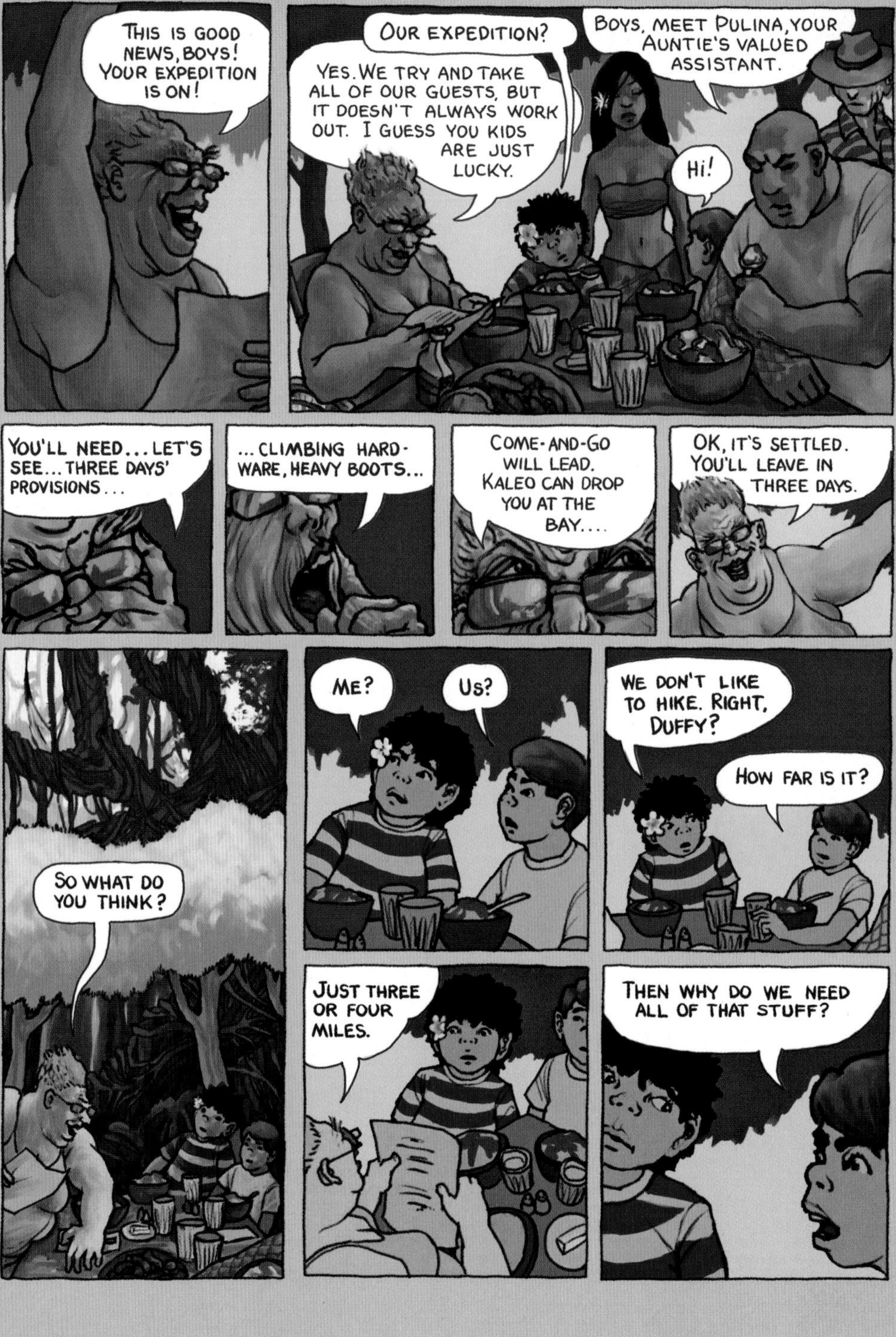
THIS IS GOOD NEWS, BOYS! YOUR EXPEDITION IS ON!
OUR EXPEDITION?
YES. WE TRY AND TAKE ALL OF OUR GUESTS, BUT IT DOESN'T ALWAYS WORK OUT. I GUESS YOU KIDS ARE JUST LUCKY.
BOYS, MEET PULINA, YOUR AUNTIE'S VALUED ASSISTANT.
HI!
YOU'LL NEED... LET'S SEE... THREE DAYS' PROVISIONS...
...CLIMBING HARDWARE, HEAVY BOOTS...
COME-AND-GO WILL LEAD. KALEO CAN DROP YOU AT THE BAY....
OK, IT'S SETTLED. YOU'LL LEAVE IN THREE DAYS.
SO WHAT DO YOU THINK?
ME?
US?
WE DON'T LIKE TO HIKE. RIGHT, DUFFY?
HOW FAR IS IT?
JUST THREE OR FOUR MILES.
THEN WHY DO WE NEED ALL OF THAT STUFF?

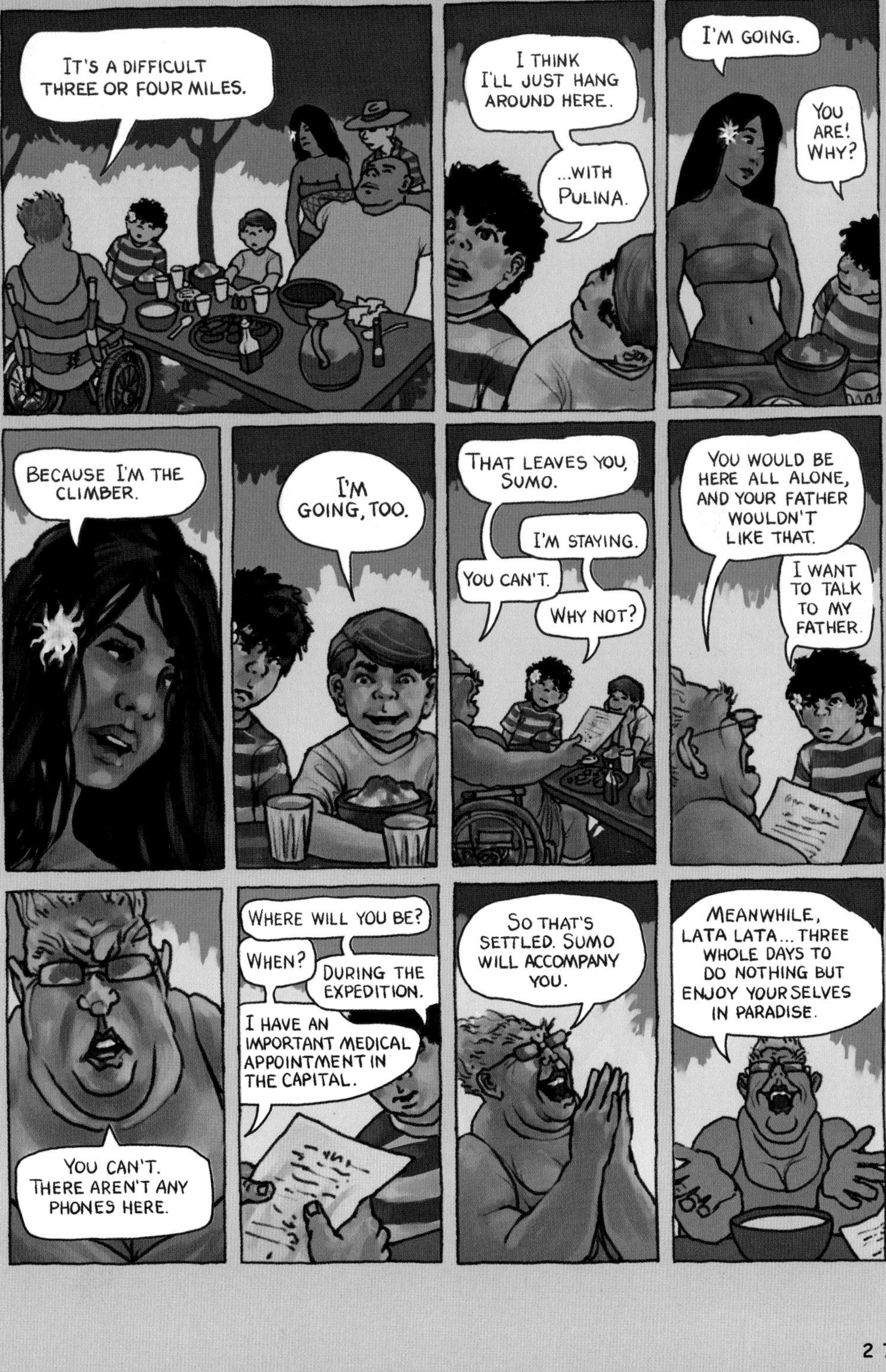
IT'S A DIFFICULT THREE OR FOUR MILES.
I THINK I'LL JUST HANG AROUND HERE.
...WITH PULINA.
I'M GOING.
YOU ARE! WHY?
BECAUSE I'M THE CLIMBER.
I'M GOING, TOO.
THAT LEAVES YOU, SUMO.
I'M STAYING.
YOU CAN'T.
WHY NOT?
YOU WOULD BE HERE ALL ALONE, AND YOUR FATHER WOULDN'T LIKE THAT.
I WANT TO TALK TO MY FATHER.
YOU CAN'T. THERE AREN'T ANY PHONES HERE.
WHERE WILL YOU BE?
WHEN?
DURING THE EXPEDITION.
I HAVE AN IMPORTANT MEDICAL APPOINTMENT IN THE CAPITAL.
SO THAT'S SETTLED. SUMO WILL ACCOMPANY YOU.
MEANWHILE, LATA LATA... THREE WHOLE DAYS TO DO NOTHING BUT ENJOY YOURSELVES IN PARADISE.

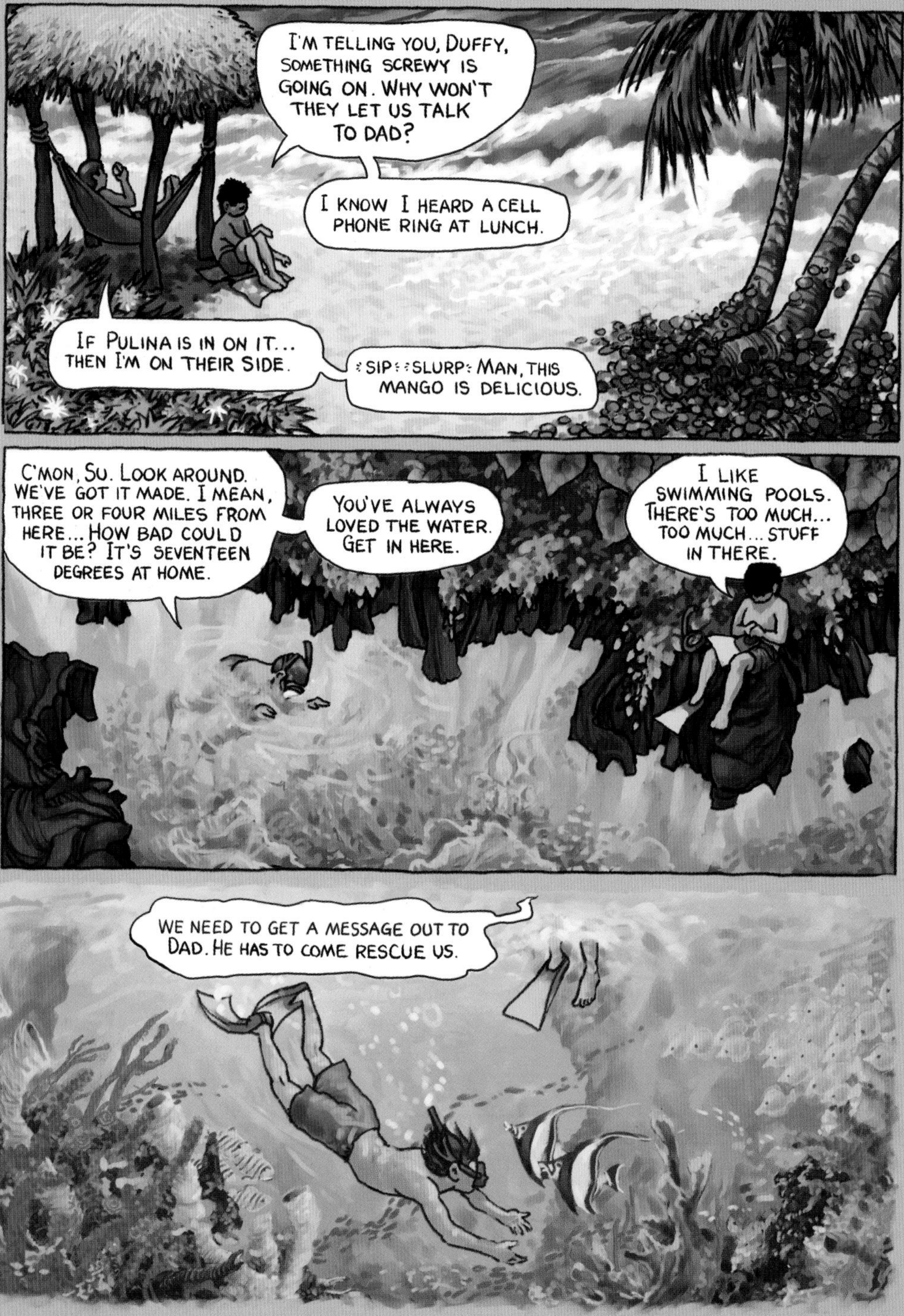
I'M TELLING YOU, DUFFY, SOMETHING SCREWY IS GOING ON. WHY WON'T THEY LET US TALK TO DAD?
I KNOW I HEARD A CELL PHONE RING AT LUNCH.
IF PULINA IS IN ON IT... THEN I'M ON THEIR SIDE.
:SIP: :SLURP: MAN, THIS MANGO IS DELICIOUS.
C'MON, SU. LOOK AROUND. WE'VE GOT IT MADE. I MEAN, THREE OR FOUR MILES FROM HERE... HOW BAD COULD IT BE? IT'S SEVENTEEN DEGREES AT HOME.
YOU'VE ALWAYS LOVED THE WATER. GET IN HERE.
I LIKE SWIMMING POOLS. THERE'S TOO MUCH... TOO MUCH... STUFF IN THERE.
WE NEED TO GET A MESSAGE OUT TO DAD. HE HAS TO COME RESCUE US.

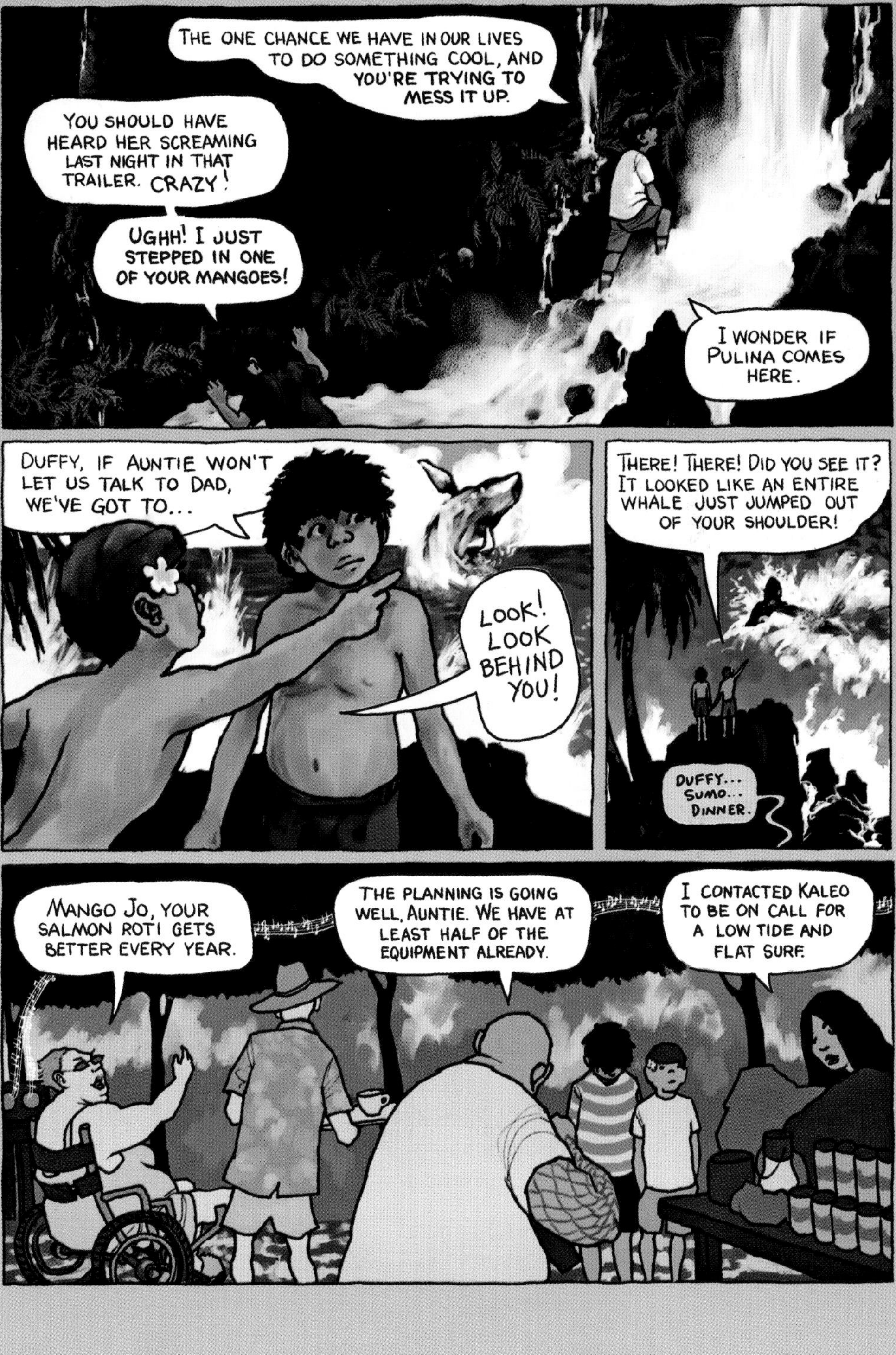
THE ONE CHANCE WE HAVE IN OUR LIVES TO DO SOMETHING COOL, AND YOU'RE TRYING TO MESS IT UP.
YOU SHOULD HAVE HEARD HER SCREAMING LAST NIGHT IN THAT TRAILER. CRAZY!
UGHH! I JUST STEPPED IN ONE OF YOUR MANGOES!
I WONDER IF PULINA COMES HERE.
DUFFY, IF AUNTIE WON'T LET US TALK TO DAD, WE'VE GOT TO...
LOOK! LOOK BEHIND YOU!
THERE! THERE! DID YOU SEE IT? IT LOOKED LIKE AN ENTIRE WHALE JUST JUMPED OUT OF YOUR SHOULDER!
DUFFY... SUMO... DINNER.
MANGO JO, YOUR SALMON ROTI GETS BETTER EVERY YEAR.
THE PLANNING IS GOING WELL, AUNTIE. WE HAVE AT LEAST HALF OF THE EQUIPMENT ALREADY.
I CONTACTED KALEO TO BE ON CALL FOR A LOW TIDE AND FLAT SURF.

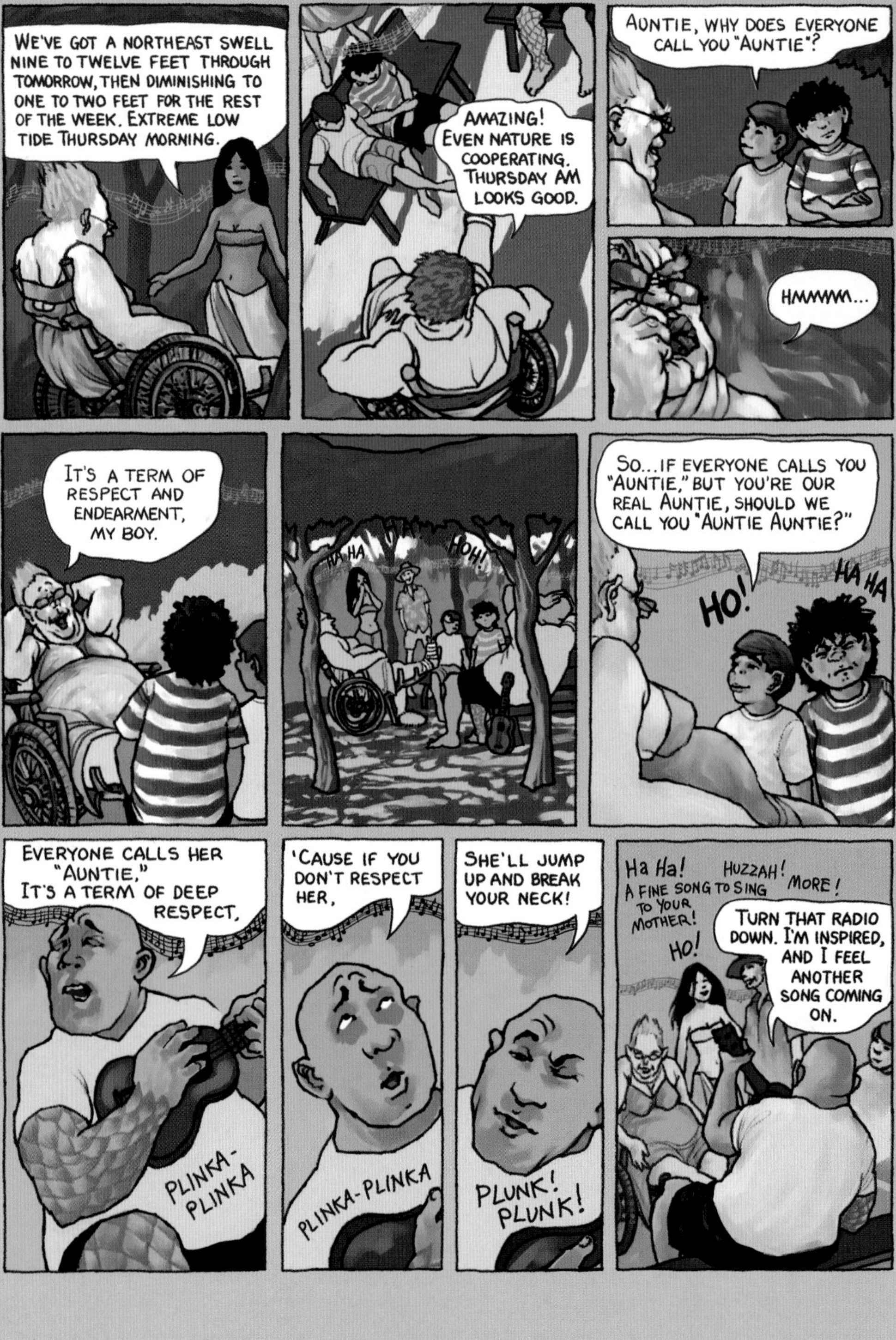
WE'VE GOT A NORTHEAST SWELL NINE TO TWELVE FEET THROUGH TOMORROW, THEN DIMINISHING TO ONE TO TWO FEET FOR THE REST OF THE WEEK. EXTREME LOW TIDE THURSDAY MORNING.
AMAZING! EVEN NATURE IS COOPERATING. THURSDAY AM LOOKS GOOD.
AUNTIE, WHY DOES EVERYONE CALL YOU "AUNTIE"?
HMMMM...
IT'S A TERM OF RESPECT AND ENDEARMENT, MY BOY.
HA HA
HA
HOH!
SO...IF EVERYONE CALLS YOU "AUNTIE," BUT YOU'RE OUR REAL AUNTIE, SHOULD WE CALL YOU "AUNTIE AUNTIE?"
HO!
HA HA
EVERYONE CALLS HER "AUNTIE," IT'S A TERM OF DEEP RESPECT.
PLINKA-PLINKA
'CAUSE IF YOU DON'T RESPECT HER,
PLINKA-PLINKA
SHE'LL JUMP UP AND BREAK YOUR NECK!
PLUNK! PLUNK!
Ha Ha!
HUZZAH!
MORE!
A FINE SONG TO SING TO YOUR MOTHER!
HO!
TURN THAT RADIO DOWN. I'M INSPIRED, AND I FEEL ANOTHER SONG COMING ON.

WE INTERRUPT THIS PROGRAM FOR A MESSAGE FROM THE KOCALAHA DEPARTMENT OF PUBLIC SAFETY. PLEASE STAND BY.

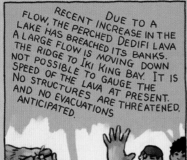

DUE TO A RECENT INCREASE IN THE FLOW, THE PERCHED DEDIFI LAVA LAKE HAS BREACHED ITS BANKS. A LARGE FLOW IS MOVING DOWN THE RIDGE TO IKI KING BAY. IT IS NOT POSSIBLE TO GAUGE THE SPEED OF THE LAVA AT PRESENT. NO STRUCTURES ARE THREATENED, AND NO EVACUATIONS ANTICIPATED.

IT'S HEADED RIGHT TO THE ACCESS POINT.

CALL NEPANKO IN THE CHOPPER. TRY TO GET AN ESTIMATE ON THE SPEED.

CALL NINI AT GEOLOGY. MAKE HER GUESS FLOW STRENGTH AND DURATION.

CALL?

PULINA?

LOW TIDE NOW, NICE LOW TOMORROW NOON. ONE-POINT-EIGHT HIGH AT FOUR-THIRTY AM. SURF IS SEVEN FEET AND RISING.

I'D LIKE TO USE THAT PHONE, PLEASE.

NEPANKO SAYS IT'S FLOWING FAST. FASTEST HE'S EVER SEEN.

NINI GUESSES THAT THIS IS A MAJOR TERMINAL EVENT, MAYBE THE TERMINAL EVENT.

YOU HAVE TO GO NOW.

PULINA, CALL KALEO. TELL HIM... WHAT DO YOU THINK, COME-AND-GO?

MIDNIGHT AT THE LAGOON.

TELL HIM TO SIGNAL US.

COME-AND-GO. WHAT ARE WE MISSING THAT'S CRUCIAL?

RADIO, GOOD LANTERNS, EXTRA BATTERIES FOR EVERYTHING, HALF THE CLIMBING EQUIPMENT, SPARE FILTERS FOR THE BREATHERS, ASBESTOS GLOVES...

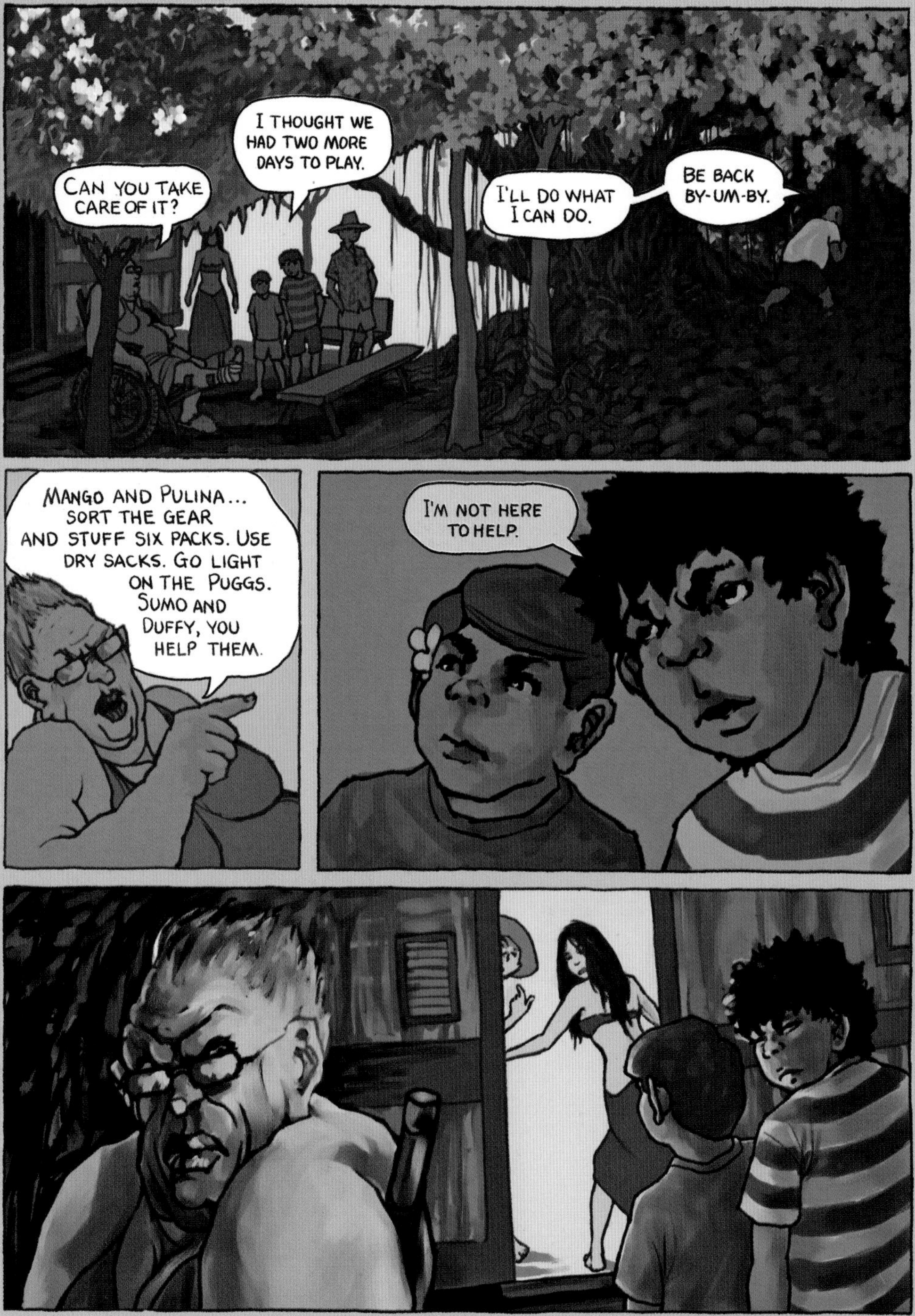
CAN YOU TAKE CARE OF IT?
I THOUGHT WE HAD TWO MORE DAYS TO PLAY.
I'LL DO WHAT I CAN DO.
BE BACK BY-UM-BY.
MANGO AND PULINA... SORT THE GEAR AND STUFF SIX PACKS. USE DRY SACKS. GO LIGHT ON THE PUGGS. SUMO AND DUFFY, YOU HELP THEM.
I'M NOT HERE TO HELP.

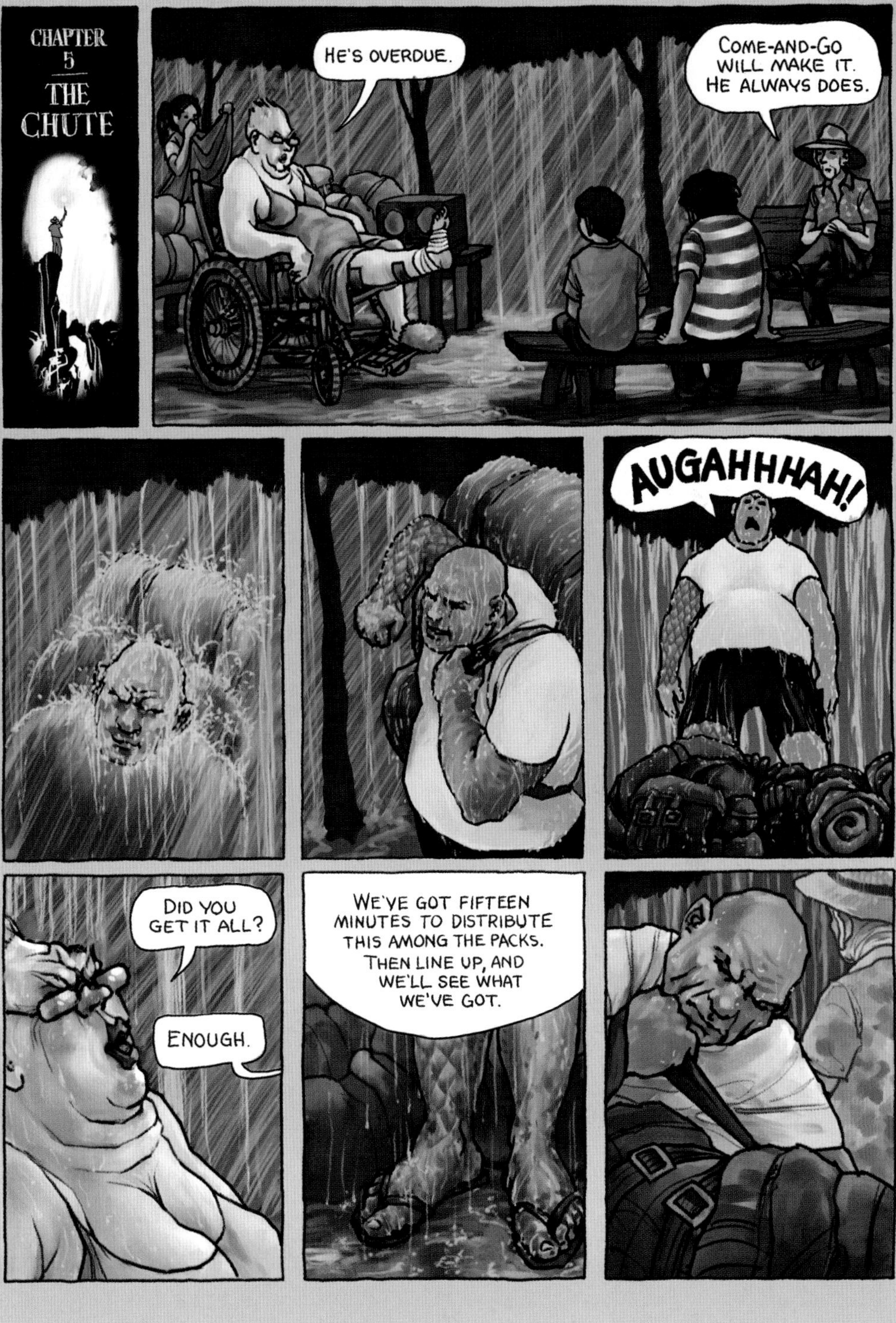
CHAPTER 5
THE CHUTE
HE'S OVERDUE.
COME-AND-GO WILL MAKE IT. HE ALWAYS DOES.
AUGAHHHAH!
DID YOU GET IT ALL?
ENOUGH.
WE'VE GOT FIFTEEN MINUTES TO DISTRIBUTE THIS AMONG THE PACKS. THEN LINE UP, AND WE'LL SEE WHAT WE'VE GOT.

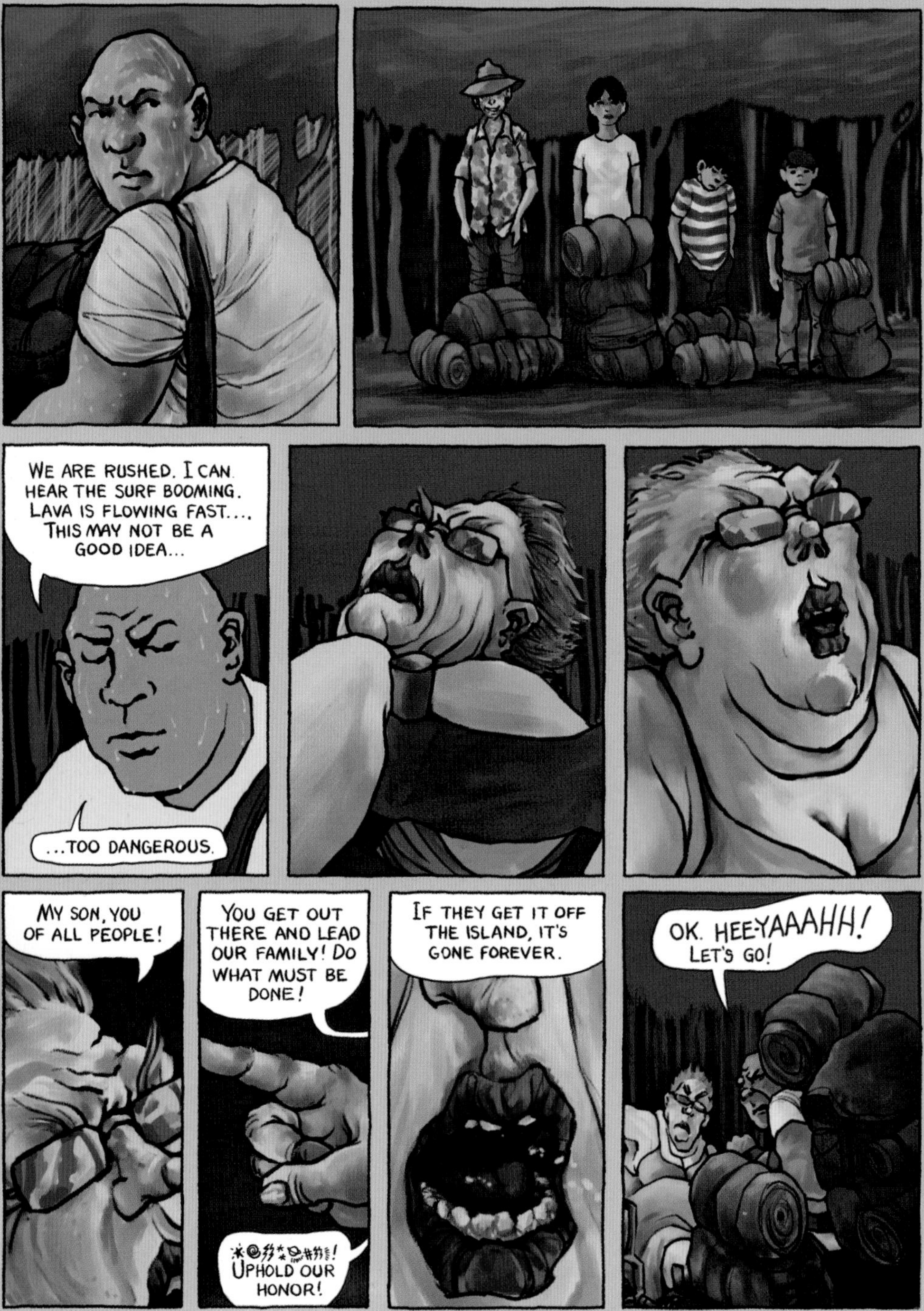
WE ARE RUSHED. I CAN HEAR THE SURF BOOMING. LAVA IS FLOWING FAST.... THIS MAY NOT BE A GOOD IDEA...
...TOO DANGEROUS.
MY SON, YOU OF ALL PEOPLE!
YOU GET OUT THERE AND LEAD OUR FAMILY! DO WHAT MUST BE DONE!
UPHOLD OUR HONOR!
IF THEY GET IT OFF THE ISLAND, IT'S GONE FOREVER.
OK. HEE-YAAAHH! LET'S GO!

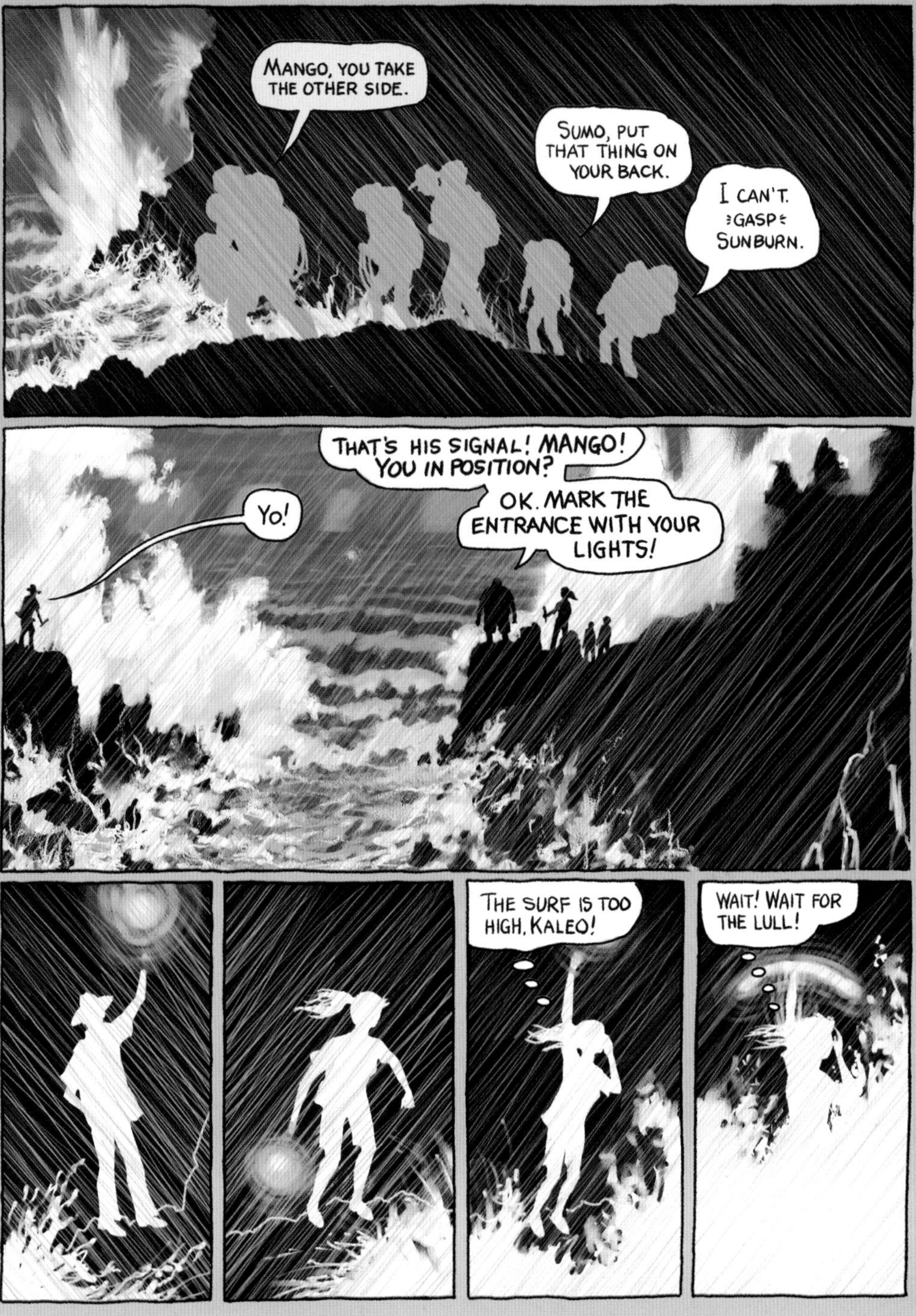
MANGO, YOU TAKE THE OTHER SIDE.
SUMO, PUT THAT THING ON YOUR BACK.
I CAN'T. ≡GASP≡ SUNBURN.
THAT'S HIS SIGNAL! MANGO! YOU IN POSITION?
YO!
OK. MARK THE ENTRANCE WITH YOUR LIGHTS!
THE SURF IS TOO HIGH, KALEO!
WAIT! WAIT FOR THE LULL!

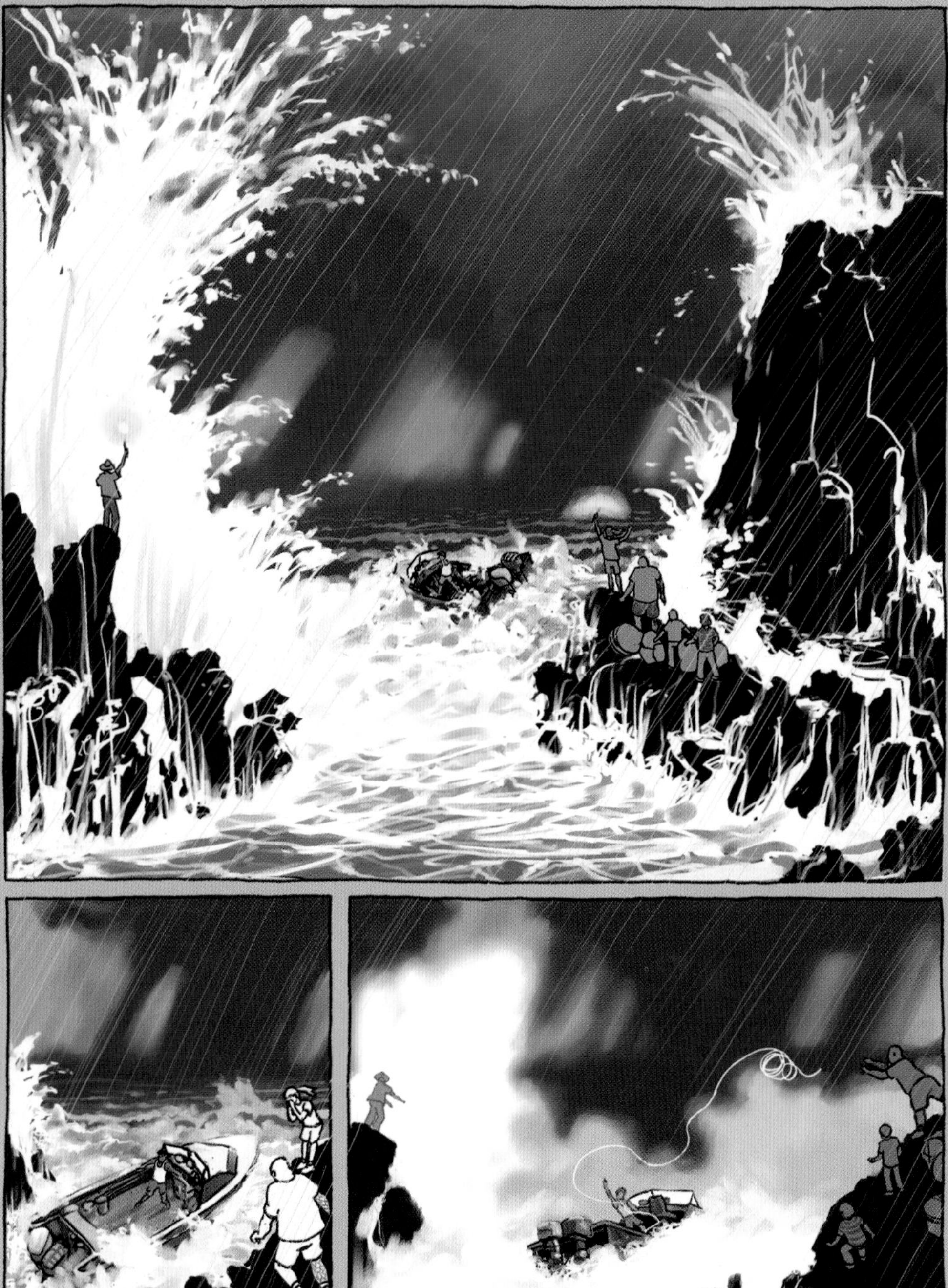

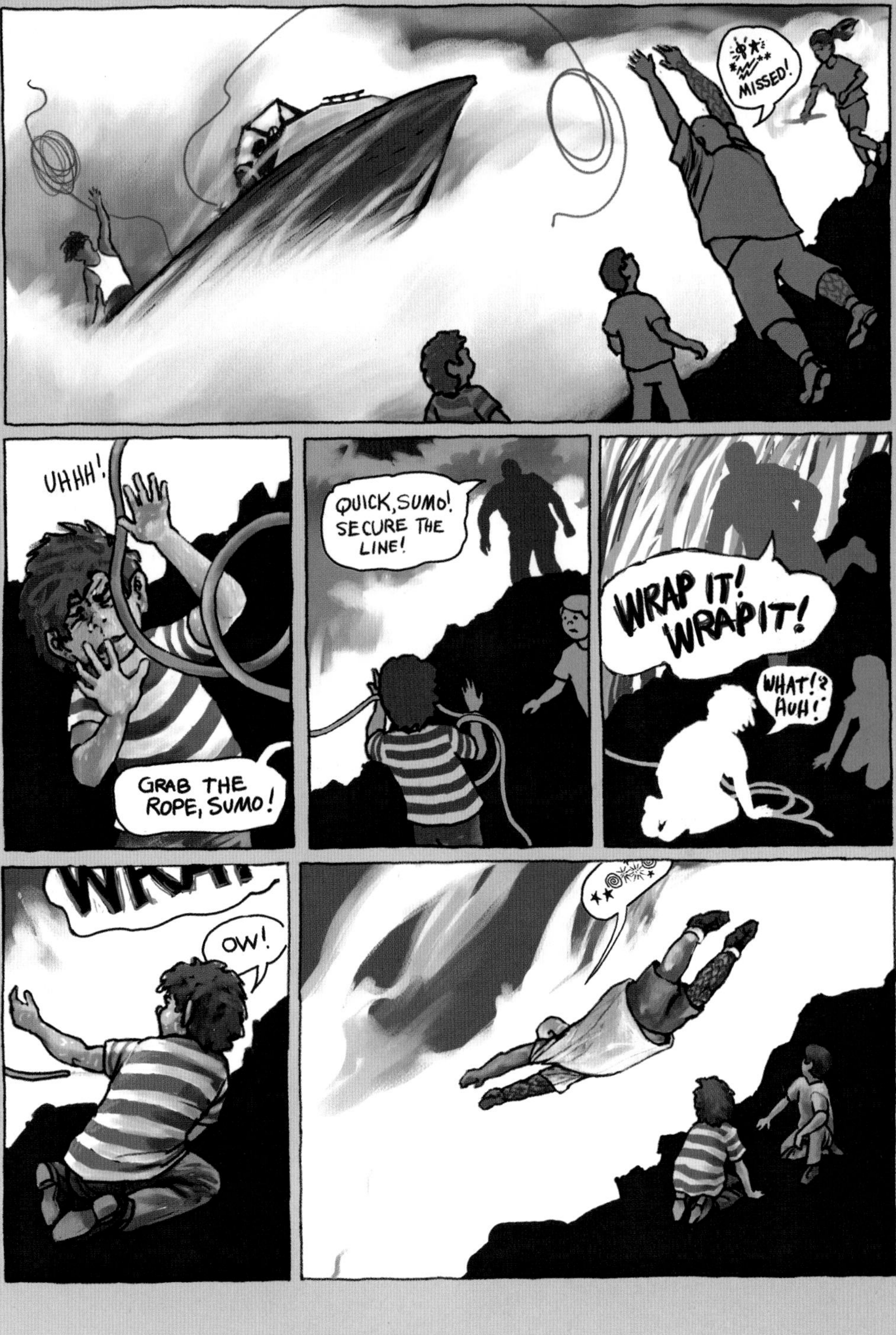
MISSED!
UHHH!
GRAB THE ROPE, SUMO!
QUICK, SUMO! SECURE THE LINE!
WRAP IT! WRAPIT!
WHAT!? AUH!
OW!

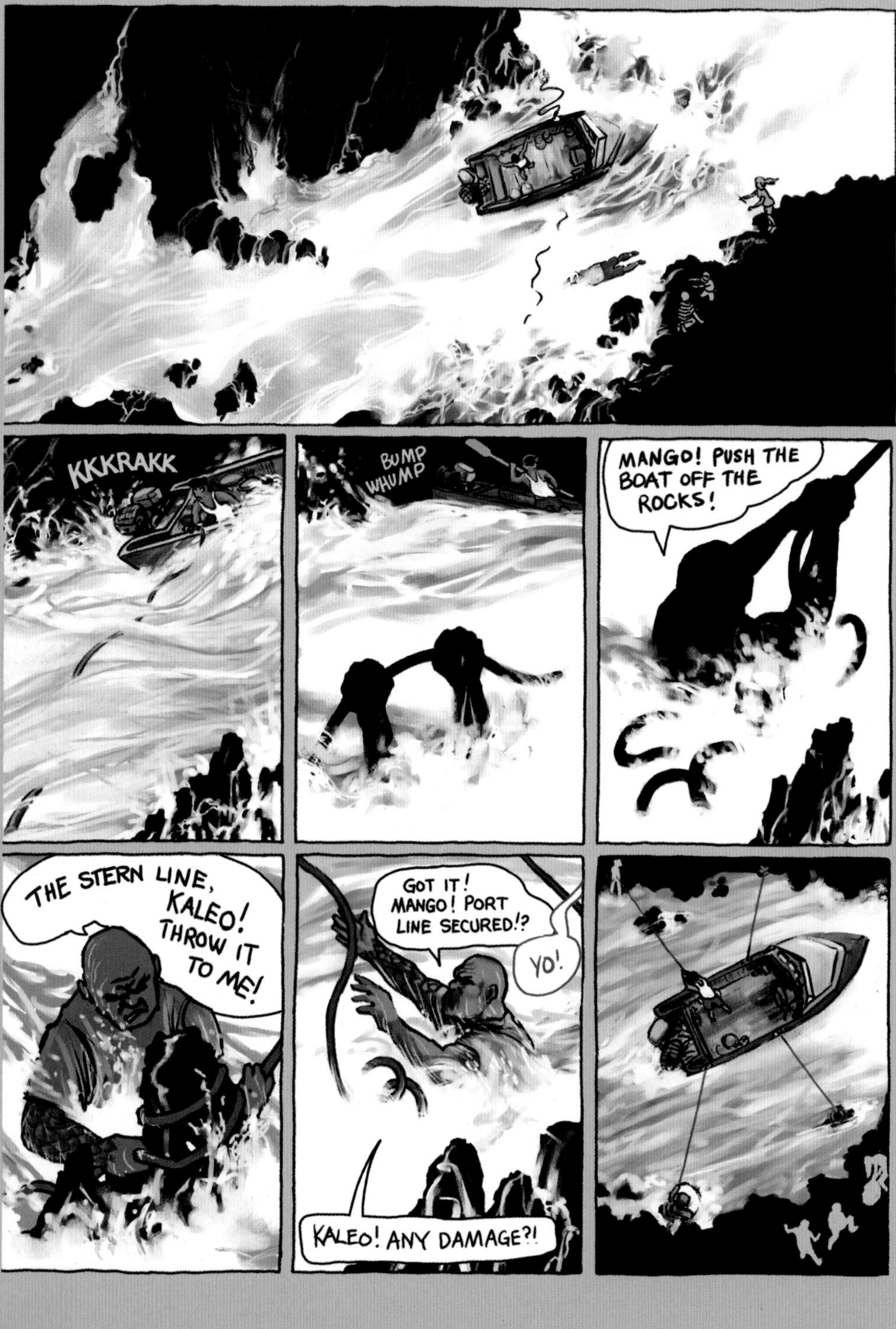
KKKRAKK
BUMP WHUMP
MANGO! PUSH THE BOAT OFF THE ROCKS!
THE STERN LINE, KALEO! THROW IT TO ME!
GOT IT! MANGO! PORT LINE SECURED!?
YO!
KALEO! ANY DAMAGE?!

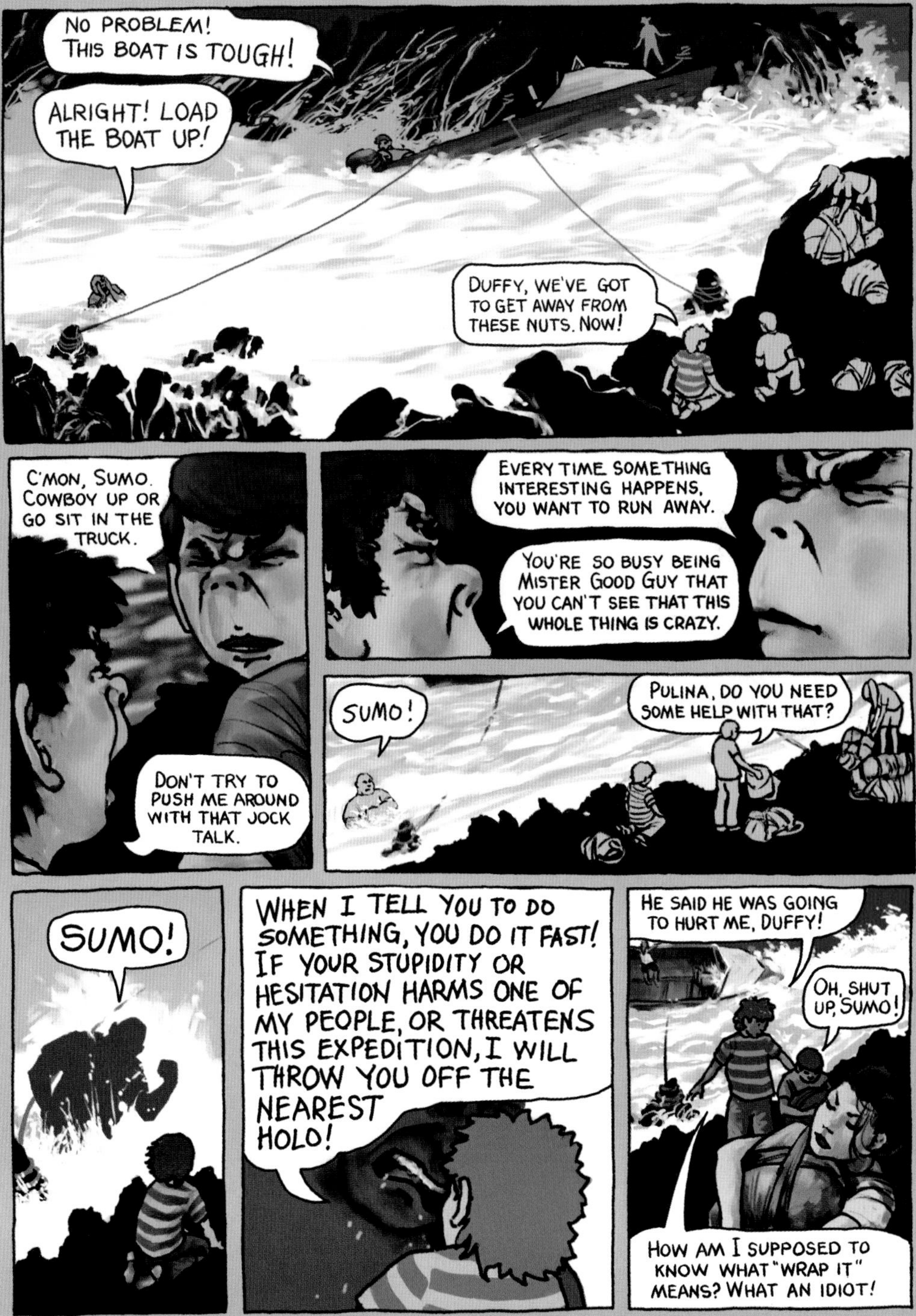
NO PROBLEM! THIS BOAT IS TOUGH!
ALRIGHT! LOAD THE BOAT UP!
DUFFY, WE'VE GOT TO GET AWAY FROM THESE NUTS. NOW!
C'MON, SUMO. COWBOY UP OR GO SIT IN THE TRUCK.
DON'T TRY TO PUSH ME AROUND WITH THAT JOCK TALK.
EVERY TIME SOMETHING INTERESTING HAPPENS, YOU WANT TO RUN AWAY.
YOU'RE SO BUSY BEING MISTER GOOD GUY THAT YOU CAN'T SEE THAT THIS WHOLE THING IS CRAZY.
SUMO!
PULINA, DO YOU NEED SOME HELP WITH THAT?
SUMO!
WHEN I TELL YOU TO DO SOMETHING, YOU DO IT FAST! IF YOUR STUPIDITY OR HESITATION HARMS ONE OF MY PEOPLE, OR THREATENS THIS EXPEDITION, I WILL THROW YOU OFF THE NEAREST HOLO!
HE SAID HE WAS GOING TO HURT ME, DUFFY!
OH, SHUT UP, SUMO!
HOW AM I SUPPOSED TO KNOW WHAT "WRAP IT" MEANS? WHAT AN IDIOT!

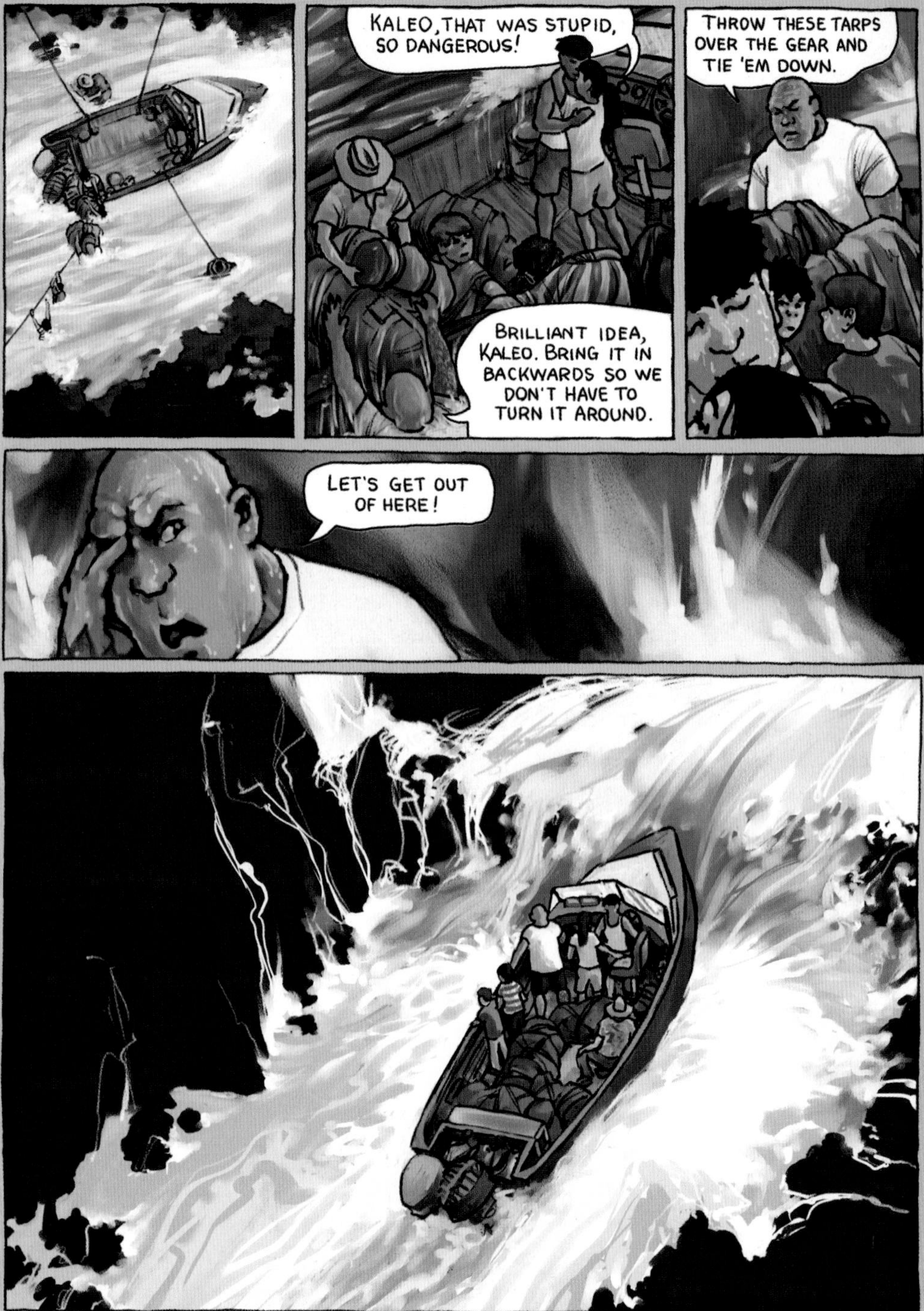
KALEO, THAT WAS STUPID, SO DANGEROUS!
BRILLIANT IDEA, KALEO. BRING IT IN BACKWARDS SO WE DON'T HAVE TO TURN IT AROUND.
THROW THESE TARPS OVER THE GEAR AND TIE 'EM DOWN.
LET'S GET OUT OF HERE!

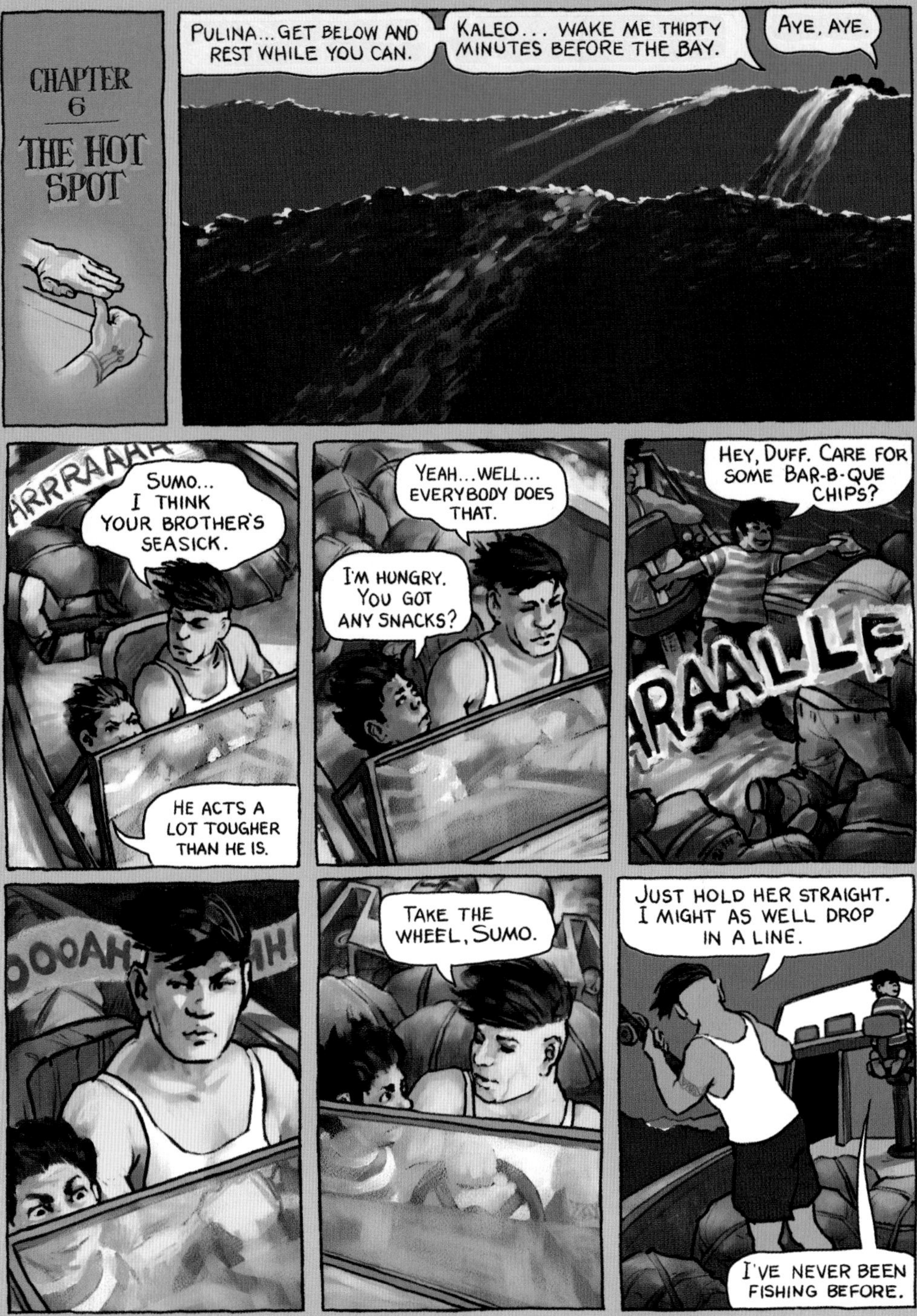
CHAPTER
6
THE HOT SPOT
PULINA... GET BELOW AND REST WHILE YOU CAN.
KALEO... WAKE ME THIRTY MINUTES BEFORE THE BAY.
AYE, AYE.
HRRRAAAH
SUMO... I THINK YOUR BROTHER'S SEASICK.
HE ACTS A LOT TOUGHER THAN HE IS.
YEAH... WELL... EVERYBODY DOES THAT.
I'M HUNGRY. YOU GOT ANY SNACKS?
HEY, DUFF. CARE FOR SOME BAR-B-QUE CHIPS?
RAALLF
OOOAH
TAKE THE WHEEL, SUMO.
JUST HOLD HER STRAIGHT. I MIGHT AS WELL DROP IN A LINE.
I'VE NEVER BEEN FISHING BEFORE.

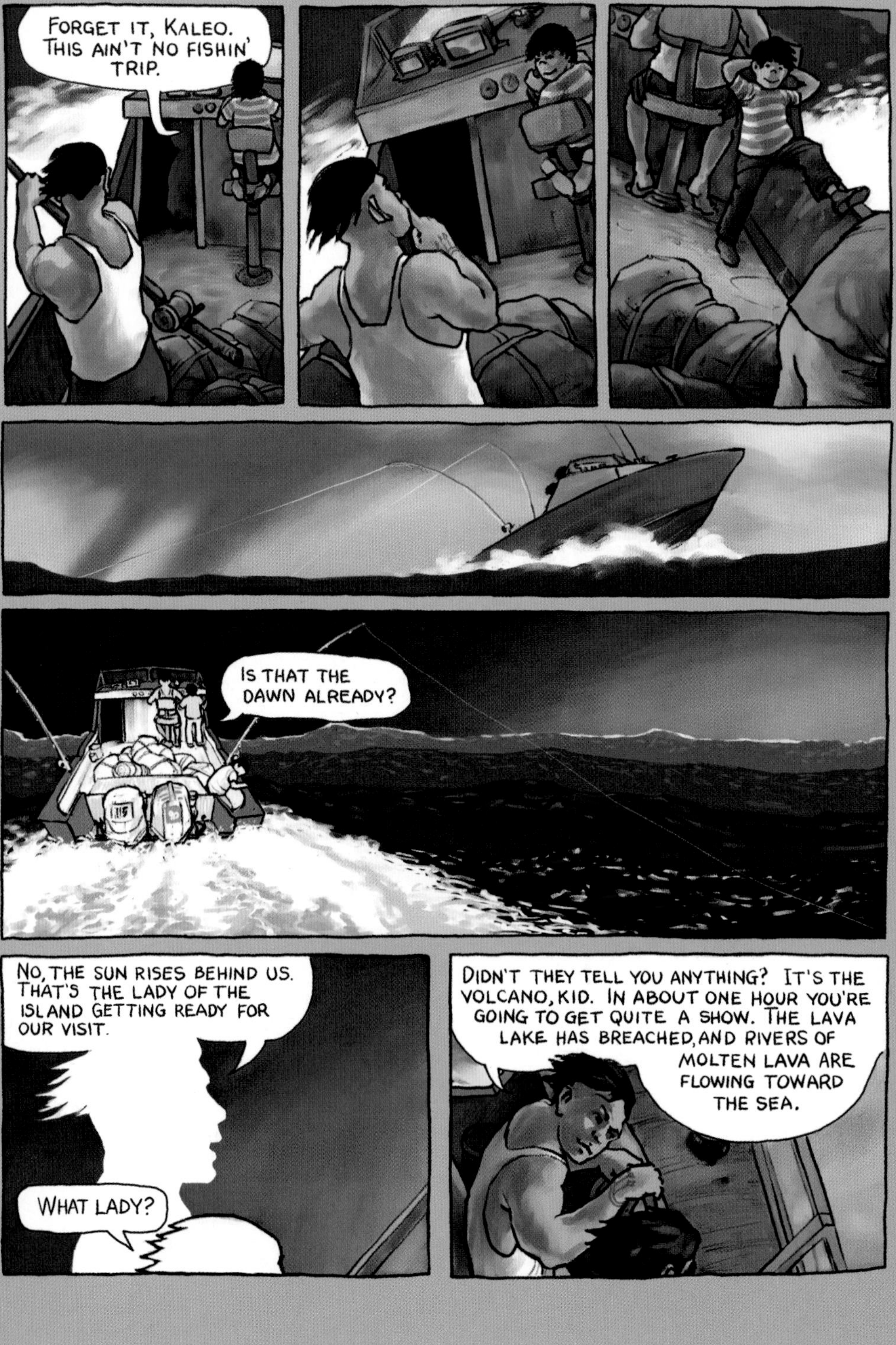
FORGET IT, KALEO. THIS AIN'T NO FISHIN' TRIP.
IS THAT THE DAWN ALREADY?
NO, THE SUN RISES BEHIND US. THAT'S THE LADY OF THE ISLAND GETTING READY FOR OUR VISIT.
WHAT LADY?
DIDN'T THEY TELL YOU ANYTHING? IT'S THE VOLCANO, KID. IN ABOUT ONE HOUR YOU'RE GOING TO GET QUITE A SHOW. THE LAVA LAKE HAS BREACHED, AND RIVERS OF MOLTEN LAVA ARE FLOWING TOWARD THE SEA.

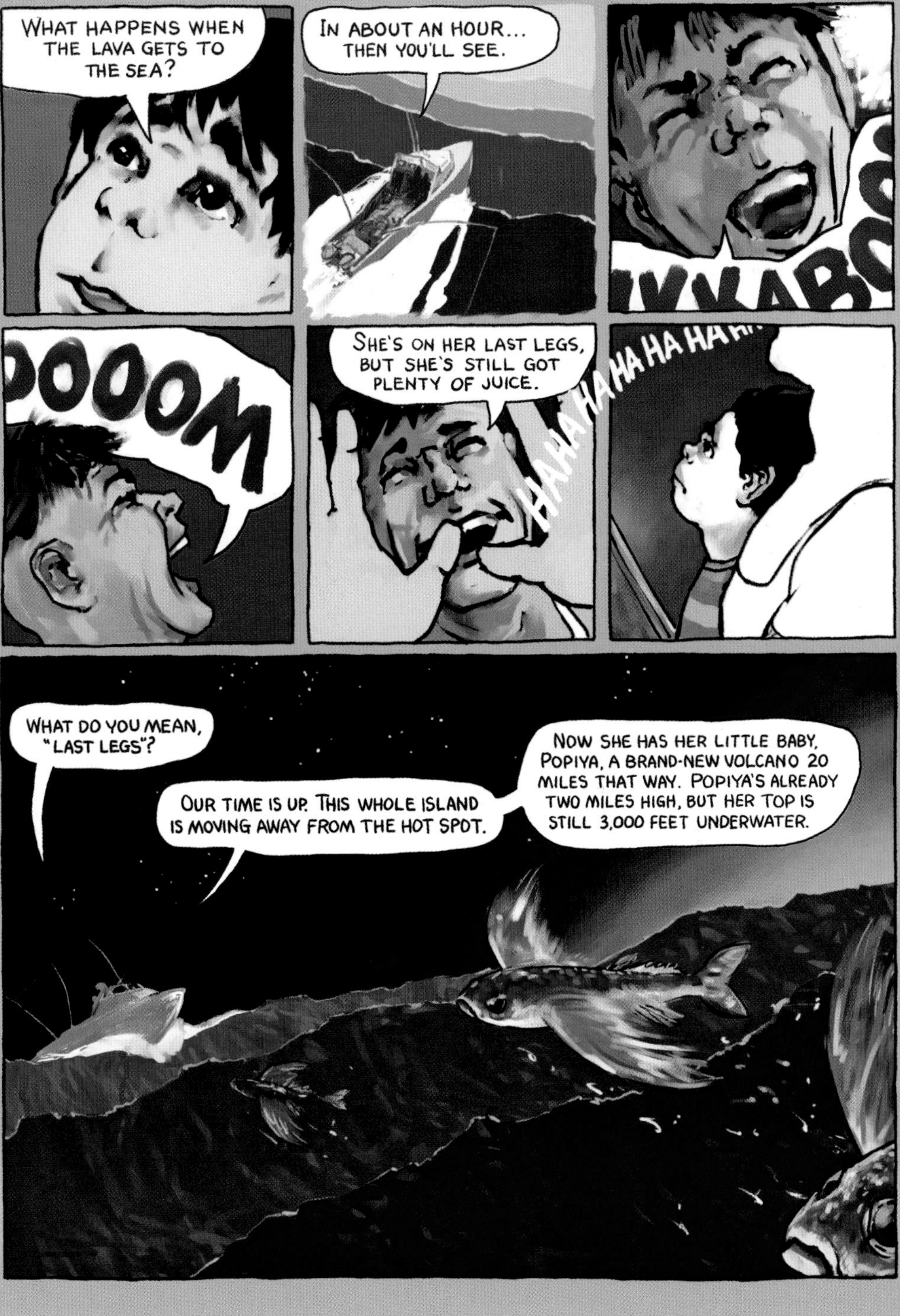
WHAT HAPPENS WHEN THE LAVA GETS TO THE SEA?
IN ABOUT AN HOUR... THEN YOU'LL SEE.
KKABO
OOOOM
SHE'S ON HER LAST LEGS, BUT SHE'S STILL GOT PLENTY OF JUICE.
HAHAHAHAHAHAHA
WHAT DO YOU MEAN, "LAST LEGS"?
OUR TIME IS UP. THIS WHOLE ISLAND IS MOVING AWAY FROM THE HOT SPOT.
NOW SHE HAS HER LITTLE BABY, POPIYA, A BRAND-NEW VOLCANO 20 MILES THAT WAY. POPIYA'S ALREADY TWO MILES HIGH, BUT HER TOP IS STILL 3,000 FEET UNDERWATER.

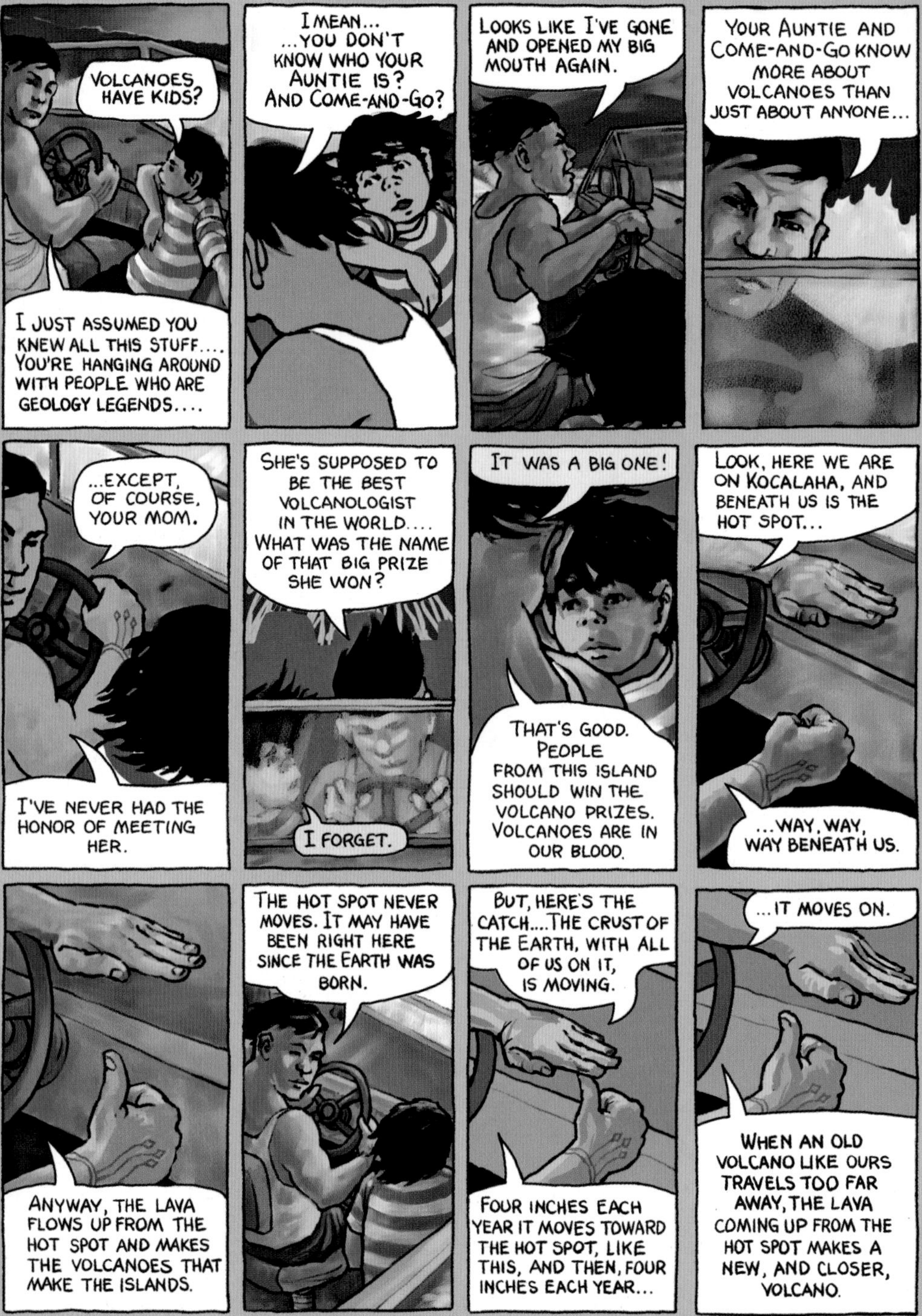
VOLCANOES HAVE KIDS?
I JUST ASSUMED YOU KNEW ALL THIS STUFF.... YOU'RE HANGING AROUND WITH PEOPLE WHO ARE GEOLOGY LEGENDS....
I MEAN... ...YOU DON'T KNOW WHO YOUR AUNTIE IS? AND COME-AND-GO?
LOOKS LIKE I'VE GONE AND OPENED MY BIG MOUTH AGAIN.
YOUR AUNTIE AND COME-AND-GO KNOW MORE ABOUT VOLCANOES THAN JUST ABOUT ANYONE...
...EXCEPT, OF COURSE, YOUR MOM.
I'VE NEVER HAD THE HONOR OF MEETING HER.
SHE'S SUPPOSED TO BE THE BEST VOLCANOLOGIST IN THE WORLD.... WHAT WAS THE NAME OF THAT BIG PRIZE SHE WON?
I FORGET.
IT WAS A BIG ONE!
THAT'S GOOD. PEOPLE FROM THIS ISLAND SHOULD WIN THE VOLCANO PRIZES. VOLCANOES ARE IN OUR BLOOD.
LOOK, HERE WE ARE ON KOCALAHA, AND BENEATH US IS THE HOT SPOT...
...WAY, WAY, WAY BENEATH US.
ANYWAY, THE LAVA FLOWS UP FROM THE HOT SPOT AND MAKES THE VOLCANOES THAT MAKE THE ISLANDS.
THE HOT SPOT NEVER MOVES. IT MAY HAVE BEEN RIGHT HERE SINCE THE EARTH WAS BORN.
BUT, HERE'S THE CATCH....THE CRUST OF THE EARTH, WITH ALL OF US ON IT, IS MOVING.
FOUR INCHES EACH YEAR IT MOVES TOWARD THE HOT SPOT, LIKE THIS, AND THEN, FOUR INCHES EACH YEAR...
...IT MOVES ON.
WHEN AN OLD VOLCANO LIKE OURS TRAVELS TOO FAR AWAY, THE LAVA COMING UP FROM THE HOT SPOT MAKES A NEW, AND CLOSER, VOLCANO.

SAY THIS SPOT OF OIL IS KOCALAHA.

HERE ARE THE SIX ISLANDS IN OUR NATION. THEY'RE ALL IN A LINE.

I TELL YOU, I LOVE THIS STUFF!

AND HERE ARE A BUNCH OF VERY OLD ISLANDS, SO OLD AND ERODED THAT NOW THEY ARE JUST REEFS, BARELY ABLE TO KEEP THEIR HEADS OUT OF THE WATER. THEY ARE IN THE SAME LINE.

NOW... HERE'S THE COOL PART, SUMO. THE LINE CONTINUES ON WITH EVEN OLDER ISLANDS SO WORN DOWN THAT THEY'RE UNDERWATER.

THERE'S 106 OF THEM OUT THERE—EVERY ONE AN OLD VOLCANO THAT WAS BORN, CREATED AN ISLAND, AND DIED.

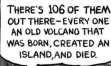

THE LINE GOES 4,000 MILES ACROSS THE PACIFIC AND UP TO SIBERIA.

WE ARE ISLAND NUMBER 107.

AND LITTLE POPIYA OVER THERE—SHE'S GOING TO BE NUMBER ONE-OH-EIGHT.

BUT THERE MAY BE EVEN MORE....

WHOA! WOULD YOU LOOK AT THAT!

A POD OF WHALES BLOWING UNDER A MOONBOW. YOU DON'T SEE THAT EVERY DAY.

45

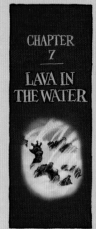

CHAPTER 7

LAVA IN THE WATER

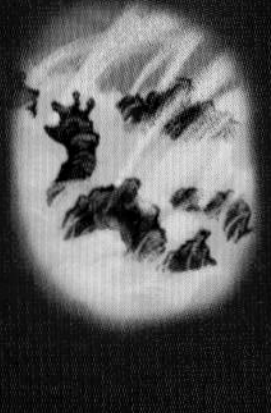

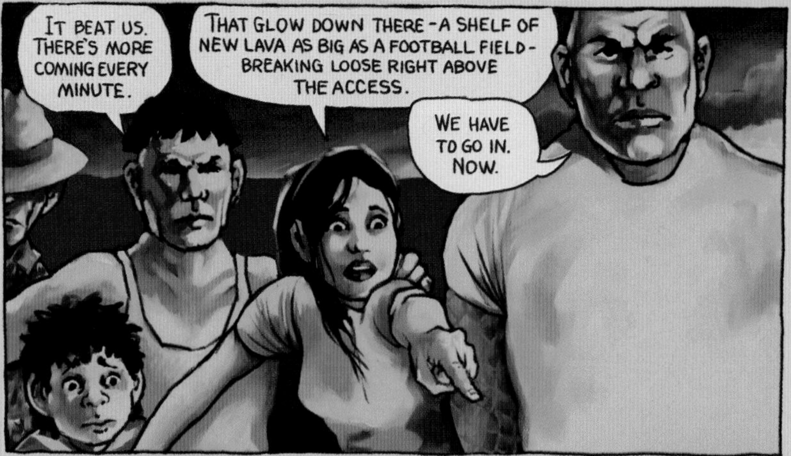
IT BEAT US. THERE'S MORE COMING EVERY MINUTE.
THAT GLOW DOWN THERE - A SHELF OF NEW LAVA AS BIG AS A FOOTBALL FIELD - BREAKING LOOSE RIGHT ABOVE THE ACCESS.
WE HAVE TO GO IN. NOW.

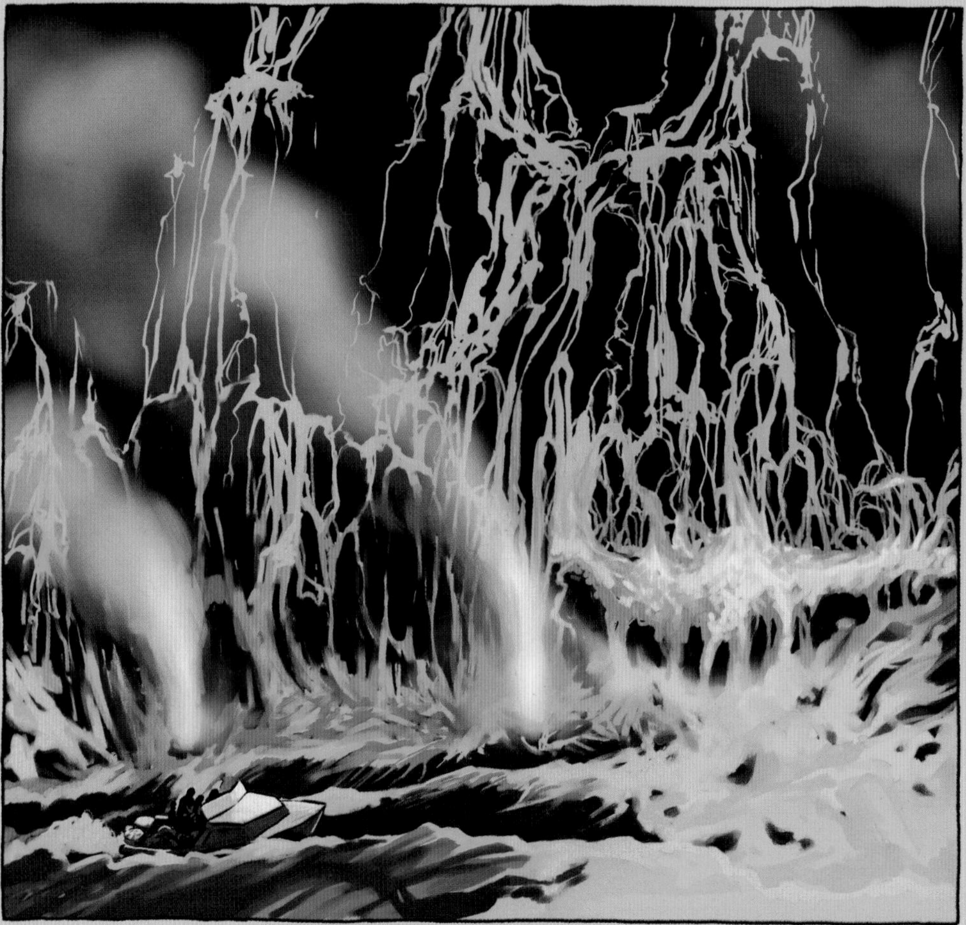

WE CAN'T. TIDE'S WRONG. SURF'S UP. IT'S ALL WORSE THAN I THOUGHT. THAT HOT LAVA WILL COME DOWN AND TRAP US.

THE FLOW OF '96, '99, THE FOUNTAIN OF '07... NOBODY KNOWS LAVA IN THE WATER LIKE ME.

TAKE US IN.

I'LL GO IN AND NOSE AROUND, BUT NO PROMISES.

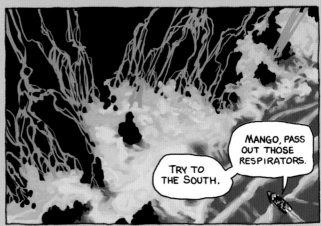

TRY TO THE SOUTH.

MANGO, PASS OUT THOSE RESPIRATORS.

I CAN'T BREATHE IN THIS THING.

PUT IT ON, AND KEEP IT ON, FOOL. THERE ARE GLASS PARTICLES IN THE SMOKE. IT WILL KILL YOU.

WITHOUT A RESPIRATOR, YOU'RE DEAD.

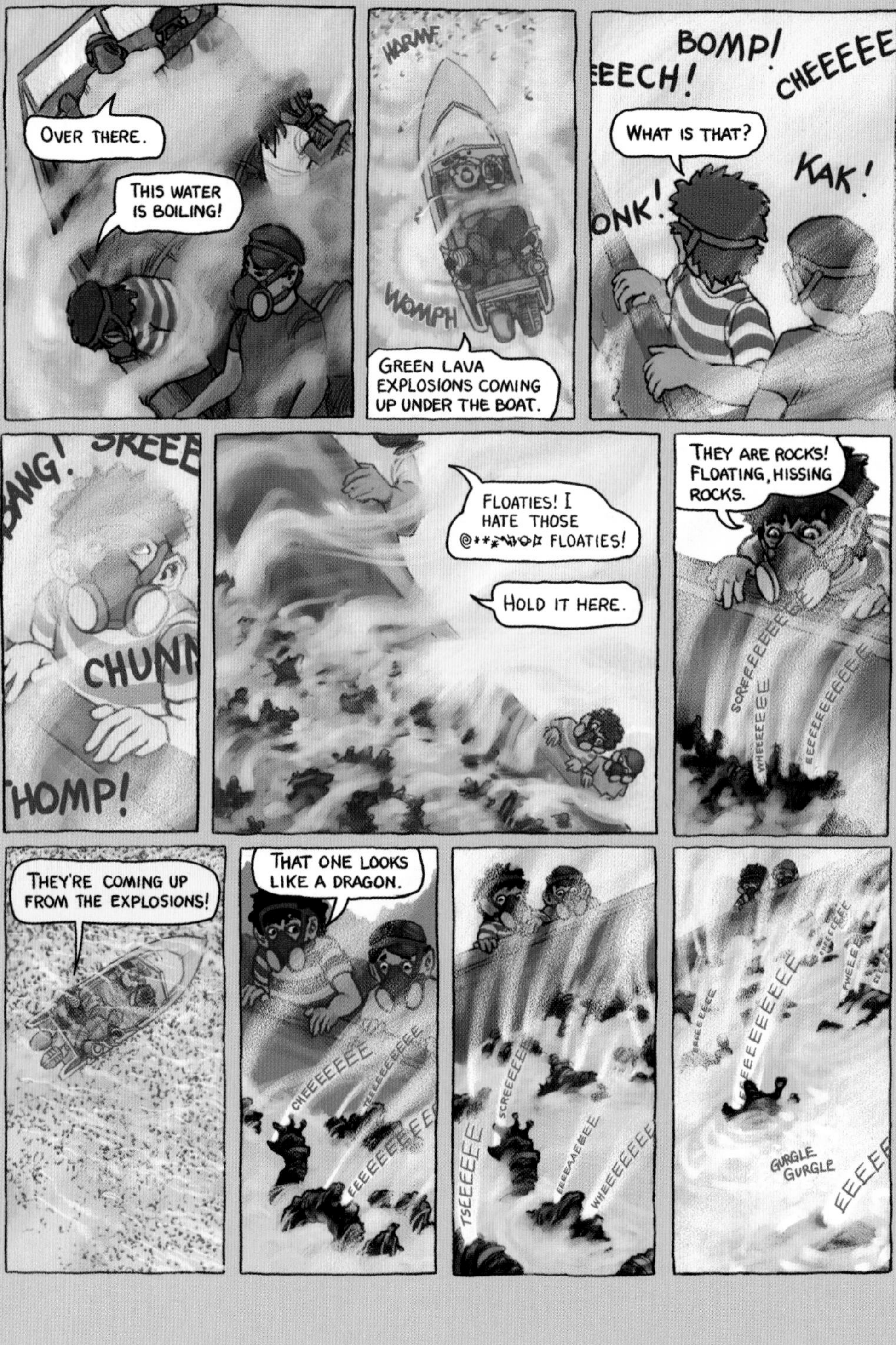
OVER THERE.
THIS WATER IS BOILING!
HARMF
WOMPH
GREEN LAVA EXPLOSIONS COMING UP UNDER THE BOAT.
BOMP!
EEECH!
CHEEEEE
WHAT IS THAT?
KAK!
ONK!
BANG!
SREEE
CHUNN
THOMP!
FLOATIES! I HATE THOSE @**%#@ FLOATIES!
HOLD IT HERE.
THEY ARE ROCKS! FLOATING, HISSING ROCKS.
SCREEEEEE
WHEEEEEE
EEEEEEEEEE
THEY'RE COMING UP FROM THE EXPLOSIONS!
THAT ONE LOOKS LIKE A DRAGON.
CHEEEEEEE
TSEEEEEEE
EEEEEEEE
SCREEEEE
TSEEEEE
EEEEAAEEEE
WHEEEEEEE
GURGLE GURGLE
EEEE

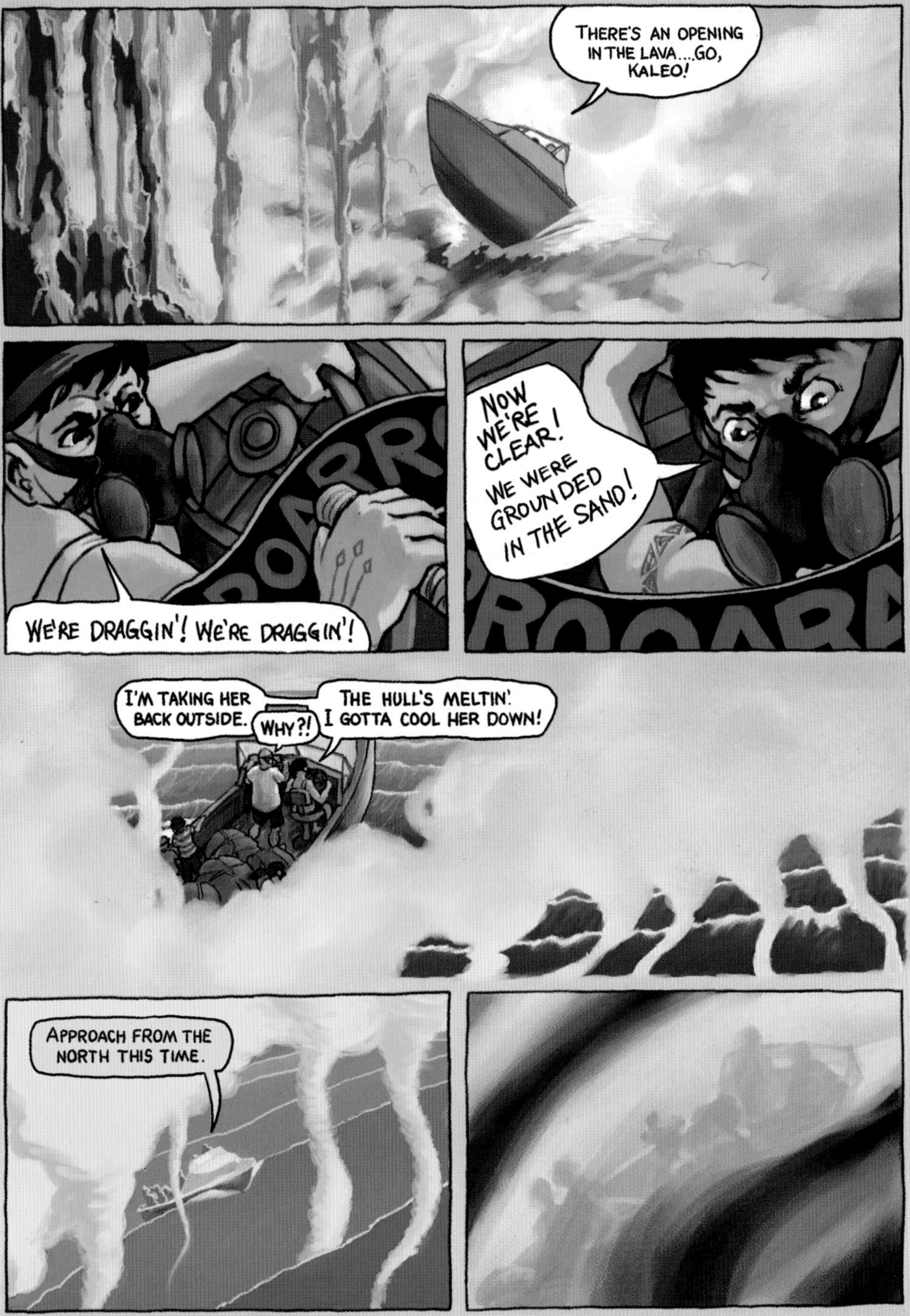
THERE'S AN OPENING IN THE LAVA....GO, KALEO!
ROARR
WE'RE DRAGGIN'! WE'RE DRAGGIN'!
NOW WE'RE CLEAR! WE WERE GROUNDED IN THE SAND!
ROOAR
I'M TAKING HER BACK OUTSIDE.
WHY?!
THE HULL'S MELTIN'. I GOTTA COOL HER DOWN!
APPROACH FROM THE NORTH THIS TIME.

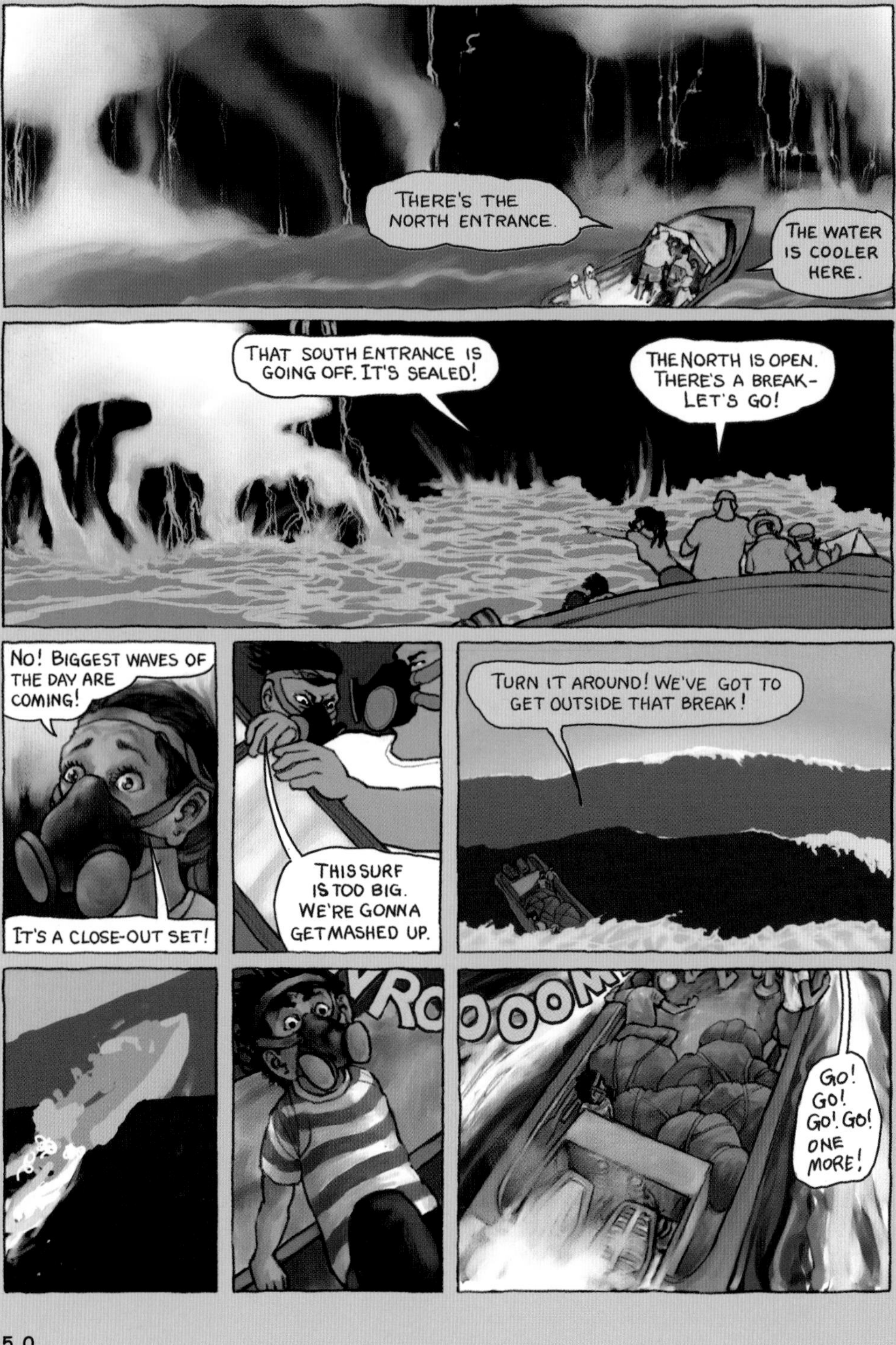
THERE'S THE NORTH ENTRANCE.
THE WATER IS COOLER HERE.
THAT SOUTH ENTRANCE IS GOING OFF. IT'S SEALED!
THE NORTH IS OPEN. THERE'S A BREAK- LET'S GO!
NO! BIGGEST WAVES OF THE DAY ARE COMING!
IT'S A CLOSE-OUT SET!
THIS SURF IS TOO BIG. WE'RE GONNA GET MASHED UP.
TURN IT AROUND! WE'VE GOT TO GET OUTSIDE THAT BREAK!
VROOOOM
GO! GO! GO! GO! ONE MORE!

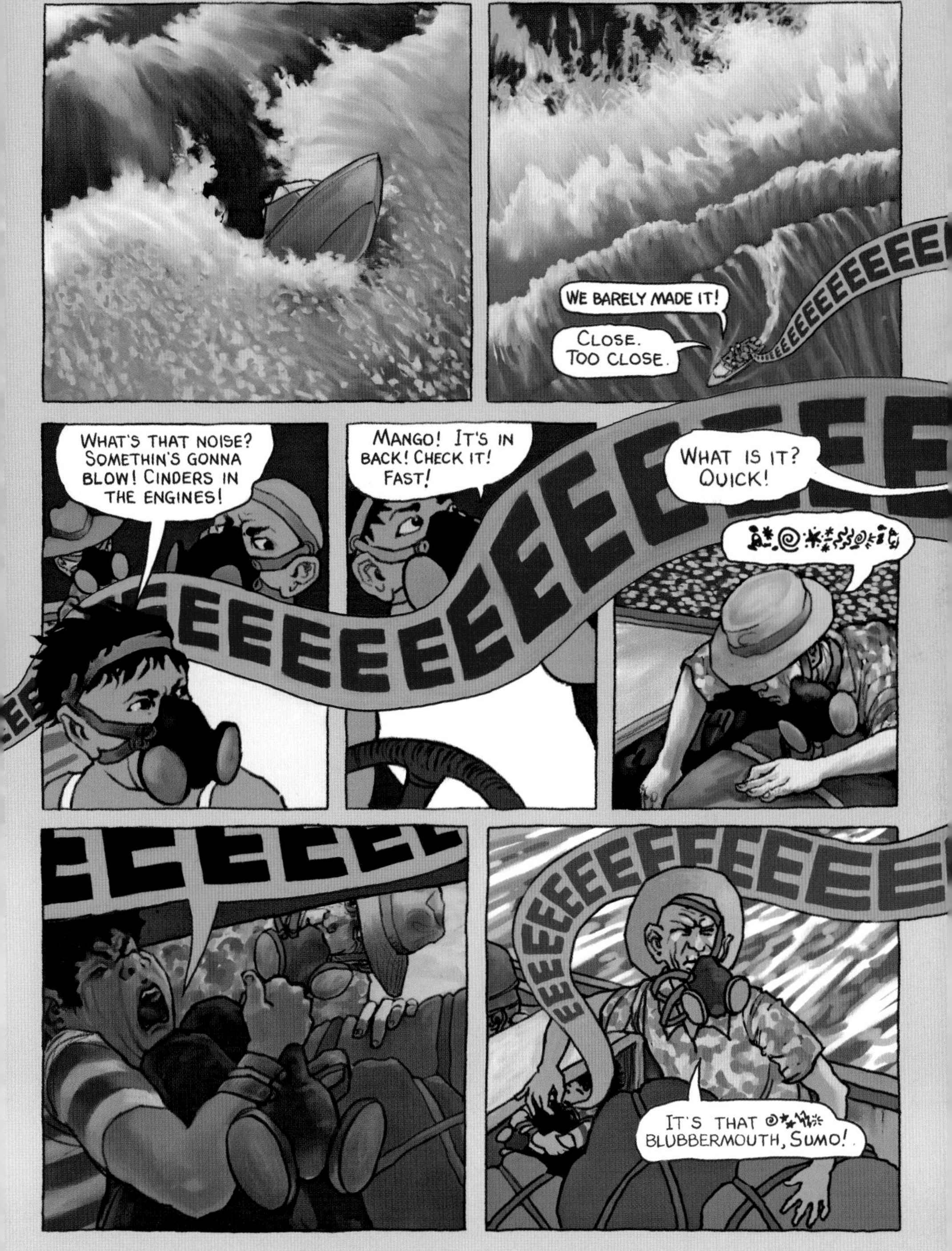
WE BARELY MADE IT!
CLOSE. TOO CLOSE.
EEEEEEEEEEEEEEEEEEEEEEE
WHAT'S THAT NOISE? SOMETHIN'S GONNA BLOW! CINDERS IN THE ENGINES!
MANGO! IT'S IN BACK! CHECK IT! FAST!
WHAT IS IT? QUICK!
EEEEEEEEEEEEEEE
IT'S THAT BLUBBERMOUTH, SUMO!

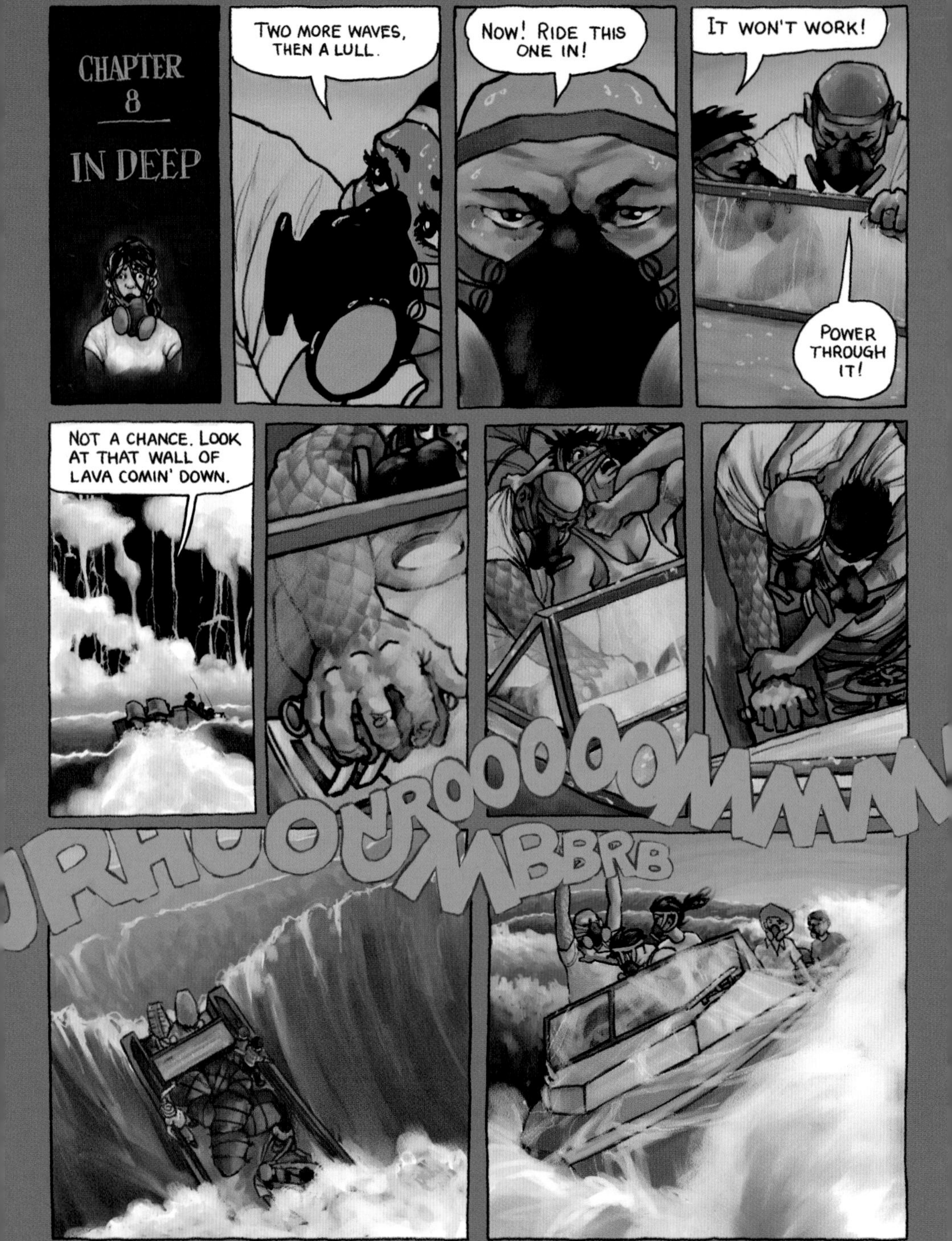
CHAPTER 8
IN DEEP
TWO MORE WAVES, THEN A LULL.
NOW! RIDE THIS ONE IN!
IT WON'T WORK!
POWER THROUGH IT!
NOT A CHANCE. LOOK AT THAT WALL OF LAVA COMIN' DOWN.
VROOOOOMMMM
RHUUUMBBRB

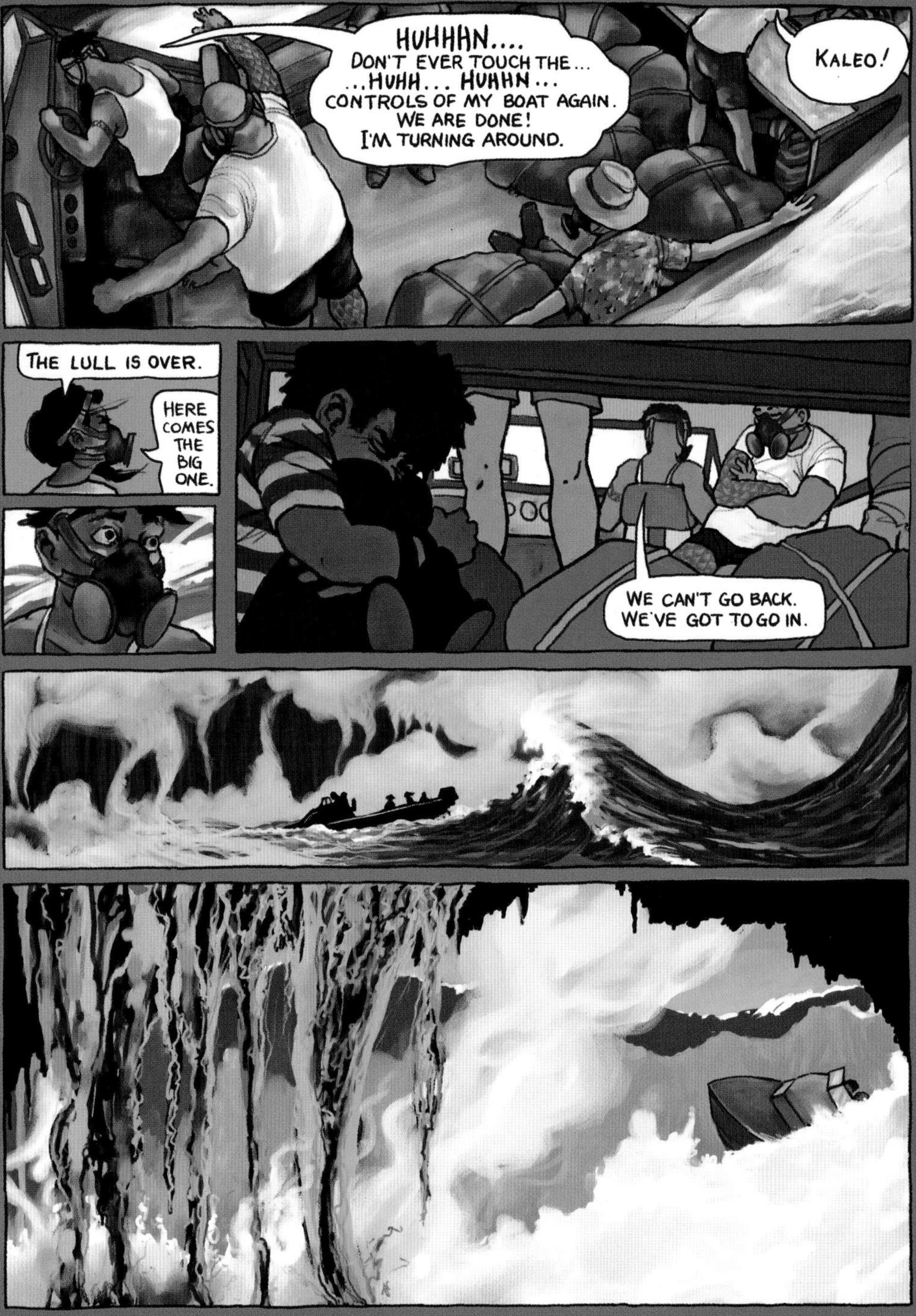
HUHHHN.... DON'T EVER TOUCH THE... ...HUHH... HUHHN... CONTROLS OF MY BOAT AGAIN. WE ARE DONE! I'M TURNING AROUND.
KALEO!
THE LULL IS OVER.
HERE COMES THE BIG ONE.
WE CAN'T GO BACK. WE'VE GOT TO GO IN.

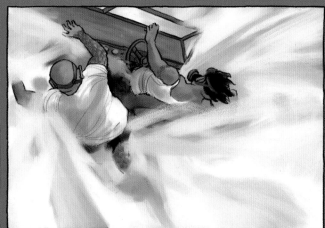

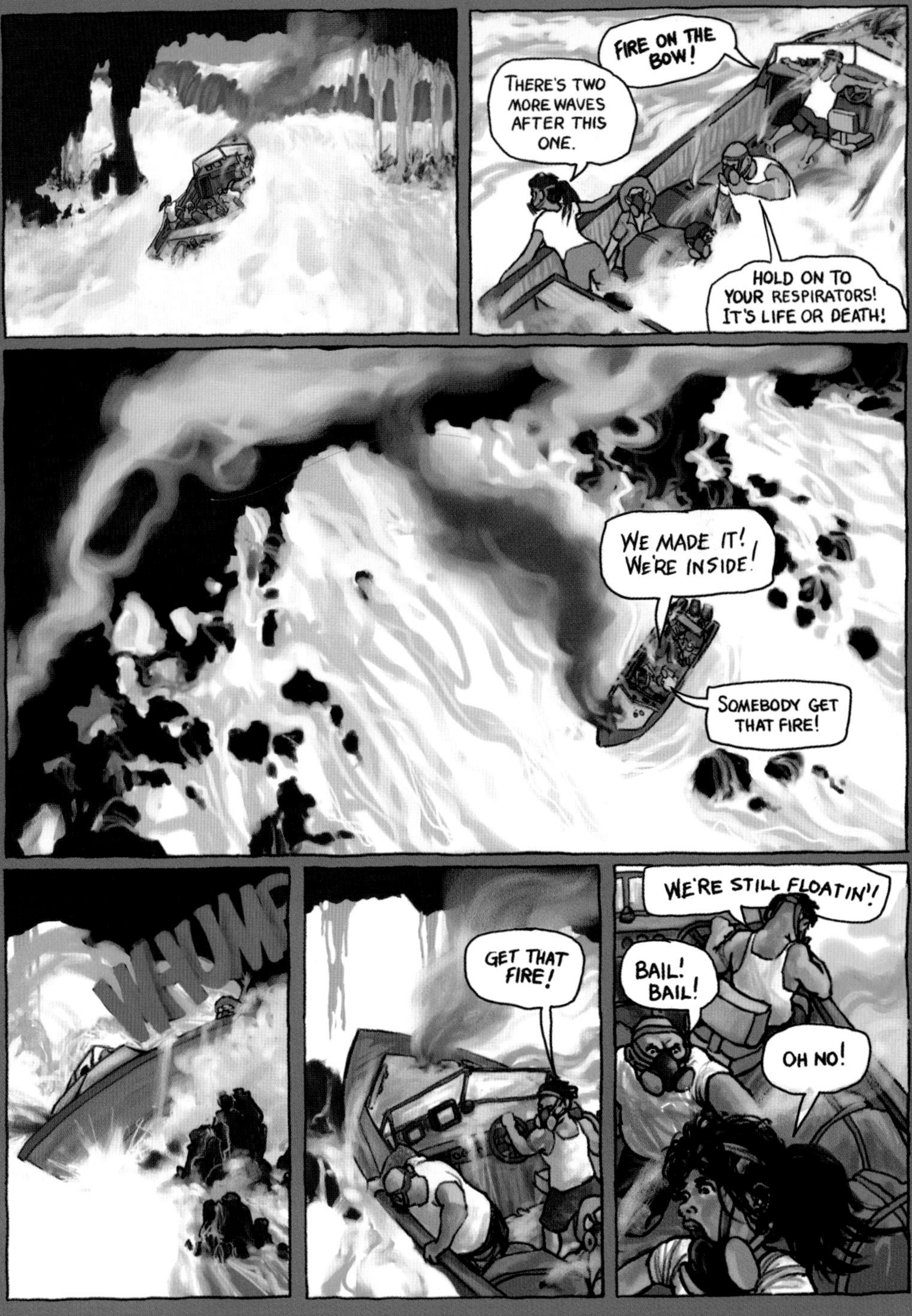
FIRE ON THE BOW!
THERE'S TWO MORE WAVES AFTER THIS ONE.
HOLD ON TO YOUR RESPIRATORS! IT'S LIFE OR DEATH!
WE MADE IT! WE'RE INSIDE!
SOMEBODY GET THAT FIRE!
WHUMF
GET THAT FIRE!
WE'RE STILL FLOATIN'!
BAIL! BAIL!
OH NO!

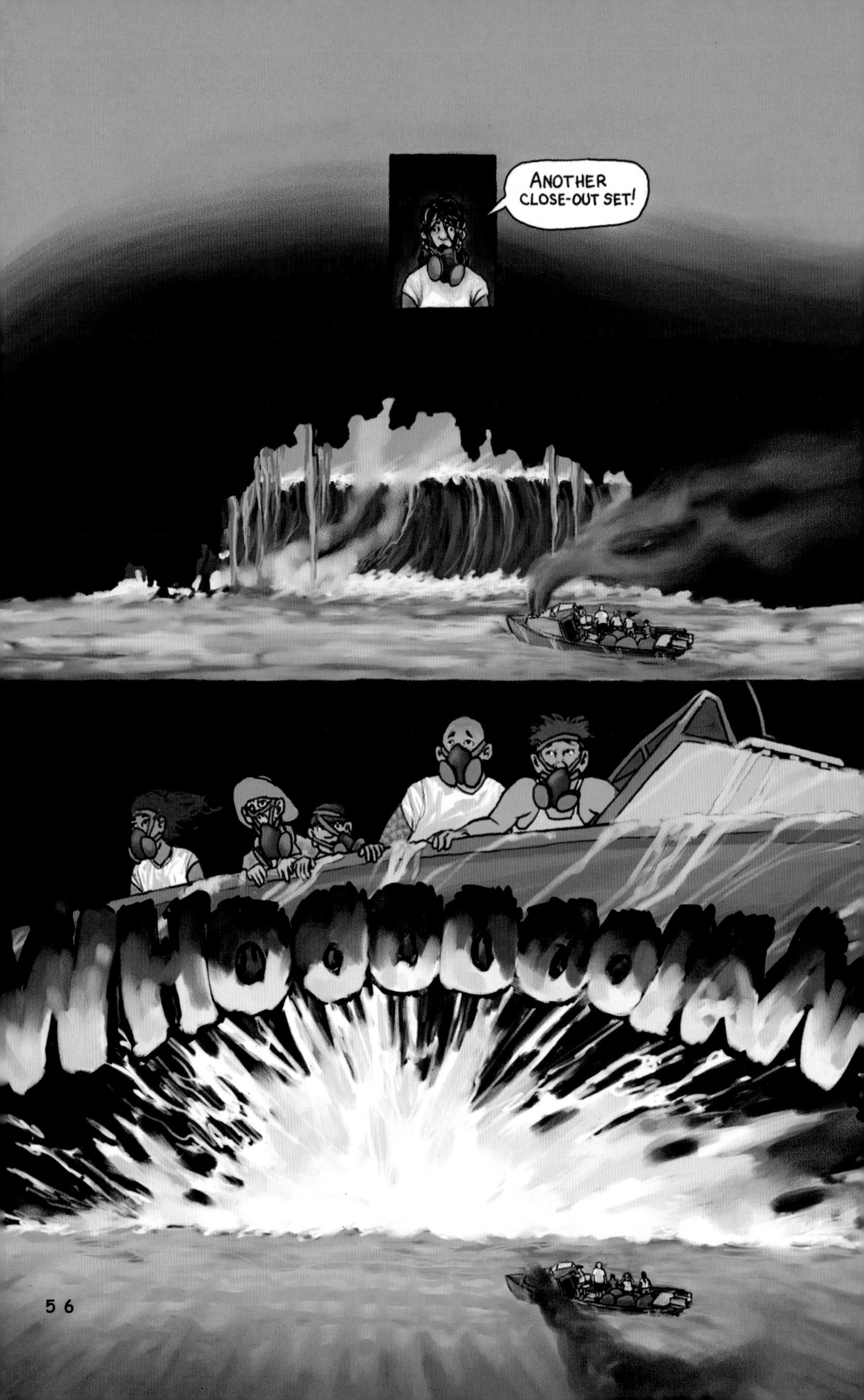
ANOTHER CLOSE-OUT SET!
WHOOOOOOOOM

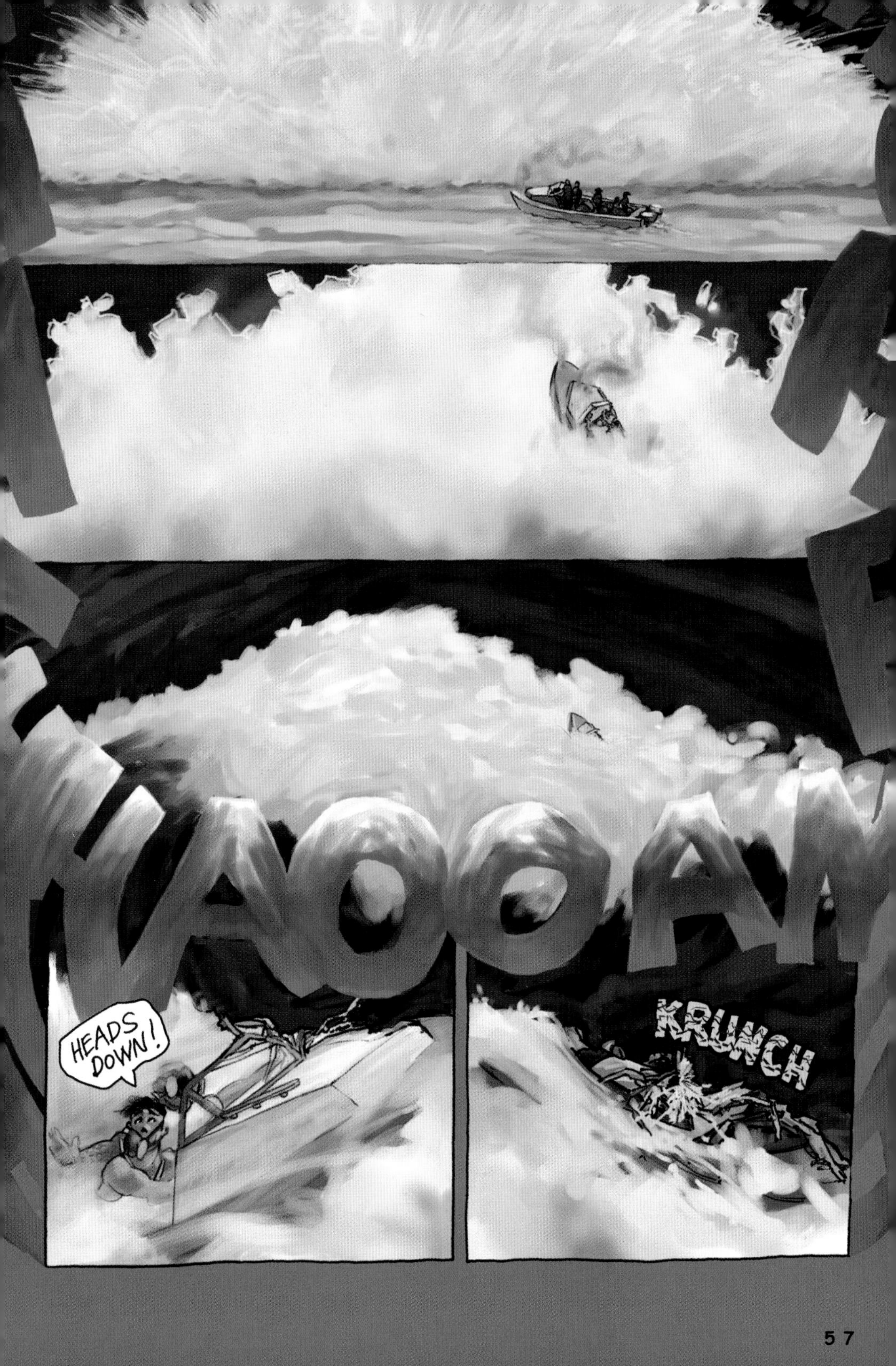

KAOOOM
HEADS DOWN!
KRUNCH

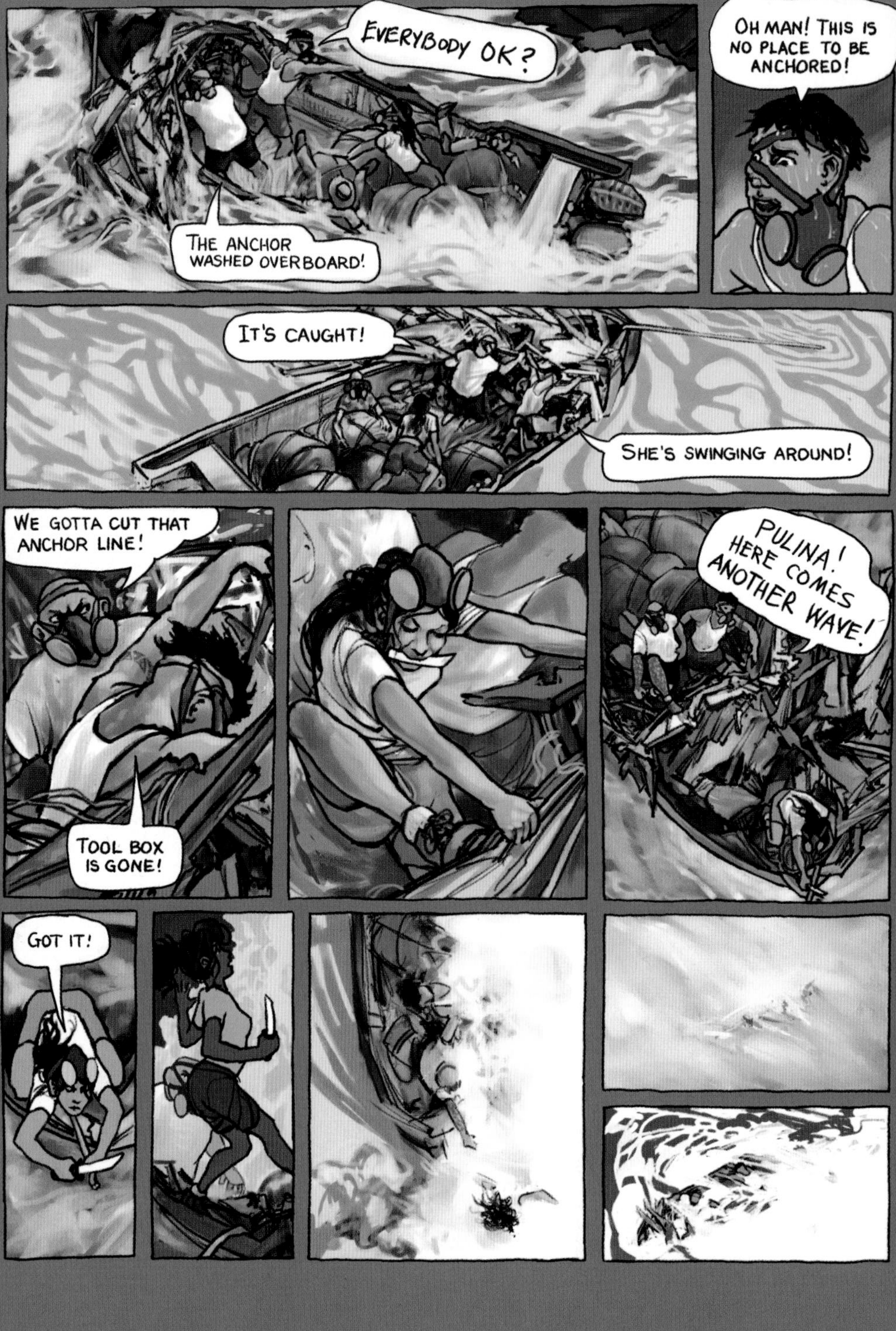
EVERYBODY OK?
THE ANCHOR WASHED OVERBOARD!
OH MAN! THIS IS NO PLACE TO BE ANCHORED!
IT'S CAUGHT!
SHE'S SWINGING AROUND!
WE GOTTA CUT THAT ANCHOR LINE!
TOOL BOX IS GONE!
PULINA! HERE COMES ANOTHER WAVE!
GOT IT!

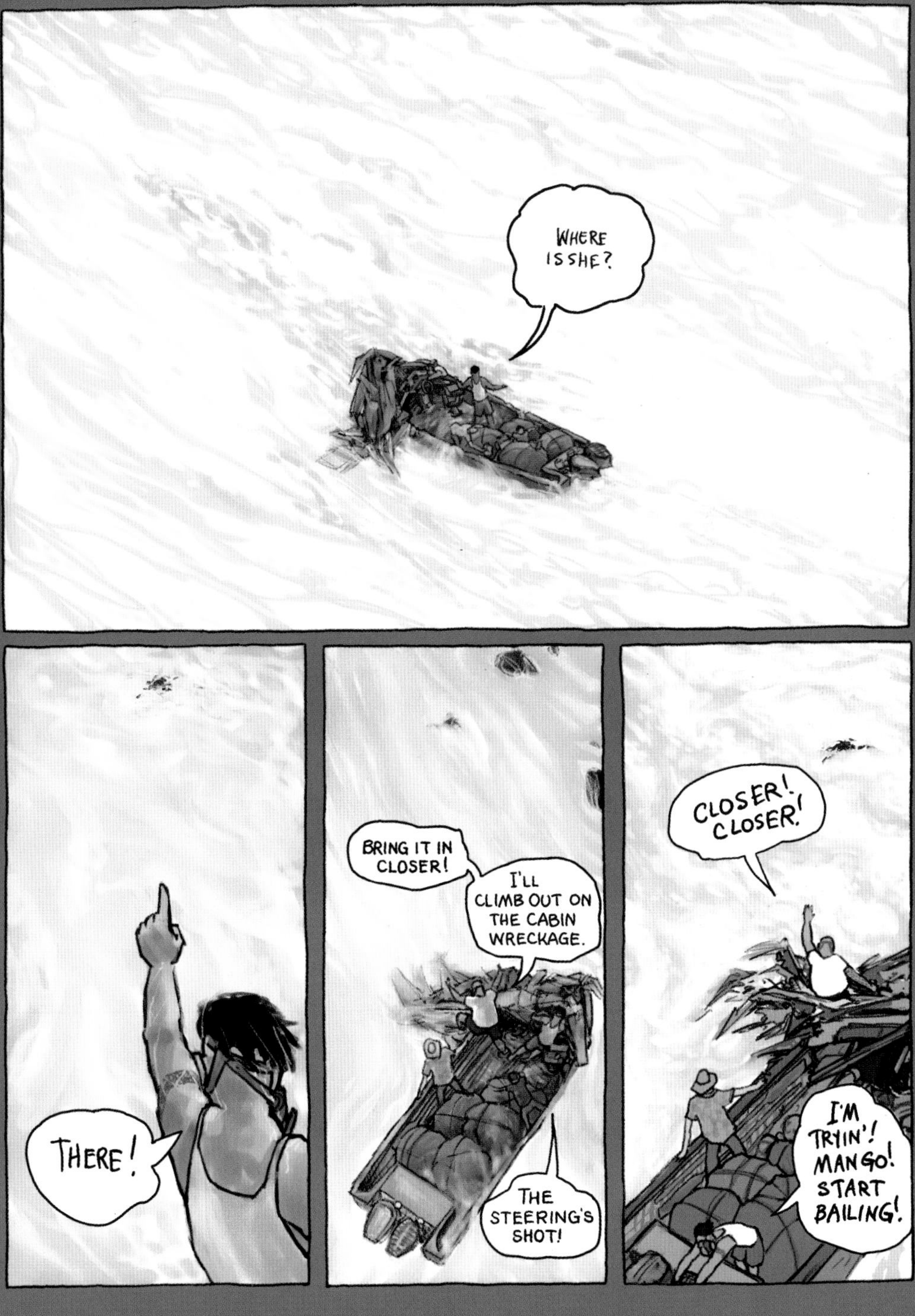
WHERE IS SHE?
THERE!
BRING IT IN CLOSER!
I'LL CLIMB OUT ON THE CABIN WRECKAGE.
THE STEERING'S SHOT!
CLOSER! CLOSER!
I'M TRYIN'! MANGO! START BAILING!

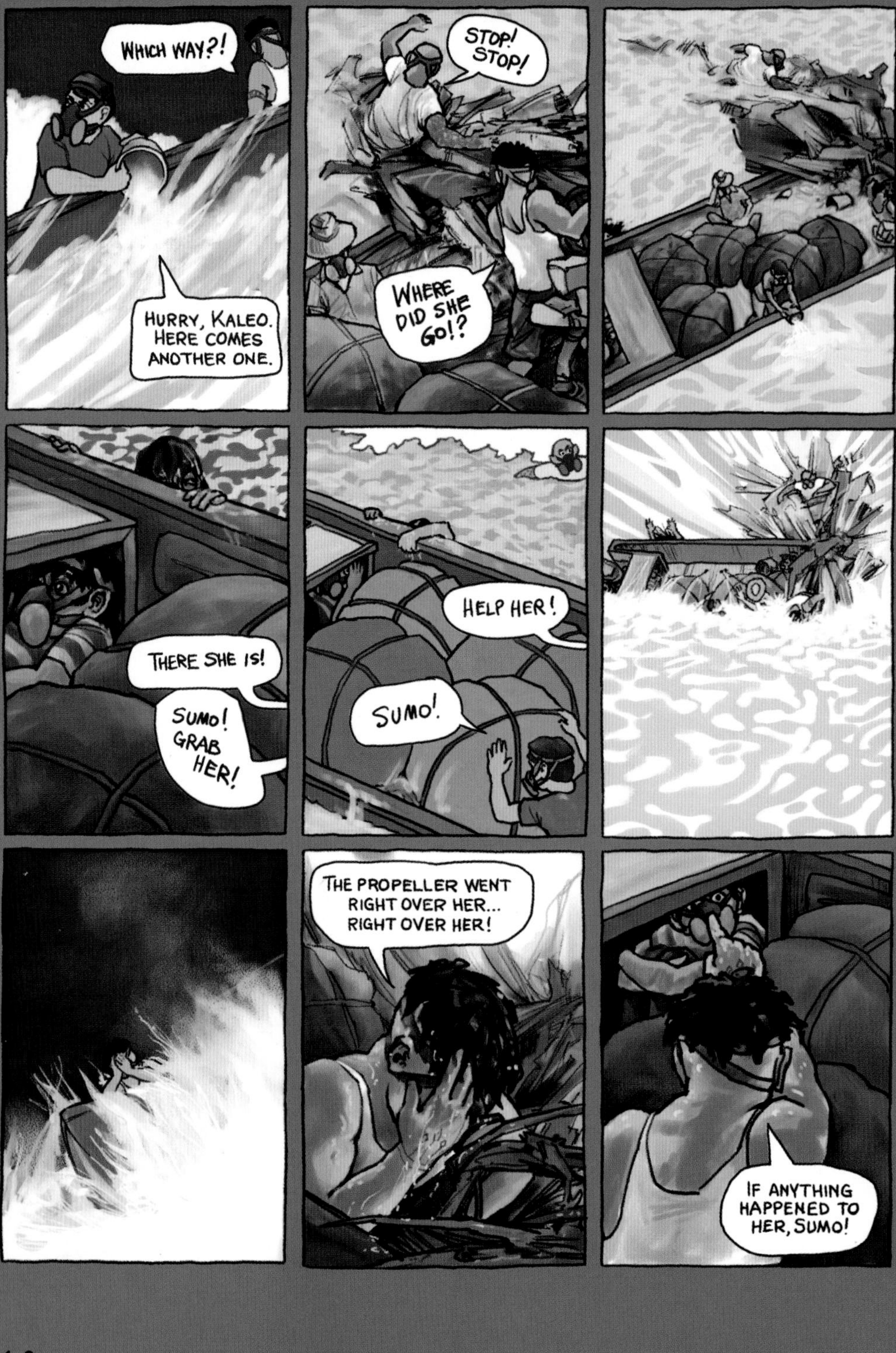
WHICH WAY?!
HURRY, KALEO. HERE COMES ANOTHER ONE.
STOP! STOP!
WHERE DID SHE GO!?
THERE SHE IS!
SUMO! GRAB HER!
HELP HER!
SUMO!
THE PROPELLER WENT RIGHT OVER HER... RIGHT OVER HER!
IF ANYTHING HAPPENED TO HER, SUMO!

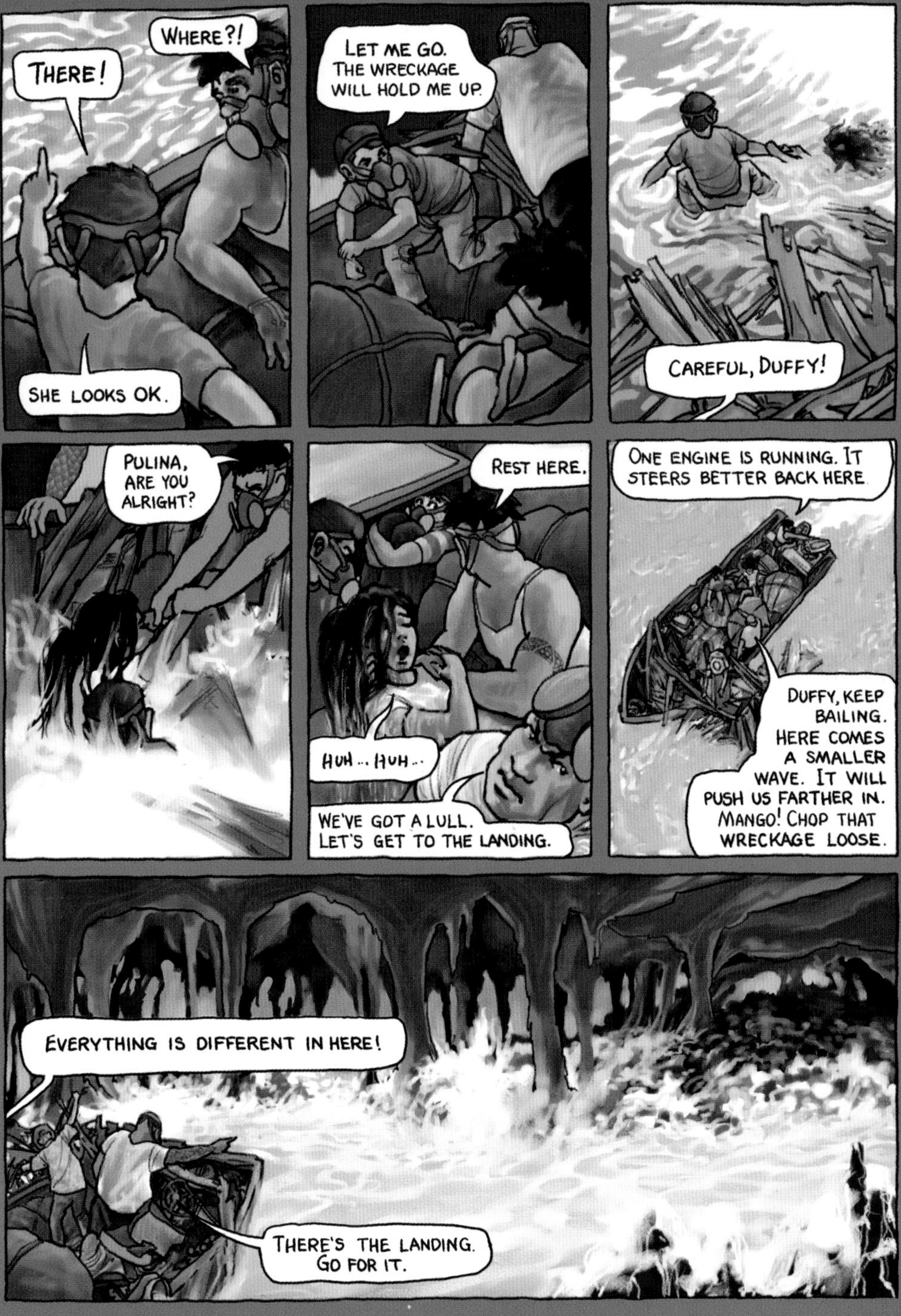
THERE!
WHERE?!
SHE LOOKS OK.
LET ME GO. THE WRECKAGE WILL HOLD ME UP.
CAREFUL, DUFFY!
PULINA, ARE YOU ALRIGHT?
REST HERE.
HUH... HUH...
WE'VE GOT A LULL. LET'S GET TO THE LANDING.
ONE ENGINE IS RUNNING. IT STEERS BETTER BACK HERE.
DUFFY, KEEP BAILING. HERE COMES A SMALLER WAVE. IT WILL PUSH US FARTHER IN. MANGO! CHOP THAT WRECKAGE LOOSE.
EVERYTHING IS DIFFERENT IN HERE!
THERE'S THE LANDING. GO FOR IT.

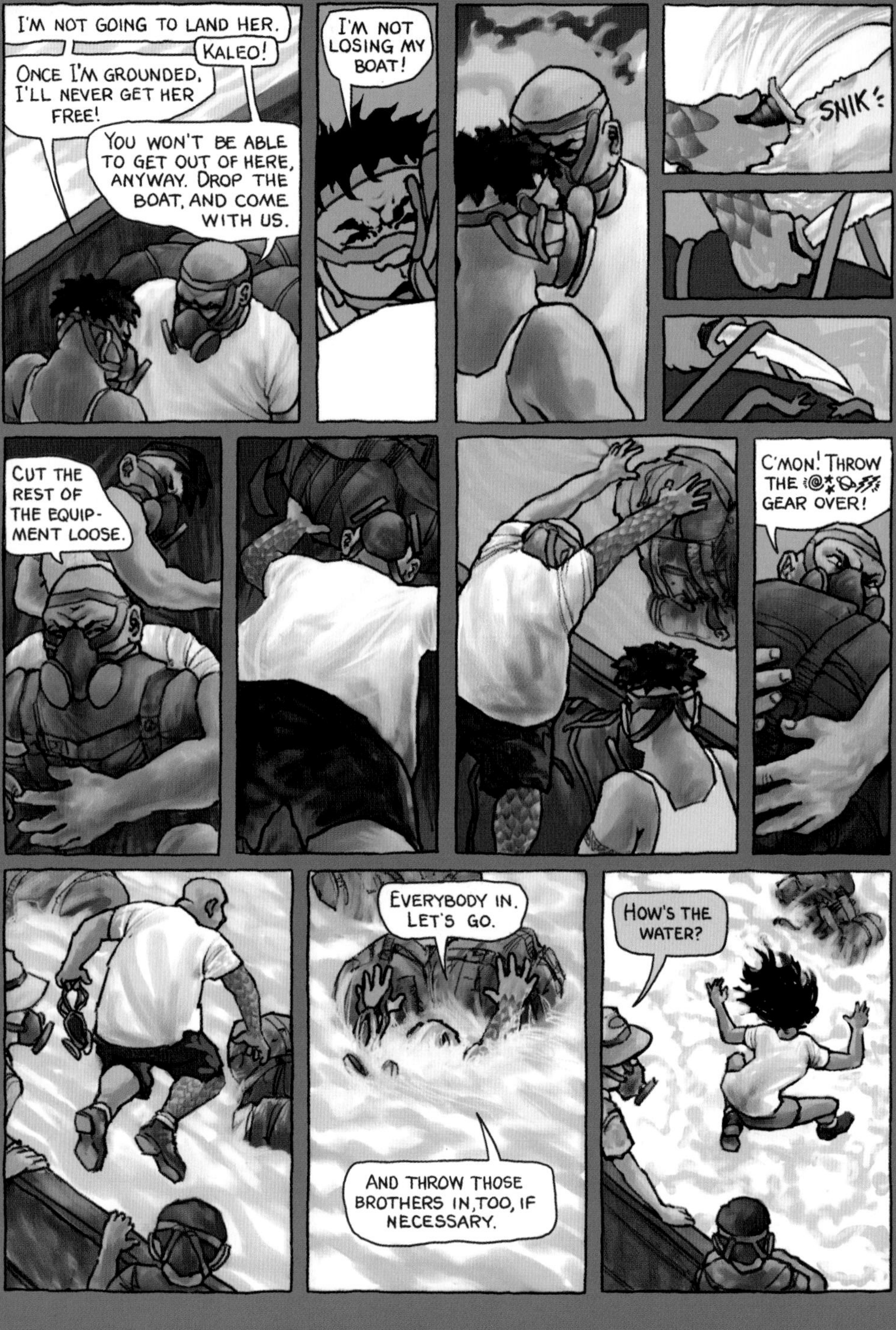
I'M NOT GOING TO LAND HER.
KALEO!
ONCE I'M GROUNDED, I'LL NEVER GET HER FREE!
YOU WON'T BE ABLE TO GET OUT OF HERE, ANYWAY. DROP THE BOAT, AND COME WITH US.
I'M NOT LOSING MY BOAT!
SNIK
CUT THE REST OF THE EQUIP-MENT LOOSE.
C'MON! THROW THE @**& GEAR OVER!
EVERYBODY IN. LET'S GO.
AND THROW THOSE BROTHERS IN,TOO, IF NECESSARY.
HOW'S THE WATER?

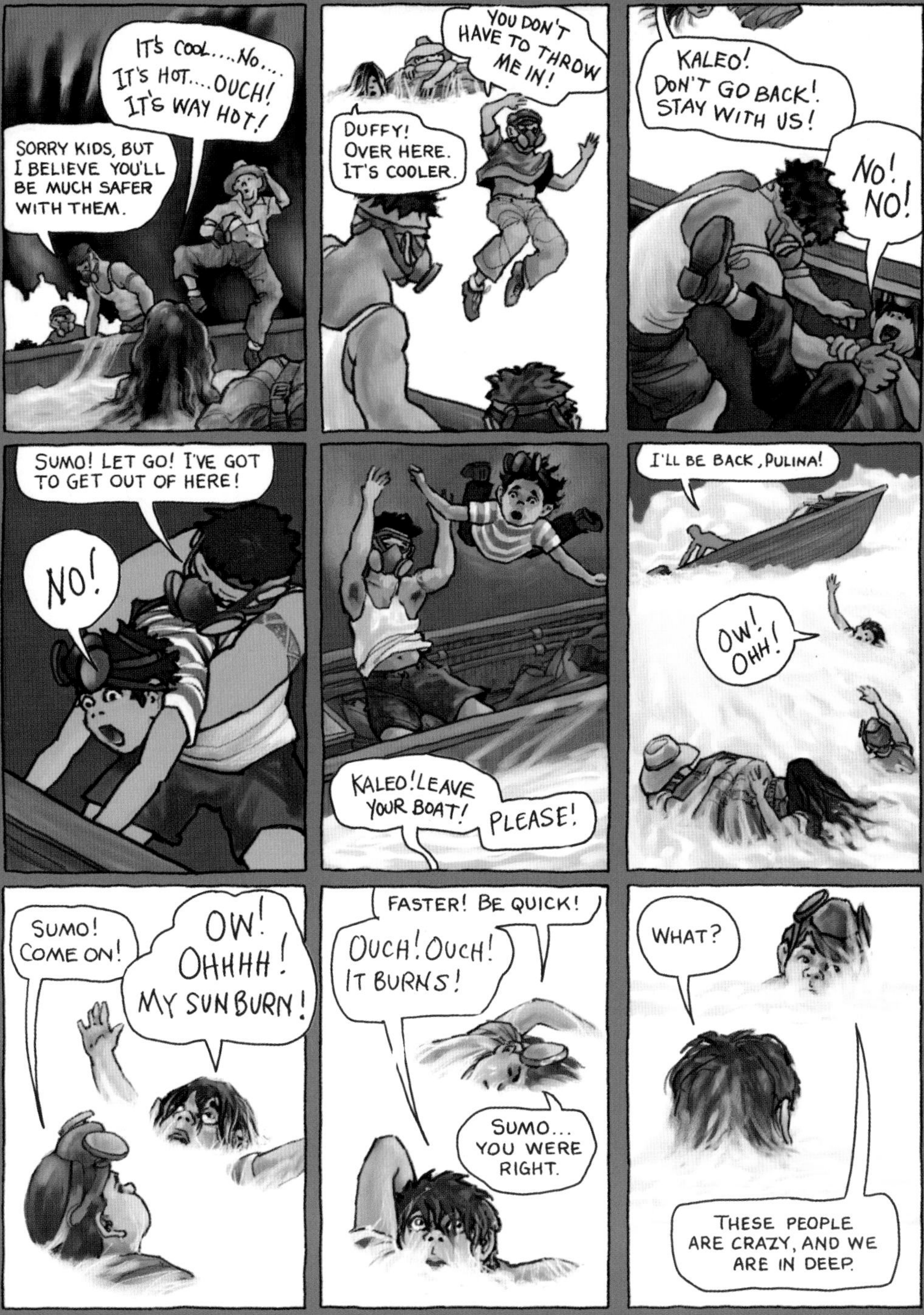
IT'S COOL....NO....
IT'S HOT....OUCH!
IT'S WAY HOT!
SORRY KIDS, BUT I BELIEVE YOU'LL BE MUCH SAFER WITH THEM.
YOU DON'T HAVE TO THROW ME IN!
DUFFY! OVER HERE. IT'S COOLER.
KALEO! DON'T GO BACK! STAY WITH US!
NO! NO!
SUMO! LET GO! I'VE GOT TO GET OUT OF HERE!
NO!
KALEO! LEAVE YOUR BOAT!
PLEASE!
I'LL BE BACK, PULINA!
OW! OHH!
SUMO! COME ON!
OW! OHHHH! MY SUNBURN!
FASTER! BE QUICK!
OUCH! OUCH! IT BURNS!
SUMO... YOU WERE RIGHT.
WHAT?
THESE PEOPLE ARE CRAZY, AND WE ARE IN DEEP.

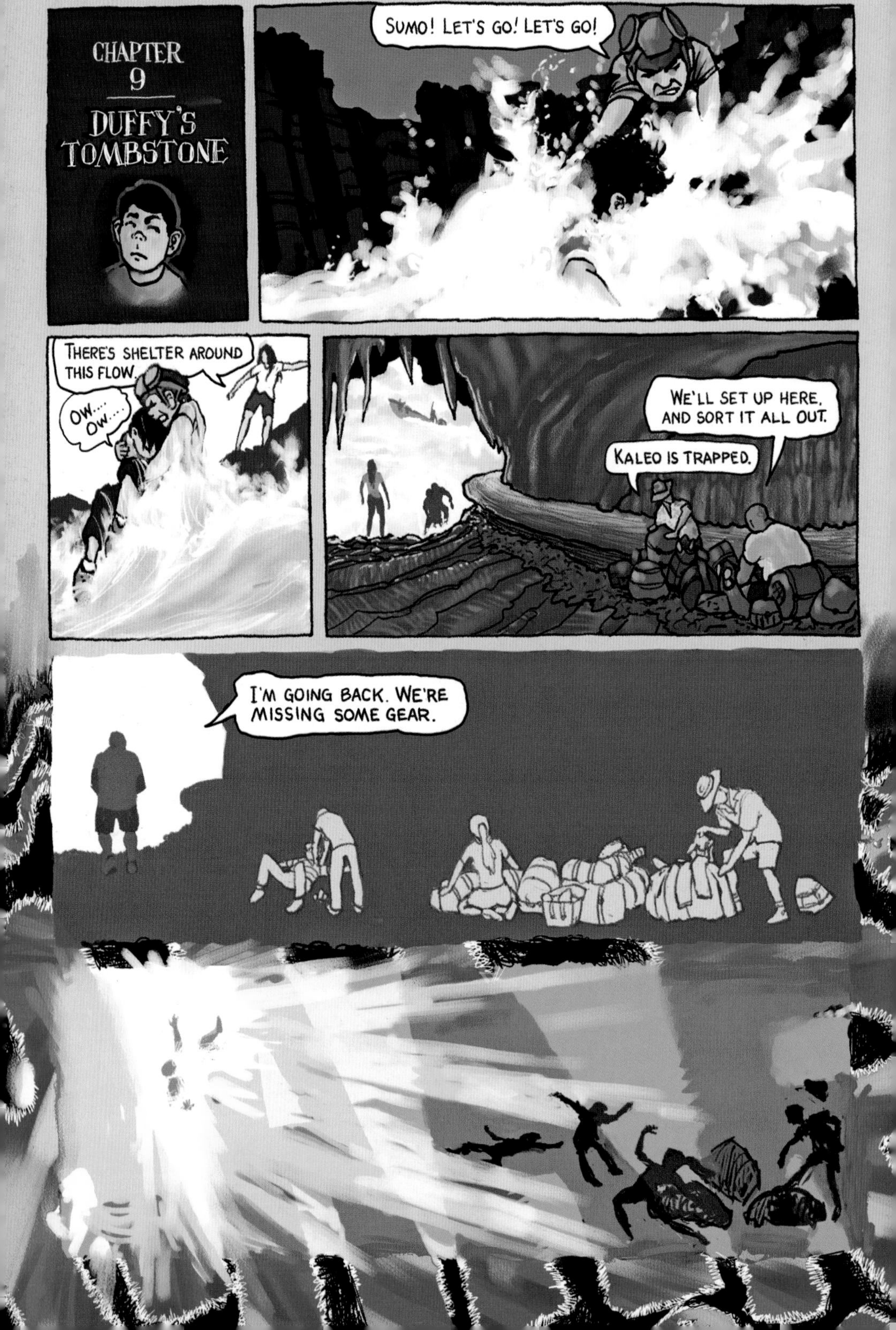
CHAPTER 9
DUFFY'S TOMBSTONE
SUMO! LET'S GO! LET'S GO!
THERE'S SHELTER AROUND THIS FLOW.
OW.... OW....
WE'LL SET UP HERE, AND SORT IT ALL OUT.
KALEO IS TRAPPED.
I'M GOING BACK. WE'RE MISSING SOME GEAR.

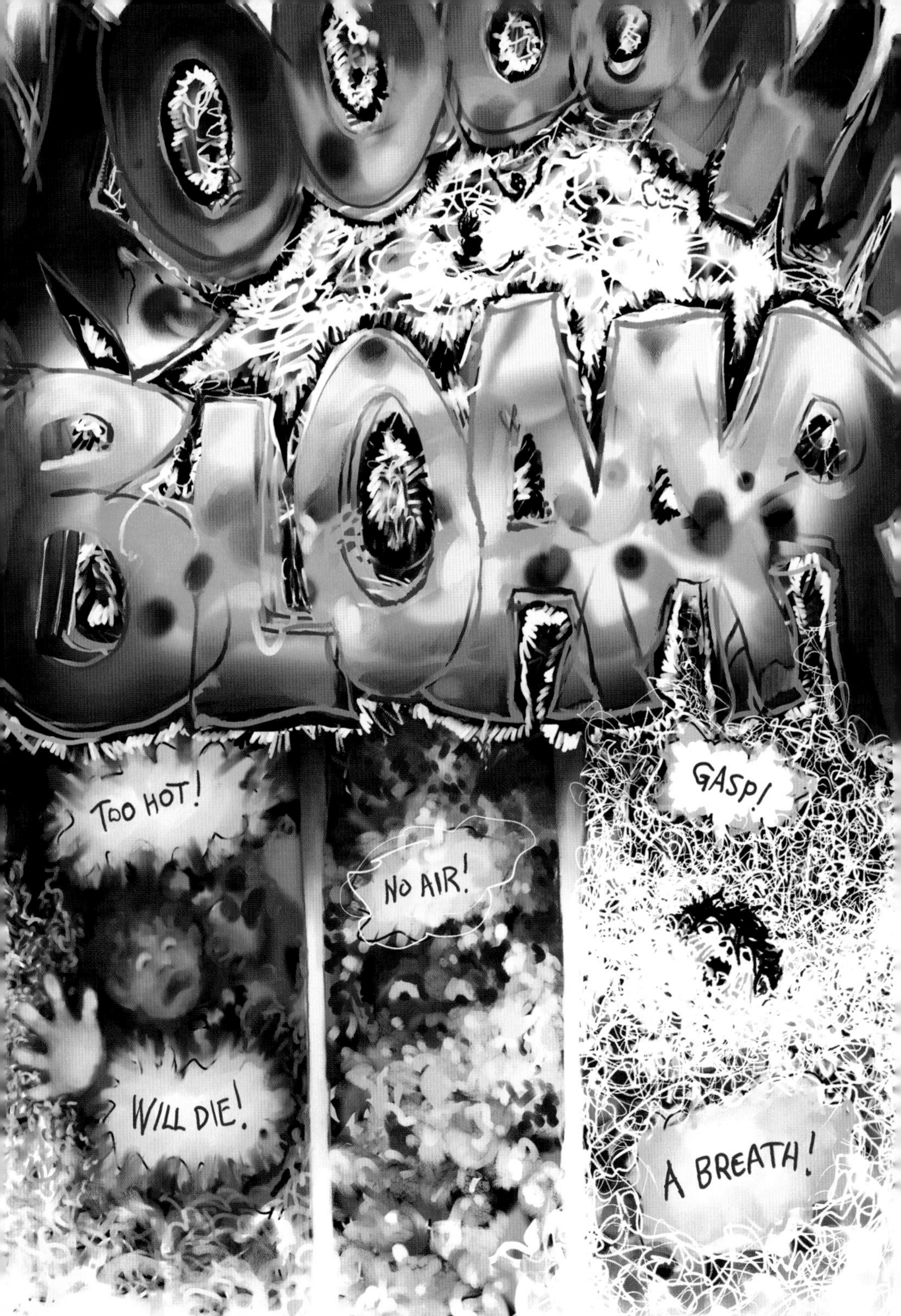
TOO HOT!
WILL DIE!
NO AIR!
GASP!
A BREATH!

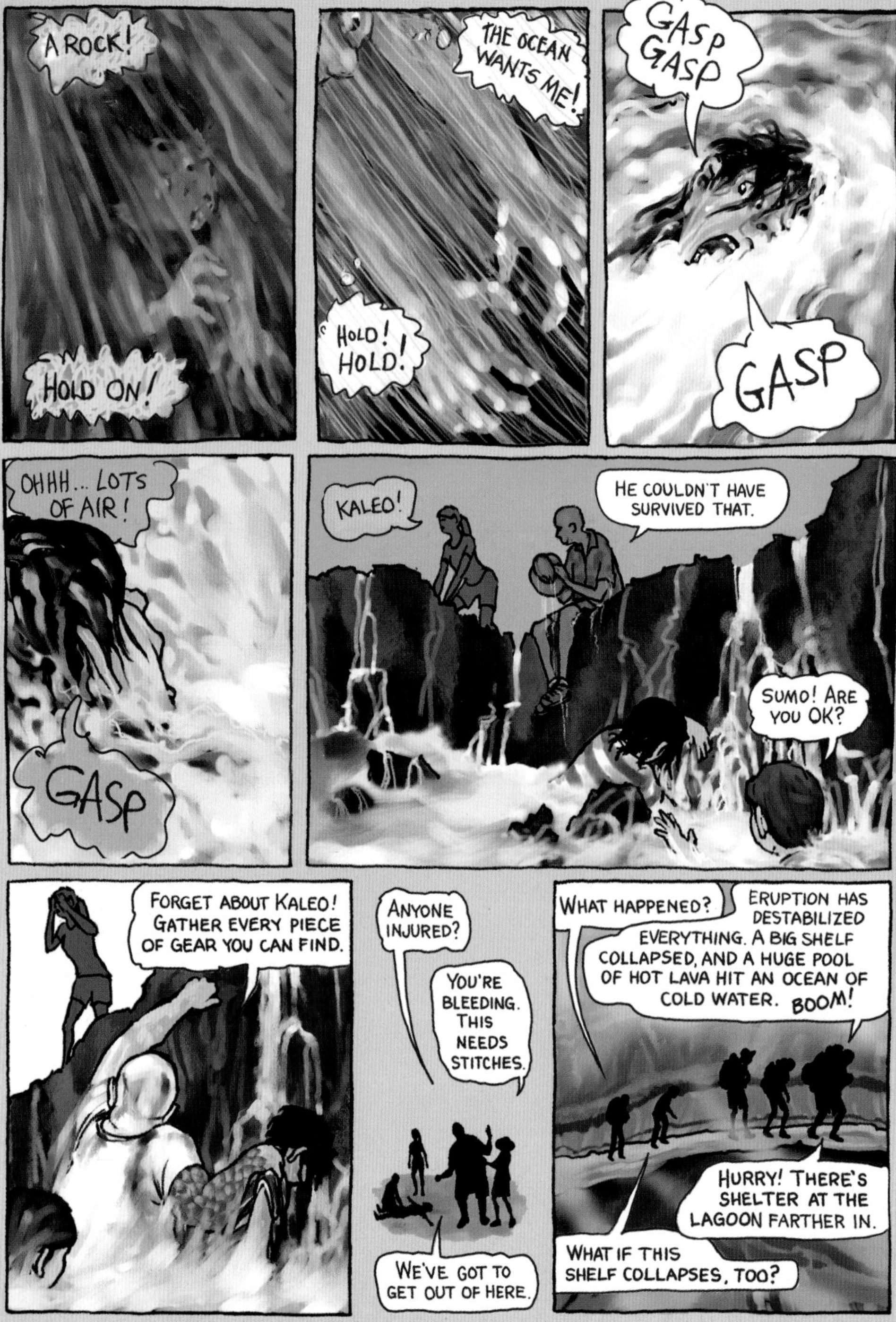
A ROCK!
HOLD ON!
THE OCEAN WANTS ME!
HOLD! HOLD!
GASP GASP
GASP
OHHH... LOTS OF AIR!
GASP
KALEO!
HE COULDN'T HAVE SURVIVED THAT.
SUMO! ARE YOU OK?
FORGET ABOUT KALEO! GATHER EVERY PIECE OF GEAR YOU CAN FIND.
ANYONE INJURED?
YOU'RE BLEEDING. THIS NEEDS STITCHES.
WE'VE GOT TO GET OUT OF HERE.
WHAT HAPPENED?
ERUPTION HAS DESTABILIZED EVERYTHING. A BIG SHELF COLLAPSED, AND A HUGE POOL OF HOT LAVA HIT AN OCEAN OF COLD WATER. BOOM!
HURRY! THERE'S SHELTER AT THE LAGOON FARTHER IN.
WHAT IF THIS SHELF COLLAPSES, TOO?

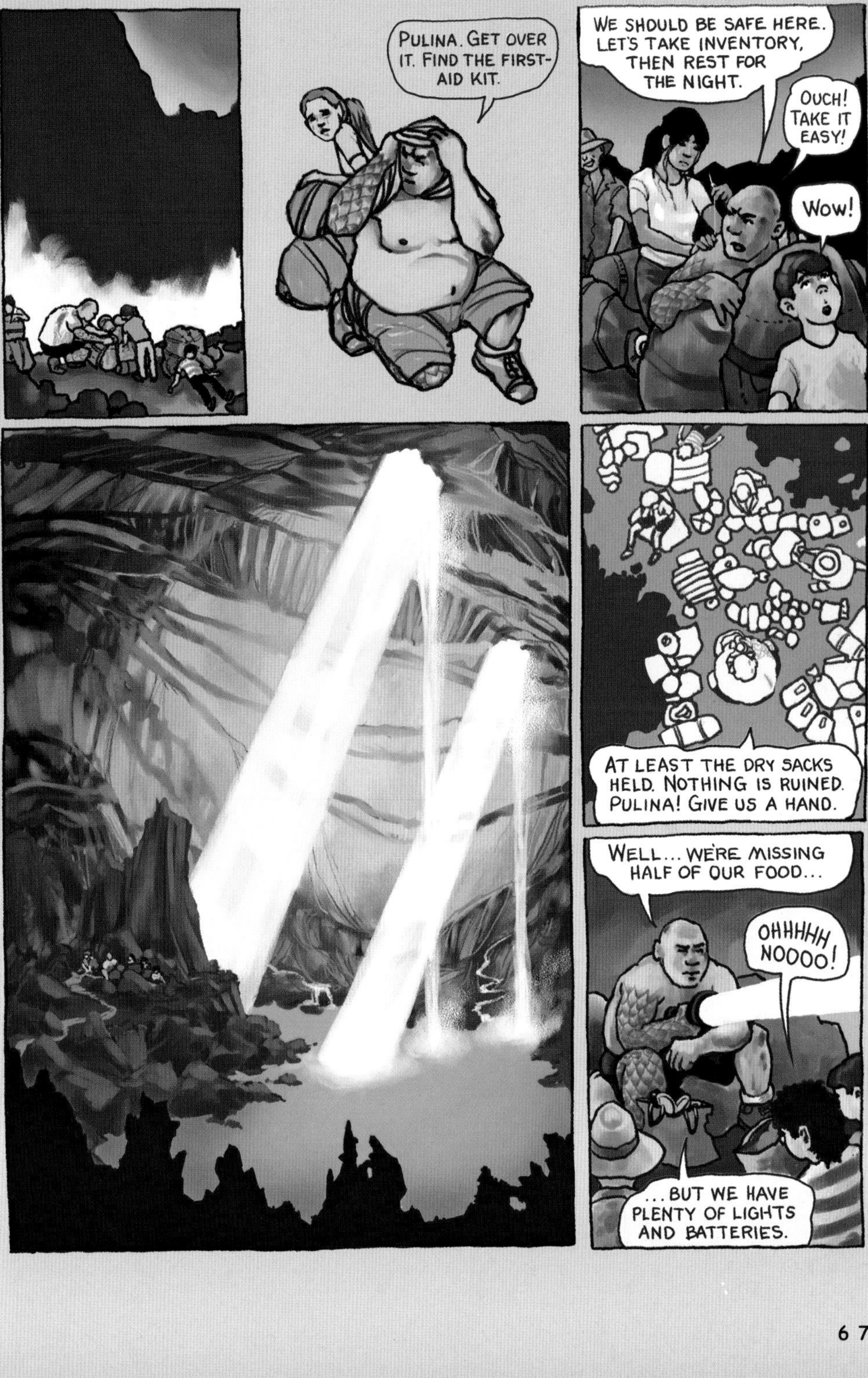
PULINA. GET OVER IT. FIND THE FIRST-AID KIT.
WE SHOULD BE SAFE HERE. LET'S TAKE INVENTORY, THEN REST FOR THE NIGHT.
OUCH! TAKE IT EASY!
WOW!
AT LEAST THE DRY SACKS HELD. NOTHING IS RUINED. PULINA! GIVE US A HAND.
WELL... WE'RE MISSING HALF OF OUR FOOD...
OHHHHH NOOOO!
...BUT WE HAVE PLENTY OF LIGHTS AND BATTERIES.

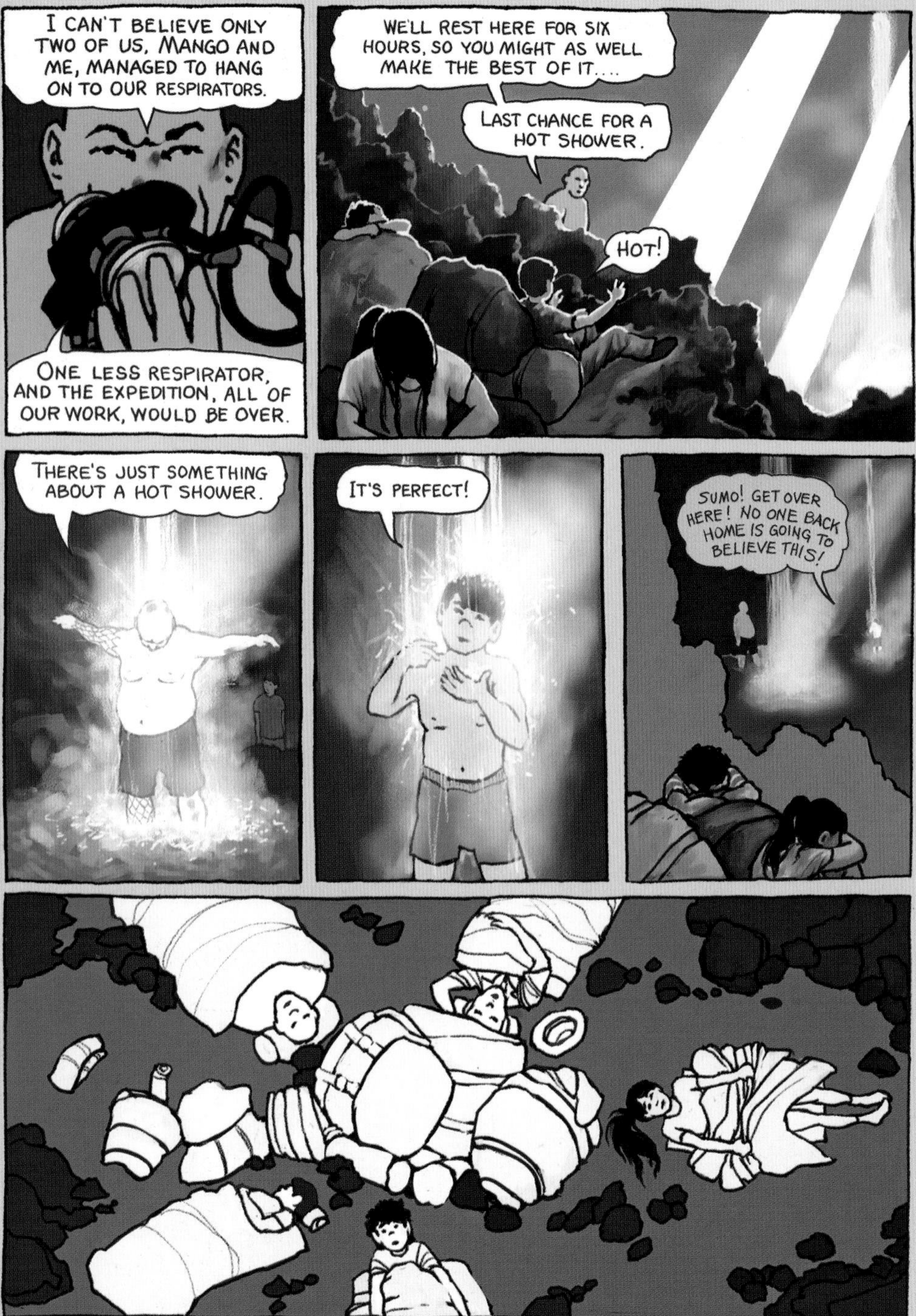
I CAN'T BELIEVE ONLY TWO OF US, MANGO AND ME, MANAGED TO HANG ON TO OUR RESPIRATORS.
ONE LESS RESPIRATOR, AND THE EXPEDITION, ALL OF OUR WORK, WOULD BE OVER.
WE'LL REST HERE FOR SIX HOURS, SO YOU MIGHT AS WELL MAKE THE BEST OF IT....
LAST CHANCE FOR A HOT SHOWER.
HOT!
THERE'S JUST SOMETHING ABOUT A HOT SHOWER.
IT'S PERFECT!
SUMO! GET OVER HERE! NO ONE BACK HOME IS GOING TO BELIEVE THIS!

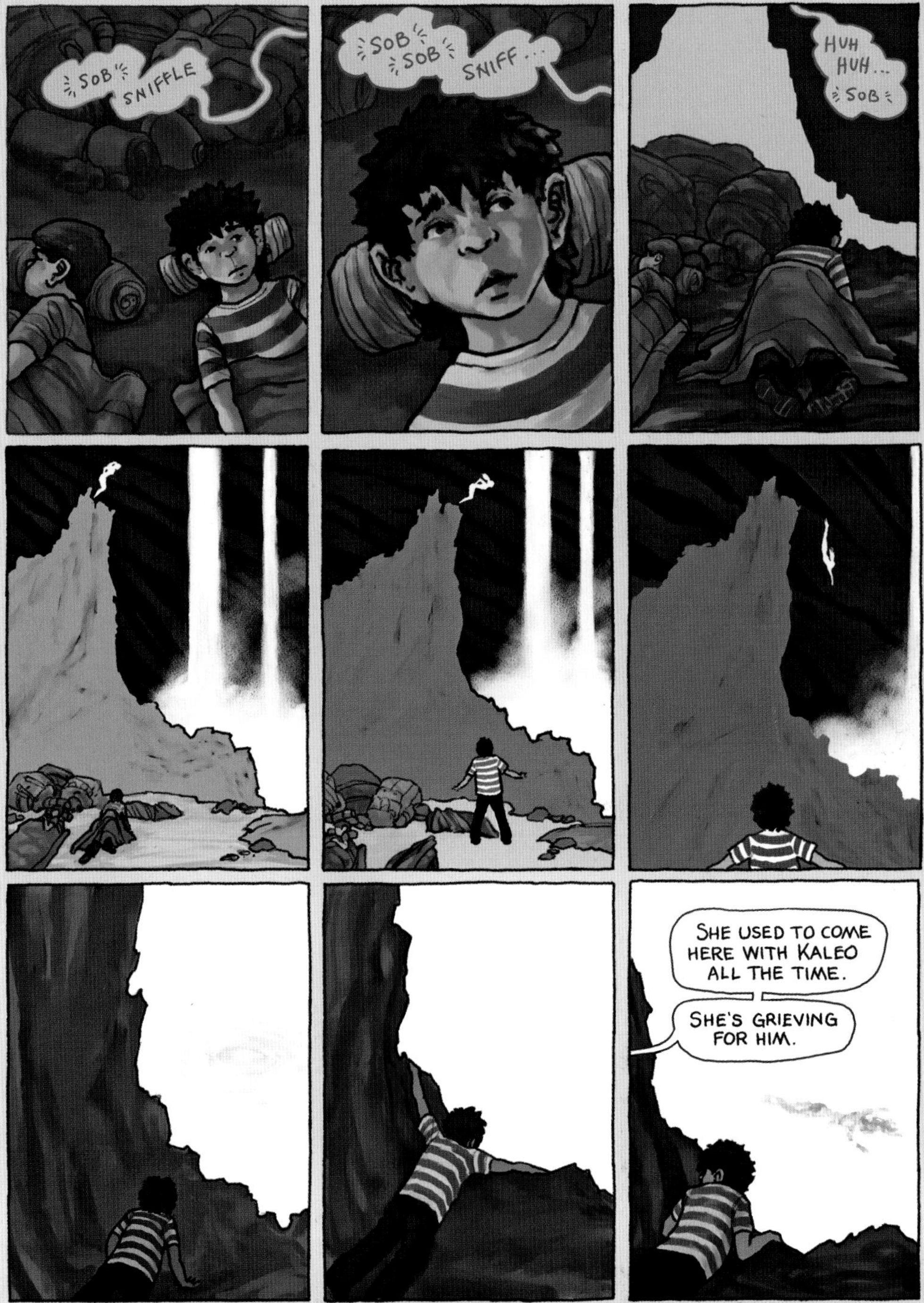
SOB SNIFFLE
SOB SOB SNIFF...
HUH HUH... SOB
SHE USED TO COME HERE WITH KALEO ALL THE TIME.
SHE'S GRIEVING FOR HIM.

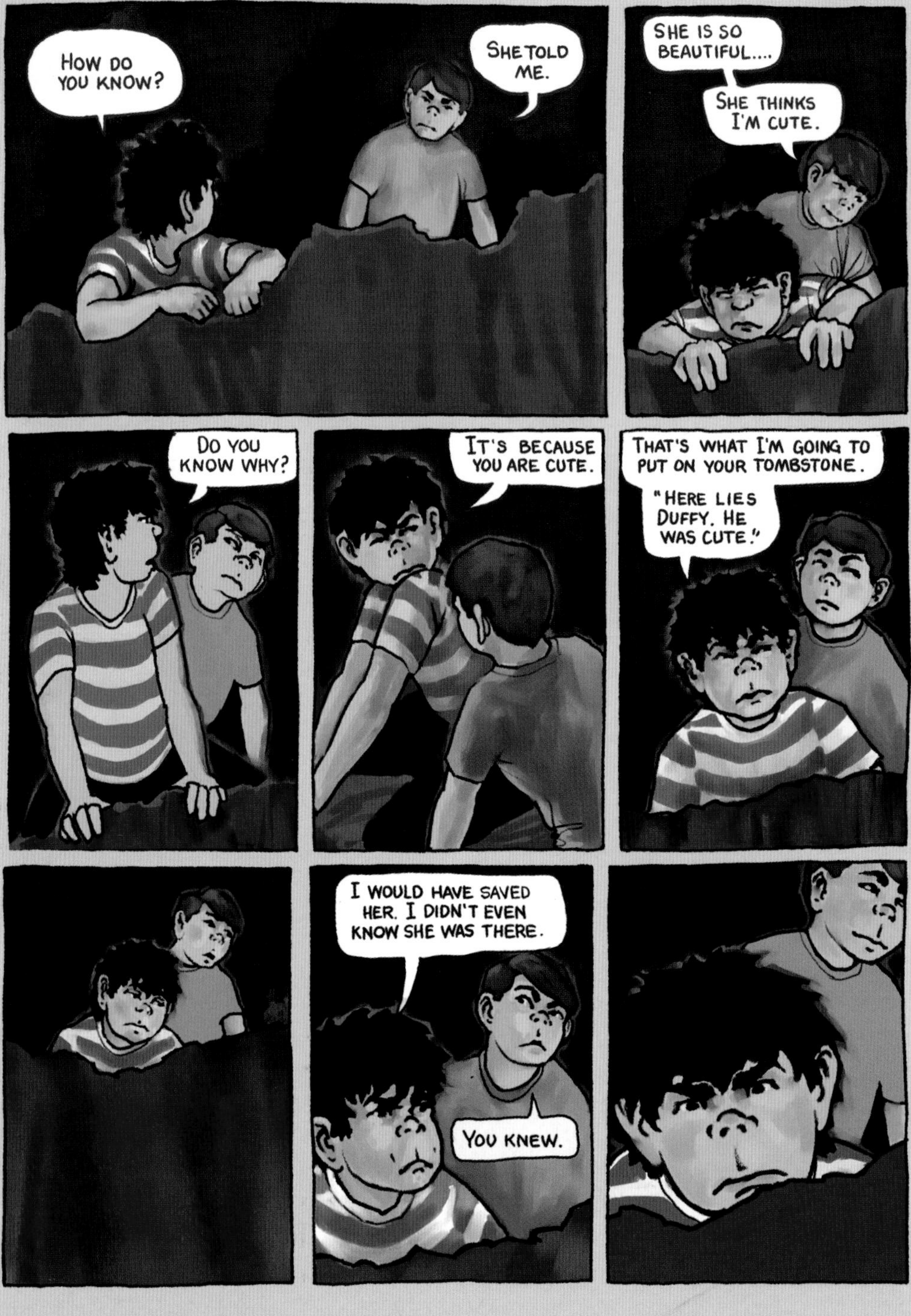
HOW DO YOU KNOW?
SHE TOLD ME.
SHE IS SO BEAUTIFUL....
SHE THINKS I'M CUTE.
DO YOU KNOW WHY?
IT'S BECAUSE YOU ARE CUTE.
THAT'S WHAT I'M GOING TO PUT ON YOUR TOMBSTONE.
"HERE LIES DUFFY. HE WAS CUTE."
I WOULD HAVE SAVED HER. I DIDN'T EVEN KNOW SHE WAS THERE.
YOU KNEW.

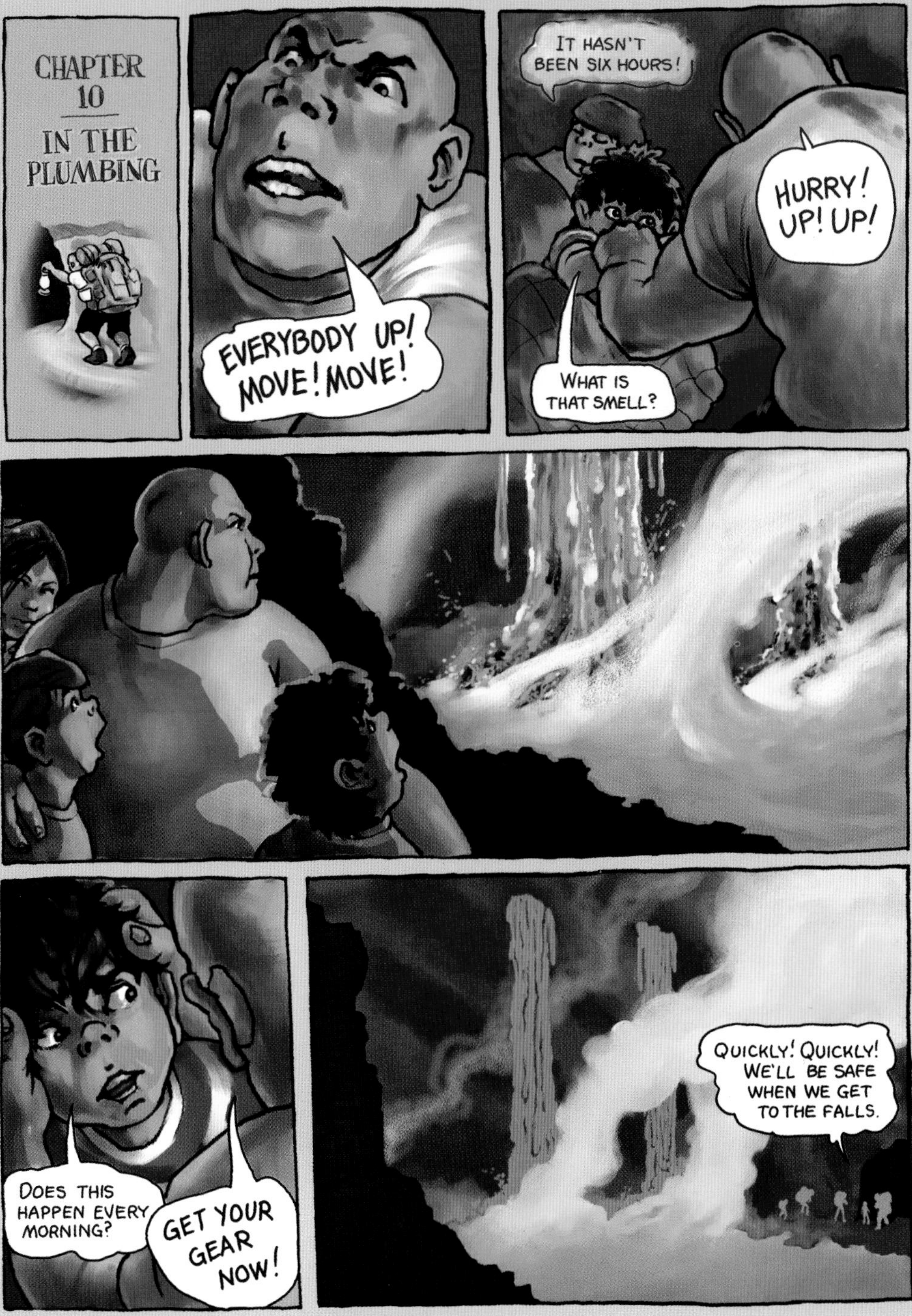
CHAPTER 10
IN THE PLUMBING
EVERYBODY UP! MOVE! MOVE!
IT HASN'T BEEN SIX HOURS!
HURRY! UP! UP!
WHAT IS THAT SMELL?
DOES THIS HAPPEN EVERY MORNING?
GET YOUR GEAR NOW!
QUICKLY! QUICKLY! WE'LL BE SAFE WHEN WE GET TO THE FALLS.

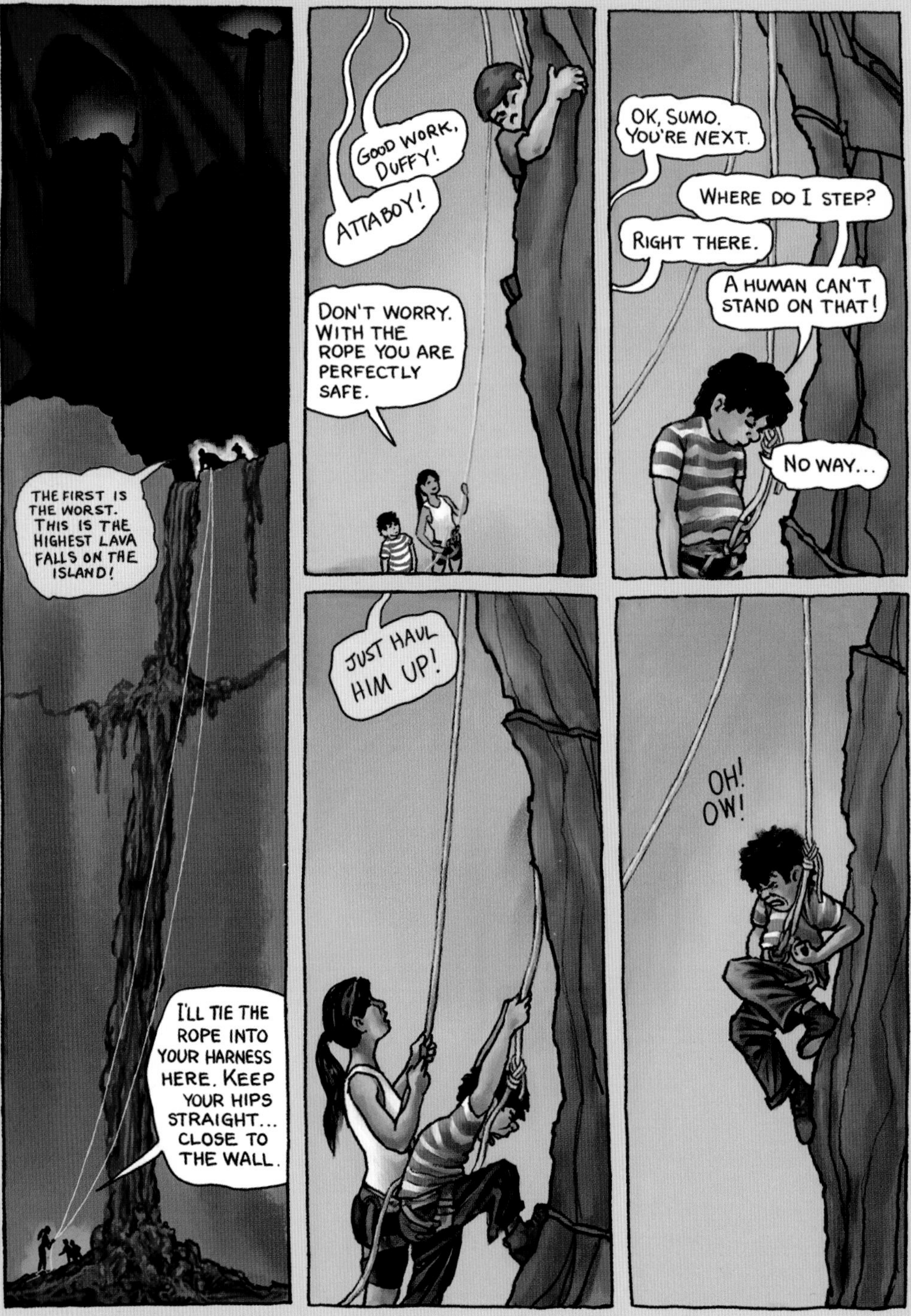
THE FIRST IS THE WORST. THIS IS THE HIGHEST LAVA FALLS ON THE ISLAND!
I'LL TIE THE ROPE INTO YOUR HARNESS HERE. KEEP YOUR HIPS STRAIGHT... CLOSE TO THE WALL.
GOOD WORK, DUFFY!
ATTABOY!
DON'T WORRY. WITH THE ROPE YOU ARE PERFECTLY SAFE.
OK, SUMO. YOU'RE NEXT.
WHERE DO I STEP?
RIGHT THERE.
A HUMAN CAN'T STAND ON THAT!
NO WAY...
JUST HAUL HIM UP!
OH! OW!

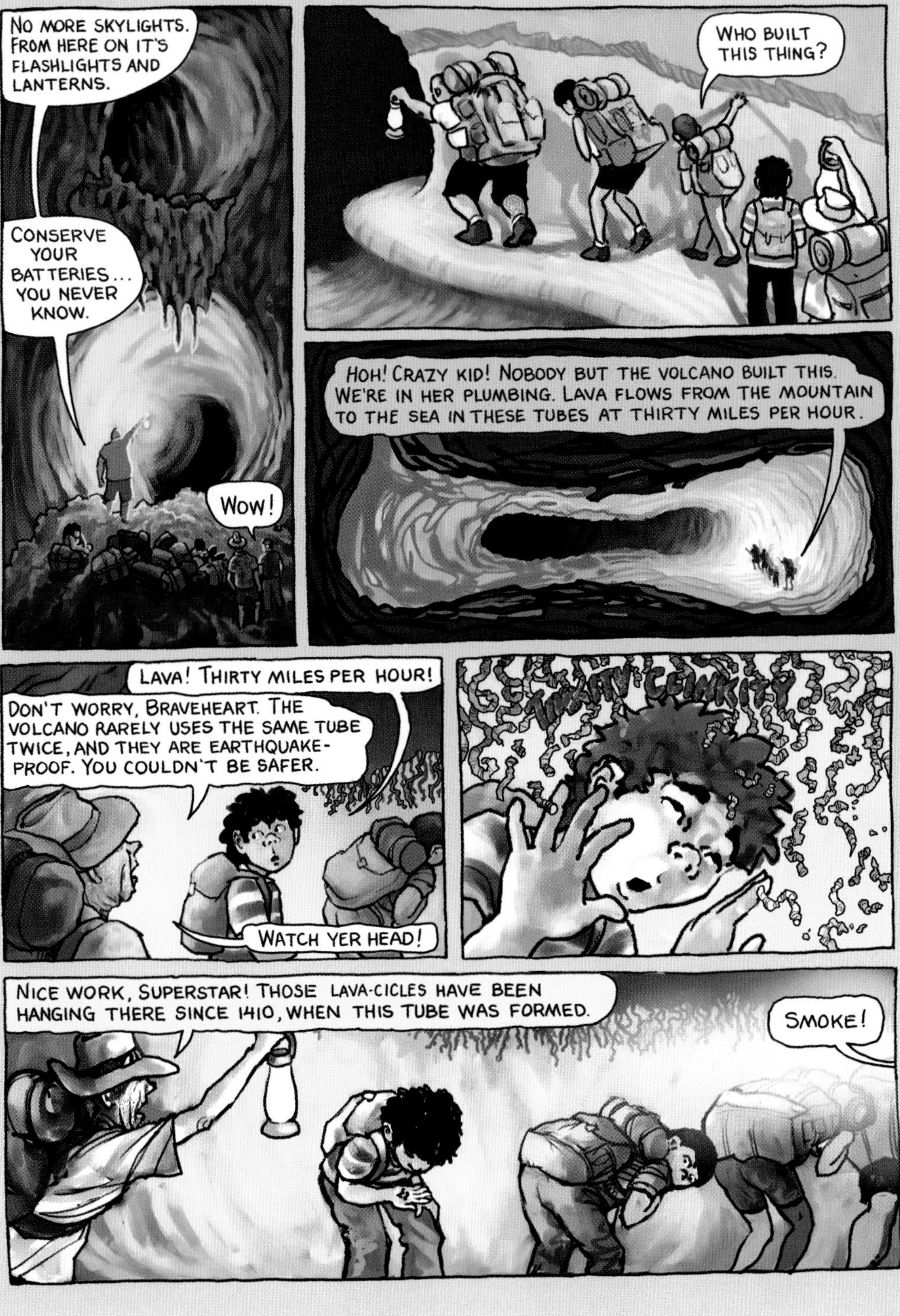
NO MORE SKYLIGHTS. FROM HERE ON IT'S FLASHLIGHTS AND LANTERNS.
CONSERVE YOUR BATTERIES... YOU NEVER KNOW.
WOW!
WHO BUILT THIS THING?
HOH! CRAZY KID! NOBODY BUT THE VOLCANO BUILT THIS. WE'RE IN HER PLUMBING. LAVA FLOWS FROM THE MOUNTAIN TO THE SEA IN THESE TUBES AT THIRTY MILES PER HOUR.
LAVA! THIRTY MILES PER HOUR!
DON'T WORRY, BRAVEHEART. THE VOLCANO RARELY USES THE SAME TUBE TWICE, AND THEY ARE EARTHQUAKE-PROOF. YOU COULDN'T BE SAFER.
WATCH YER HEAD!
NICE WORK, SUPERSTAR! THOSE LAVA-CICLES HAVE BEEN HANGING THERE SINCE 1410, WHEN THIS TUBE WAS FORMED.
SMOKE!

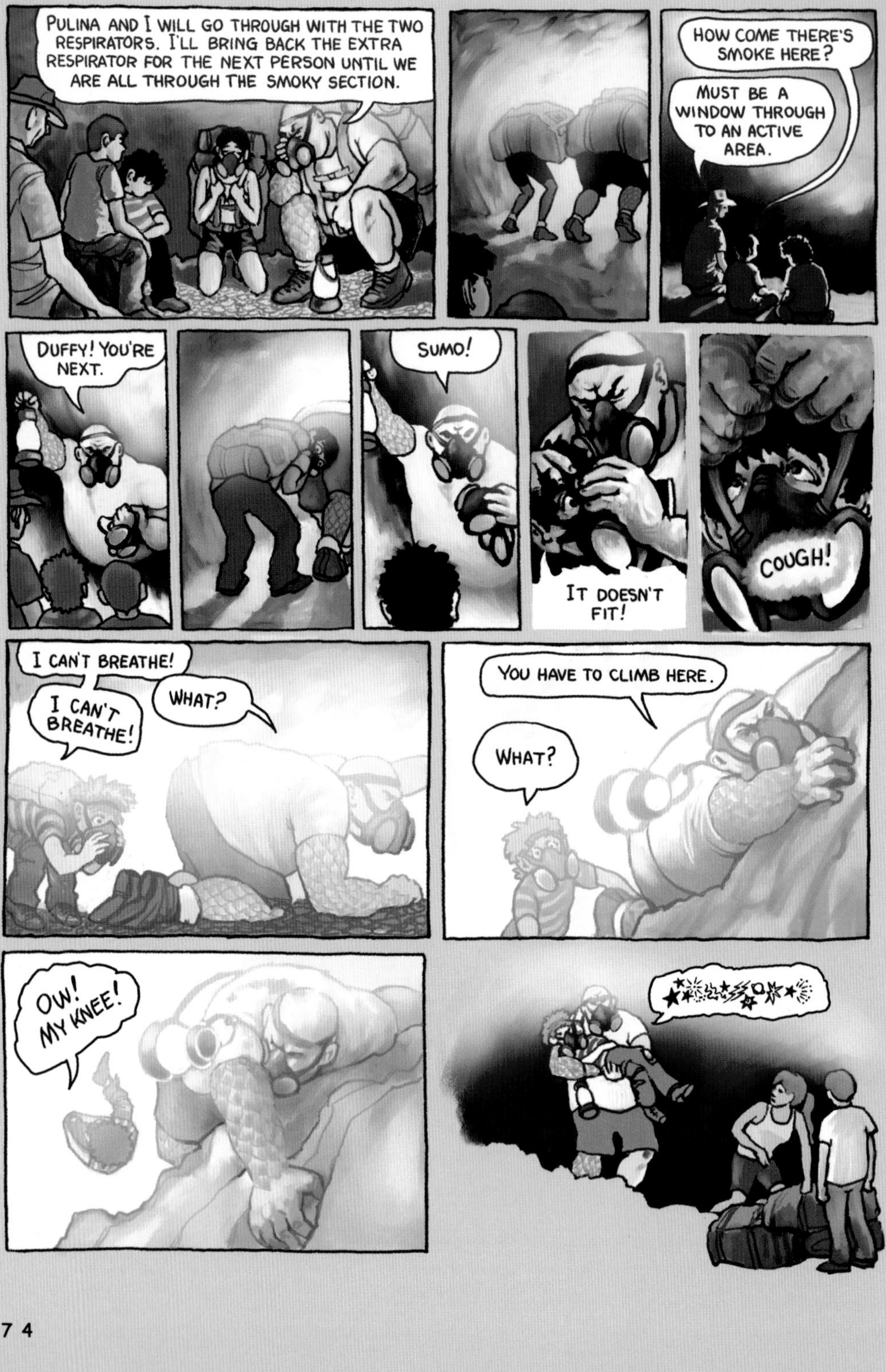
PULINA AND I WILL GO THROUGH WITH THE TWO RESPIRATORS. I'LL BRING BACK THE EXTRA RESPIRATOR FOR THE NEXT PERSON UNTIL WE ARE ALL THROUGH THE SMOKY SECTION.
HOW COME THERE'S SMOKE HERE?
MUST BE A WINDOW THROUGH TO AN ACTIVE AREA.
DUFFY! YOU'RE NEXT.
SUMO!
IT DOESN'T FIT!
COUGH!
I CAN'T BREATHE!
I CAN'T BREATHE!
WHAT?
YOU HAVE TO CLIMB HERE.
WHAT?
OW! MY KNEE!

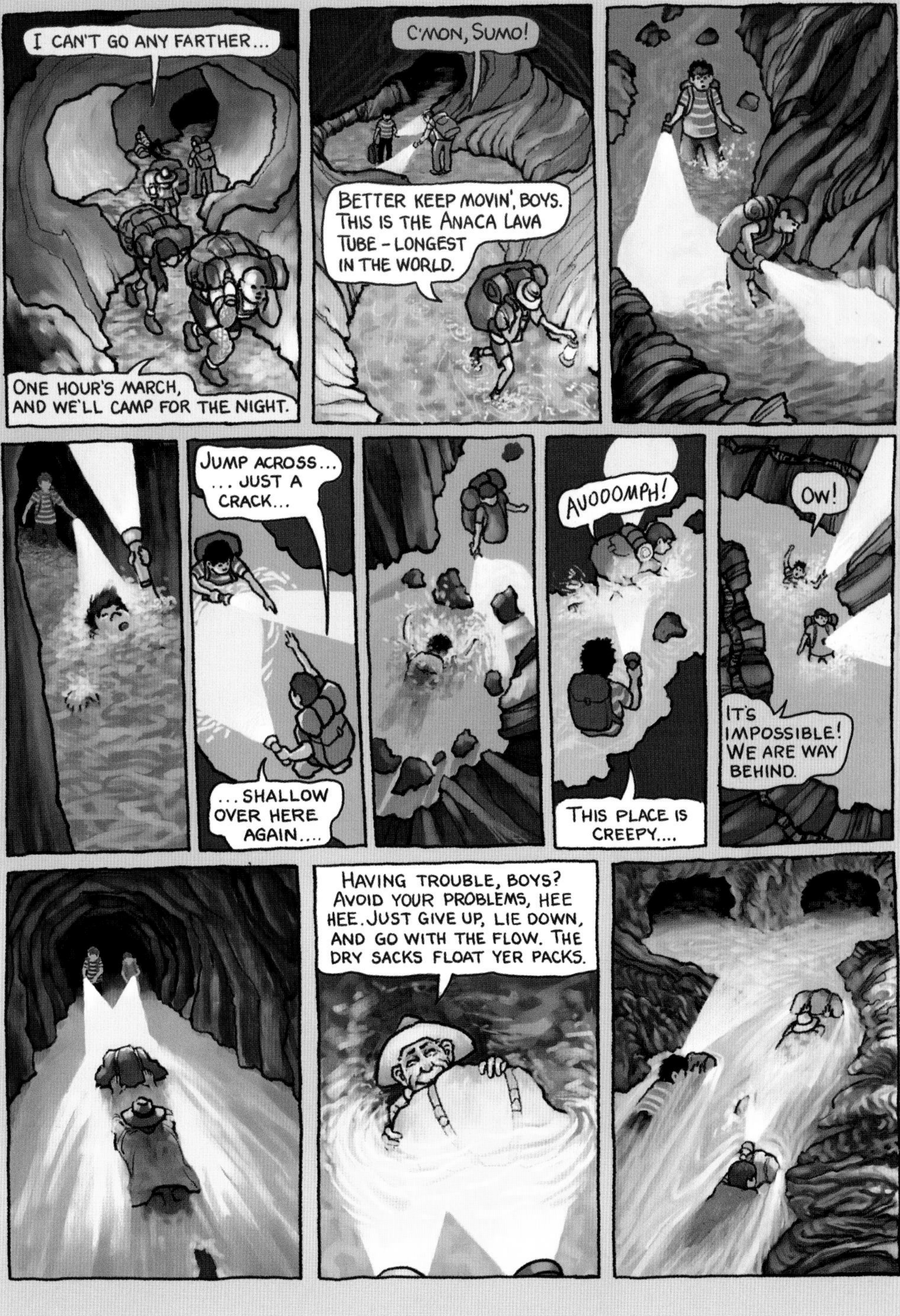
I CAN'T GO ANY FARTHER...
ONE HOUR'S MARCH, AND WE'LL CAMP FOR THE NIGHT.
C'MON, SUMO!
BETTER KEEP MOVIN', BOYS. THIS IS THE ANACA LAVA TUBE - LONGEST IN THE WORLD.
JUMP ACROSS... ... JUST A CRACK...
... SHALLOW OVER HERE AGAIN....
AVOOOMPH!
THIS PLACE IS CREEPY....
OW!
IT'S IMPOSSIBLE! WE ARE WAY BEHIND.
HAVING TROUBLE, BOYS? AVOID YOUR PROBLEMS, HEE HEE. JUST GIVE UP, LIE DOWN, AND GO WITH THE FLOW. THE DRY SACKS FLOAT YER PACKS.

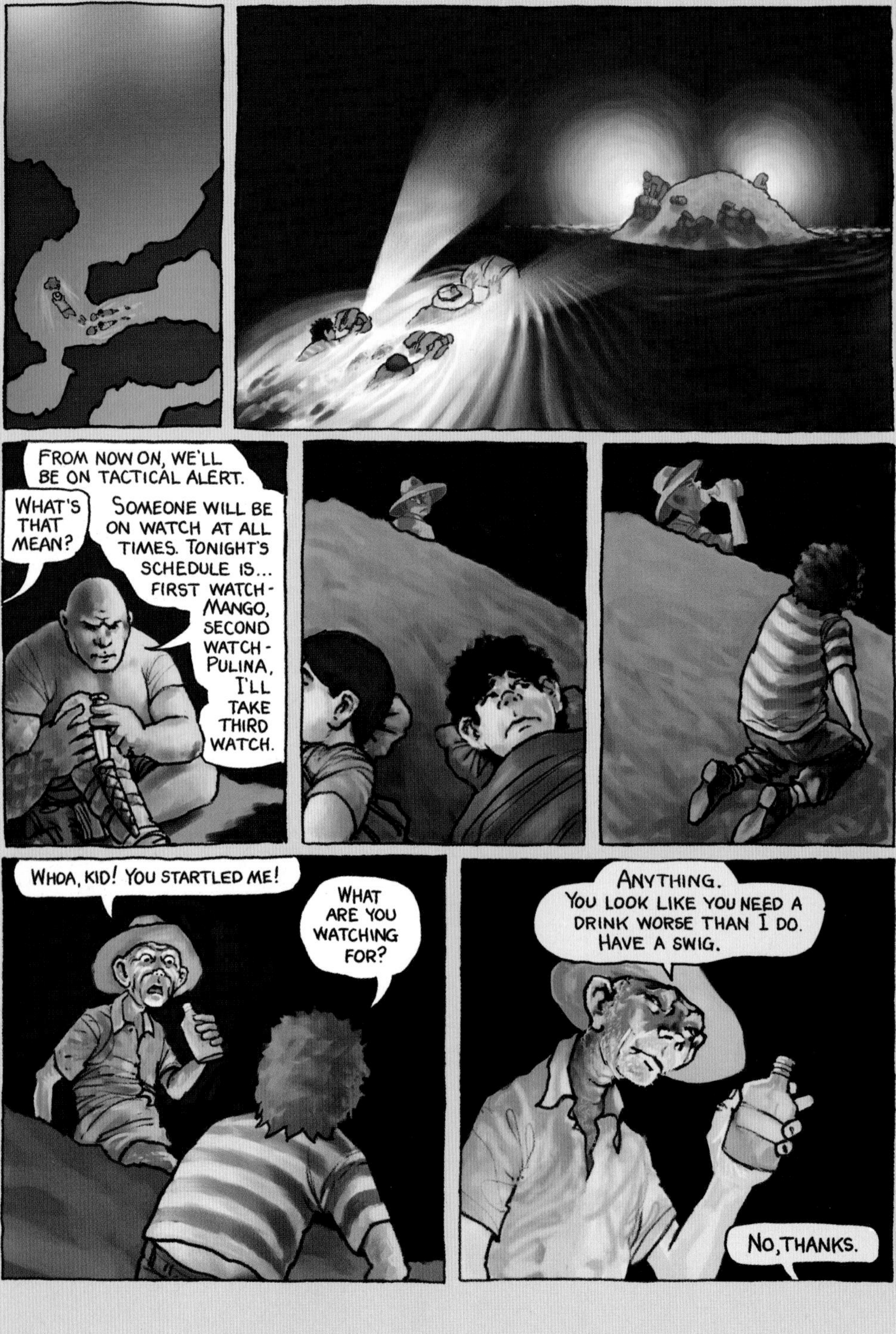
FROM NOW ON, WE'LL BE ON TACTICAL ALERT.
WHAT'S THAT MEAN?
SOMEONE WILL BE ON WATCH AT ALL TIMES. TONIGHT'S SCHEDULE IS... FIRST WATCH - MANGO, SECOND WATCH - PULINA, I'LL TAKE THIRD WATCH.
WHOA, KID! YOU STARTLED ME!
WHAT ARE YOU WATCHING FOR?
ANYTHING. YOU LOOK LIKE YOU NEED A DRINK WORSE THAN I DO. HAVE A SWIG.
NO, THANKS.

SAY... DON'T TELL COME-AND-GO ABOUT THIS. IT'LL BE OUR LITTLE SECRET.

YEAH, SURE.

YOU'RE HAVING TROUBLES, KID. I UNDERSTAND THAT.... I'VE GOT TROUBLES, TOO.

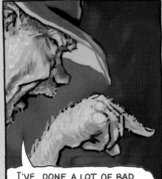

I'VE DONE A LOT OF BAD THINGS IN MY LIFE... A LOT OF 'EM... AND THEY'RE STILL RIGHT THERE, RIGHT IN FRONT OF ME.

IF I COULD DO IT ALL OVER AGAIN... I WOULD ONLY DO RIGHT THINGS... STRONG AND RIGHT.. ✱⊛✳✿❋ I'M STILL DOING BAD THINGS.

WHAT ARE YOU DOING NOW THAT'S BAD?

HO HO!

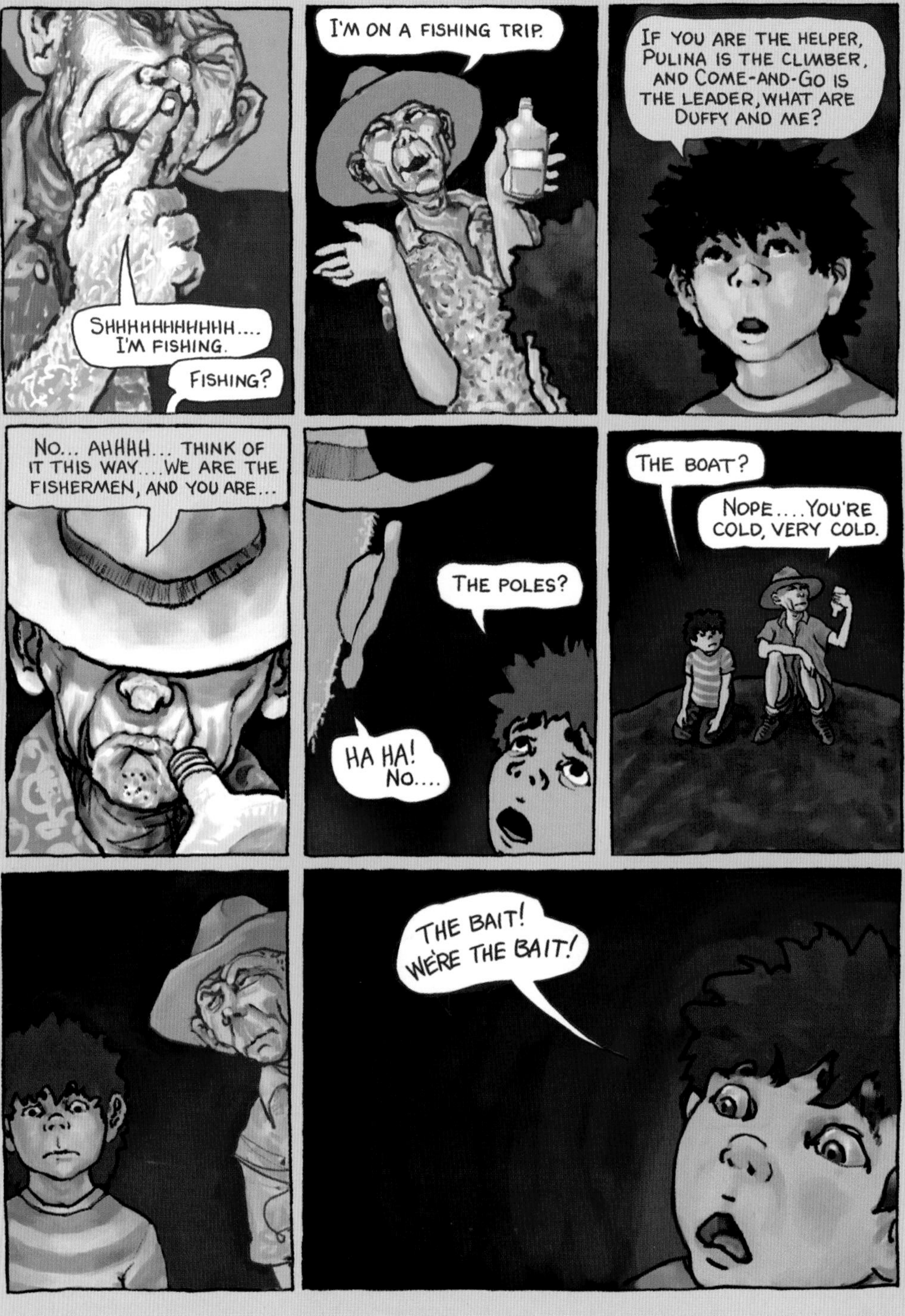
SHHHHHHHHHHH....
I'M FISHING.
FISHING?
I'M ON A FISHING TRIP.
IF YOU ARE THE HELPER, PULINA IS THE CLIMBER, AND COME-AND-GO IS THE LEADER, WHAT ARE DUFFY AND ME?
NO... AHHHH... THINK OF IT THIS WAY....WE ARE THE FISHERMEN, AND YOU ARE...
THE POLES?
HA HA! NO....
THE BOAT?
NOPE....YOU'RE COLD, VERY COLD.
THE BAIT! WE'RE THE BAIT!

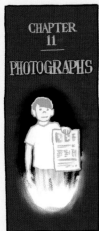

CHAPTER
11

PHOTOGRAPHS

PSSSST... DUFFY!
I TALKED WITH
MANGO LAST NIGHT....
HE SAID THEY'RE ON A
FISHING TRIP, AND WE
ARE THE BAIT!

BAIT?

BAIT FOR WHAT?
THAT DOESN'T MAKE
ANY SENSE.

ONE THING'S FOR SURE.
THIS IS NO TOURIST
TRIP. THEY'RE AFTER
SOMETHING.

I KNOW... I KNOW...
YOU TOLD ME SO.

WHAT DO THEY
WANT US FOR?

MAYBE IT'S BECAUSE
WE'RE SMALL, AND
THEY NEED US TO GET
INTO A SMALL PLACE...
LIKE THE WAY THEY
USED TO USE CHILDREN
AS CHIMNEY SWEEPS.

I HATE
SMALL
PLACES.

NOOO! IT MUST BE
SOMETHING WE KNOW.
WHAT DO WE KNOW?

I DON'T KNOW
NOTHIN'!

YEAH... I DON'T
KNOW ANYTHING
EITHER.

KEEP YOUR EYES OPEN
AND BE SMART, SUMO....

TELL ME EVERYTHING
YOU HEAR. THE SLIGHTEST
BIT OF INFORMATION
COULD GIVE US A CLUE.

TIME TO GO. HERE'S
SOME SPRING WATER.... IT'S
THE FRESHEST, PUREST....

OH!

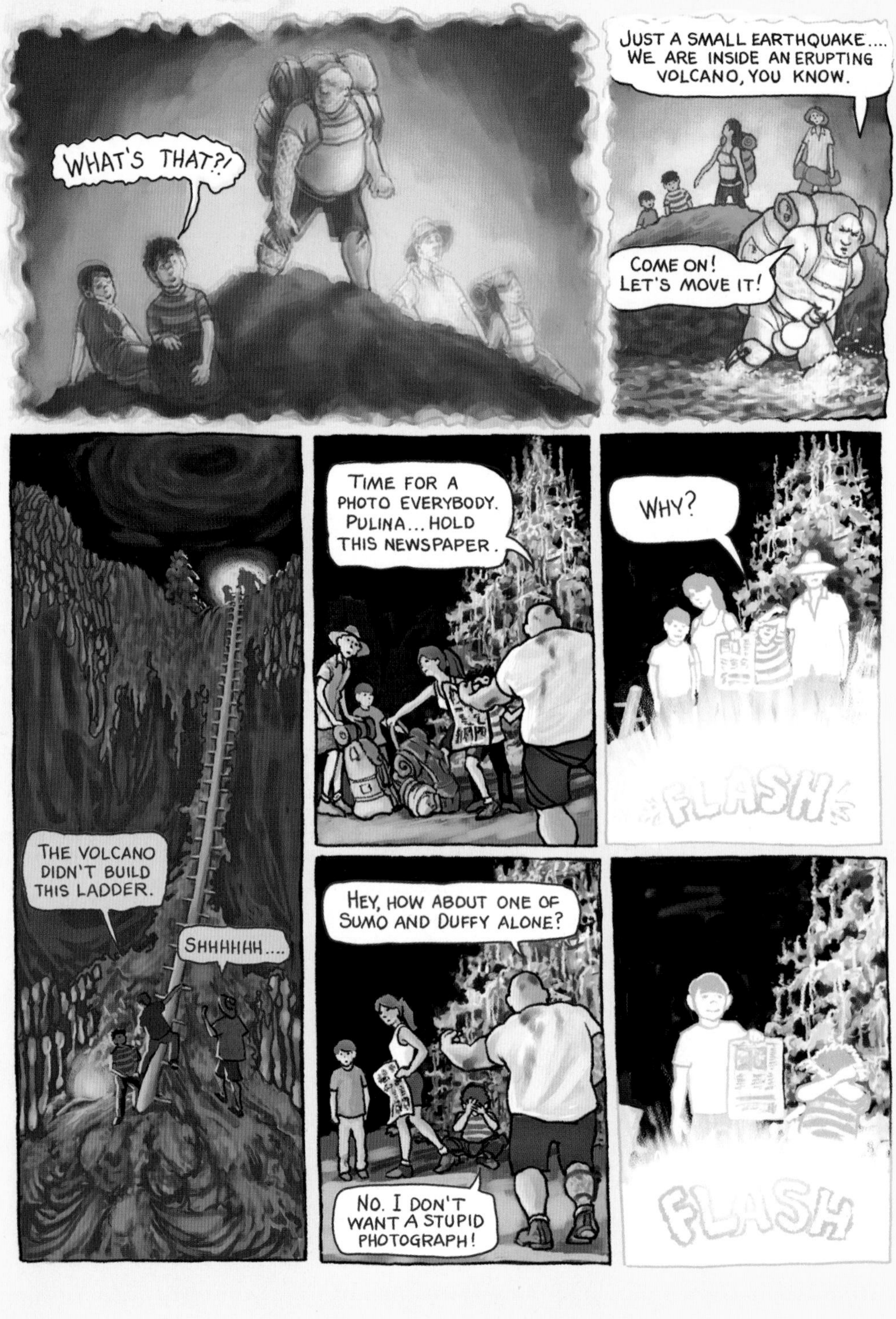
WHAT'S THAT?!
JUST A SMALL EARTHQUAKE.... WE ARE INSIDE AN ERUPTING VOLCANO, YOU KNOW.
COME ON! LET'S MOVE IT!
THE VOLCANO DIDN'T BUILD THIS LADDER.
SHHHHHH....
TIME FOR A PHOTO EVERYBODY. PULINA... HOLD THIS NEWSPAPER.
WHY?
FLASH
HEY, HOW ABOUT ONE OF SUMO AND DUFFY ALONE?
NO. I DON'T WANT A STUPID PHOTOGRAPH!
FLASH

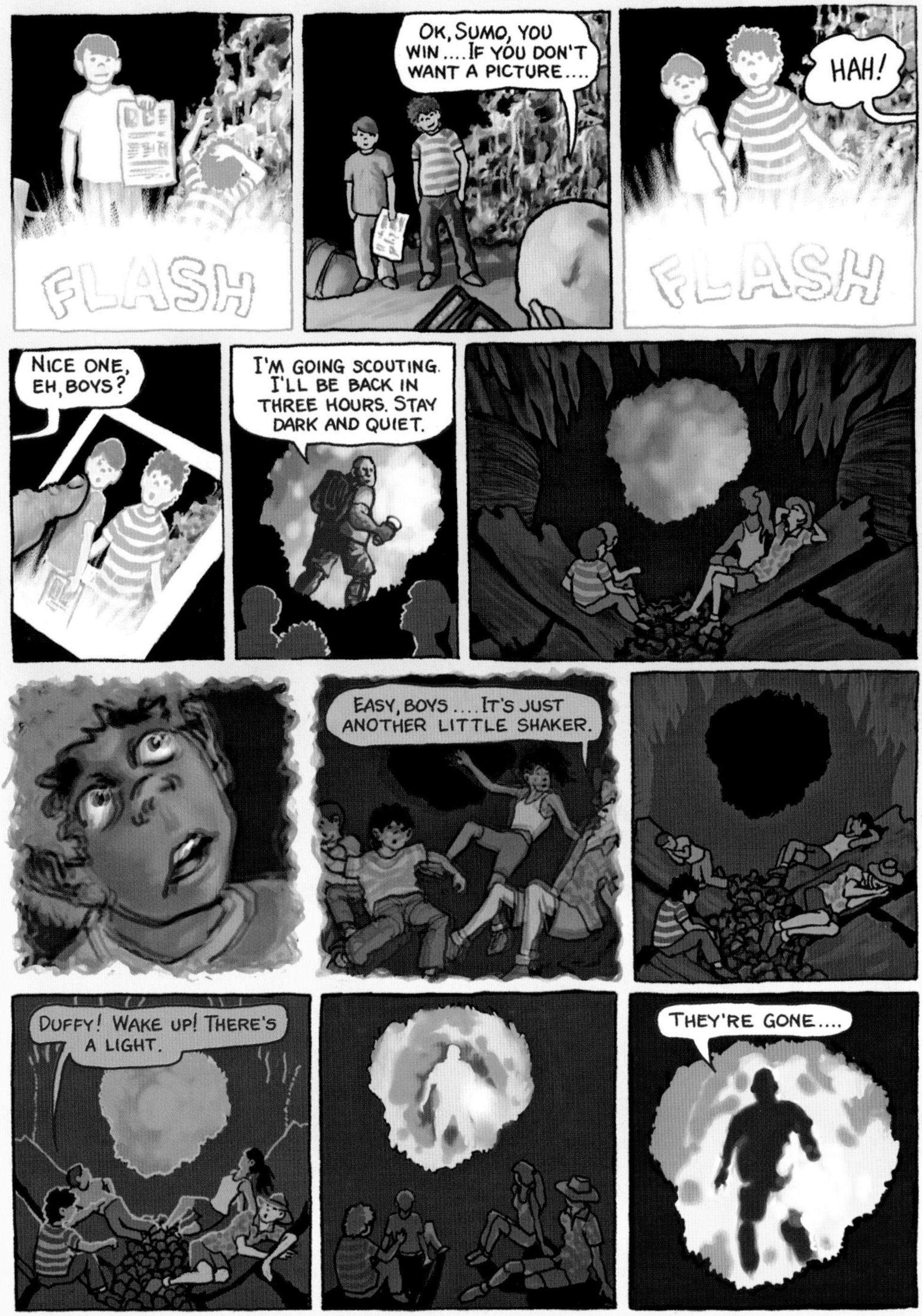
FLASH
OK, SUMO, YOU WIN.... IF YOU DON'T WANT A PICTURE....
HAH!
FLASH
NICE ONE, EH, BOYS?
I'M GOING SCOUTING. I'LL BE BACK IN THREE HOURS. STAY DARK AND QUIET.
EASY, BOYS.... IT'S JUST ANOTHER LITTLE SHAKER.
DUFFY! WAKE UP! THERE'S A LIGHT.
THEY'RE GONE....

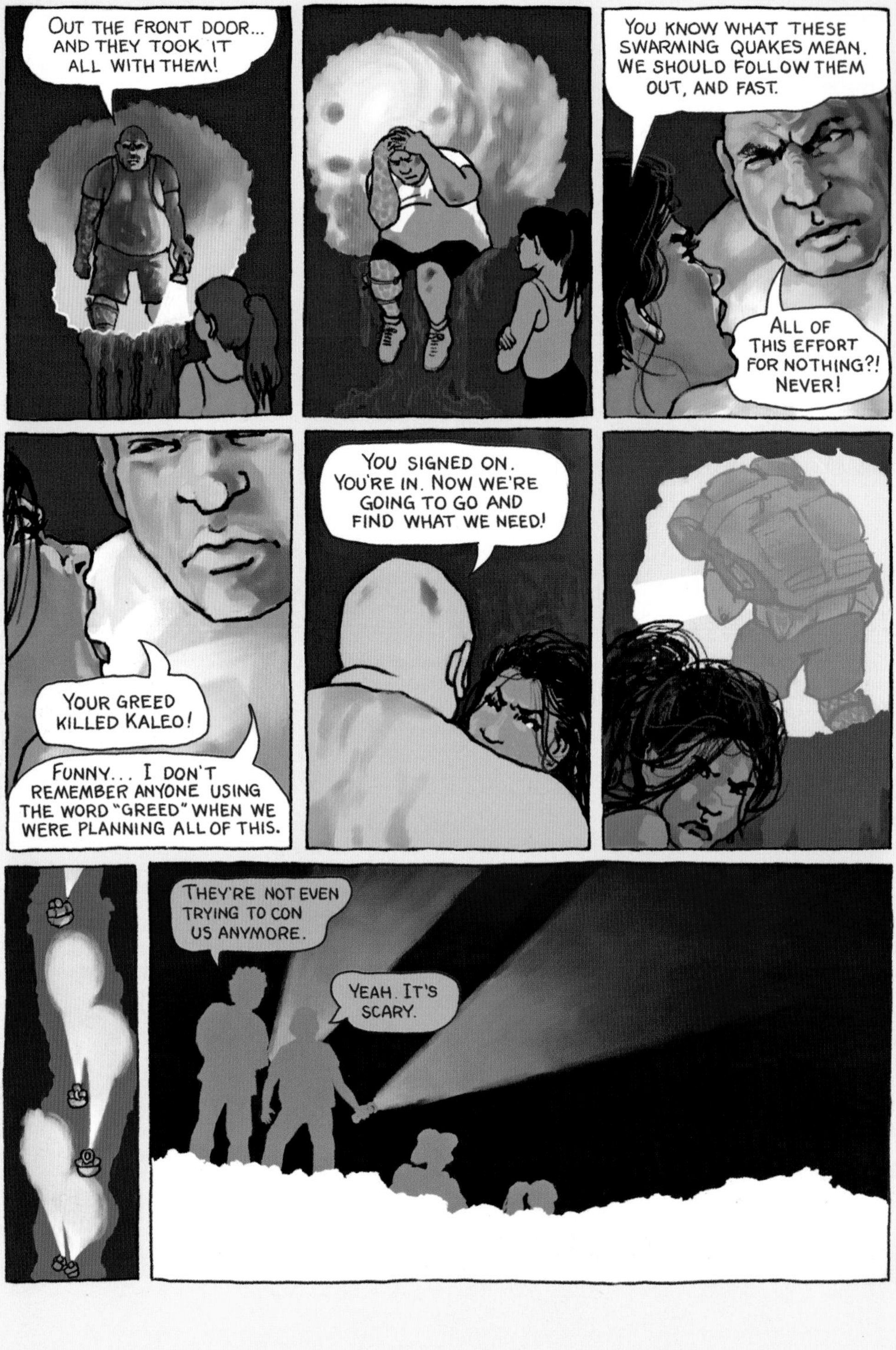
OUT THE FRONT DOOR... AND THEY TOOK IT ALL WITH THEM!
YOU KNOW WHAT THESE SWARMING QUAKES MEAN. WE SHOULD FOLLOW THEM OUT, AND FAST.
ALL OF THIS EFFORT FOR NOTHING?! NEVER!
YOUR GREED KILLED KALEO!
FUNNY... I DON'T REMEMBER ANYONE USING THE WORD "GREED" WHEN WE WERE PLANNING ALL OF THIS.
YOU SIGNED ON. YOU'RE IN. NOW WE'RE GOING TO GO AND FIND WHAT WE NEED!
THEY'RE NOT EVEN TRYING TO CON US ANYMORE.
YEAH. IT'S SCARY.

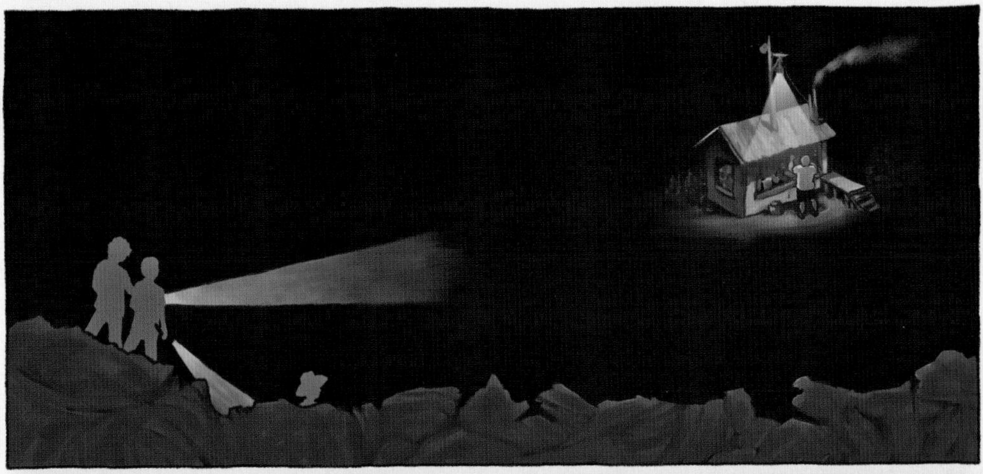

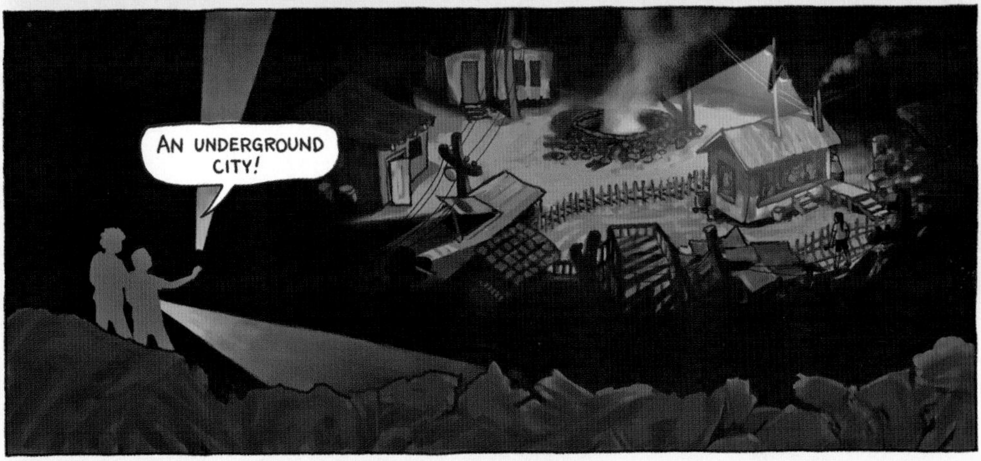
AN UNDERGROUND CITY!

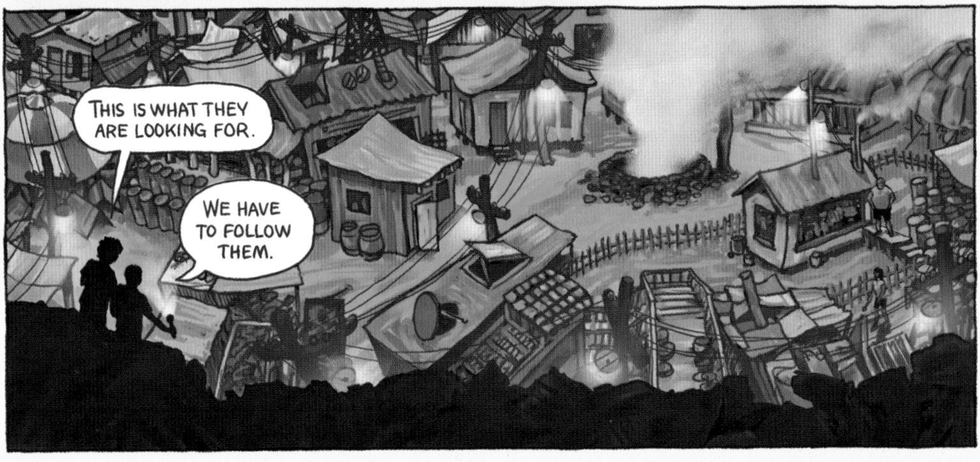
THIS IS WHAT THEY ARE LOOKING FOR.
WE HAVE TO FOLLOW THEM.

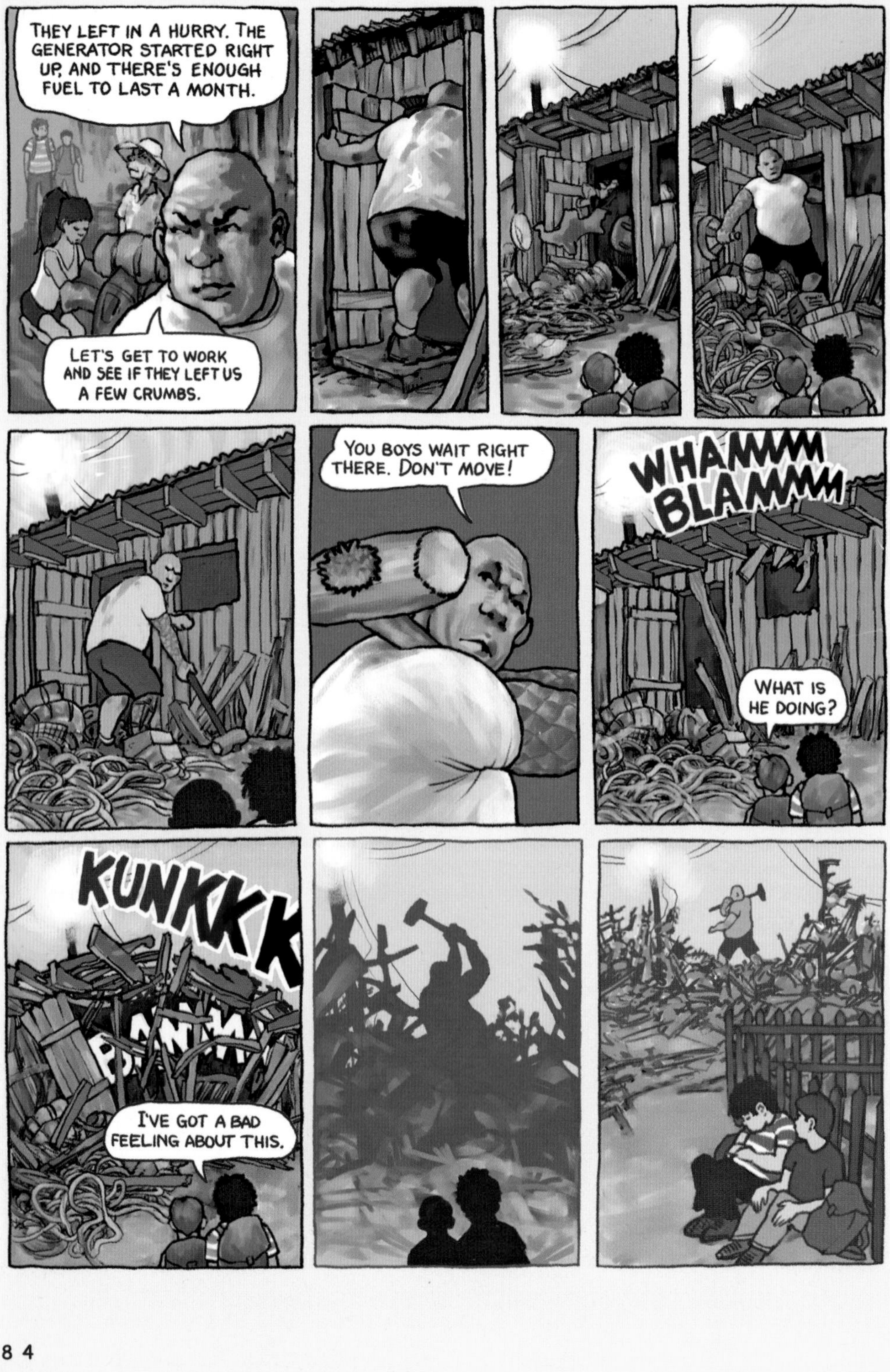
THEY LEFT IN A HURRY. THE GENERATOR STARTED RIGHT UP, AND THERE'S ENOUGH FUEL TO LAST A MONTH.
LET'S GET TO WORK AND SEE IF THEY LEFT US A FEW CRUMBS.
YOU BOYS WAIT RIGHT THERE. DON'T MOVE!
WHAMMM
BLAMMM
WHAT IS HE DOING?
KUNKKK
I'VE GOT A BAD FEELING ABOUT THIS.

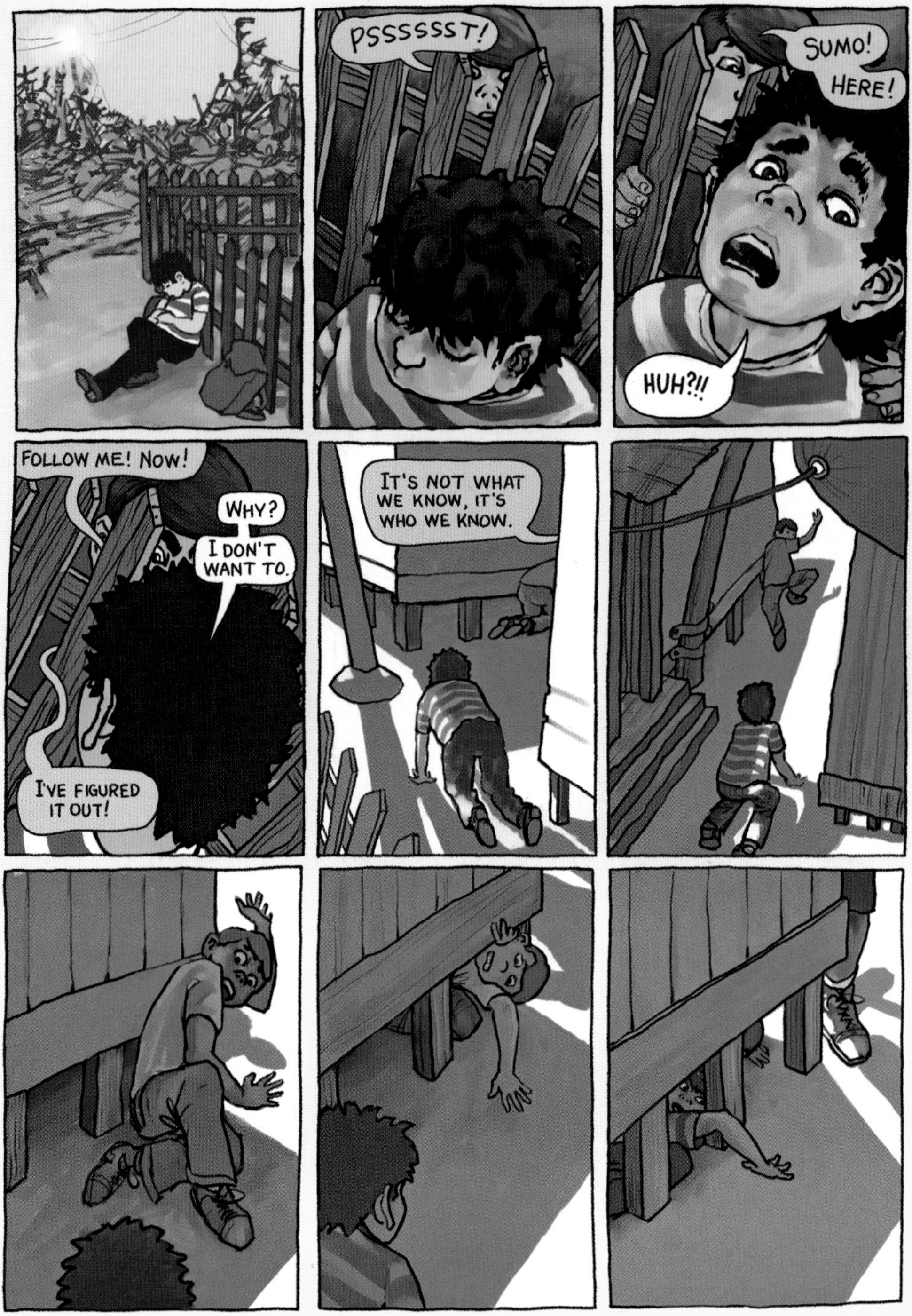
PSSSSSST!
SUMO! HERE!
HUH?!!
FOLLOW ME! NOW!
WHY?
I DON'T WANT TO.
I'VE FIGURED IT OUT!
IT'S NOT WHAT WE KNOW, IT'S WHO WE KNOW.

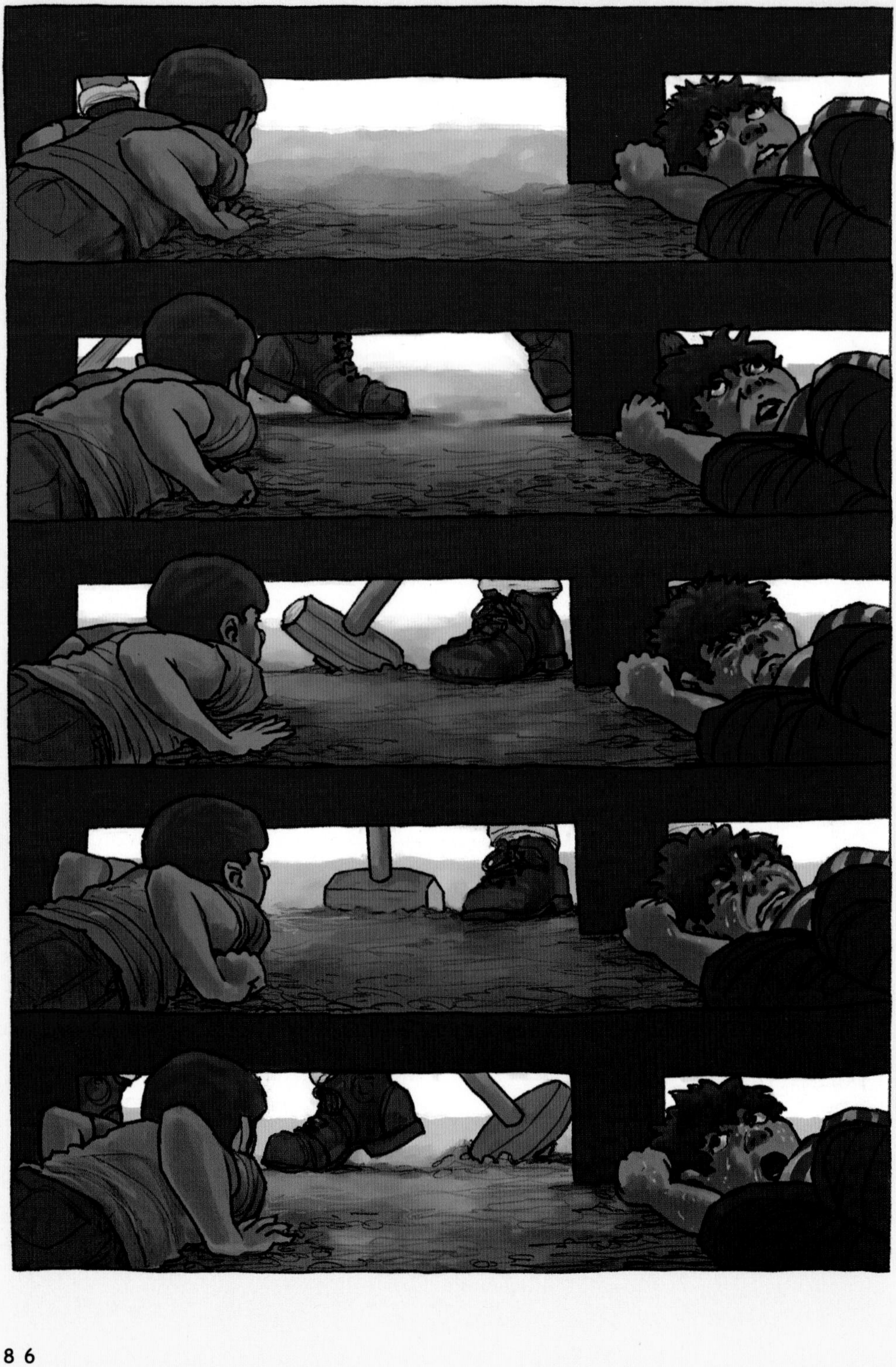

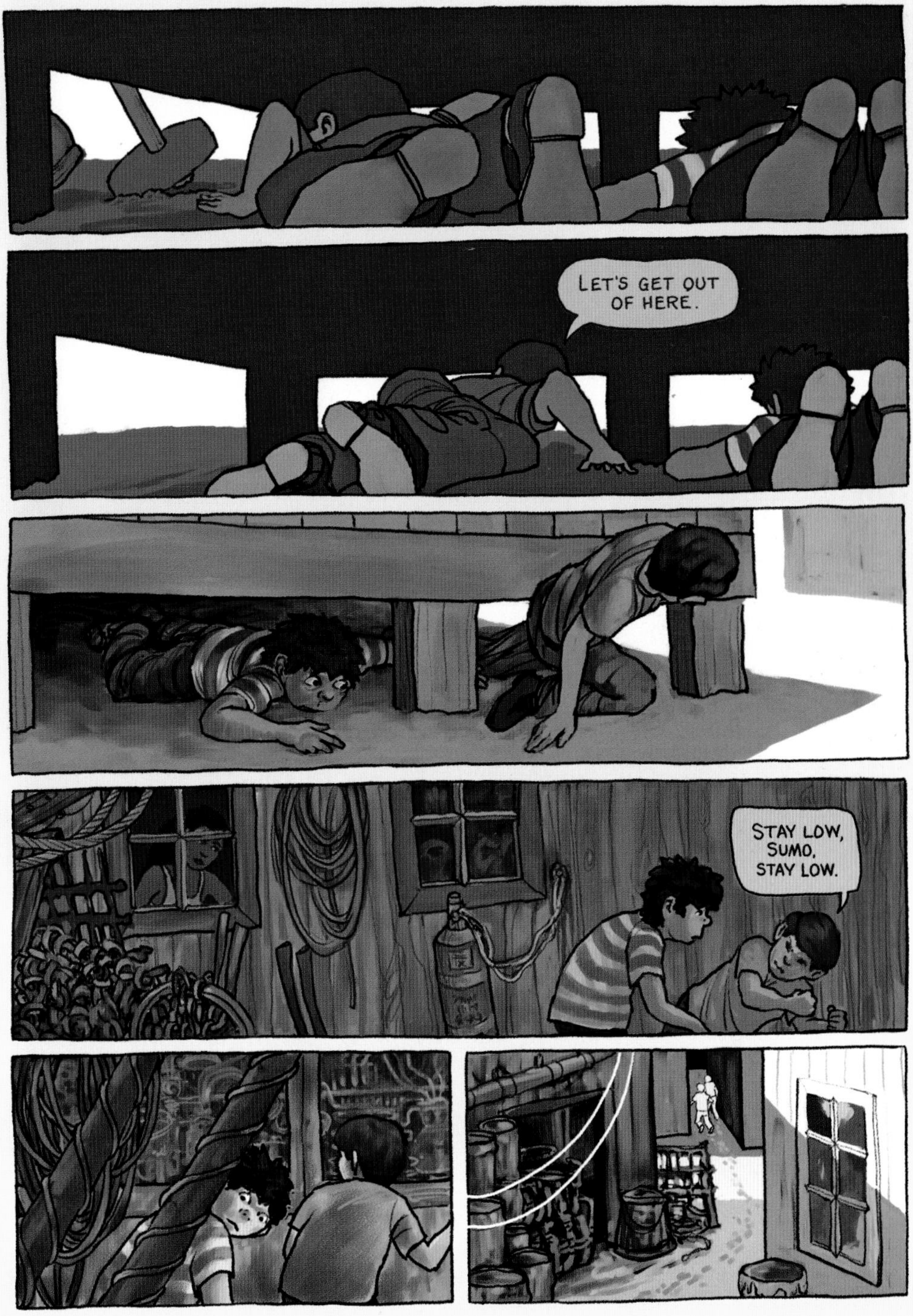
LET'S GET OUT OF HERE.
STAY LOW, SUMO, STAY LOW.

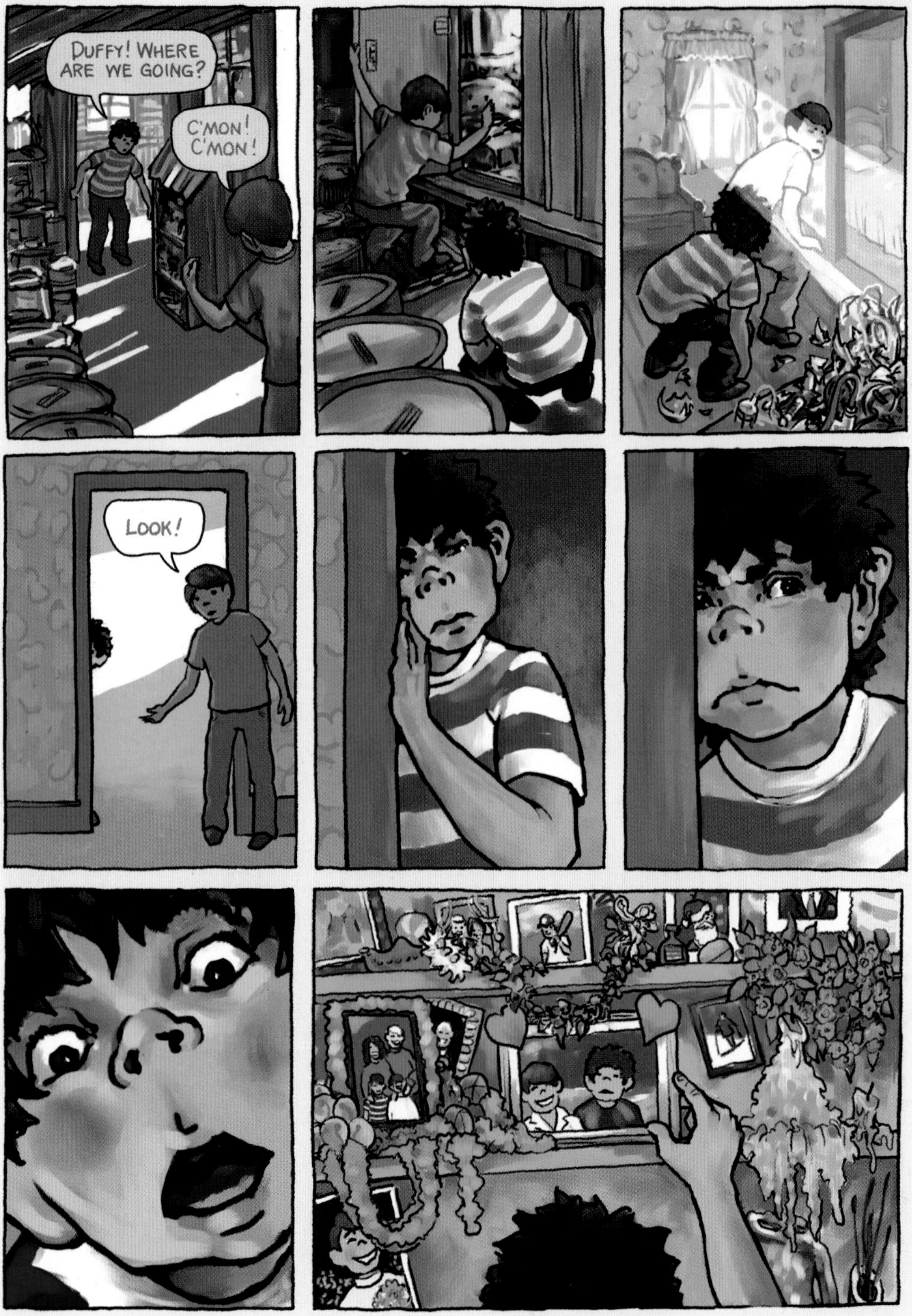
DUFFY! WHERE ARE WE GOING?
C'MON! C'MON!
LOOK!

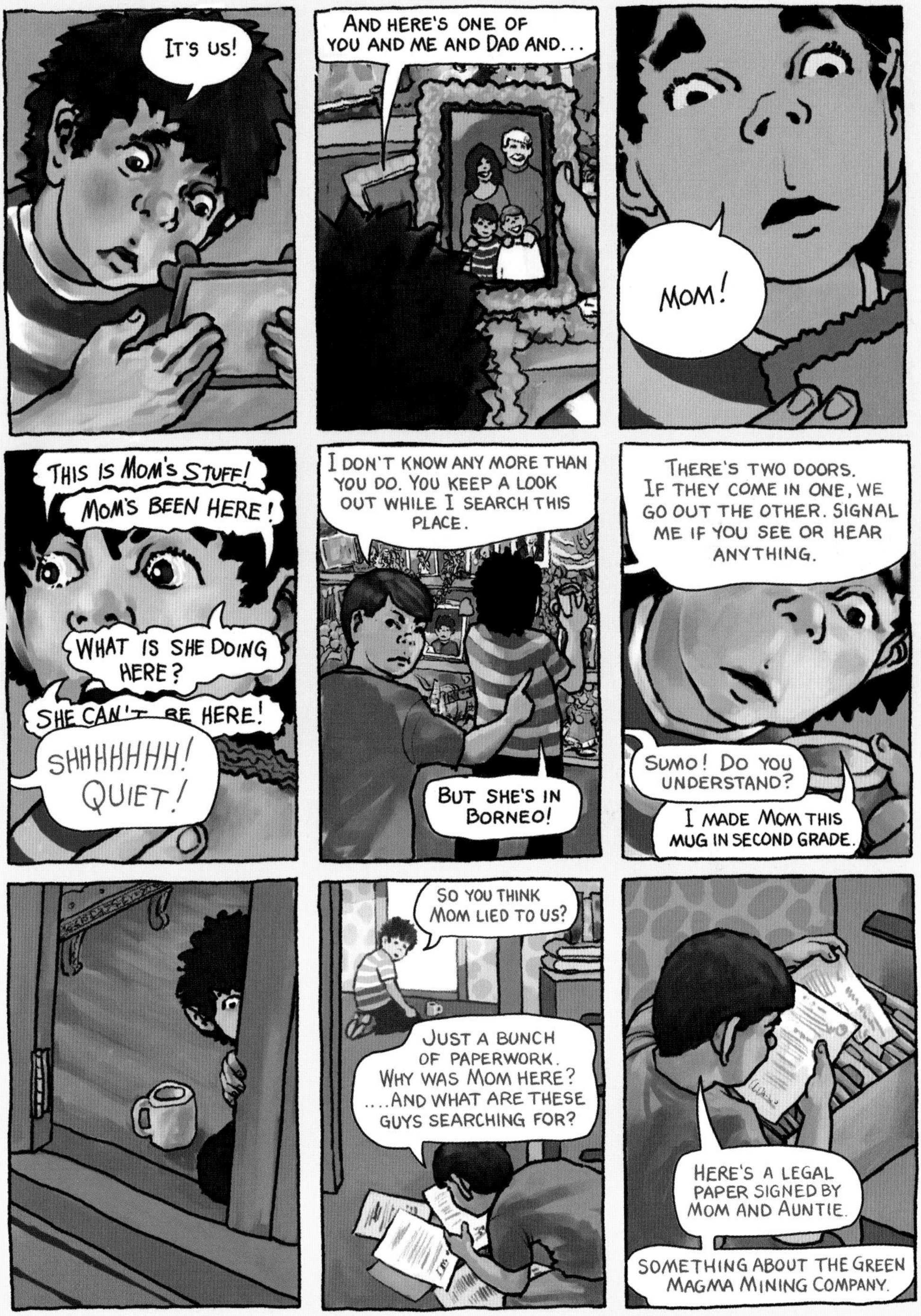
IT'S US!
AND HERE'S ONE OF YOU AND ME AND DAD AND...
MOM!
THIS IS MOM'S STUFF!
MOM'S BEEN HERE!
WHAT IS SHE DOING HERE?
SHE CAN'T BE HERE!
SHHHHHHH! QUIET!
I DON'T KNOW ANY MORE THAN YOU DO. YOU KEEP A LOOK OUT WHILE I SEARCH THIS PLACE.
BUT SHE'S IN BORNEO!
THERE'S TWO DOORS. IF THEY COME IN ONE, WE GO OUT THE OTHER. SIGNAL ME IF YOU SEE OR HEAR ANYTHING.
SUMO! DO YOU UNDERSTAND?
I MADE MOM THIS MUG IN SECOND GRADE.
SO YOU THINK MOM LIED TO US?
JUST A BUNCH OF PAPERWORK. WHY WAS MOM HERE? ....AND WHAT ARE THESE GUYS SEARCHING FOR?
HERE'S A LEGAL PAPER SIGNED BY MOM AND AUNTIE.
SOMETHING ABOUT THE GREEN MAGMA MINING COMPANY.

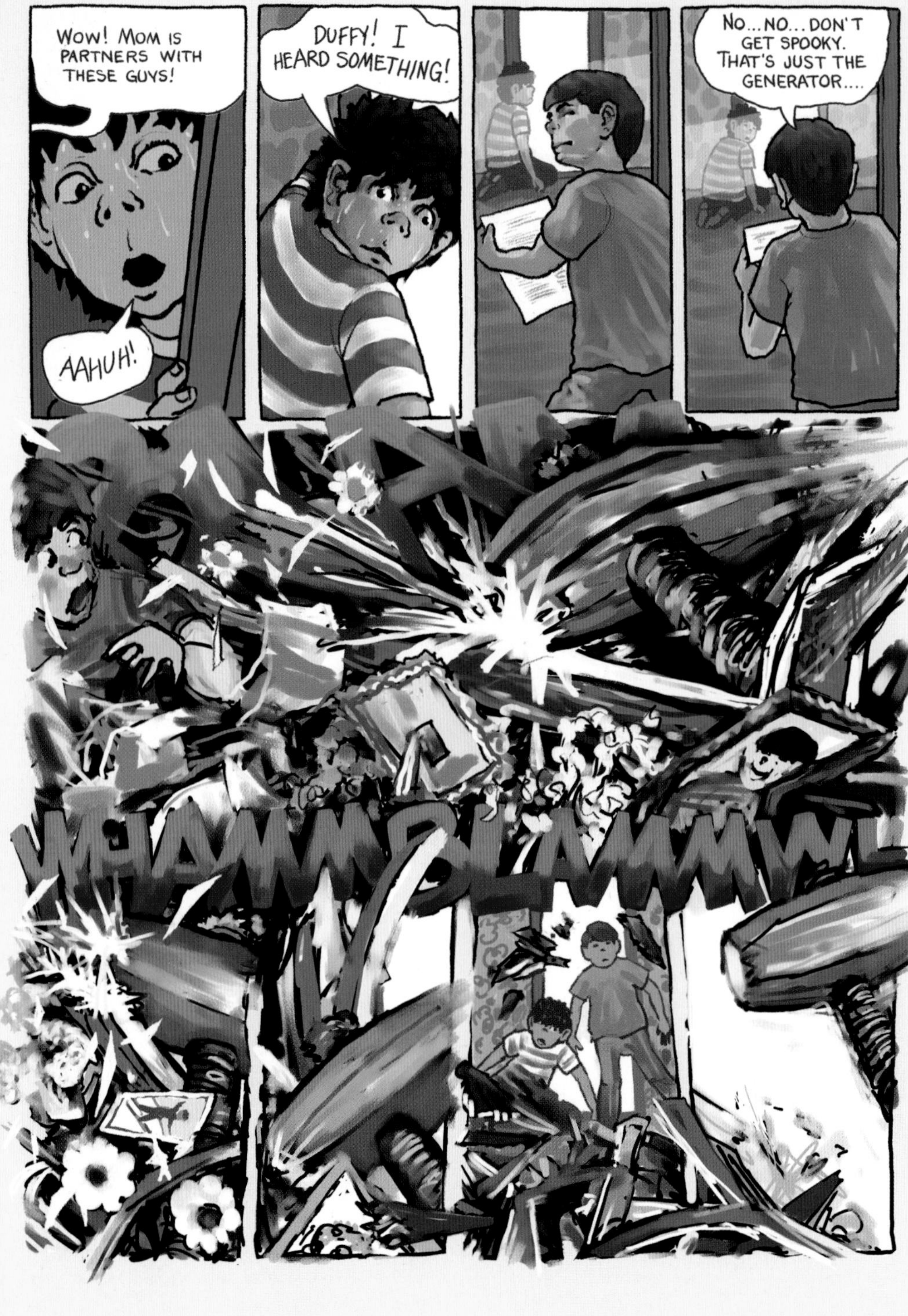
WOW! MOM IS PARTNERS WITH THESE GUYS!
AAHUH!
DUFFY! I HEARD SOMETHING!
NO...NO...DON'T GET SPOOKY. THAT'S JUST THE GENERATOR....
WHAMMBLAMMM!

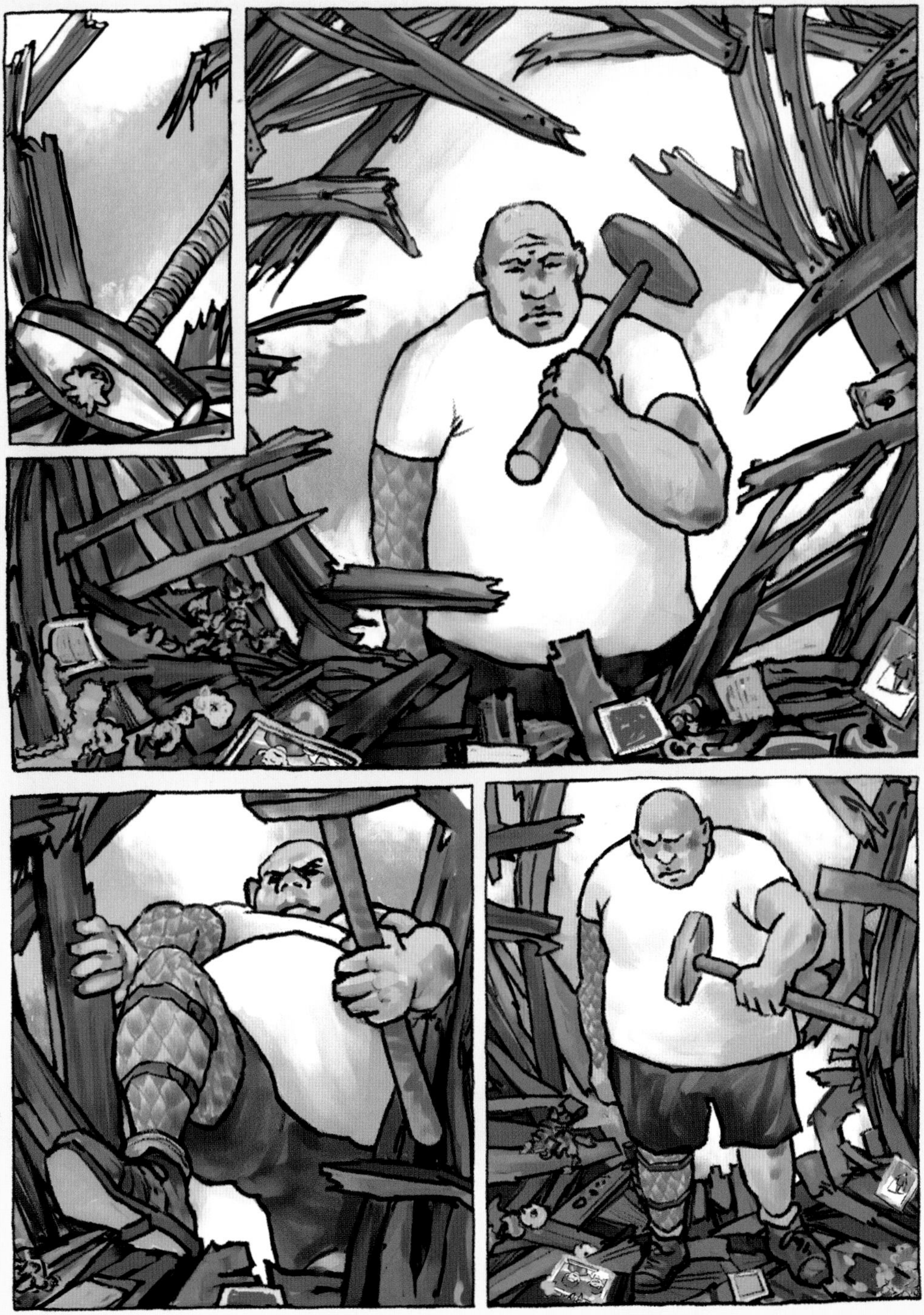

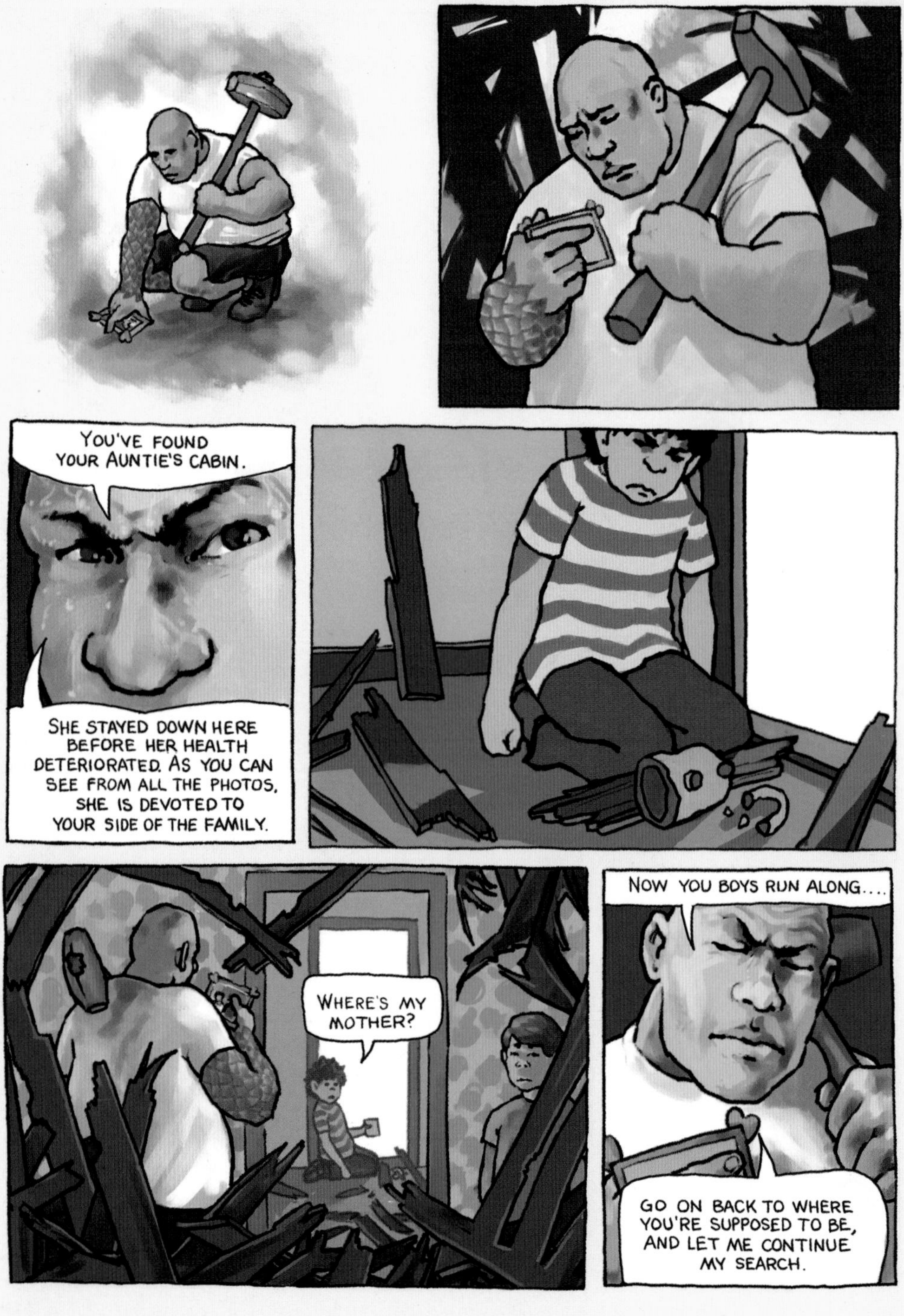
YOU'VE FOUND YOUR AUNTIE'S CABIN.
SHE STAYED DOWN HERE BEFORE HER HEALTH DETERIORATED. AS YOU CAN SEE FROM ALL THE PHOTOS, SHE IS DEVOTED TO YOUR SIDE OF THE FAMILY.
WHERE'S MY MOTHER?
NOW YOU BOYS RUN ALONG....
GO ON BACK TO WHERE YOU'RE SUPPOSED TO BE, AND LET ME CONTINUE MY SEARCH.

CHAPTER 12
STRAIGHT DOWN

HEY! HEY, COME-AND-GO! GET OVER HERE!

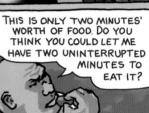
THIS IS ONLY TWO MINUTES' WORTH OF FOOD. DO YOU THINK YOU COULD LET ME HAVE TWO UNINTERRUPTED MINUTES TO EAT IT?

YOU'RE GONNA BE INTERESTED IN THIS! IT'S BETTER'N FOOD!

MAYBE WE'LL FIND SOMETHIN' AFTER ALL.

CHECK OUT THE ASH AT THE MOUTH OF THIS TUBE. SOMEBODY WENT DOWN AND DIDN'T COME BACK UP.

GOOD EYE, MANGO. THAT PASSAGE GOES STRAIGHT DOWN TO THE CHAMBER. THEY RAN DOWN THERE AND TOOK IT WITH THEM.

THE CHAMBER'S A DEAD END.

SHALL WE WAIT?

THERE'S NOT ENOUGH TIME. WE'LL HAVE TO GO DOWN AND GET THEM.

MANGO AND I NEED TWO HOURS' SLEEP, THEN WE'RE GOING DOWN. PULINA, YOU'RE ON WATCH.

I WANT TO GO, TOO.

YOU CAN'T. WE ONLY HAVE TWO RESPIRATORS. YOU'D BE DEAD IN FIVE MINUTES DOWN THERE WITHOUT ONE.

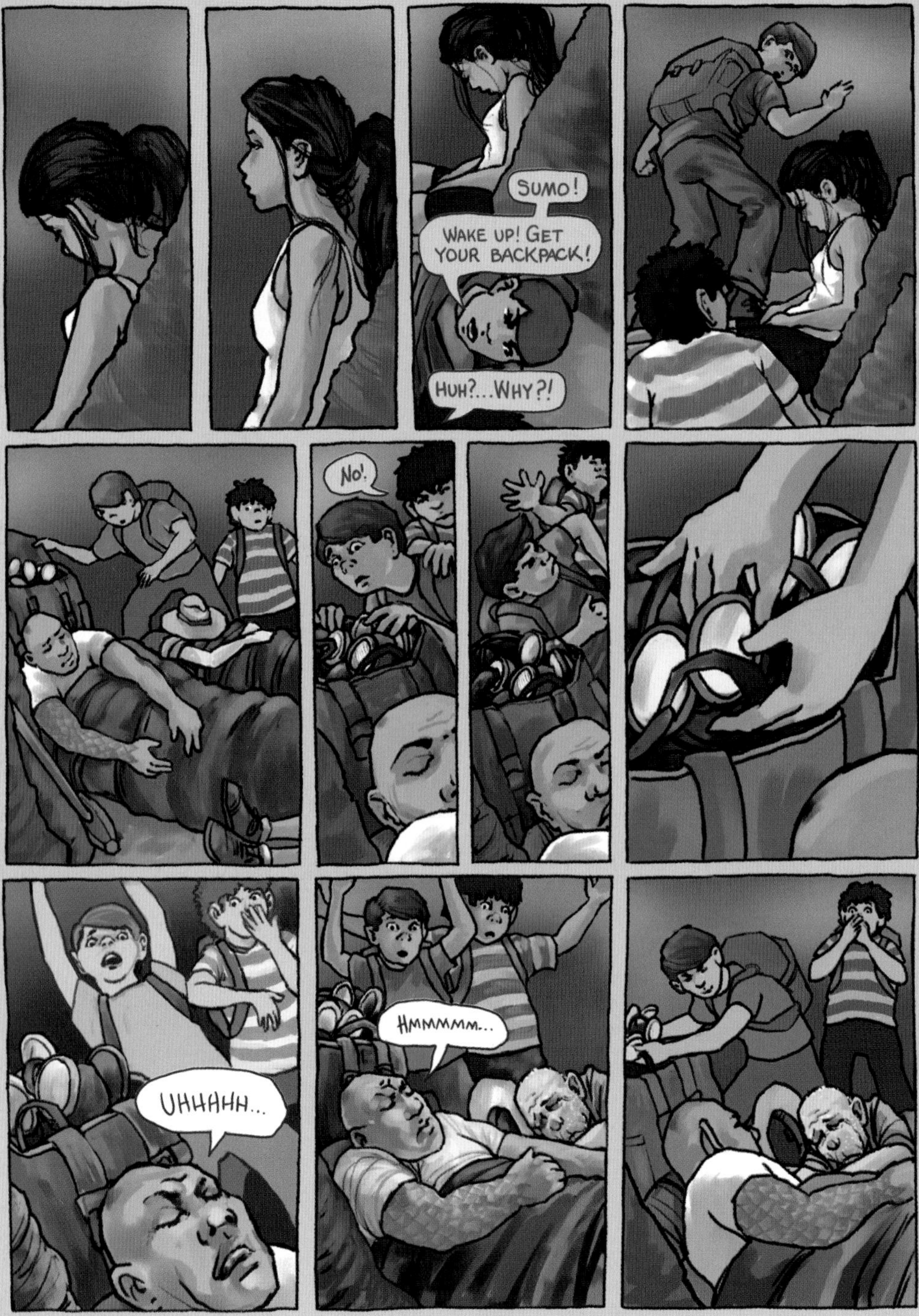
SUMO!
WAKE UP! GET YOUR BACKPACK!
HUH?...WHY?!
No!
UHHAHH...
HMMMMM...

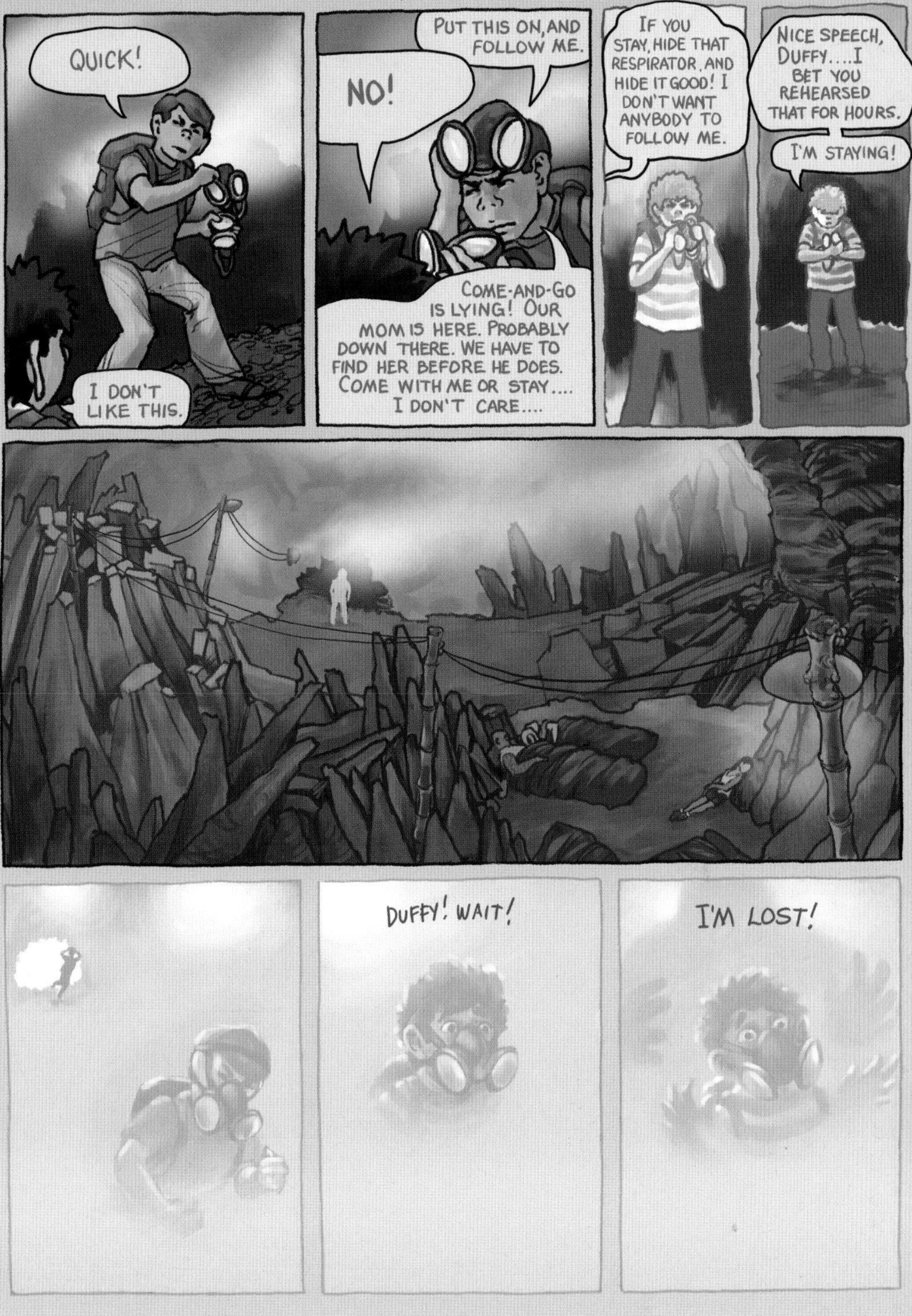
QUICK!
I DON'T LIKE THIS.
PUT THIS ON, AND FOLLOW ME.
NO!
COME-AND-GO IS LYING! OUR MOM IS HERE. PROBABLY DOWN THERE. WE HAVE TO FIND HER BEFORE HE DOES. COME WITH ME OR STAY.... I DON'T CARE....
IF YOU STAY, HIDE THAT RESPIRATOR, AND HIDE IT GOOD! I DON'T WANT ANYBODY TO FOLLOW ME.
NICE SPEECH, DUFFY....I BET YOU REHEARSED THAT FOR HOURS.
I'M STAYING!
DUFFY! WAIT!
I'M LOST!

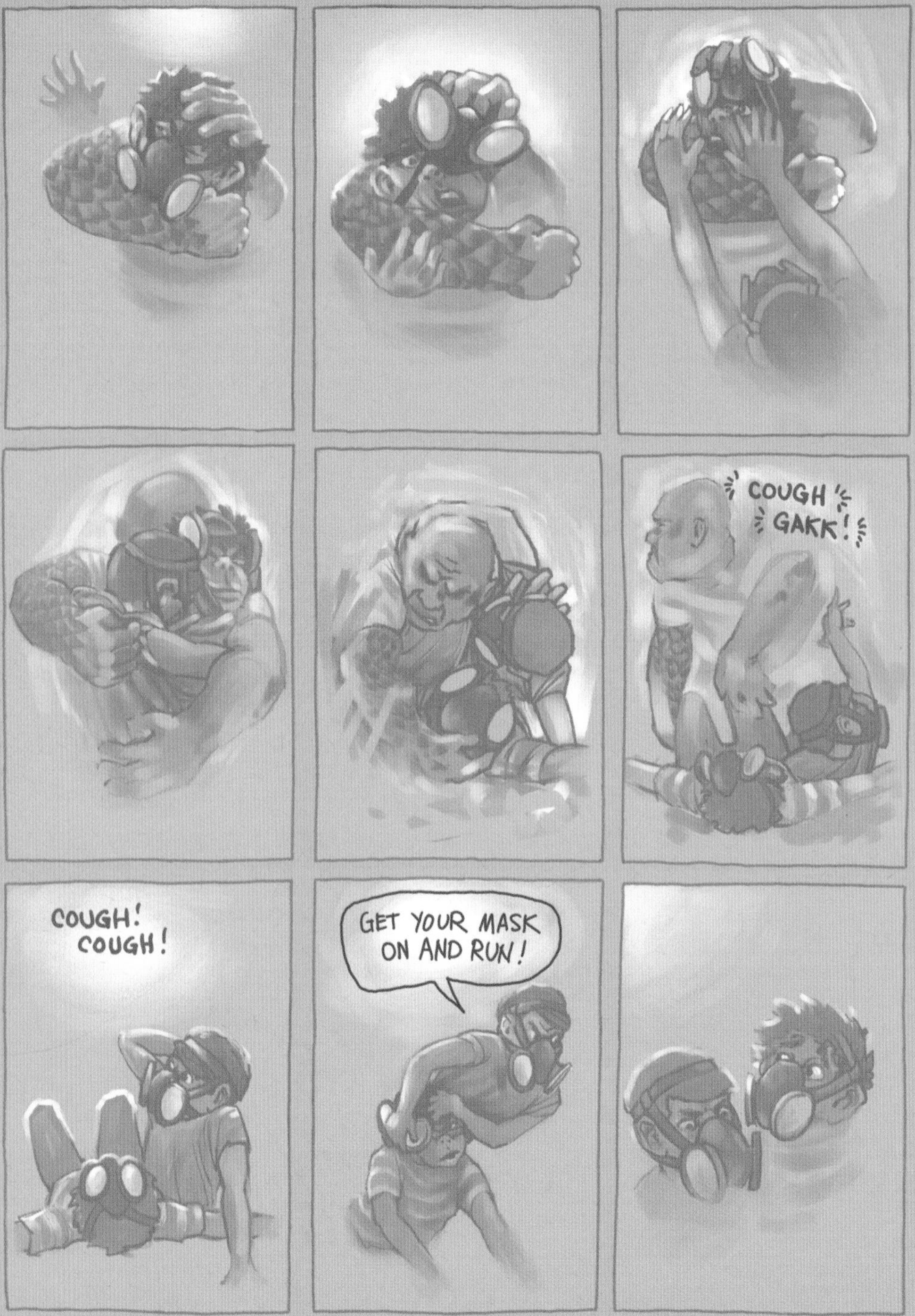
COUGH
GAKK!
COUGH!
COUGH!
GET YOUR MASK ON AND RUN!

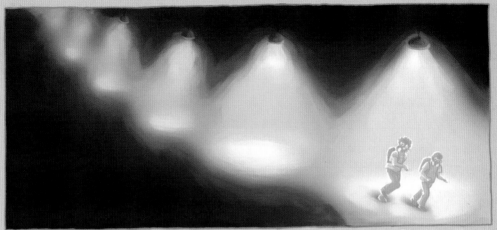

WAIT A SECOND! WHAT (WHU! WHUUU! AH!) ARE YOU DOING? (GASP!)

GETTING MY LIGHT. THEY KNOW WE'RE GONE, SO THEY'LL CUT OUR ELECTRICITY. LOOK AT ALL THIS STUFF. THIS MUST BE GREEN MAGMA MINING.

RUMBLERUMBLERUMBL

NOT AGAIN!

THERE GOES THE POWER.

EARTHQUAKES... DARKNESS... LOST! WE'LL BE BURIED ALIVE!

HE SAID, "STRAIGHT DOWN." HOW DIFFICULT IS THAT?

NO MORE SMOKE. WE'RE CLEAR.

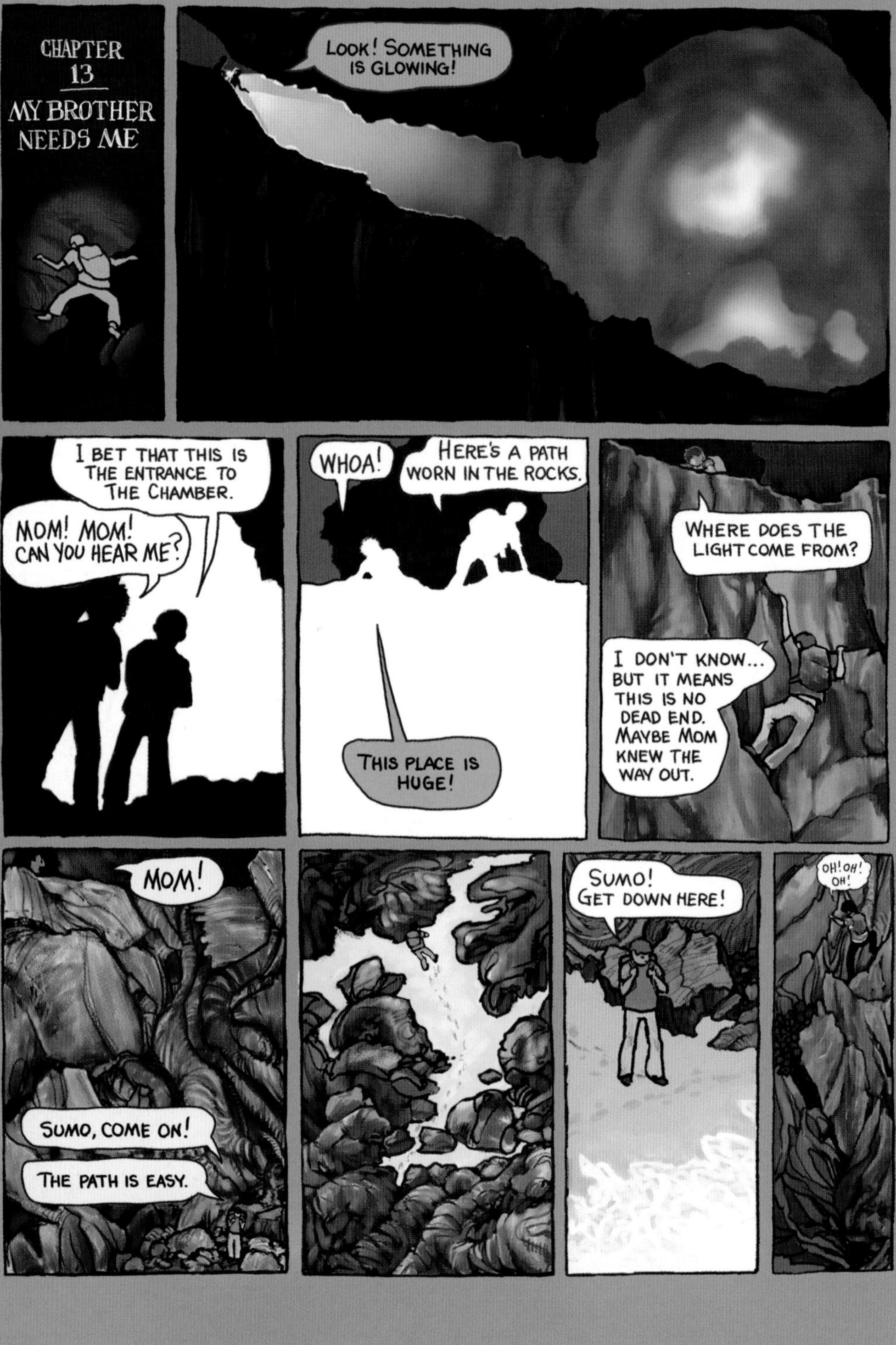
CHAPTER 13
MY BROTHER NEEDS ME
LOOK! SOMETHING IS GLOWING!
I BET THAT THIS IS THE ENTRANCE TO THE CHAMBER.
MOM! MOM! CAN YOU HEAR ME?
WHOA!
HERE'S A PATH WORN IN THE ROCKS.
THIS PLACE IS HUGE!
WHERE DOES THE LIGHT COME FROM?
I DON'T KNOW... BUT IT MEANS THIS IS NO DEAD END. MAYBE MOM KNEW THE WAY OUT.
MOM!
SUMO, COME ON!
THE PATH IS EASY.
SUMO! GET DOWN HERE!
OH! OH! OH!

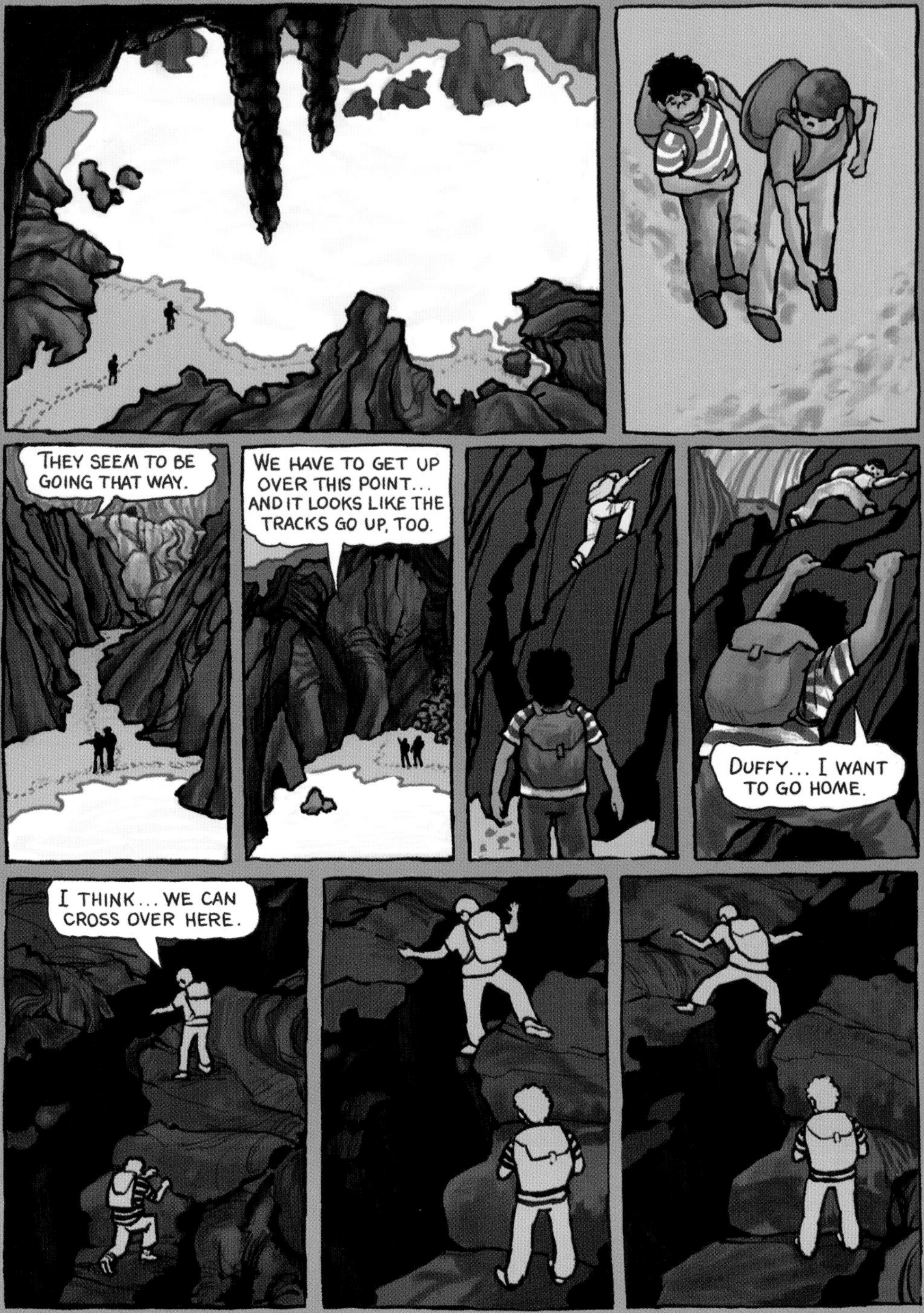
THEY SEEM TO BE GOING THAT WAY.
WE HAVE TO GET UP OVER THIS POINT... AND IT LOOKS LIKE THE TRACKS GO UP, TOO.
DUFFY... I WANT TO GO HOME.
I THINK... WE CAN CROSS OVER HERE.

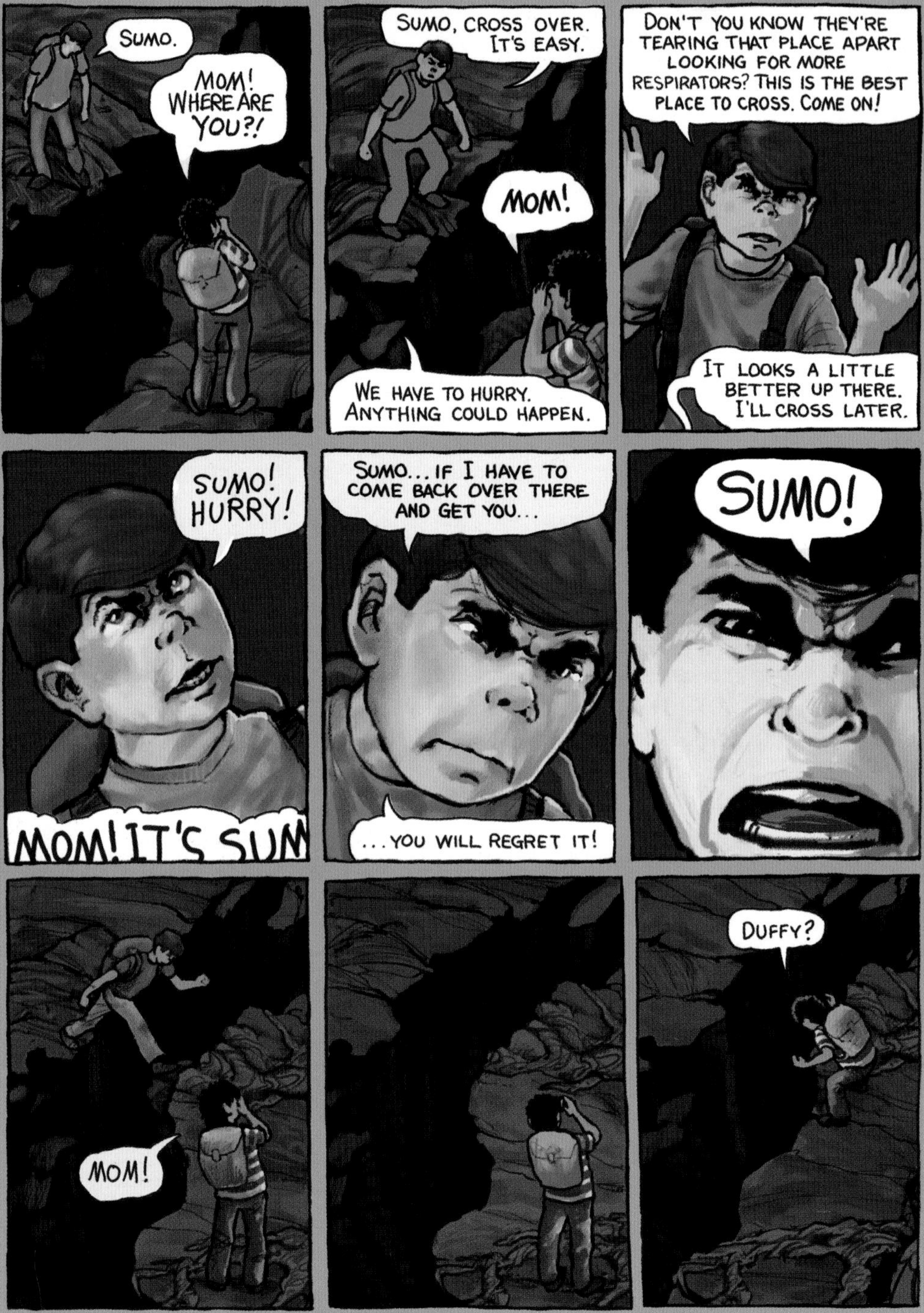
SUMO.
MOM! WHERE ARE YOU?!
SUMO, CROSS OVER. IT'S EASY.
MOM!
WE HAVE TO HURRY. ANYTHING COULD HAPPEN.
DON'T YOU KNOW THEY'RE TEARING THAT PLACE APART LOOKING FOR MORE RESPIRATORS? THIS IS THE BEST PLACE TO CROSS. COME ON!
IT LOOKS A LITTLE BETTER UP THERE. I'LL CROSS LATER.
SUMO! HURRY!
MOM! IT'S SUM
SUMO... IF I HAVE TO COME BACK OVER THERE AND GET YOU...
...YOU WILL REGRET IT!
SUMO!
MOM!
DUFFY?

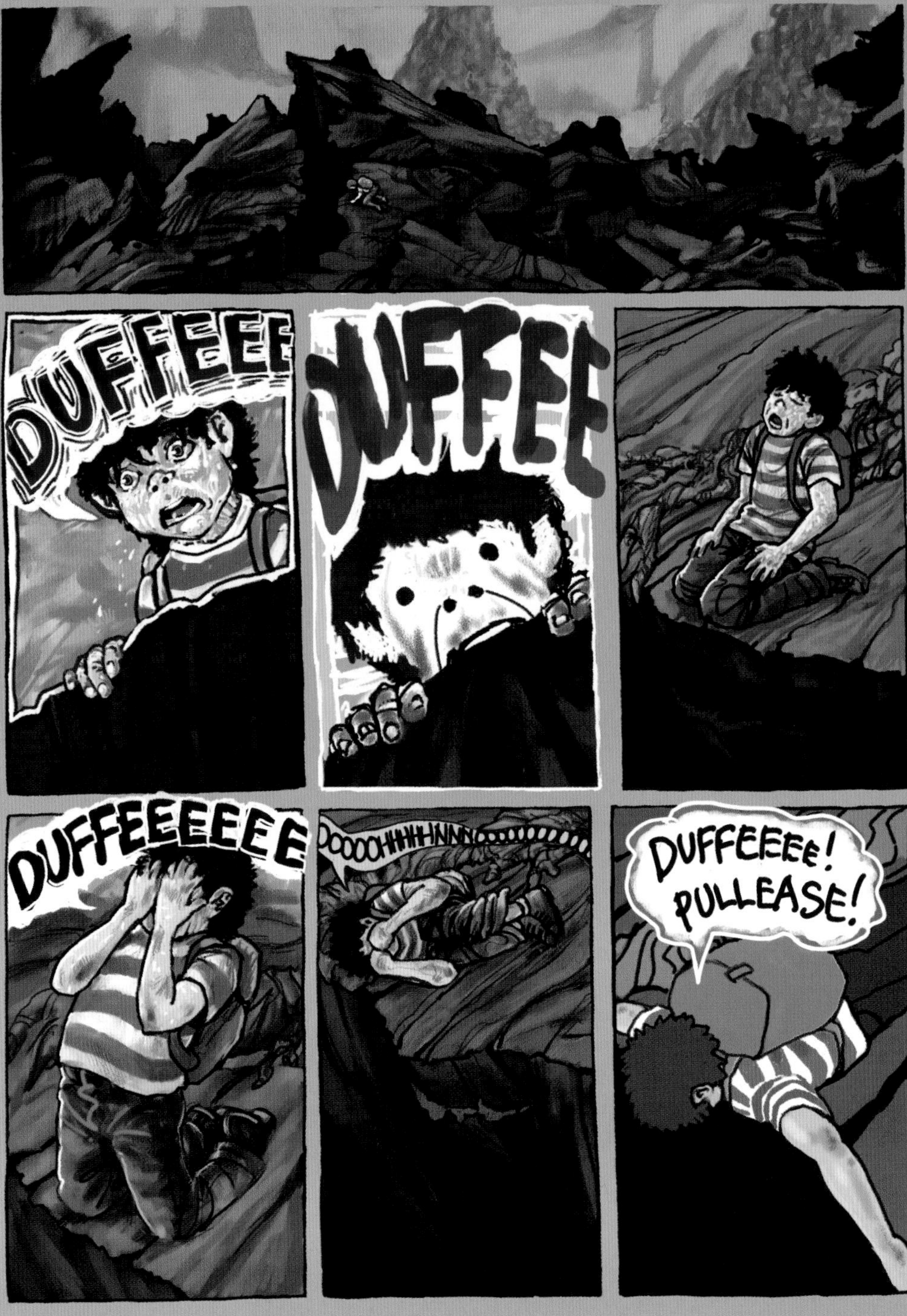
DUFFEEE
DUFFEE
DUFFEEEEEEE
OOOOOHHHHHNNNoooooooo
DUFFEEEE! PULLEASE!

SOB
YOU CAN'T LEAVE ME, DUFFY....
OHHHHHHH
DUFFY! DUFFY! IS THAT YOU?
THANK YOU! THANK YOU! ARE YOU OK? CAN YOU CLIMB OUT?
DUFFY! TALK TO ME!
HURT... CAN'T MOVE SO GOOD....
OH NO! I'LL HELP YOU!
THERE'S ROPE IN THE MINES. I'LL GET ROPE!

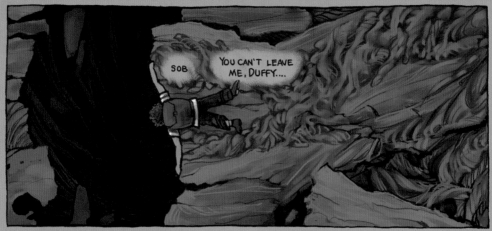

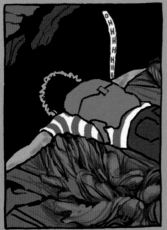

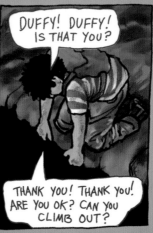

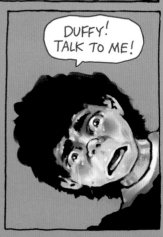

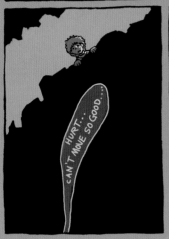

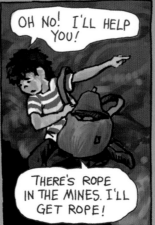

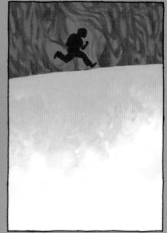

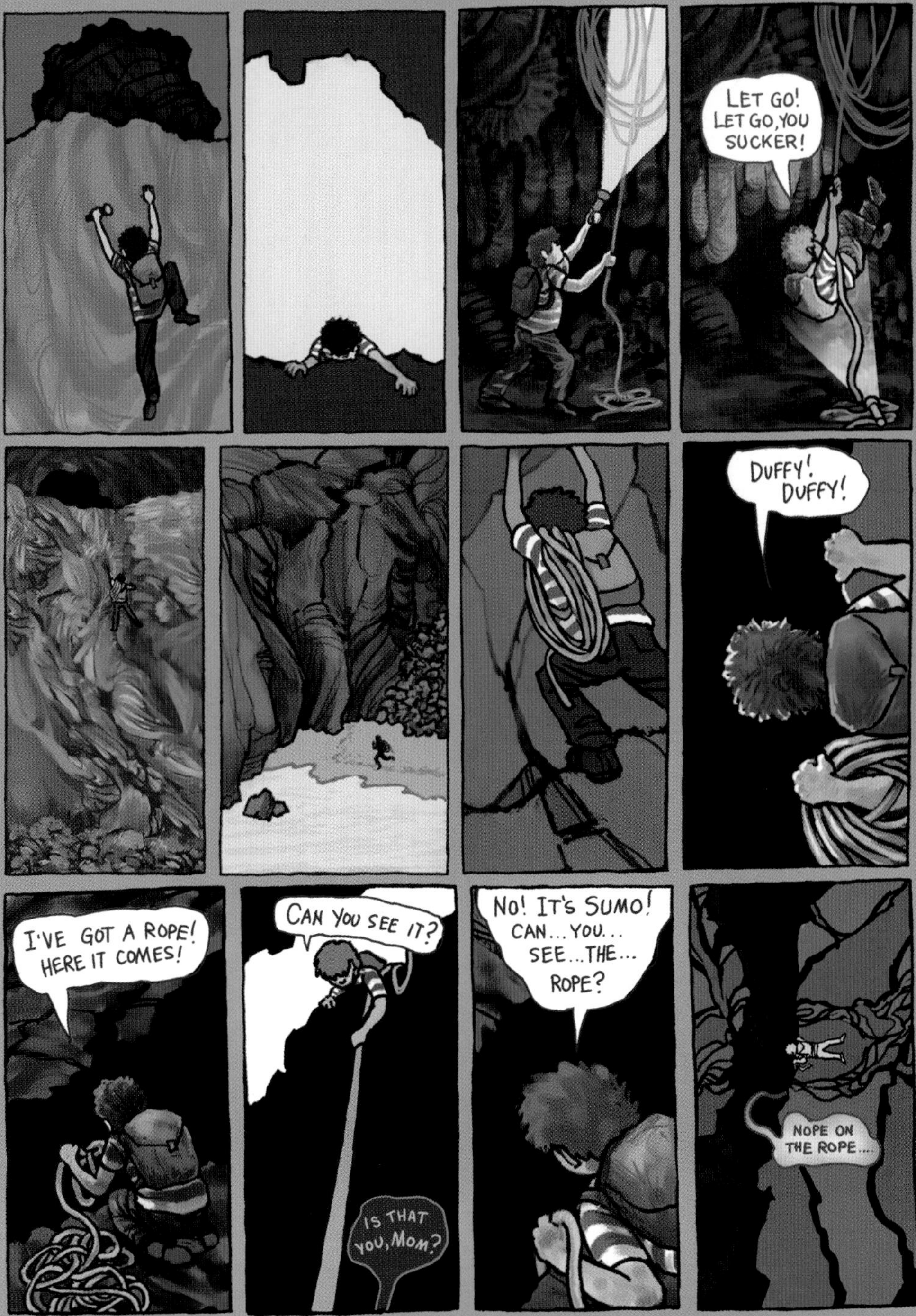
LET GO! LET GO, YOU SUCKER!
DUFFY! DUFFY!
I'VE GOT A ROPE! HERE IT COMES!
CAN YOU SEE IT?
IS THAT YOU, MOM?
NO! IT'S SUMO! CAN... YOU... SEE... THE... ROPE?
NOPE ON THE ROPE....

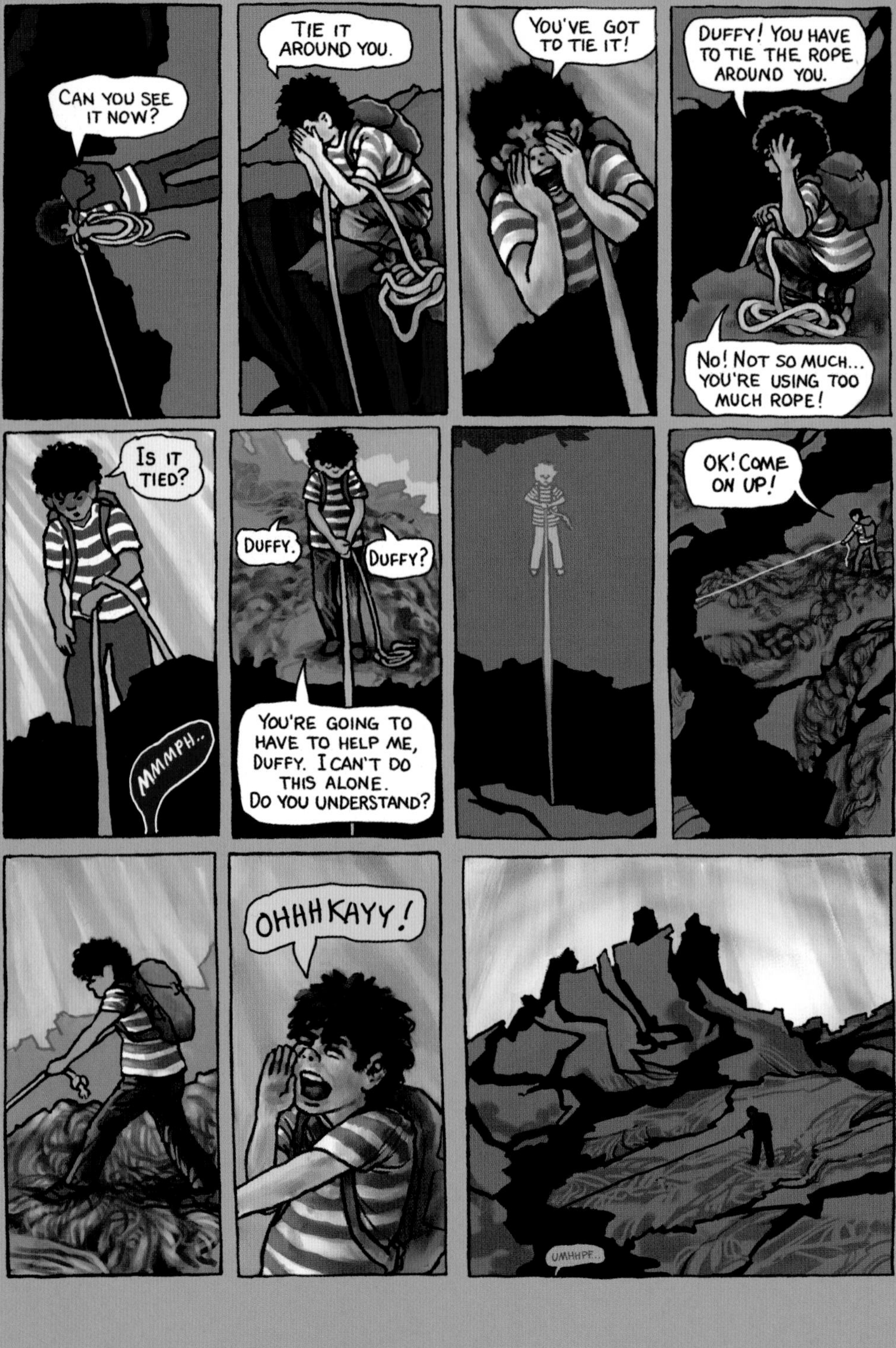
CAN YOU SEE IT NOW?
TIE IT AROUND YOU.
YOU'VE GOT TO TIE IT!
DUFFY! YOU HAVE TO TIE THE ROPE AROUND YOU.
NO! NOT SO MUCH... YOU'RE USING TOO MUCH ROPE!
IS IT TIED?
MMMPH..
DUFFY.
DUFFY?
YOU'RE GOING TO HAVE TO HELP ME, DUFFY. I CAN'T DO THIS ALONE. DO YOU UNDERSTAND?
OK! COME ON UP!
OHHHKAYY!
UMHHPF..

AHHEEEEEEEEEE
AAHHHHHHHHHHHH
DUFFY! WORK WITH ME!!
GOT TO TAKE A WRAP!
YESSS! THAT'S GOOD. WE'RE SAFE!
DUFFY! CAN YOU CLIMB? IF YOU WILL WORK WITH ME, WE'LL GET YOU OUT!
OHHHHHHHH
YOU'RE THE JOCK, BROTHER! WHEN THE GOING GETS TOUGH, THE TOUGH GET GOING. RIGHT?
NOW'S THE TIME TO GET GOING!
I'M GOING TO UNWRAP THIS AND PULL, AND YOU'RE GOING TO CLIMB. RIGHT!
RIGHT....

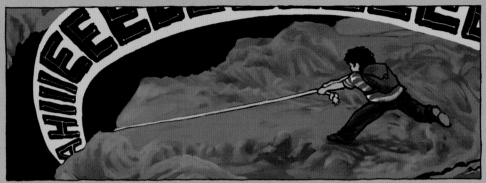

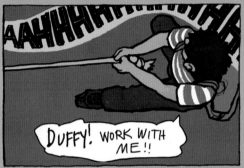

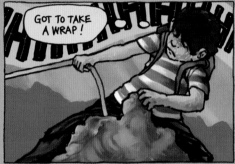

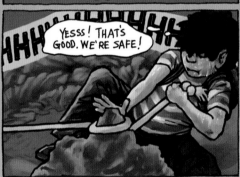

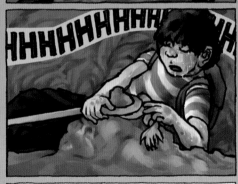

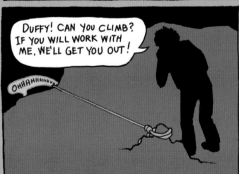

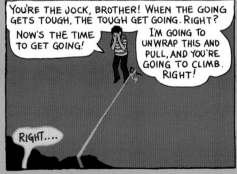

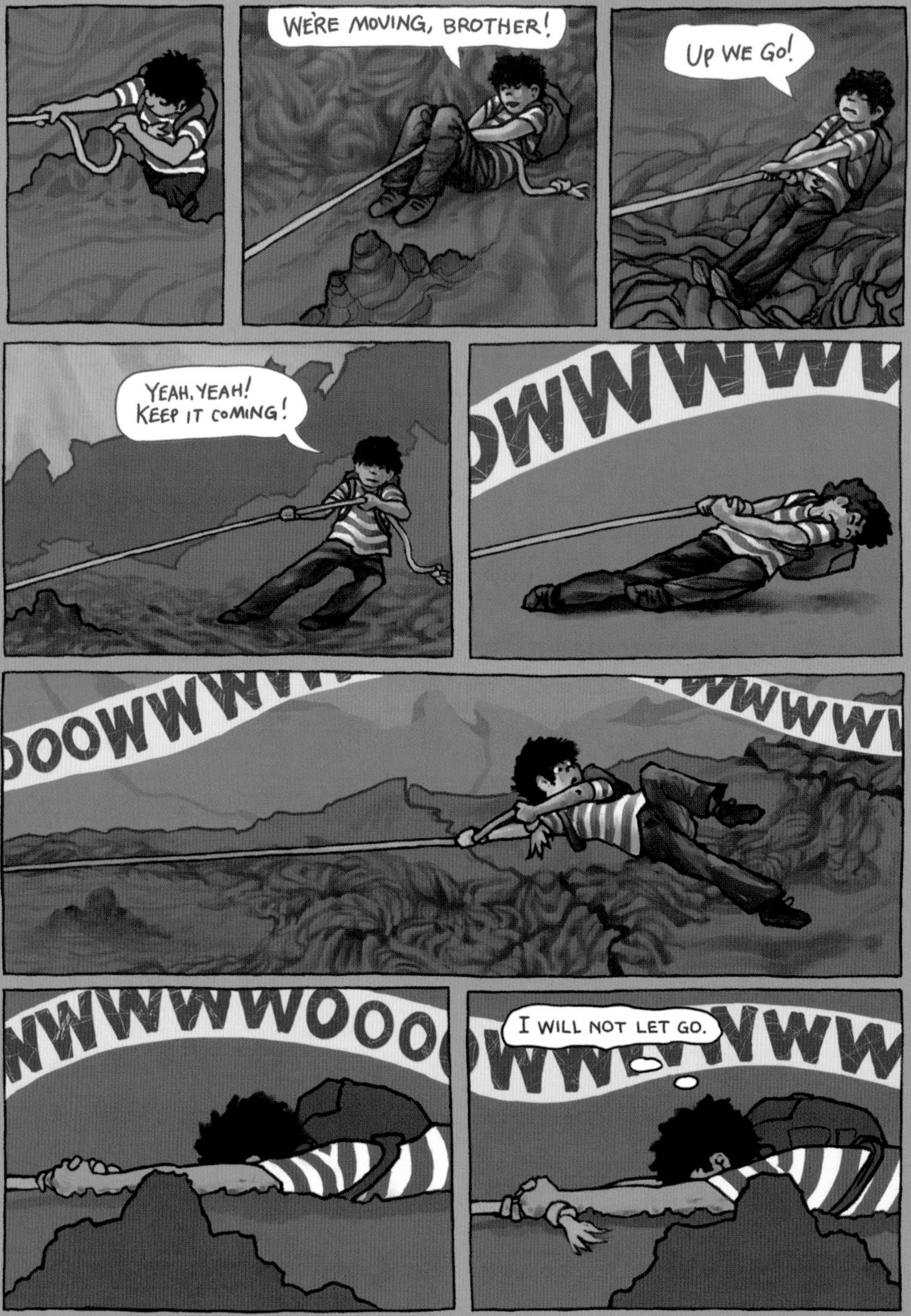
WE'RE MOVING, BROTHER!
UP WE GO!
YEAH, YEAH!
KEEP IT COMING!
OWWWWW
OOOWWWWW
WWWWWI
WWWWWOOOO
OWWWWWW
I WILL NOT LET GO.

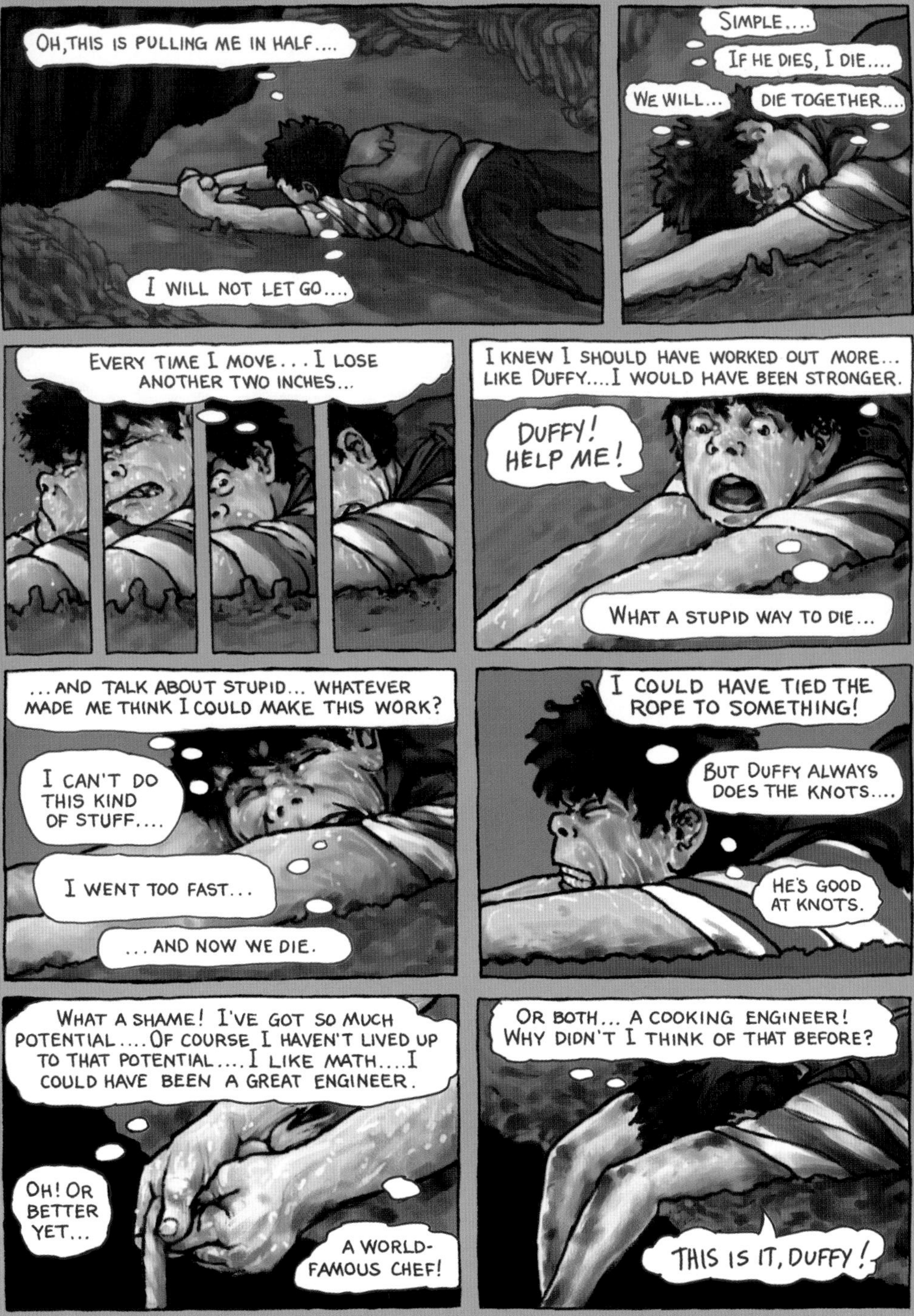
OH, THIS IS PULLING ME IN HALF....
I WILL NOT LET GO....
SIMPLE....
IF HE DIES, I DIE....
WE WILL...
DIE TOGETHER....
EVERY TIME I MOVE... I LOSE ANOTHER TWO INCHES...
I KNEW I SHOULD HAVE WORKED OUT MORE... LIKE DUFFY....I WOULD HAVE BEEN STRONGER.
DUFFY! HELP ME!
WHAT A STUPID WAY TO DIE...
...AND TALK ABOUT STUPID... WHATEVER MADE ME THINK I COULD MAKE THIS WORK?
I CAN'T DO THIS KIND OF STUFF....
I WENT TOO FAST...
...AND NOW WE DIE.
I COULD HAVE TIED THE ROPE TO SOMETHING!
BUT DUFFY ALWAYS DOES THE KNOTS....
HE'S GOOD AT KNOTS.
WHAT A SHAME! I'VE GOT SO MUCH POTENTIAL....OF COURSE I HAVEN'T LIVED UP TO THAT POTENTIAL....I LIKE MATH....I COULD HAVE BEEN A GREAT ENGINEER.
OH! OR BETTER YET...
A WORLD-FAMOUS CHEF!
OR BOTH... A COOKING ENGINEER! WHY DIDN'T I THINK OF THAT BEFORE?
THIS IS IT, DUFFY!

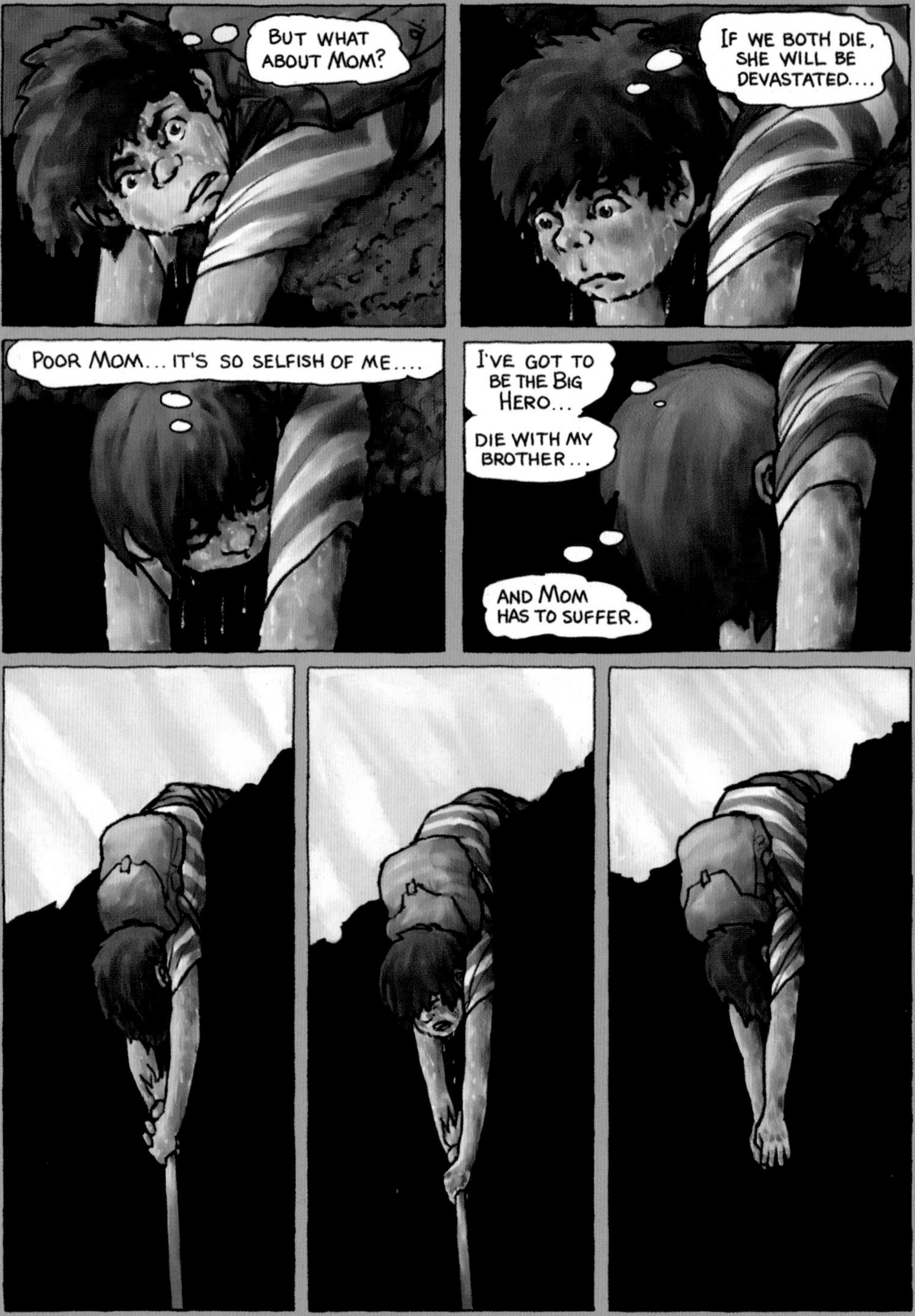
BUT WHAT ABOUT MOM?
IF WE BOTH DIE, SHE WILL BE DEVASTATED....
POOR MOM... IT'S SO SELFISH OF ME....
I'VE GOT TO BE THE BIG HERO...
DIE WITH MY BROTHER...
AND MOM HAS TO SUFFER.

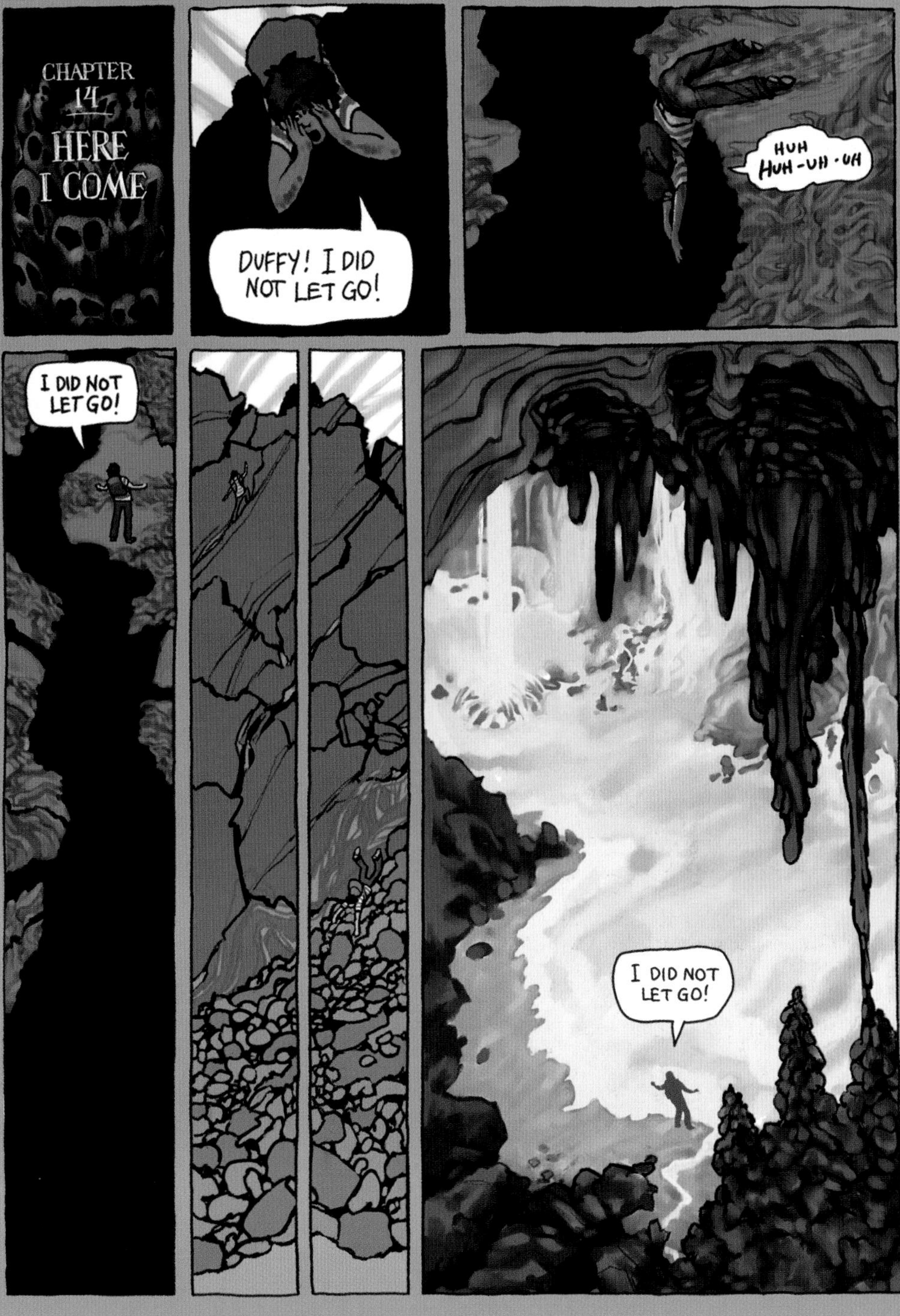
CHAPTER
14
HERE
I COME
DUFFY! I DID NOT LET GO!
HUH
HUH-UH-UH
I DID NOT LET GO!
I DID NOT LET GO!

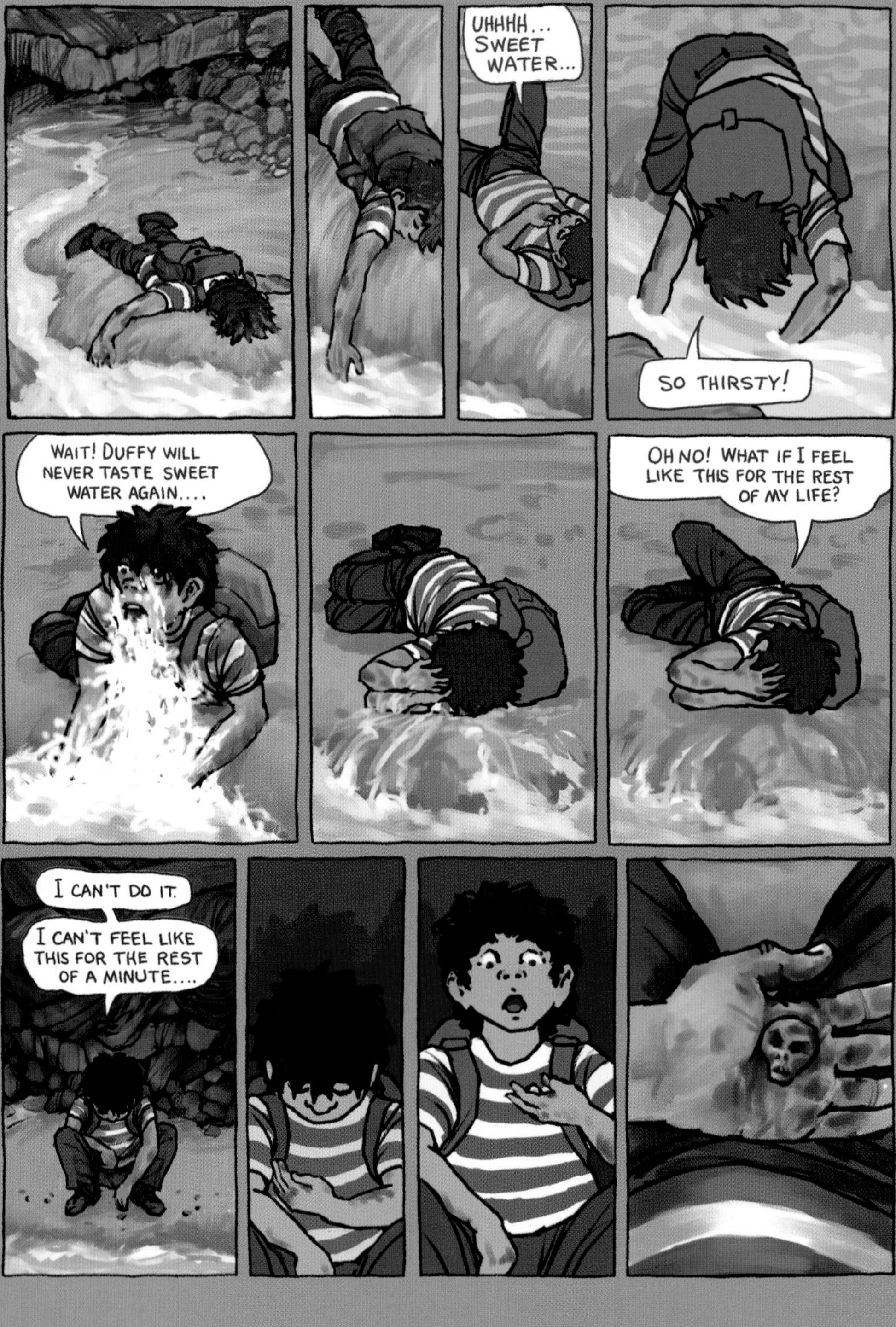
UHHHH... SWEET WATER...
SO THIRSTY!
WAIT! DUFFY WILL NEVER TASTE SWEET WATER AGAIN....
OH NO! WHAT IF I FEEL LIKE THIS FOR THE REST OF MY LIFE?
I CAN'T DO IT.
I CAN'T FEEL LIKE THIS FOR THE REST OF A MINUTE....

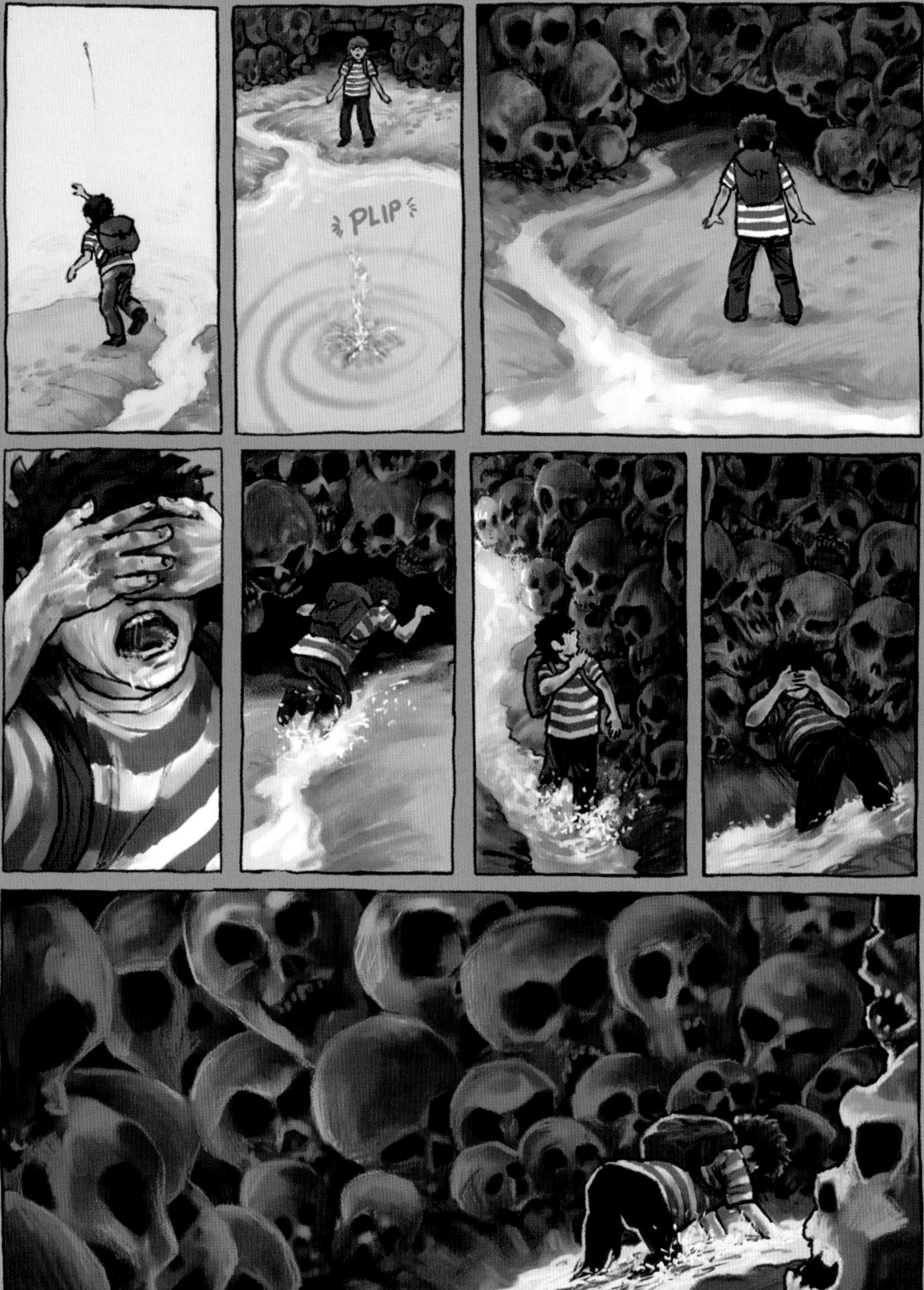
PLIP

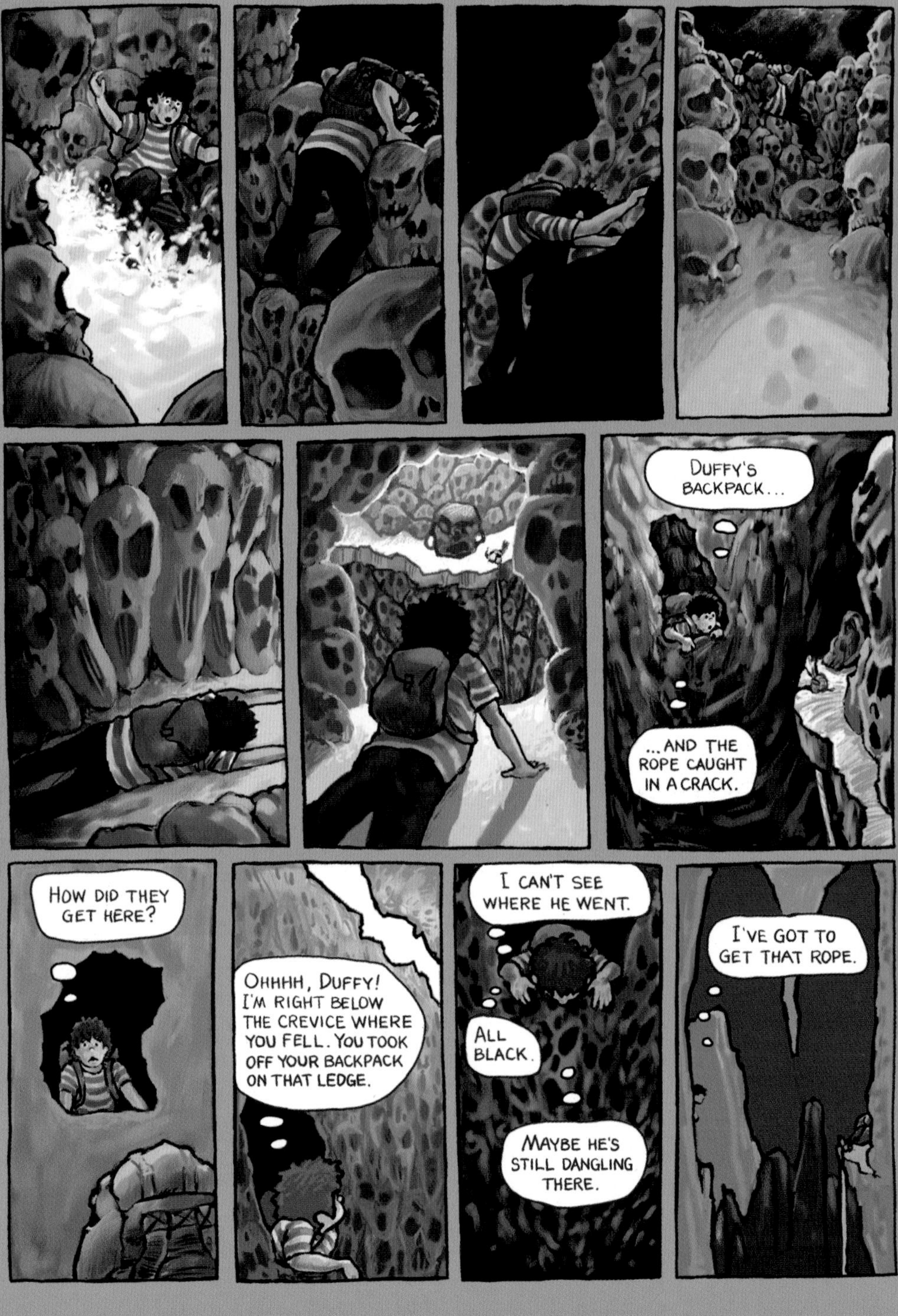
DUFFY'S BACKPACK...
...AND THE ROPE CAUGHT IN A CRACK.
HOW DID THEY GET HERE?
OHHHH, DUFFY! I'M RIGHT BELOW THE CREVICE WHERE YOU FELL. YOU TOOK OFF YOUR BACKPACK ON THAT LEDGE.
I CAN'T SEE WHERE HE WENT.
ALL BLACK.
MAYBE HE'S STILL DANGLING THERE.
I'VE GOT TO GET THAT ROPE.

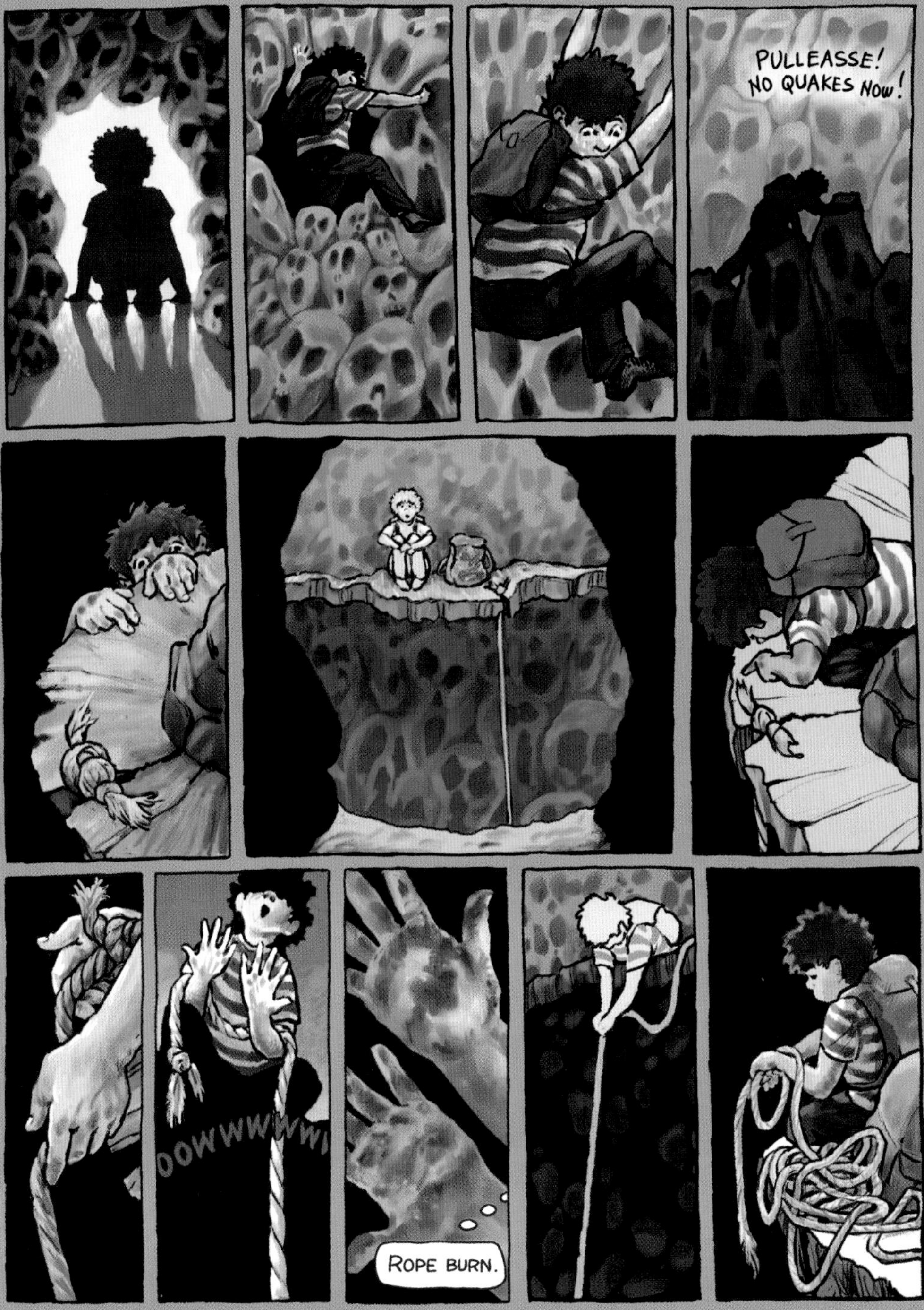
PULLEASSE!
NO QUAKES NOW!
OOWWWWWWW
ROPE BURN.

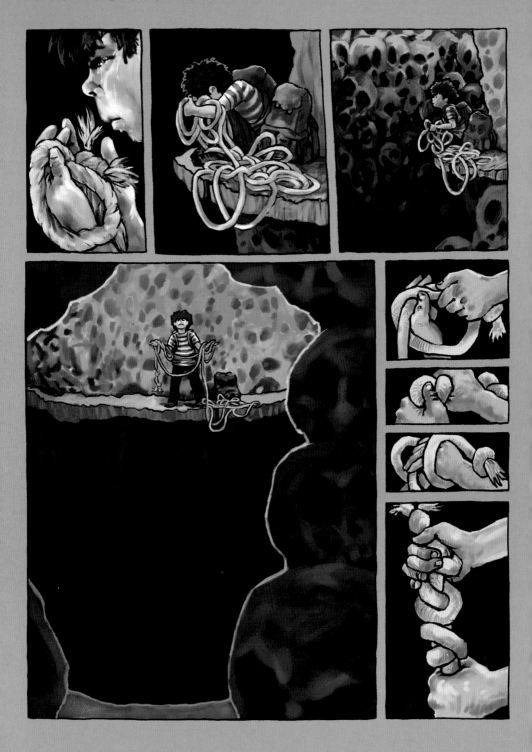

THE KNOT IN THE CRACK HELD ONCE. IT SHOULD HOLD AGAIN.

I'M NOT GONNA LEAVE YOU TO ROT, DUFFY.

I'M COMIN' DOWN TO GET YOU!

HERE GOES NOTHIN'.

BUT WHAT ABOUT HIS BACKPACK?

HIS FOOD!

I SHOULDN'T EAT DUFFY'S FOOD.... HOW CAN I EAT DUFFY'S FOOD?

DUFFY, I'LL USE THE ENERGY FROM YOUR FOOD TO FIND YOUR BODY.

WOW...HE HAD A LOT MORE THAN ME!

EXTRA BATTERIES AND LIGHTS....

WHAT AM I DOING?

ALL I HAVE TO DO IS GO BACK THE WAY I CAME AND WAIT ON THE BEACH AND SOMEONE WILL RESCUE ME.

DUFFY!

OW!

HERE I COME!

OW! OW!

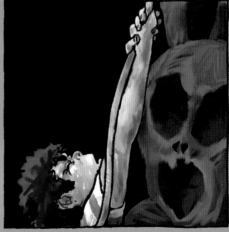

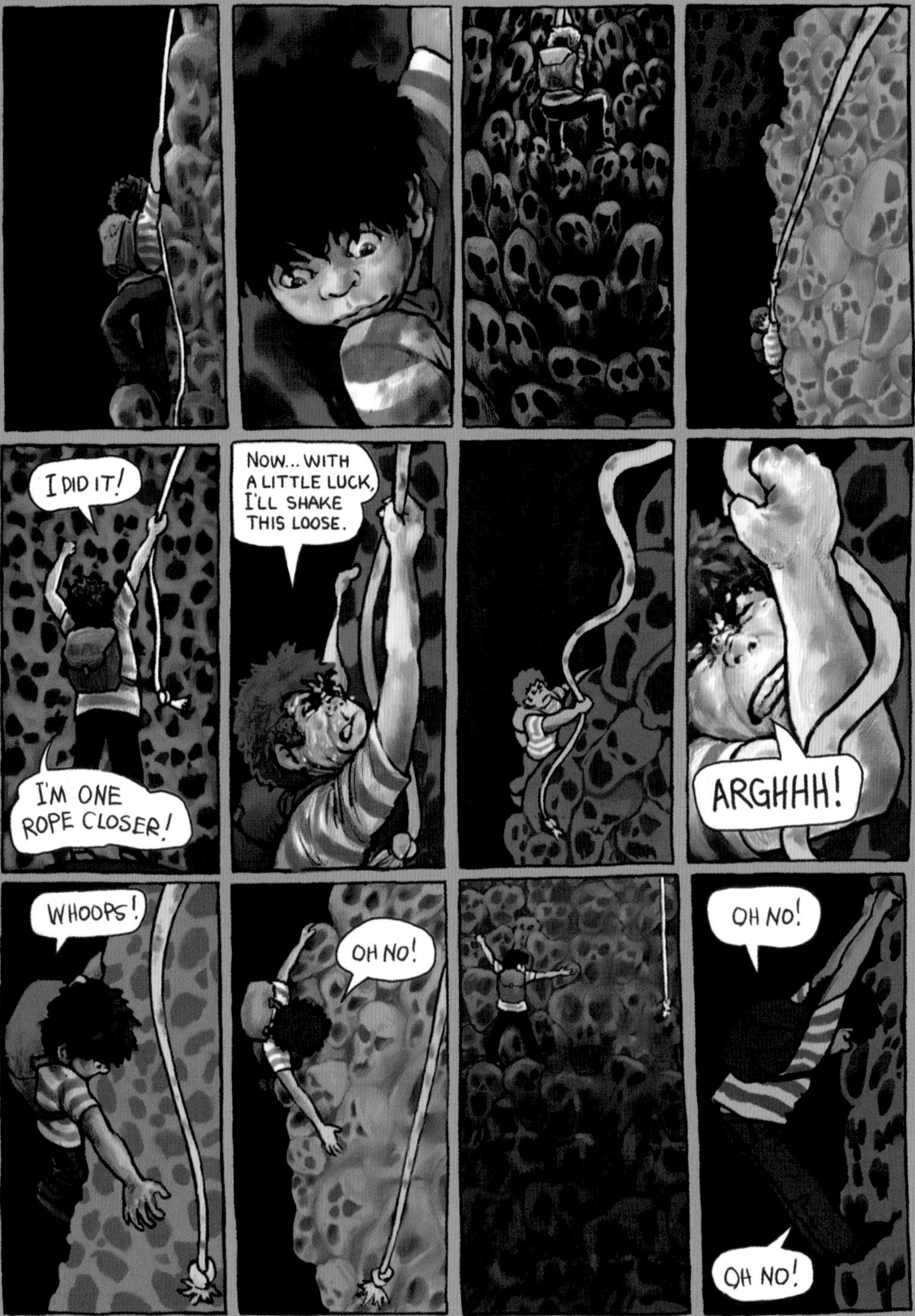
I DID IT!
I'M ONE ROPE CLOSER!
NOW... WITH A LITTLE LUCK, I'LL SHAKE THIS LOOSE.
ARGHHH!
WHOOPS!
OH NO!
OH NO!
OH NO!

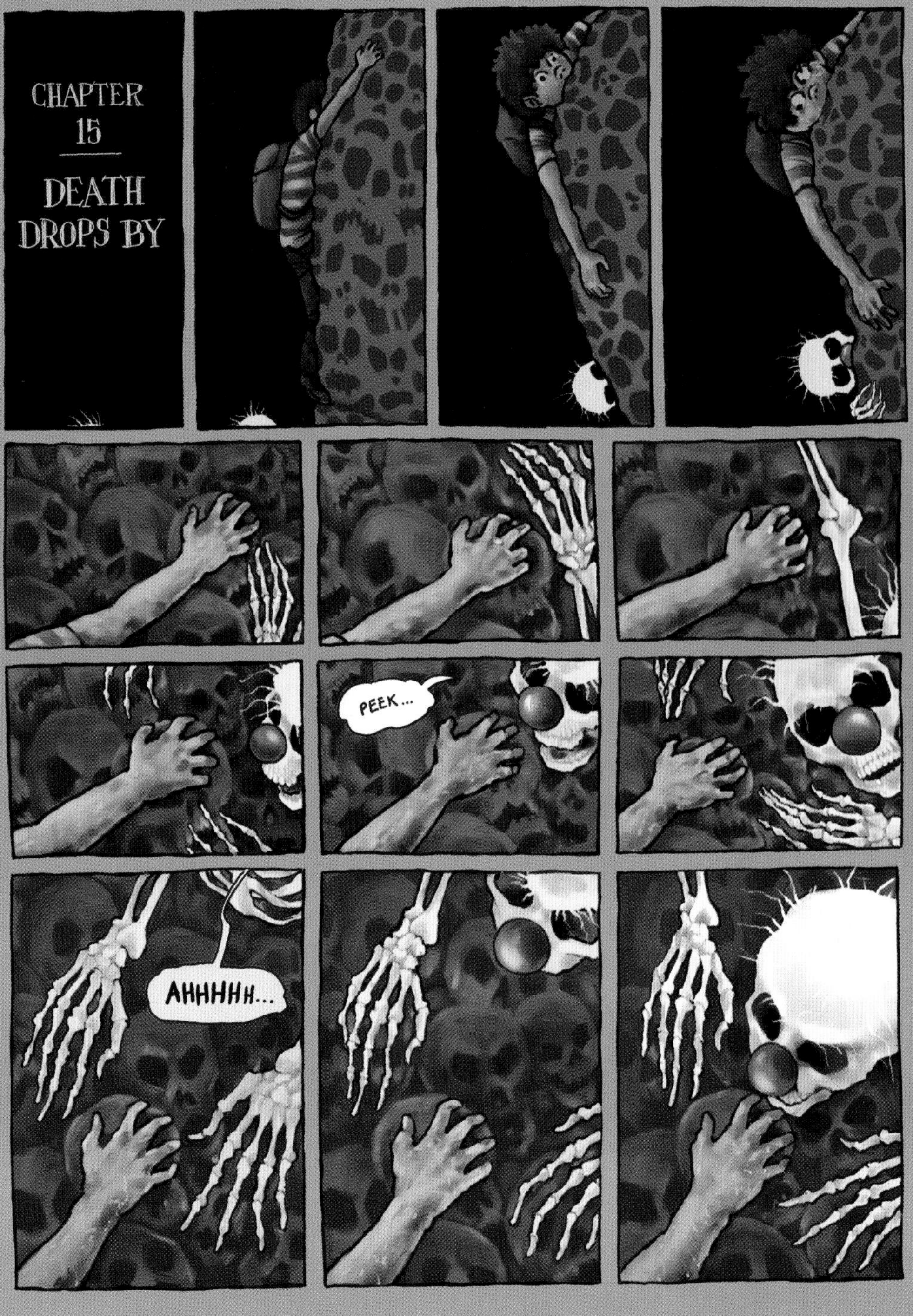
CHAPTER
15
DEATH
DROPS BY
PEEK...
AHHHHH...

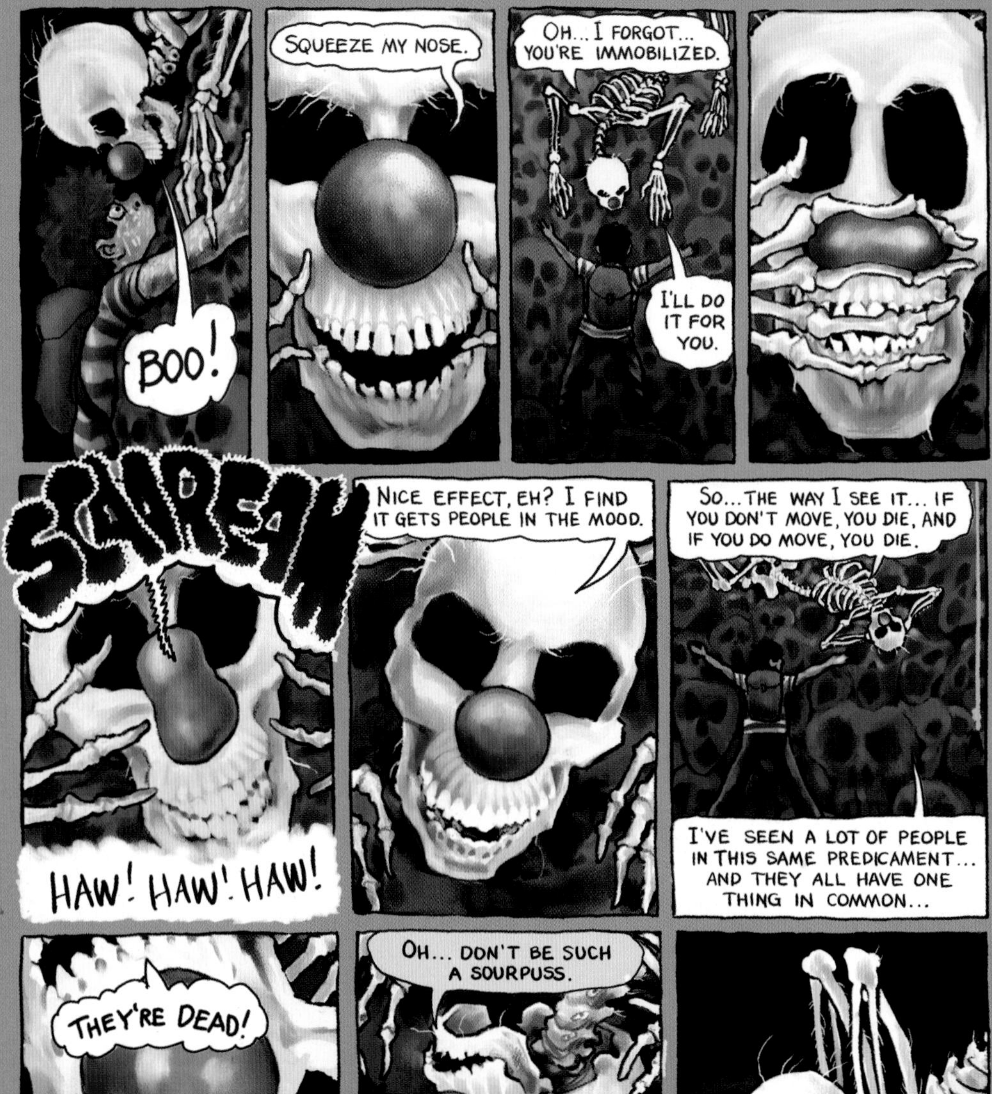
BOO!
SQUEEZE MY NOSE.
OH... I FORGOT... YOU'RE IMMOBILIZED.
I'LL DO IT FOR YOU.
SCWREEH
HAW! HAW! HAW!
NICE EFFECT, EH? I FIND IT GETS PEOPLE IN THE MOOD.
SO... THE WAY I SEE IT... IF YOU DON'T MOVE, YOU DIE, AND IF YOU DO MOVE, YOU DIE.
I'VE SEEN A LOT OF PEOPLE IN THIS SAME PREDICAMENT... AND THEY ALL HAVE ONE THING IN COMMON...
THEY'RE DEAD!
HEE-HEEEEE
OH... DON'T BE SUCH A SOURPUSS.
I KNOW WHAT'S BOTHERING YOU.... OH MY! IT'S SUCH A STUPID DEATH.
WELL... I'VE GOT NEWS FOR YOU, KID. THEY'RE NEARLY ALL STUPID.

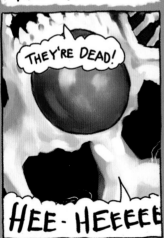

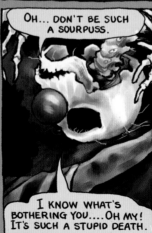

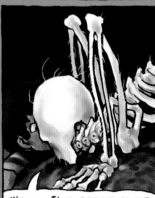

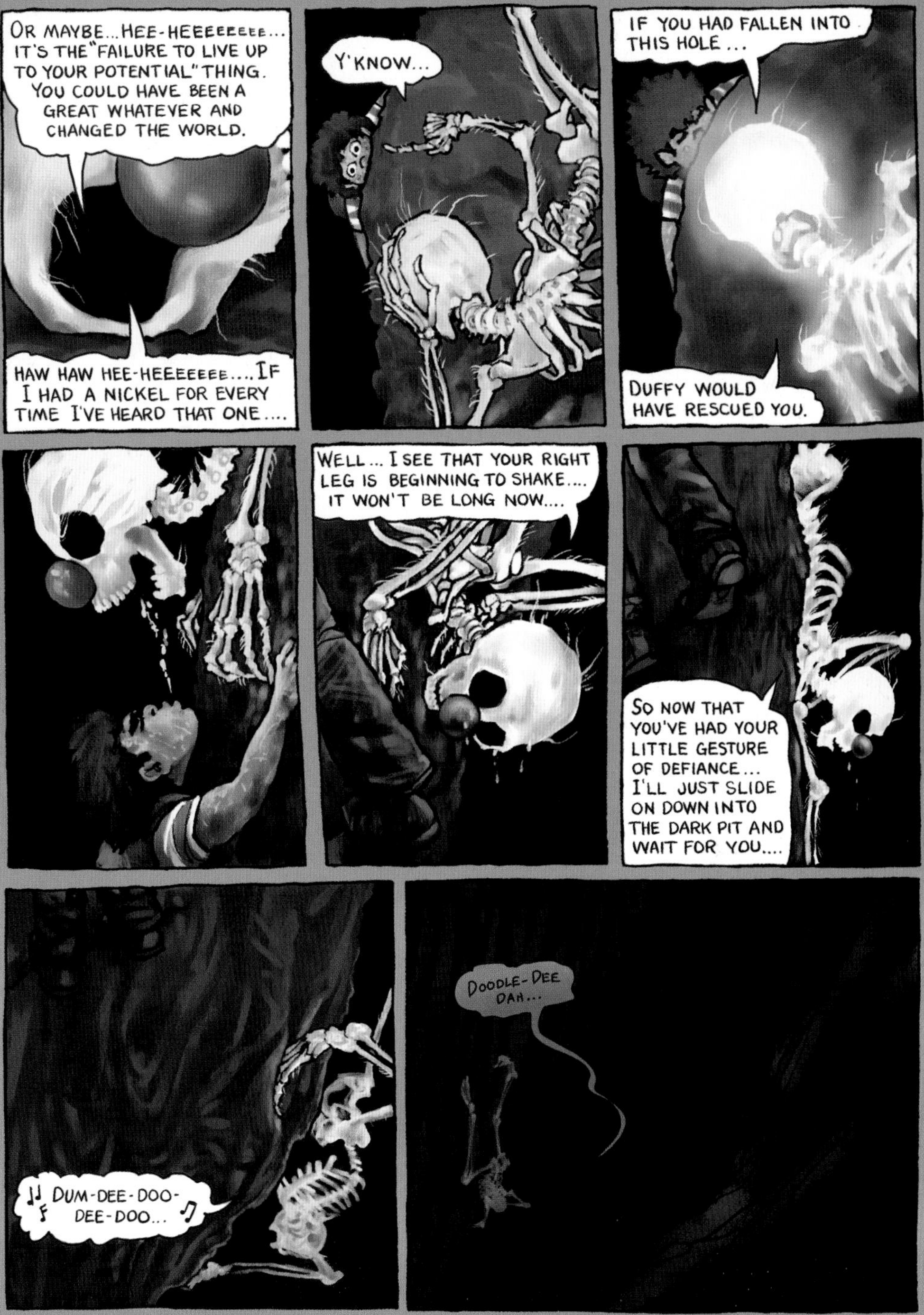
OR MAYBE...HEE-HEEEEEEEE... IT'S THE "FAILURE TO LIVE UP TO YOUR POTENTIAL" THING. YOU COULD HAVE BEEN A GREAT WHATEVER AND CHANGED THE WORLD.
HAW HAW HEE-HEEEEEEE.... IF I HAD A NICKEL FOR EVERY TIME I'VE HEARD THAT ONE....
Y'KNOW...
IF YOU HAD FALLEN INTO THIS HOLE...
DUFFY WOULD HAVE RESCUED YOU.
WELL... I SEE THAT YOUR RIGHT LEG IS BEGINNING TO SHAKE.... IT WON'T BE LONG NOW....
SO NOW THAT YOU'VE HAD YOUR LITTLE GESTURE OF DEFIANCE... I'LL JUST SLIDE ON DOWN INTO THE DARK PIT AND WAIT FOR YOU....
DUM-DEE-DOO-DEE-DOO...
DOODLE-DEE DAH...

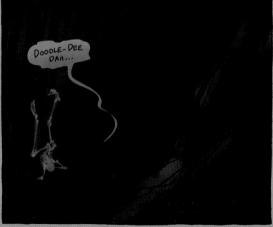

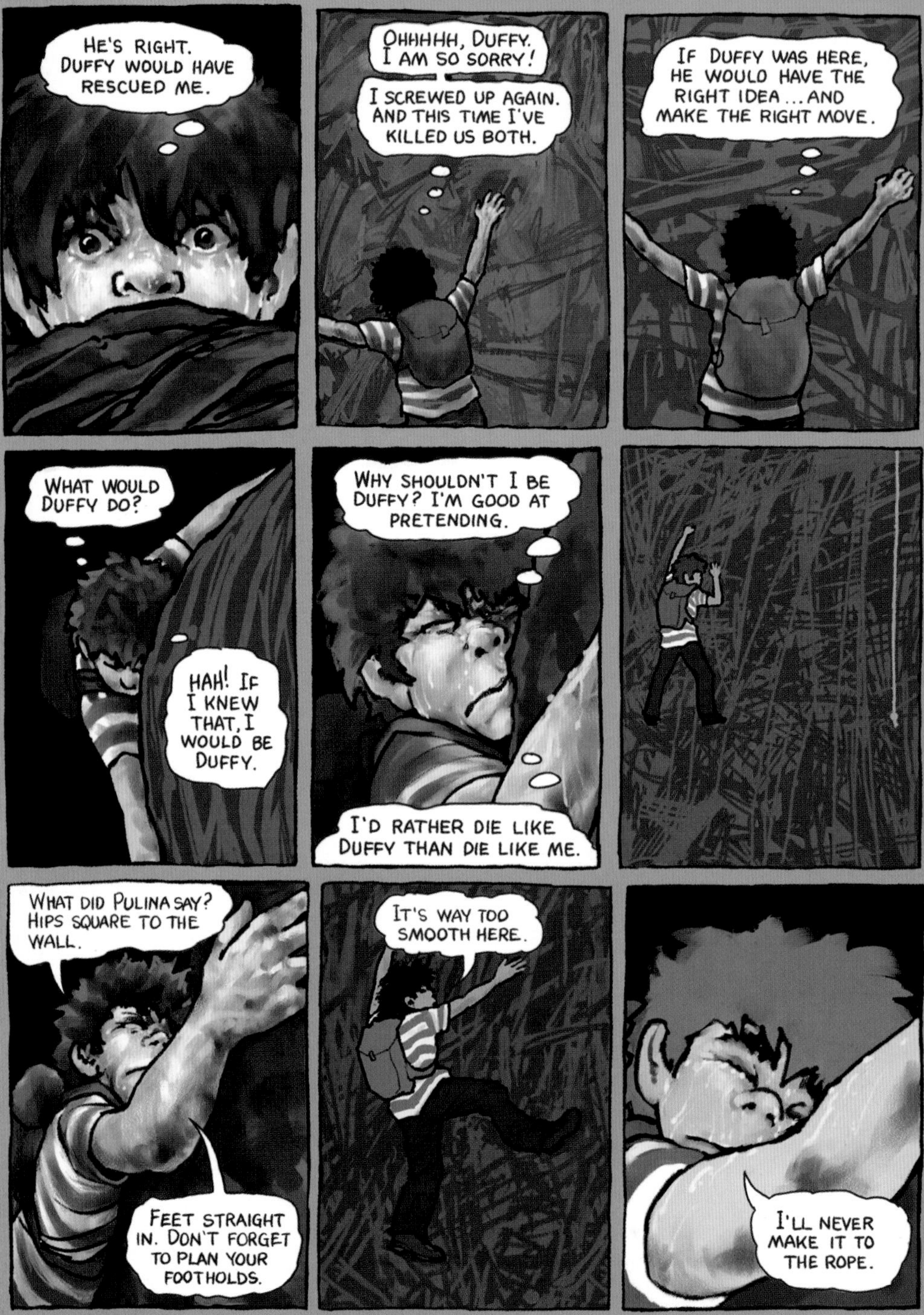
HE'S RIGHT. DUFFY WOULD HAVE RESCUED ME.
OHHHHH, DUFFY. I AM SO SORRY!
I SCREWED UP AGAIN. AND THIS TIME I'VE KILLED US BOTH.
IF DUFFY WAS HERE, HE WOULD HAVE THE RIGHT IDEA ... AND MAKE THE RIGHT MOVE.
WHAT WOULD DUFFY DO?
HAH! IF I KNEW THAT, I WOULD BE DUFFY.
WHY SHOULDN'T I BE DUFFY? I'M GOOD AT PRETENDING.
I'D RATHER DIE LIKE DUFFY THAN DIE LIKE ME.
WHAT DID PULINA SAY? HIPS SQUARE TO THE WALL.
FEET STRAIGHT IN. DON'T FORGET TO PLAN YOUR FOOTHOLDS.
IT'S WAY TOO SMOOTH HERE.
I'LL NEVER MAKE IT TO THE ROPE.

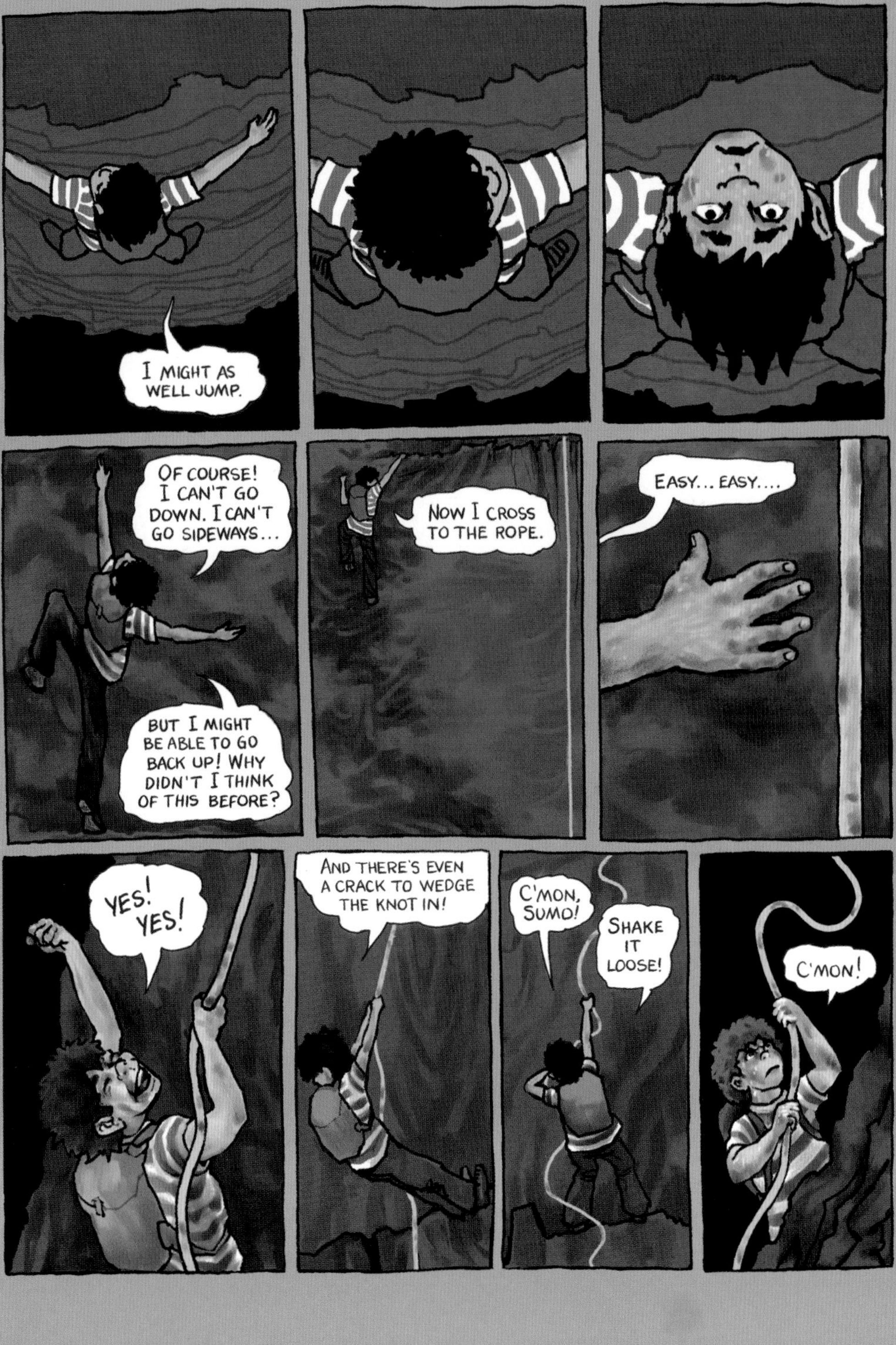
I MIGHT AS WELL JUMP.
OF COURSE! I CAN'T GO DOWN. I CAN'T GO SIDEWAYS...
BUT I MIGHT BE ABLE TO GO BACK UP! WHY DIDN'T I THINK OF THIS BEFORE?
NOW I CROSS TO THE ROPE.
EASY... EASY....
YES! YES!
AND THERE'S EVEN A CRACK TO WEDGE THE KNOT IN!
C'MON, SUMO!
SHAKE IT LOOSE!
C'MON!

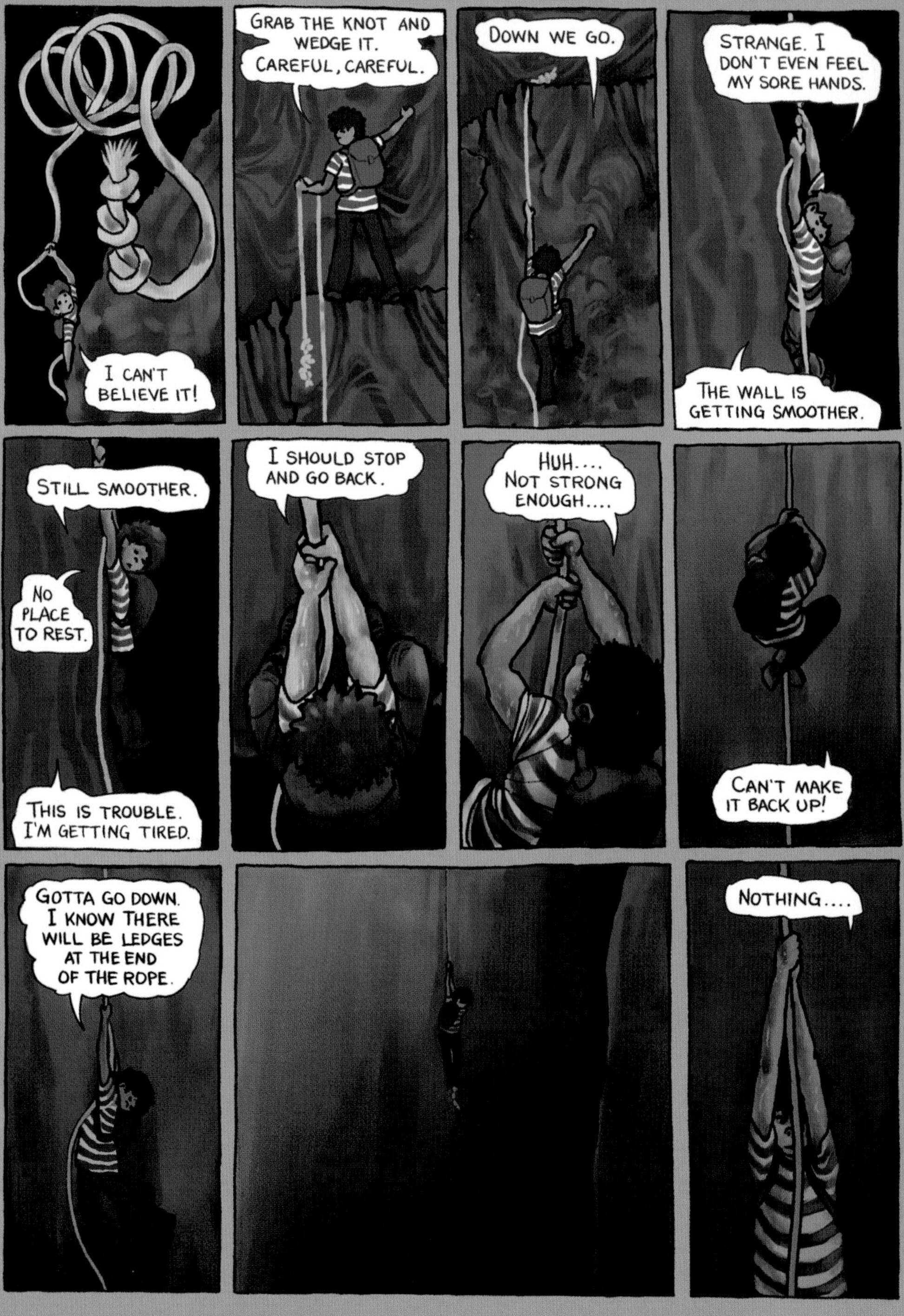
I CAN'T BELIEVE IT!
GRAB THE KNOT AND WEDGE IT. CAREFUL, CAREFUL.
DOWN WE GO.
STRANGE. I DON'T EVEN FEEL MY SORE HANDS.
THE WALL IS GETTING SMOOTHER.
STILL SMOOTHER.
NO PLACE TO REST.
THIS IS TROUBLE. I'M GETTING TIRED.
I SHOULD STOP AND GO BACK.
HUH.... NOT STRONG ENOUGH....
CAN'T MAKE IT BACK UP!
GOTTA GO DOWN. I KNOW THERE WILL BE LEDGES AT THE END OF THE ROPE.
NOTHING....

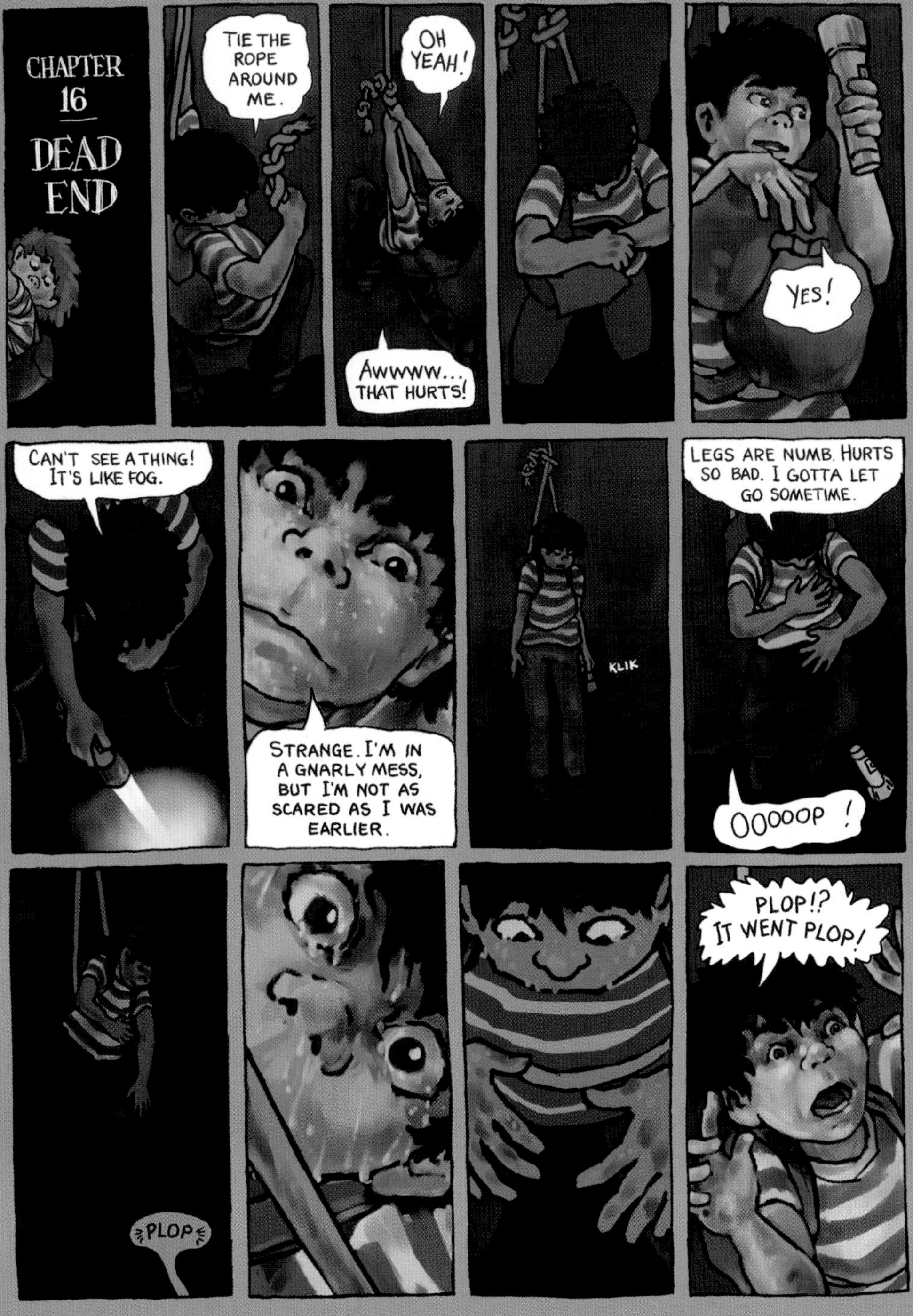
CHAPTER
16
DEAD END
TIE THE ROPE AROUND ME.
OH YEAH!
AWWWW... THAT HURTS!
YES!
CAN'T SEE A THING! IT'S LIKE FOG.
STRANGE. I'M IN A GNARLY MESS, BUT I'M NOT AS SCARED AS I WAS EARLIER.
KLIK
LEGS ARE NUMB. HURTS SO BAD. I GOTTA LET GO SOMETIME.
OOOOOP!
PLOP
PLOP!? IT WENT PLOP!

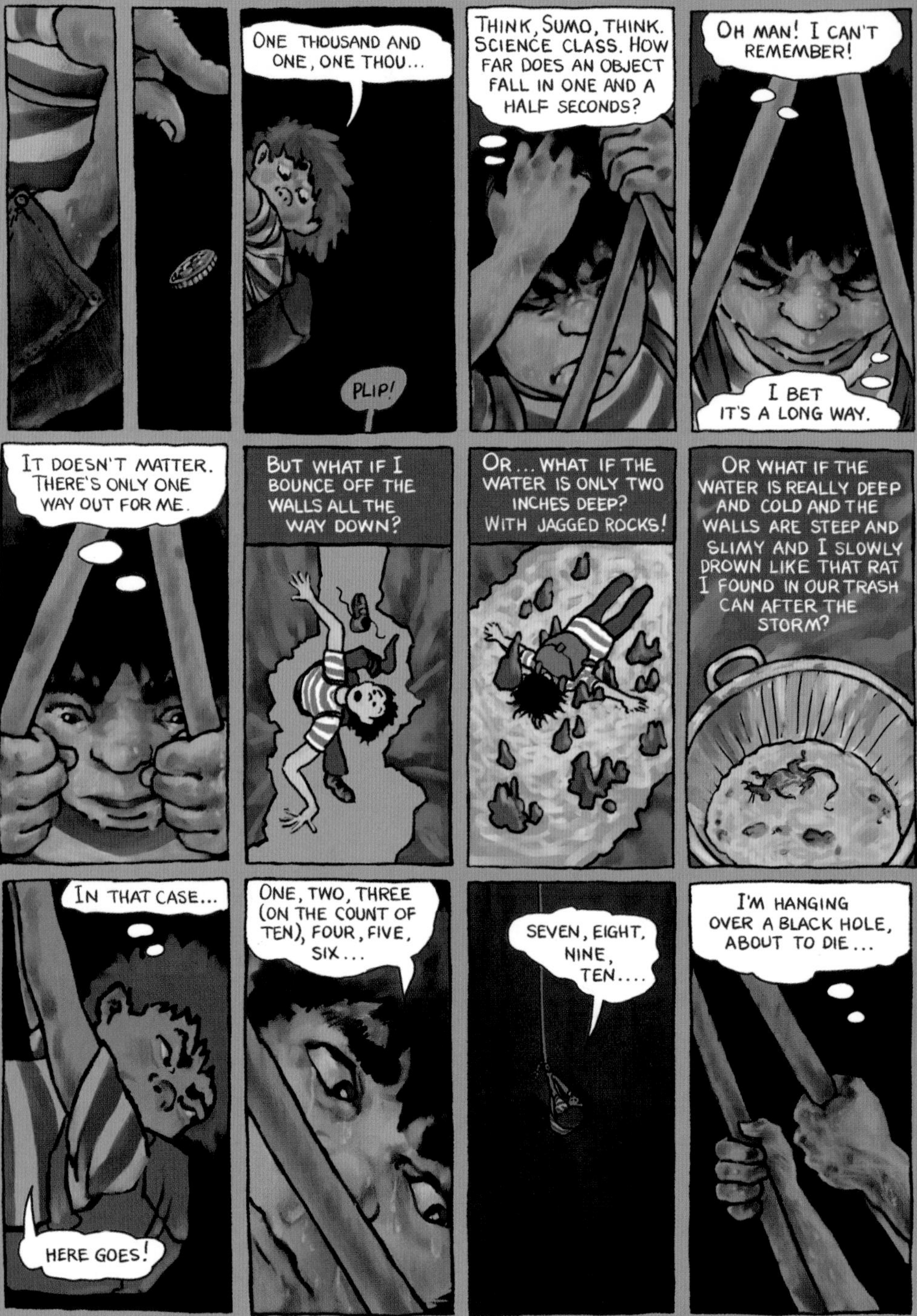
ONE THOUSAND AND ONE, ONE THOU...
PLIP!
THINK, SUMO, THINK. SCIENCE CLASS. HOW FAR DOES AN OBJECT FALL IN ONE AND A HALF SECONDS?
OH MAN! I CAN'T REMEMBER!
I BET IT'S A LONG WAY.
IT DOESN'T MATTER. THERE'S ONLY ONE WAY OUT FOR ME.
BUT WHAT IF I BOUNCE OFF THE WALLS ALL THE WAY DOWN?
OR... WHAT IF THE WATER IS ONLY TWO INCHES DEEP? WITH JAGGED ROCKS!
OR WHAT IF THE WATER IS REALLY DEEP AND COLD AND THE WALLS ARE STEEP AND SLIMY AND I SLOWLY DROWN LIKE THAT RAT I FOUND IN OUR TRASH CAN AFTER THE STORM?
IN THAT CASE...
HERE GOES!
ONE, TWO, THREE (ON THE COUNT OF TEN), FOUR, FIVE, SIX...
SEVEN, EIGHT, NINE, TEN....
I'M HANGING OVER A BLACK HOLE, ABOUT TO DIE...

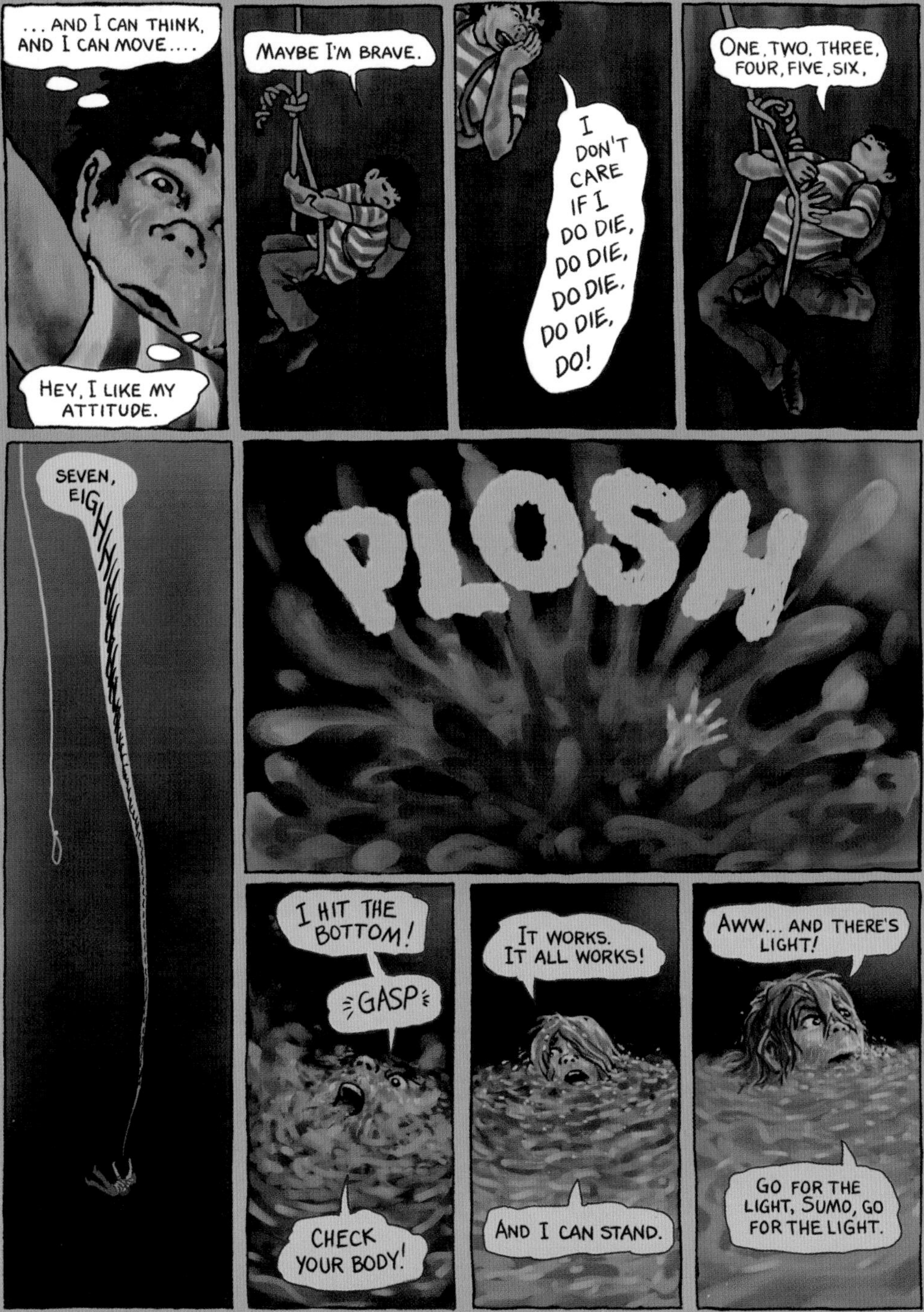
... AND I CAN THINK, AND I CAN MOVE....
HEY, I LIKE MY ATTITUDE.
MAYBE I'M BRAVE.
I DON'T CARE IF I DO DIE, DO DIE, DO DIE, DO DIE, DO!
ONE, TWO, THREE, FOUR, FIVE, SIX,
SEVEN, EIGHHHHHHHHHH
PLOSH
I HIT THE BOTTOM!
GASP
CHECK YOUR BODY!
IT WORKS. IT ALL WORKS!
AND I CAN STAND.
AWW... AND THERE'S LIGHT!
GO FOR THE LIGHT, SUMO, GO FOR THE LIGHT.

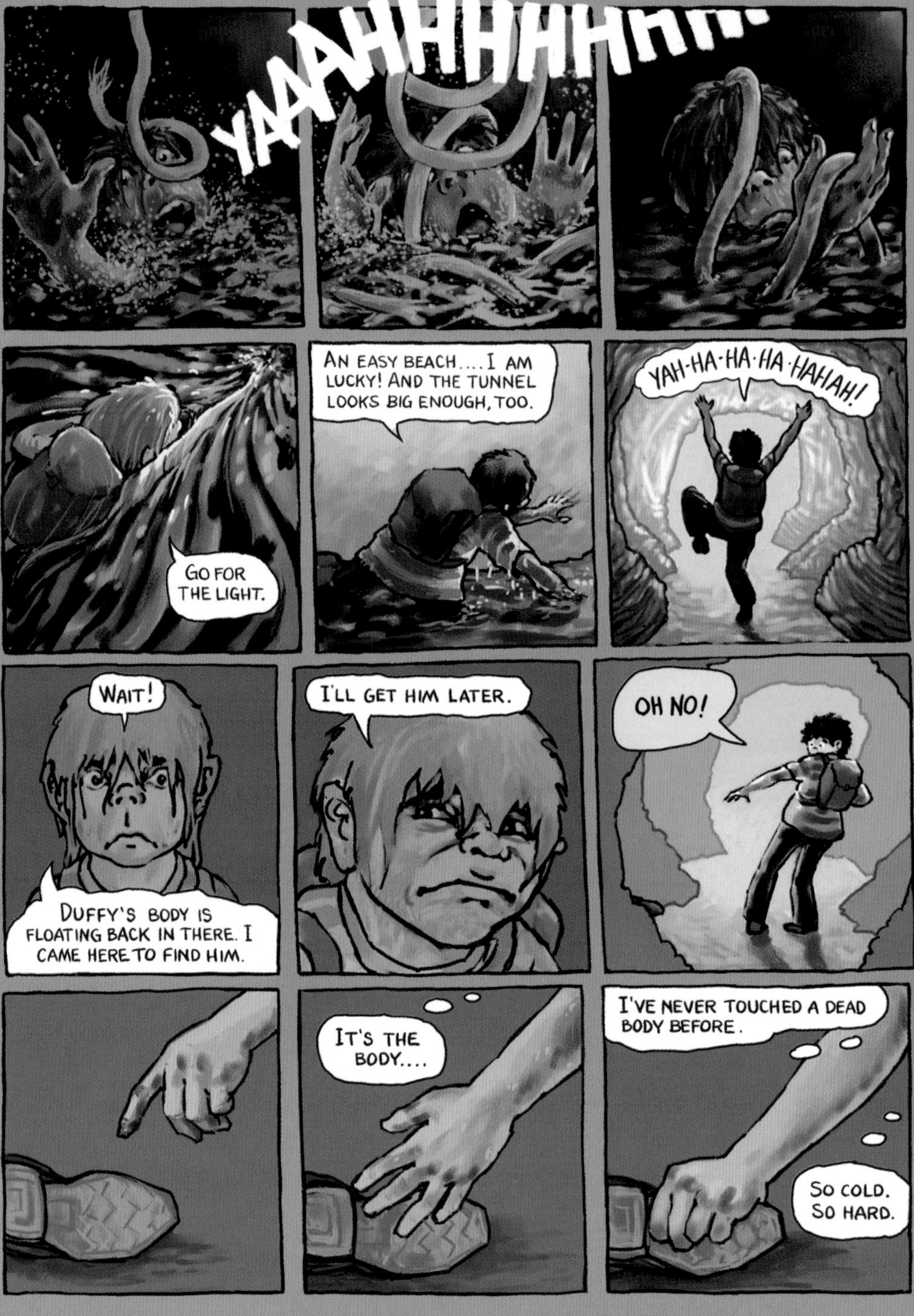
YAAAHHHHHHH!!
GO FOR THE LIGHT.
AN EASY BEACH.... I AM LUCKY! AND THE TUNNEL LOOKS BIG ENOUGH, TOO.
YAH-HA-HA-HA-HAHAH!
WAIT!
DUFFY'S BODY IS FLOATING BACK IN THERE. I CAME HERE TO FIND HIM.
I'LL GET HIM LATER.
OH NO!
IT'S THE BODY....
I'VE NEVER TOUCHED A DEAD BODY BEFORE.
SO COLD. SO HARD.

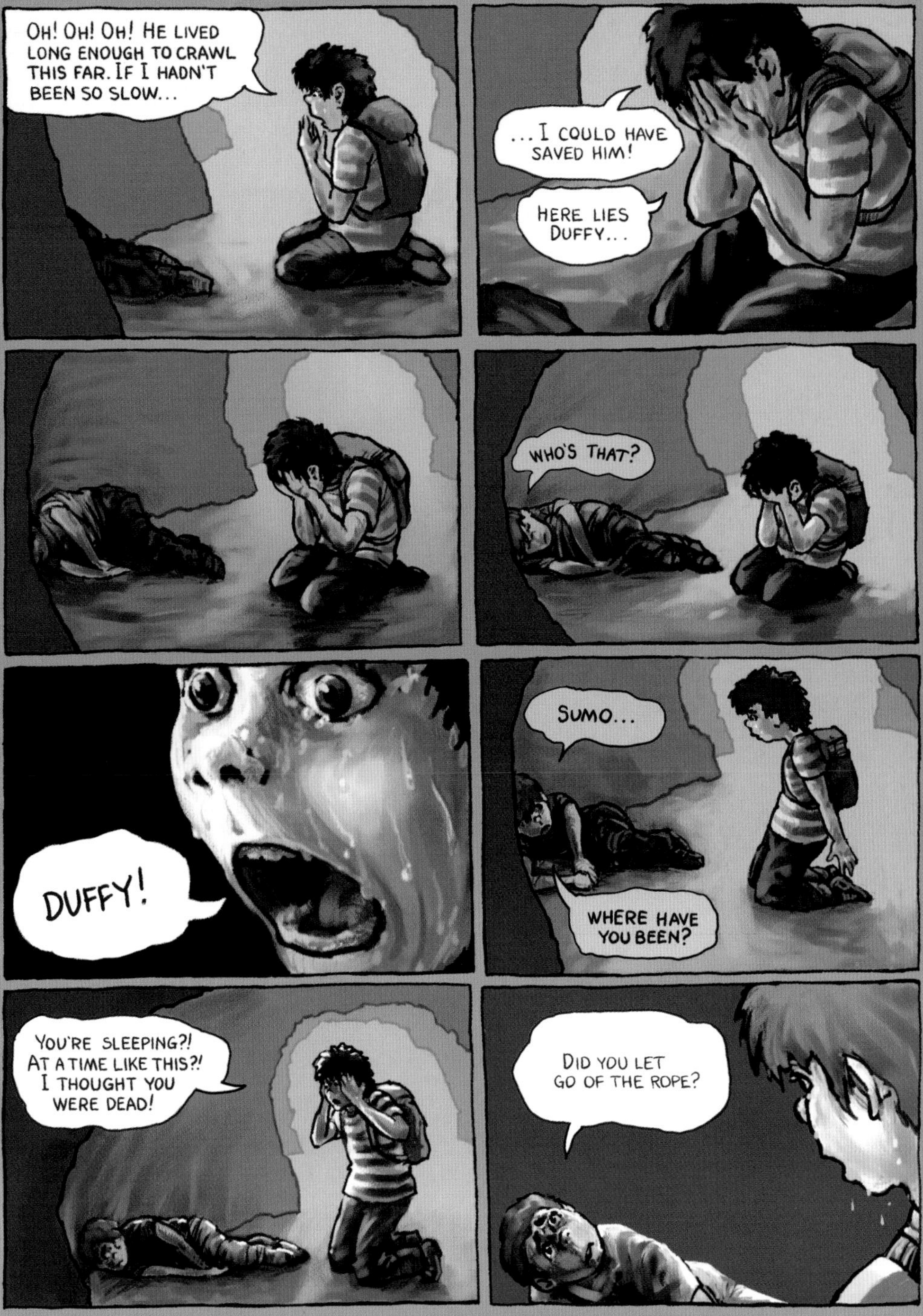
OH! OH! OH! HE LIVED LONG ENOUGH TO CRAWL THIS FAR. IF I HADN'T BEEN SO SLOW...
...I COULD HAVE SAVED HIM!
HERE LIES DUFFY...
WHO'S THAT?
DUFFY!
SUMO...
WHERE HAVE YOU BEEN?
YOU'RE SLEEPING?! AT A TIME LIKE THIS?! I THOUGHT YOU WERE DEAD!
DID YOU LET GO OF THE ROPE?

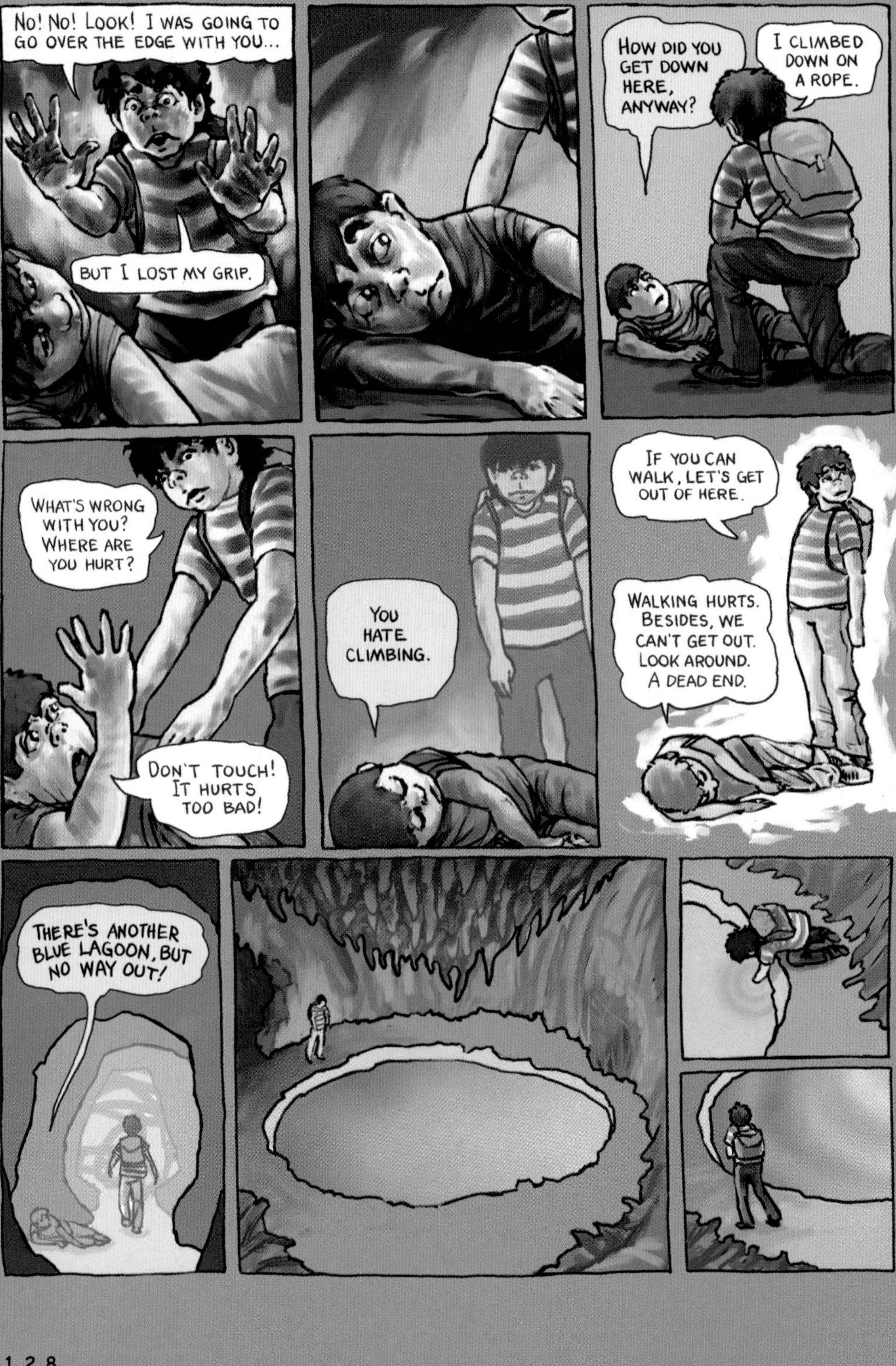
No! No! Look! I was going to go over the edge with you...
But I lost my grip.
How did you get down here, anyway?
I climbed down on a rope.
What's wrong with you? Where are you hurt?
Don't touch! It hurts too bad!
You hate climbing.
If you can walk, let's get out of here.
Walking hurts. Besides, we can't get out. Look around. A dead end.
There's another blue lagoon, but no way out!

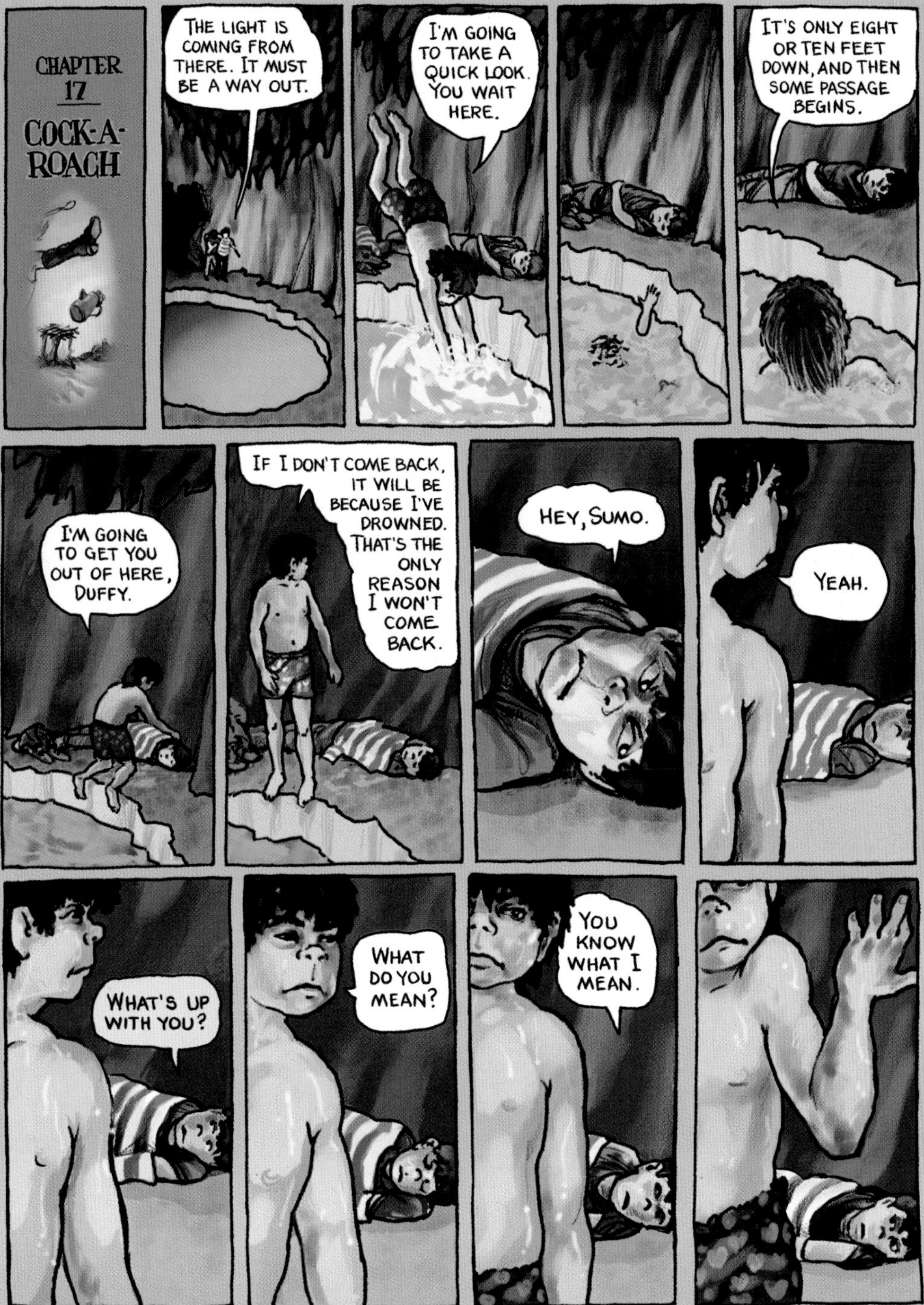
CHAPTER 17
COCK-A-ROACH
THE LIGHT IS COMING FROM THERE. IT MUST BE A WAY OUT.
I'M GOING TO TAKE A QUICK LOOK. YOU WAIT HERE.
IT'S ONLY EIGHT OR TEN FEET DOWN, AND THEN SOME PASSAGE BEGINS.
I'M GOING TO GET YOU OUT OF HERE, DUFFY.
IF I DON'T COME BACK, IT WILL BE BECAUSE I'VE DROWNED. THAT'S THE ONLY REASON I WON'T COME BACK.
HEY, SUMO.
YEAH.
WHAT'S UP WITH YOU?
WHAT DO YOU MEAN?
YOU KNOW WHAT I MEAN.

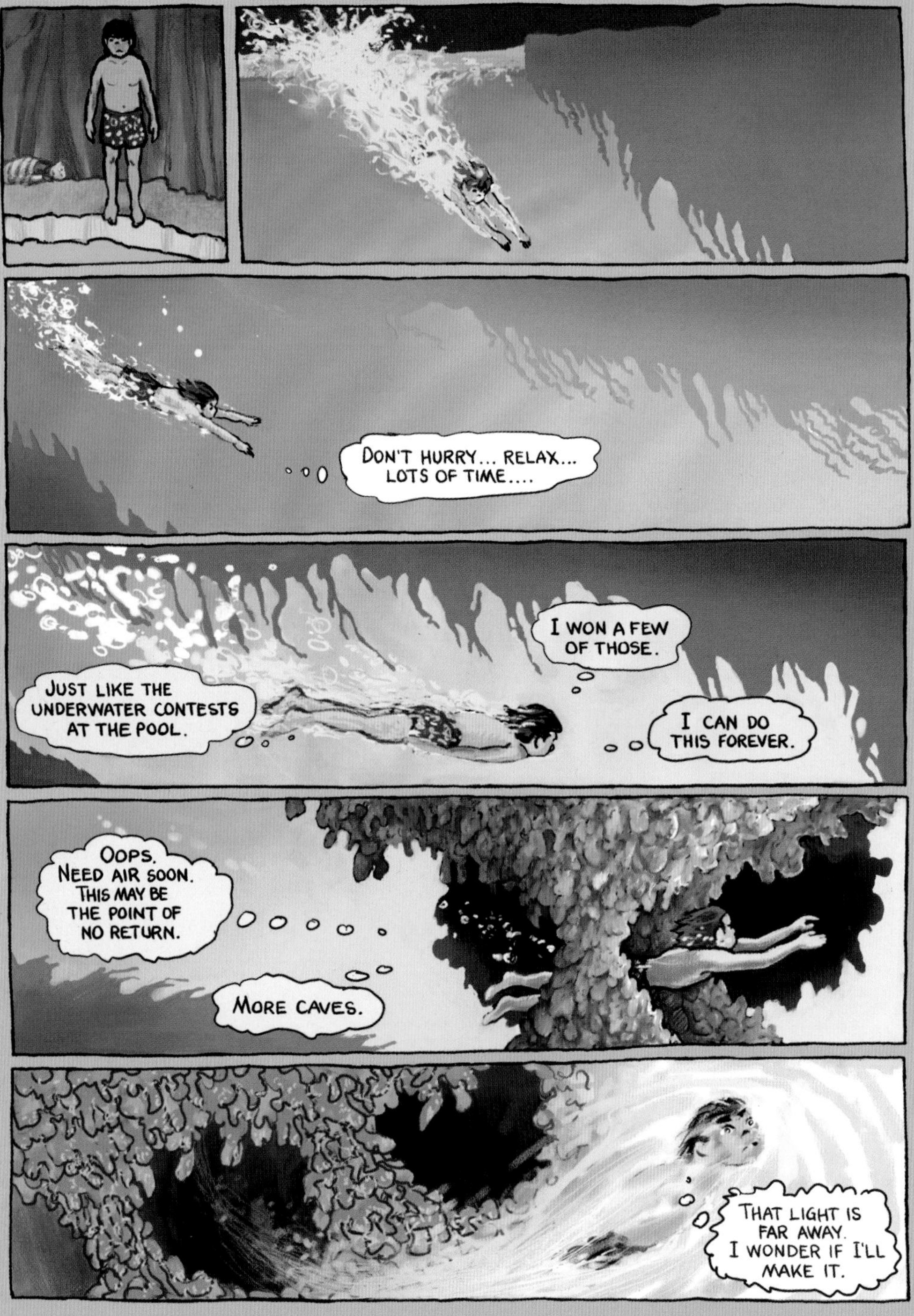
DON'T HURRY... RELAX...
LOTS OF TIME....
JUST LIKE THE UNDERWATER CONTESTS AT THE POOL.
I WON A FEW OF THOSE.
I CAN DO THIS FOREVER.
OOPS. NEED AIR SOON. THIS MAY BE THE POINT OF NO RETURN.
MORE CAVES.
THAT LIGHT IS FAR AWAY. I WONDER IF I'LL MAKE IT.

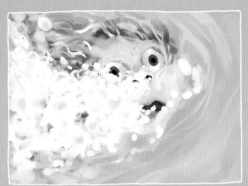

FWWAHH!

STAY WHERE
YOU ARE!

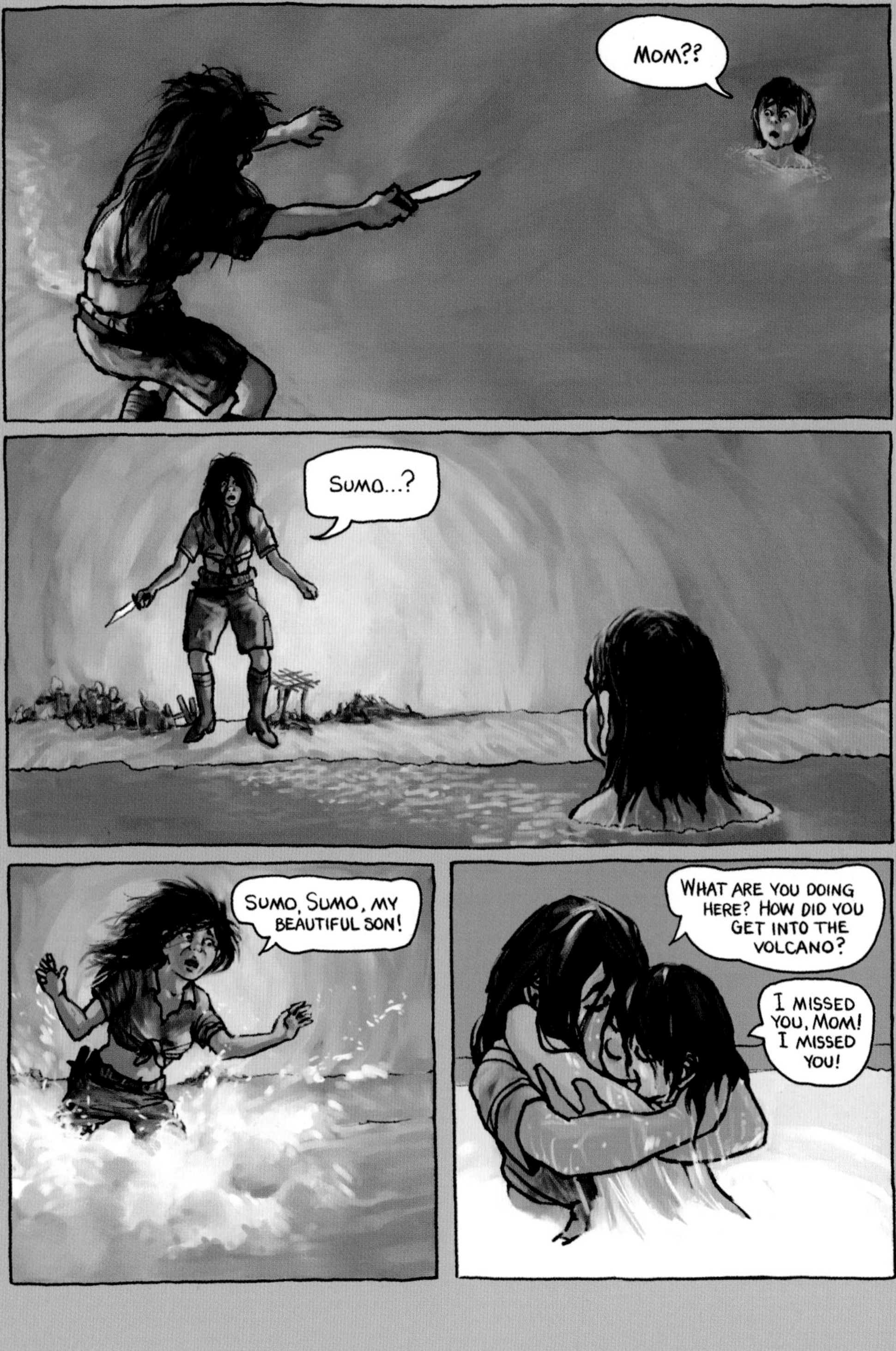
MOM??
SUMO...?
SUMO, SUMO, MY BEAUTIFUL SON!
WHAT ARE YOU DOING HERE? HOW DID YOU GET INTO THE VOLCANO?
I MISSED YOU, MOM! I MISSED YOU!

WE'VE BEEN LOOKING FOR YOU.

FOR ME! OH NO! THAT'S TERRIBLE. I'M SO SORRY!

BUT WHERE'S YOUR BROTHER? IS HE OK? DID SOMETHING HAPPEN TO DUFFY? YOU BOYS HAVE TO STICK TOGETHER!

DUFFY'S BACK THERE. HE'S HURT.

HURT! HOW BAD? WHAT HAPPENED? CAN HE TALK? WHY DID YOU LEAVE HIM? IS HE BLEEDING?!

YES, YES, I MEAN, NO, HE'S NOT BLEEDING, YES, HE CAN TALK. HE FELL IN A CRACK AND BROKE A BONE AND IT HURTS A LOT! HE CAN'T SWIM.

I HAVE TO GO BACK AND GET HIM RIGHT NOW. I PROMISED.

WE CAN'T RIGHT NOW. IT'S IMPOSSIBLE. THE TIDE IS AGAINST US. WE WOULD BE SWIMMING UPSTREAM. THE TIDE WILL CHANGE IN AN HOUR OR SO. THEN WE CAN GET HIM.

BUT I PROMISED.

WE'LL KEEP YOUR PROMISE, MY SON. HE WILL JUST HAVE TO LAST ANOTHER HOUR.

WHY DID YOU LIE TO US, MOM? THIS ISN'T BORNEO.

I'VE GOT TO GET YOU DRY. YOU MUST BE FREEZING!

MOM, WHY DID YOU PULL THAT KNIFE ON ME?

(SIGH...) I THOUGHT YOU WERE... A COCK-A-ROACH.

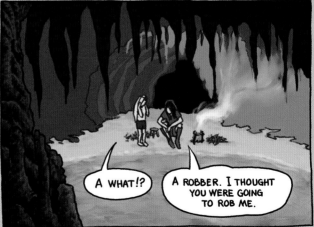

A WHAT!?

A ROBBER. I THOUGHT YOU WERE GOING TO ROB ME.

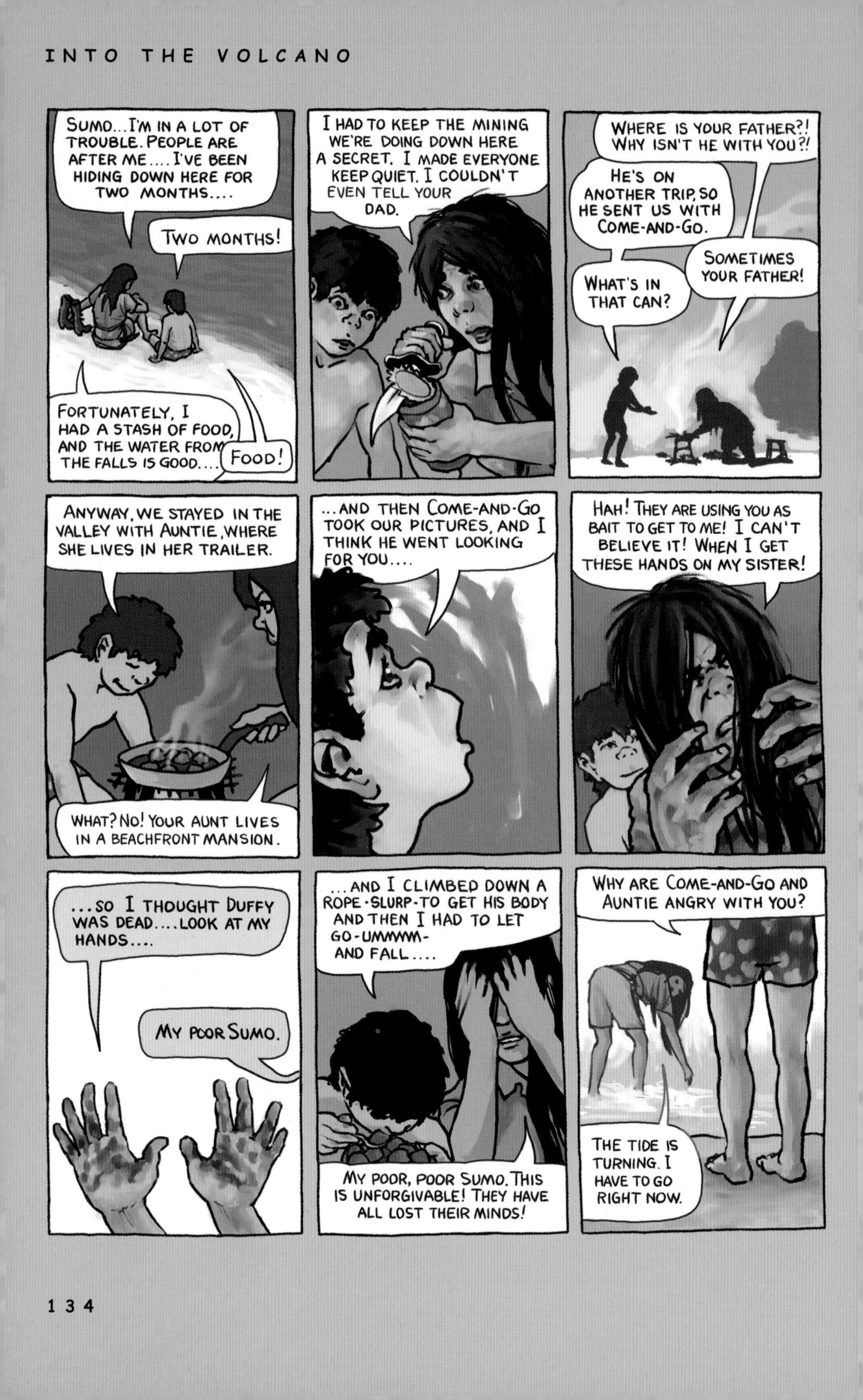
SUMO... I'M IN A LOT OF TROUBLE. PEOPLE ARE AFTER ME.... I'VE BEEN HIDING DOWN HERE FOR TWO MONTHS....
TWO MONTHS!
FORTUNATELY, I HAD A STASH OF FOOD, AND THE WATER FROM THE FALLS IS GOOD....
FOOD!
I HAD TO KEEP THE MINING WE'RE DOING DOWN HERE A SECRET. I MADE EVERYONE KEEP QUIET. I COULDN'T EVEN TELL YOUR DAD.
WHERE IS YOUR FATHER?! WHY ISN'T HE WITH YOU?!
HE'S ON ANOTHER TRIP, SO HE SENT US WITH COME-AND-GO.
SOMETIMES YOUR FATHER!
WHAT'S IN THAT CAN?
ANYWAY, WE STAYED IN THE VALLEY WITH AUNTIE, WHERE SHE LIVES IN HER TRAILER.
WHAT? NO! YOUR AUNT LIVES IN A BEACHFRONT MANSION.
...AND THEN COME-AND-GO TOOK OUR PICTURES, AND I THINK HE WENT LOOKING FOR YOU....
HAH! THEY ARE USING YOU AS BAIT TO GET TO ME! I CAN'T BELIEVE IT! WHEN I GET THESE HANDS ON MY SISTER!
...SO I THOUGHT DUFFY WAS DEAD.... LOOK AT MY HANDS....
MY POOR SUMO.
...AND I CLIMBED DOWN A ROPE-SLURP-TO GET HIS BODY AND THEN I HAD TO LET GO-UMMMM- AND FALL....
MY POOR, POOR SUMO. THIS IS UNFORGIVABLE! THEY HAVE ALL LOST THEIR MINDS!
WHY ARE COME-AND-GO AND AUNTIE ANGRY WITH YOU?
THE TIDE IS TURNING. I HAVE TO GO RIGHT NOW.

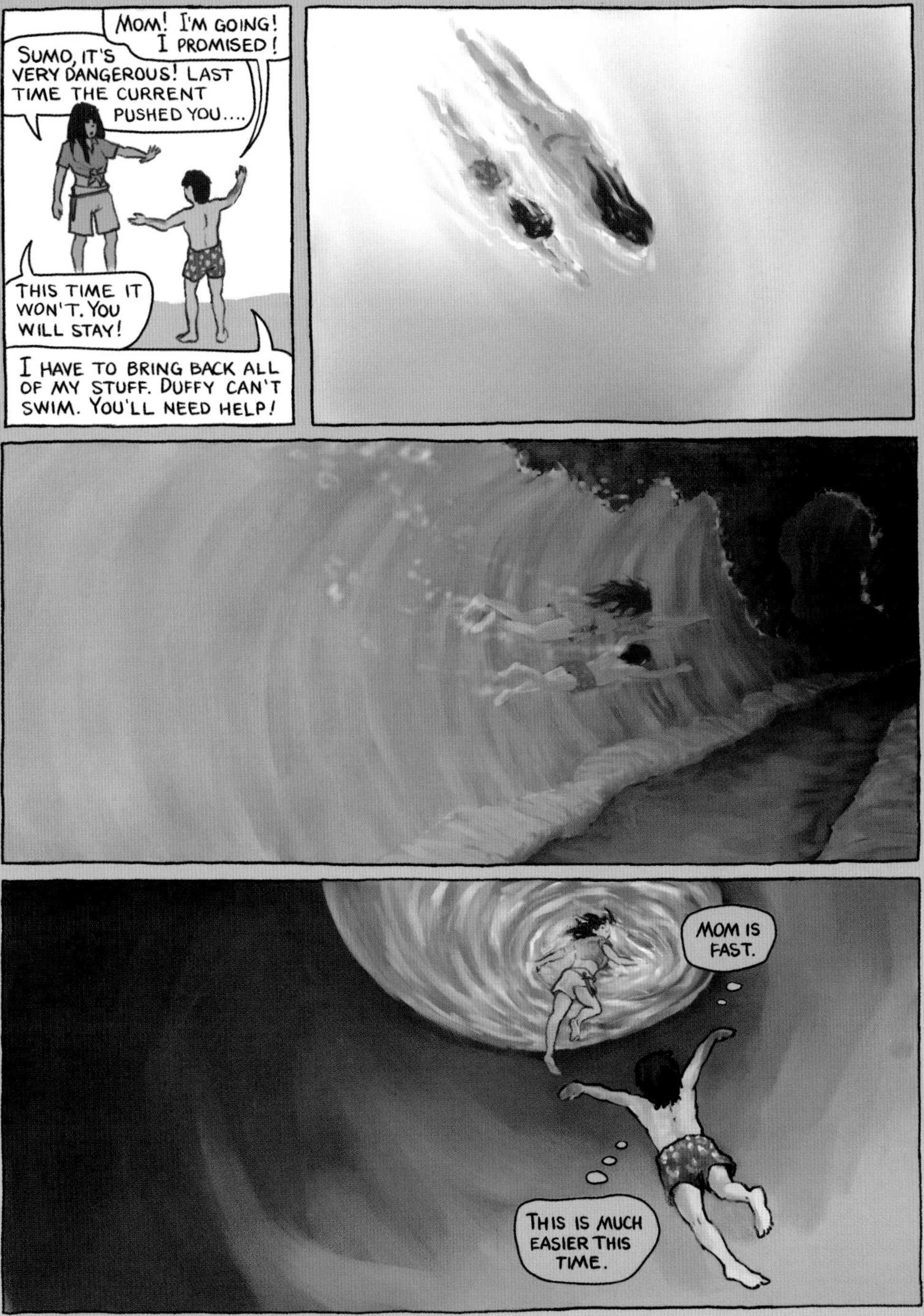
MOM! I'M GOING! I PROMISED!
SUMO, IT'S VERY DANGEROUS! LAST TIME THE CURRENT PUSHED YOU....
THIS TIME IT WON'T. YOU WILL STAY!
I HAVE TO BRING BACK ALL OF MY STUFF. DUFFY CAN'T SWIM. YOU'LL NEED HELP!
MOM IS FAST.
THIS IS MUCH EASIER THIS TIME.

CHAPTER 18

SUMO IN THAT NEXT CHAMBER

SUMO...WHO'S THAT?

IT'S MOM! I FOUND HER!

MOM? NOW EVERYTHING WILL BE OK.

DUFFY... I LOVE YOU, AND WE HAVE TO HURRY VERY, VERY FAST.

WHERE ARE YOU INJURED?

MOM?

HIS COLLARBONE IS FRACTURED.

WE HAVE TO BIND HIM. SUMO, TEAR UP YOUR SHIRT.

WOULD A ROPE BE BETTER?

MUCH BETTER. WE'LL PAD IT WITH THE SHIRT.

DUFFY... I AM SO SORRY... SO SORRY I GOT YOU INTO THIS....

OUCH!

I'LL BE RIGHT BACK.

HURRY!

DUFFY, MY SON, THIS IS GOING TO HURT... A LOT... BUT YOU'VE ALWAYS BEEN TOUGH.

AFTER WE FINISH, IT WILL FEEL MUCH BETTER.

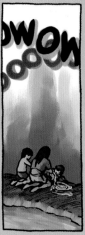

OHH! THAT DOES FEEL BETTER!

NO TIME TO REST. THE TIDE IS TURNING. WHEN I GET YOU INTO THE WATER, HOLD ON TO MY BELT WITH YOUR GOOD ARM. SUMO, GRAB YOUR GEAR.

You can't drag him alone, Mom. You'll never make it.

Let's make something to share the load.

No! Don't tie! Too dangerous! Put this loop loosely over your shoulder.

Practice getting out of it quickly. If anything goes wrong, let the rope go.

What about Duffy?

I'll get him by myself, if necessary.

Duffy, hold on for your life. Your legs are ok, right? Good. Then kick as hard as you can!

Everybody ready? Keep the rope tight! No snags.

Mom.

Don't worry. We'll make it. One...two....

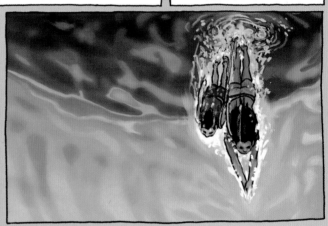

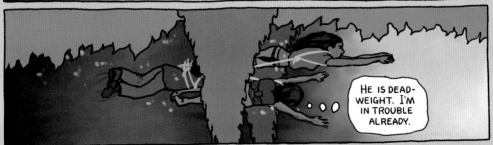

He is dead-weight. I'm in trouble already.

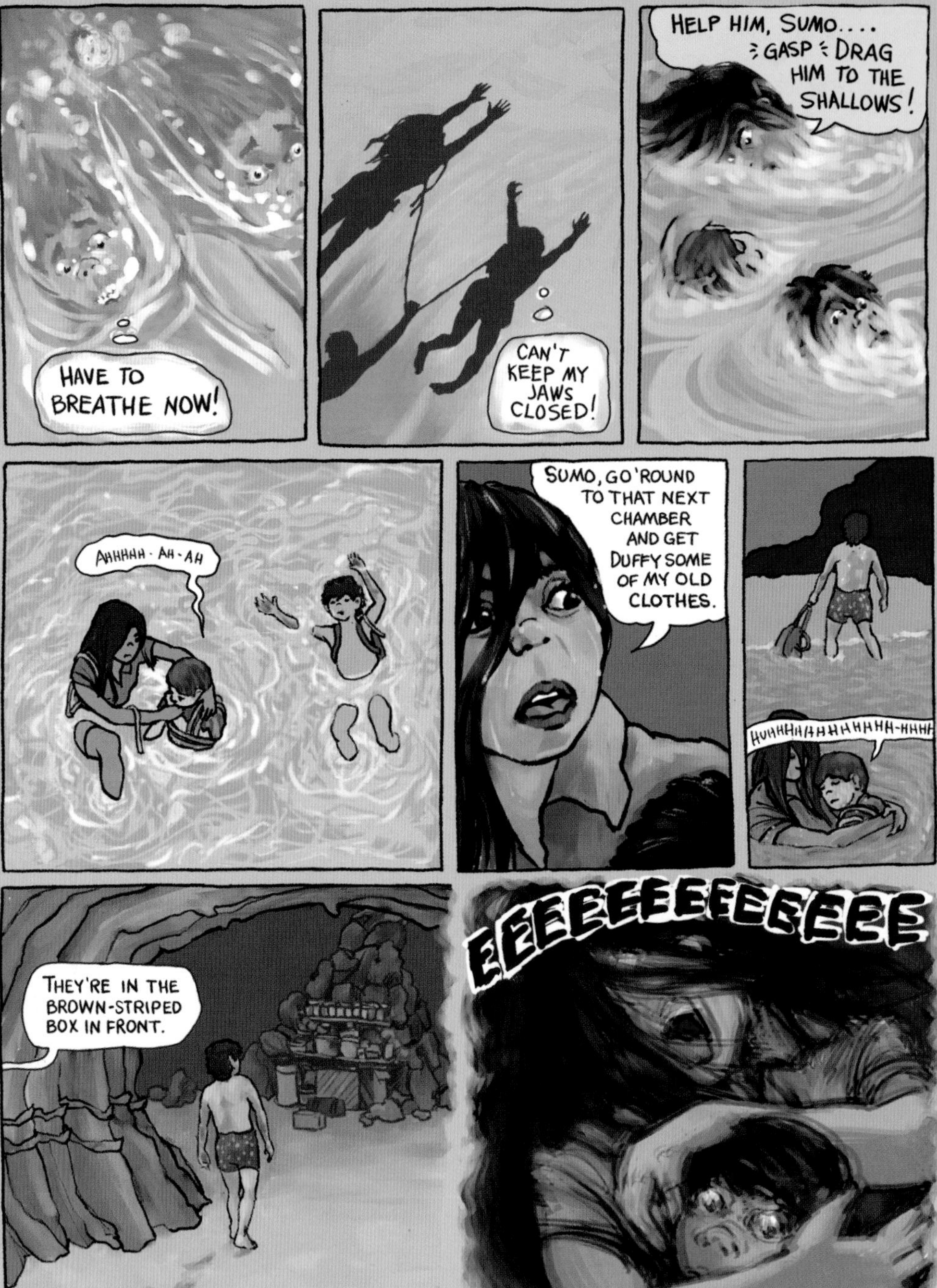
HAVE TO BREATHE NOW!
CAN'T KEEP MY JAWS CLOSED!
HELP HIM, SUMO.... GASP DRAG HIM TO THE SHALLOWS!
AHHHHH - AH - AH
SUMO, GO 'ROUND TO THAT NEXT CHAMBER AND GET DUFFY SOME OF MY OLD CLOTHES.
HUHHHAHHHHHHHH-HHHH
THEY'RE IN THE BROWN-STRIPED BOX IN FRONT.
EEEEEEEEEEEEEE

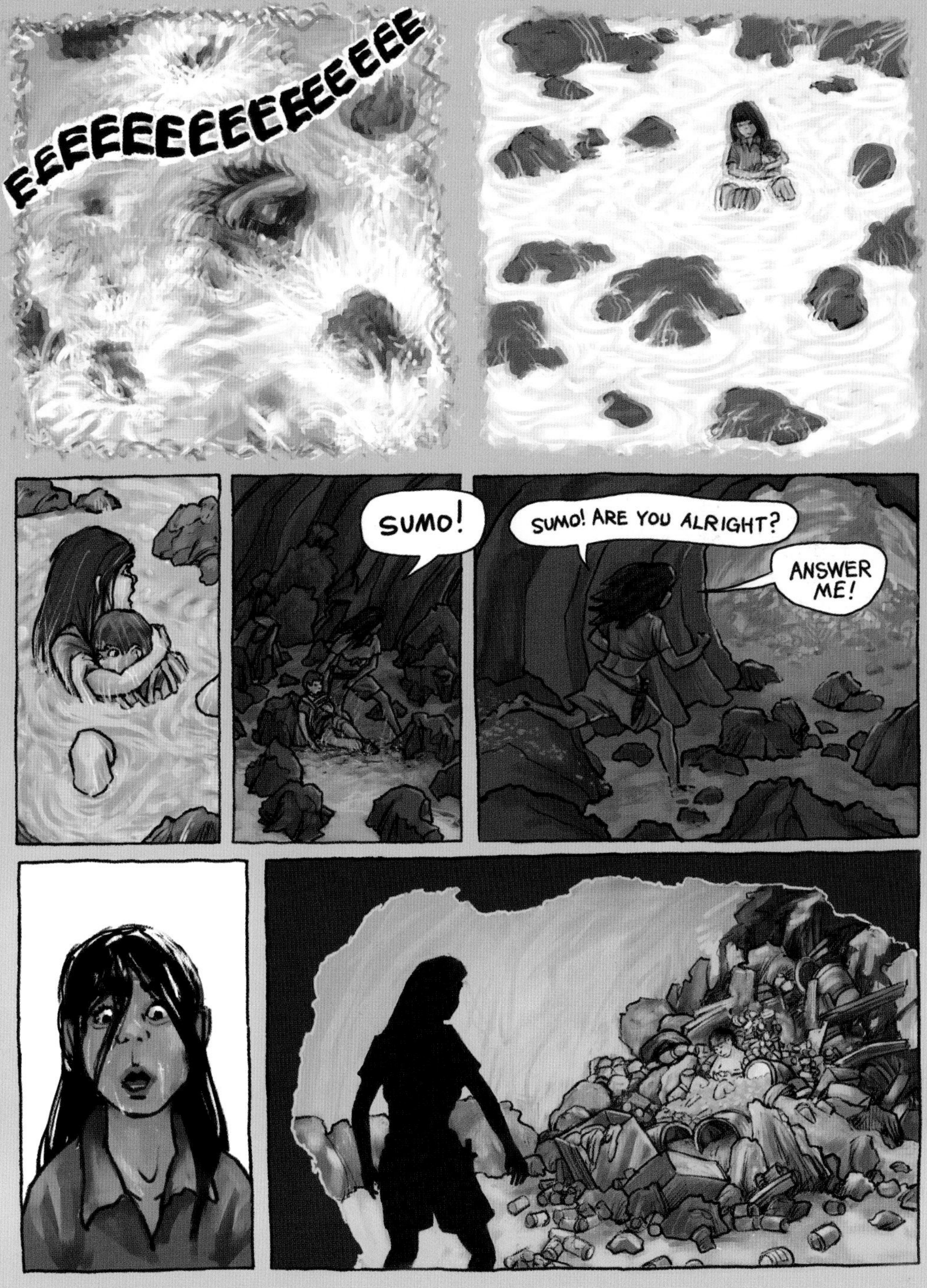
EEEEEEEEEEEEEEEEE
SUMO!
SUMO! ARE YOU ALRIGHT?
ANSWER ME!

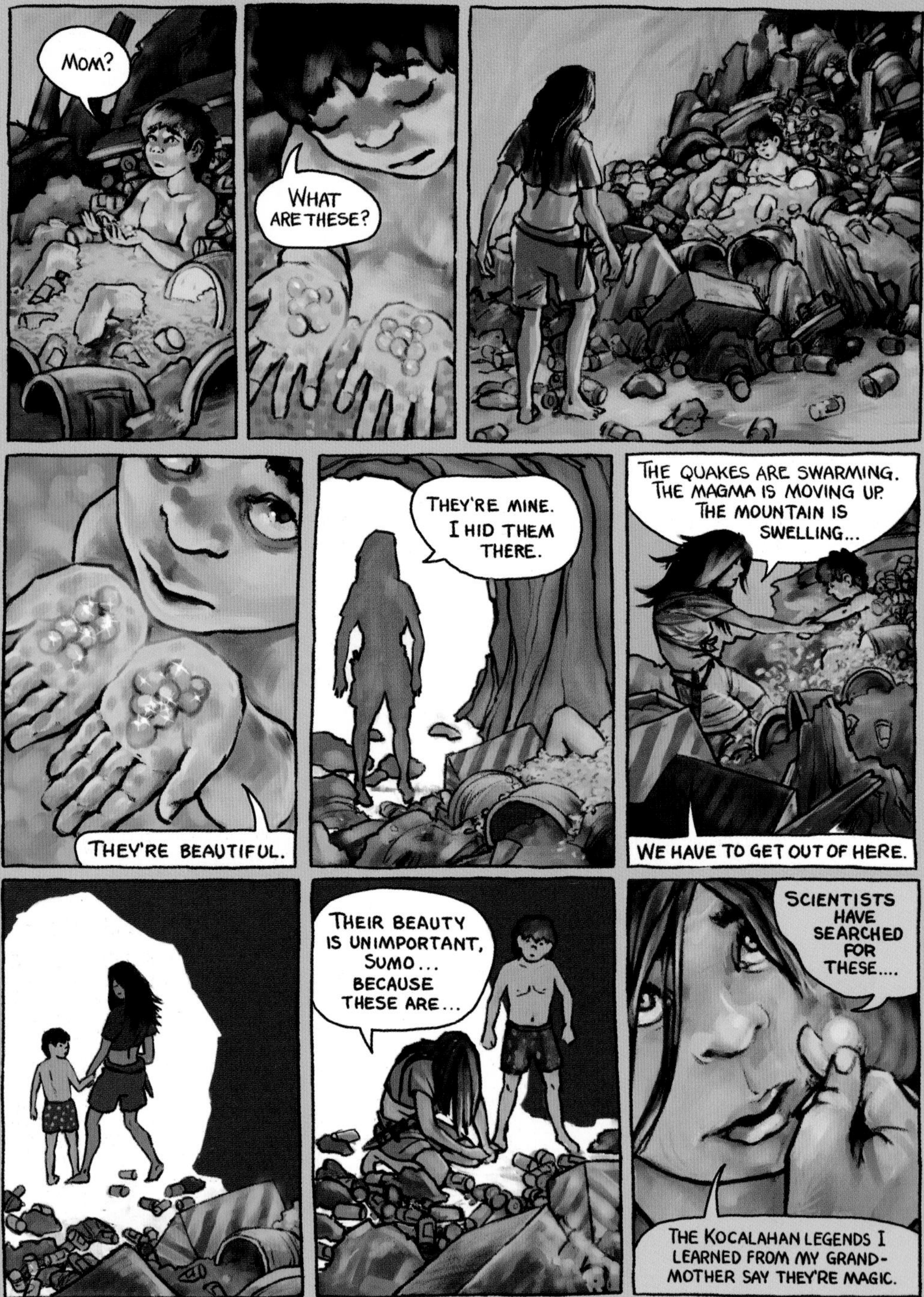
MOM?
WHAT ARE THESE?
THEY'RE BEAUTIFUL.
THEY'RE MINE. I HID THEM THERE.
THE QUAKES ARE SWARMING. THE MAGMA IS MOVING UP. THE MOUNTAIN IS SWELLING...
WE HAVE TO GET OUT OF HERE.
THEIR BEAUTY IS UNIMPORTANT, SUMO... BECAUSE THESE ARE...
SCIENTISTS HAVE SEARCHED FOR THESE....
THE KOCALAHAN LEGENDS I LEARNED FROM MY GRAND-MOTHER SAY THEY'RE MAGIC.

AND MAYBE THEY ARE.

THIS IS THE MOST VALUABLE MATERIAL ON EARTH. COMBINE IT WITH COPPER AND IT BECOMES...

A ROOM-TEMPERATURE SUPER CONDUCTOR. MIX IT WITH SILICON, AND I BELIEVE I CAN MAKE A POWER RING APPROACHING 100 PERCENT SOLAR EFFICIENCY.

ADD A LITTLE TO CALCIUM, AND IT ALTERS YOUR TASTE BUDS. EVERYTHING TASTES SWEET.

AND I'VE JUST BEGUN TO EXPERIMENT. THERE IS SO MUCH MORE.

IN OTHER WORDS, THIS STUFF WILL CHANGE THE WORLD. GO GET YOUR BACKPACK. THROW EVERYTHING AWAY. COME BACK HERE AND FILL IT UP WITH THESE - EVERY COMPARTMENT. GET THEM ALL!

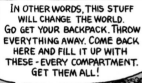

THERE'S MUCH MORE BURIED IN A BOX BEHIND YOU, BUT WE'LL HAVE TO LEAVE THAT.

ONE BACKPACK FULL WILL BE ENOUGH FOR A LIFETIME OF EXPERIMENTS.

AND INCIDENTALLY... IT WILL ALSO MAKE US COMPLETELY RICH.

YOU USED TO SAY WE WERE ALREADY RICH.

SUMO, DON'T BE DIFFICULT.

YOU KNOW WHAT I MEAN.

DUFFY, WE HAVE TO GET OUT OF HERE . I KNOW YOU NEED TO REST, BUT....

UGH!

OH, THERE'S ANOTHER QUAKE! DID YOU FEEL IT?

MANGO LIED. HE SAID THESE TUBES WERE EARTHQUAKE - PROOF.

NOTHING IS EARTHQUAKE-PROOF.

THIS WAY! HURRY!

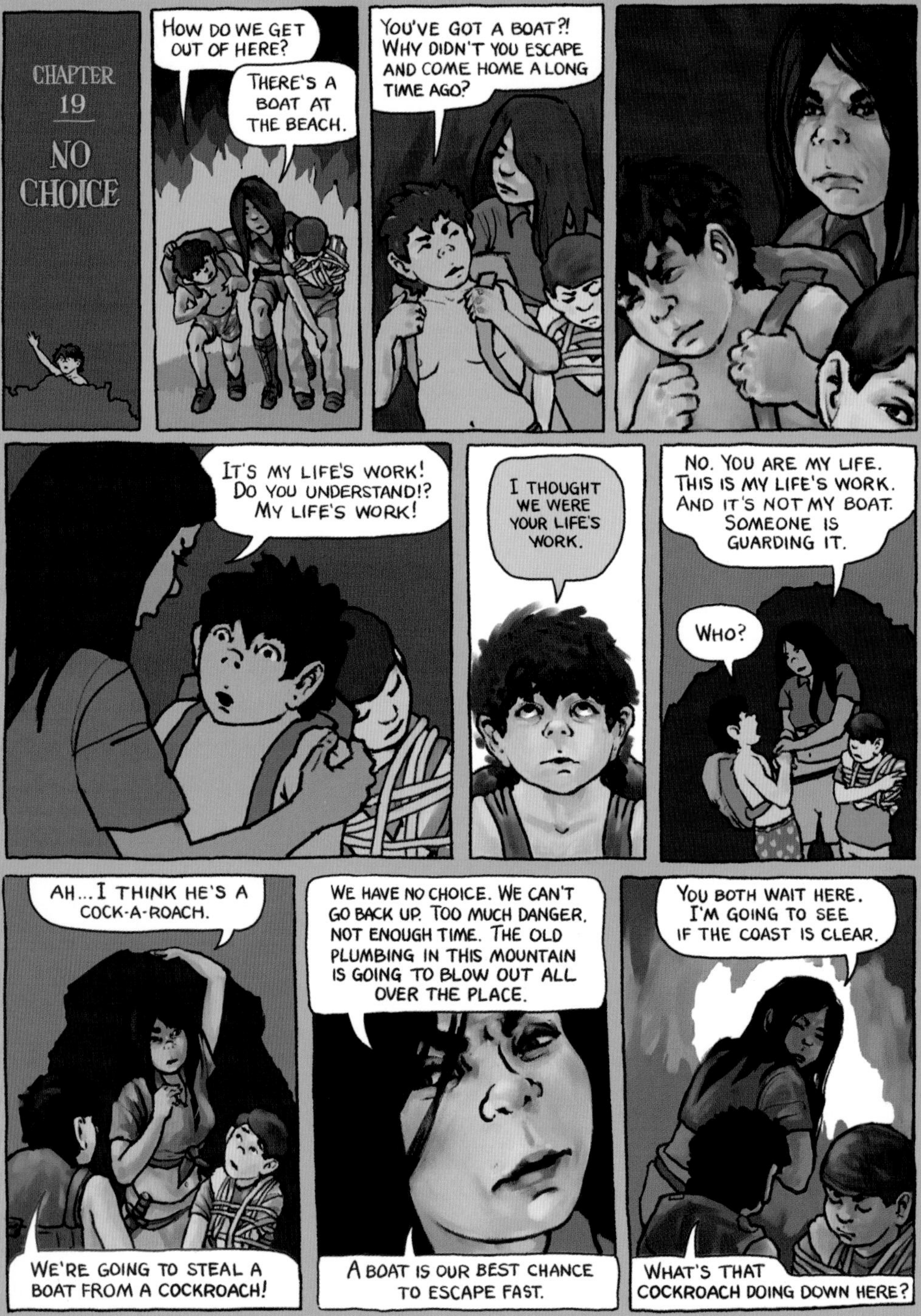
CHAPTER 19
NO CHOICE
HOW DO WE GET OUT OF HERE?
THERE'S A BOAT AT THE BEACH.
YOU'VE GOT A BOAT?! WHY DIDN'T YOU ESCAPE AND COME HOME A LONG TIME AGO?
IT'S MY LIFE'S WORK! DO YOU UNDERSTAND!? MY LIFE'S WORK!
I THOUGHT WE WERE YOUR LIFE'S WORK.
NO. YOU ARE MY LIFE. THIS IS MY LIFE'S WORK. AND IT'S NOT MY BOAT. SOMEONE IS GUARDING IT.
WHO?
AH... I THINK HE'S A COCK-A-ROACH.
WE'RE GOING TO STEAL A BOAT FROM A COCKROACH!
WE HAVE NO CHOICE. WE CAN'T GO BACK UP. TOO MUCH DANGER. NOT ENOUGH TIME. THE OLD PLUMBING IN THIS MOUNTAIN IS GOING TO BLOW OUT ALL OVER THE PLACE.
A BOAT IS OUR BEST CHANCE TO ESCAPE FAST.
YOU BOTH WAIT HERE. I'M GOING TO SEE IF THE COAST IS CLEAR.
WHAT'S THAT COCKROACH DOING DOWN HERE?

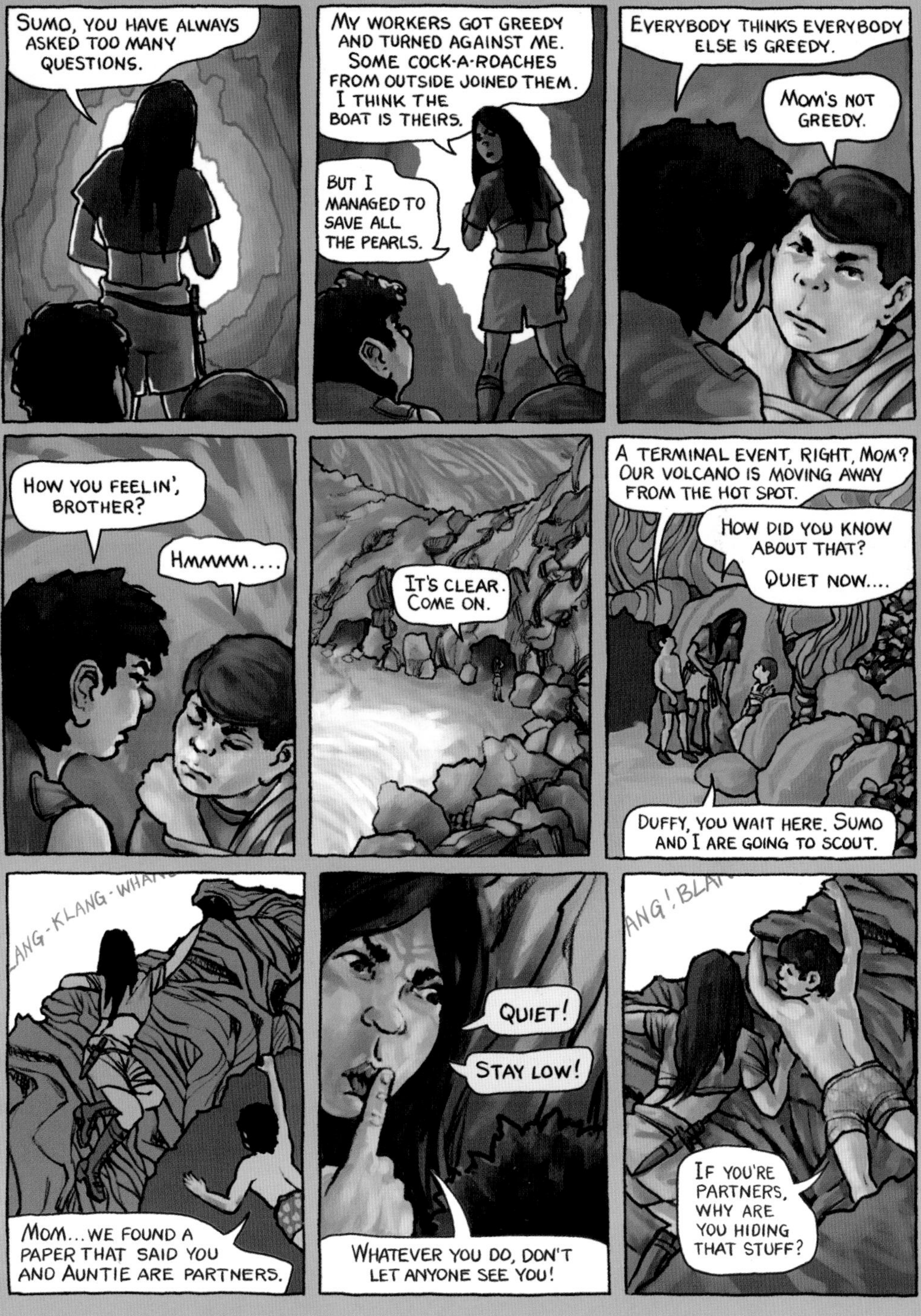
SUMO, YOU HAVE ALWAYS ASKED TOO MANY QUESTIONS.
MY WORKERS GOT GREEDY AND TURNED AGAINST ME. SOME COCK-A-ROACHES FROM OUTSIDE JOINED THEM. I THINK THE BOAT IS THEIRS.
BUT I MANAGED TO SAVE ALL THE PEARLS.
EVERYBODY THINKS EVERYBODY ELSE IS GREEDY.
MOM'S NOT GREEDY.
HOW YOU FEELIN', BROTHER?
HMMMM....
IT'S CLEAR. COME ON.
A TERMINAL EVENT, RIGHT, MOM? OUR VOLCANO IS MOVING AWAY FROM THE HOT SPOT.
HOW DID YOU KNOW ABOUT THAT?
QUIET NOW....
DUFFY, YOU WAIT HERE. SUMO AND I ARE GOING TO SCOUT.
LANG-KLANG-WHAN
MOM...WE FOUND A PAPER THAT SAID YOU AND AUNTIE ARE PARTNERS.
QUIET!
STAY LOW!
WHATEVER YOU DO, DON'T LET ANYONE SEE YOU!
ANG!, BLAN
IF YOU'RE PARTNERS, WHY ARE YOU HIDING THAT STUFF?

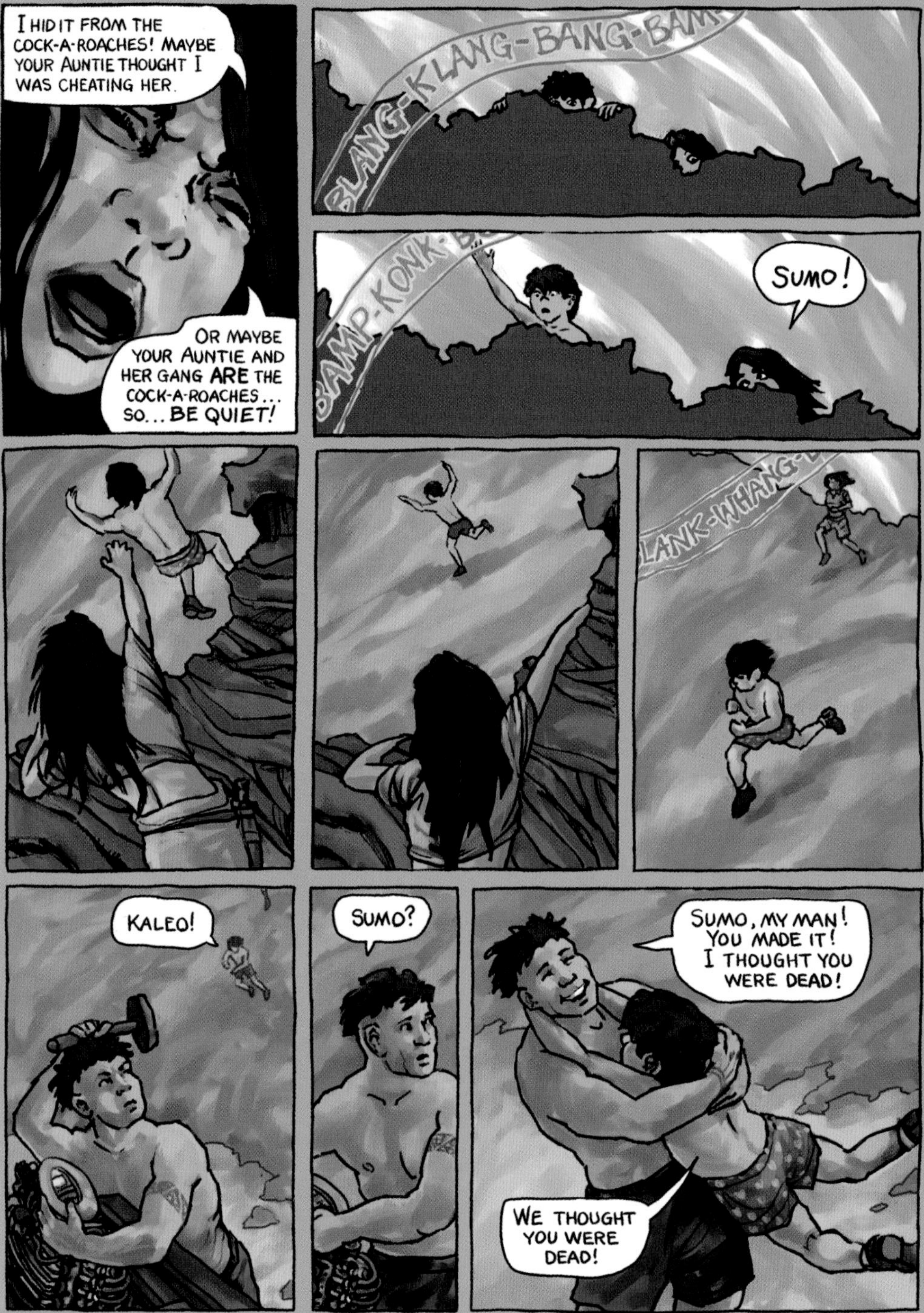
I HID IT FROM THE COCK-A-ROACHES! MAYBE YOUR AUNTIE THOUGHT I WAS CHEATING HER.
OR MAYBE YOUR AUNTIE AND HER GANG ARE THE COCK-A-ROACHES... SO... BE QUIET!
BLANG-KLANG-BANG-BAM
BAMP-KONK-B
SUMO!
LANK-WHANG-
KALEO!
SUMO?
SUMO, MY MAN! YOU MADE IT! I THOUGHT YOU WERE DEAD!
WE THOUGHT YOU WERE DEAD!

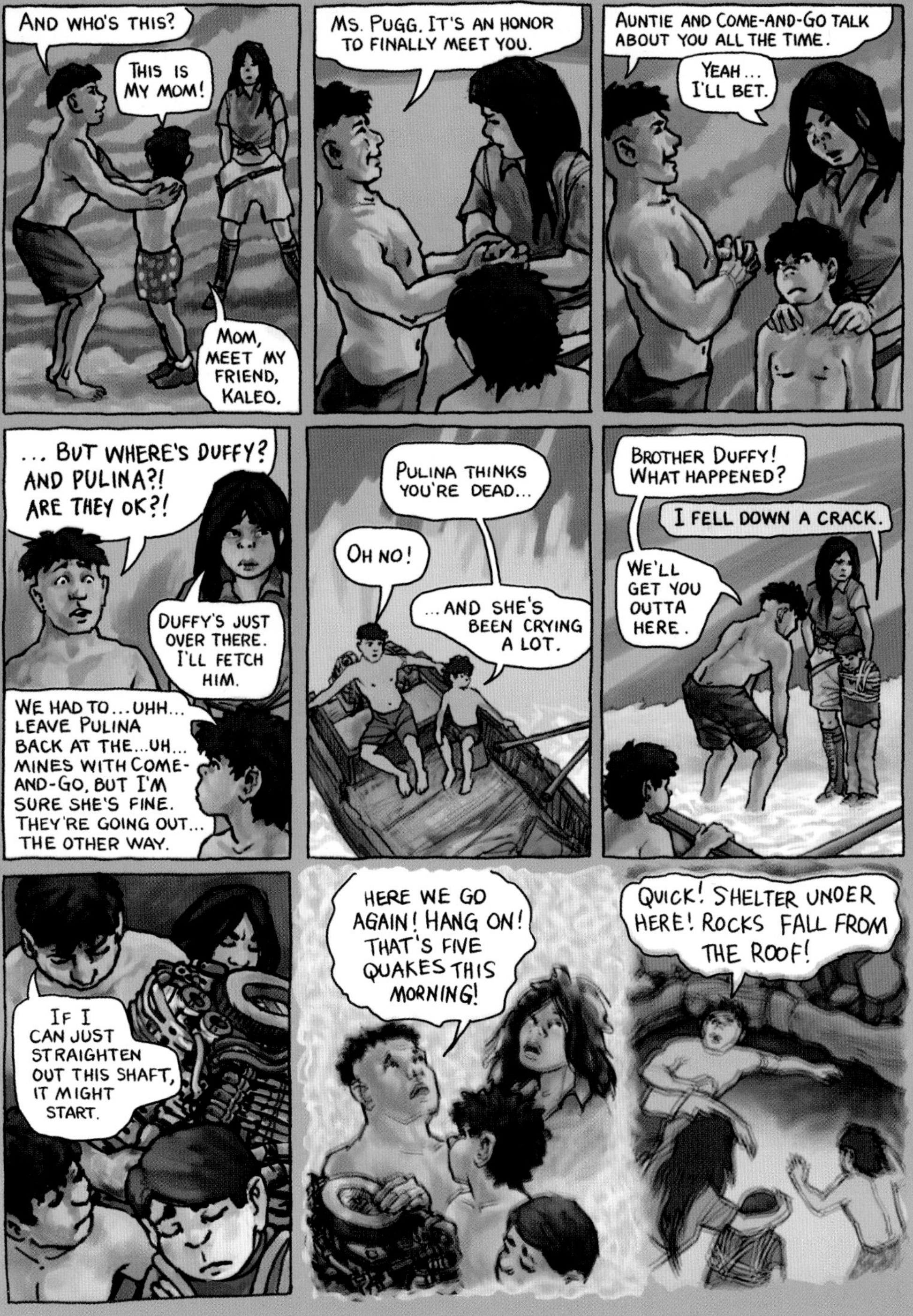
AND WHO'S THIS?
THIS IS MY MOM!
MOM, MEET MY FRIEND, KALEO.
MS. PUGG. IT'S AN HONOR TO FINALLY MEET YOU.
AUNTIE AND COME-AND-GO TALK ABOUT YOU ALL THE TIME.
YEAH... I'LL BET.
... BUT WHERE'S DUFFY? AND PULINA?! ARE THEY OK?!
DUFFY'S JUST OVER THERE. I'LL FETCH HIM.
WE HAD TO... UHH... LEAVE PULINA BACK AT THE... UH... MINES WITH COME-AND-GO, BUT I'M SURE SHE'S FINE. THEY'RE GOING OUT... THE OTHER WAY.
PULINA THINKS YOU'RE DEAD...
OH NO!
...AND SHE'S BEEN CRYING A LOT.
BROTHER DUFFY! WHAT HAPPENED?
I FELL DOWN A CRACK.
WE'LL GET YOU OUTTA HERE.
IF I CAN JUST STRAIGHTEN OUT THIS SHAFT, IT MIGHT START.
HERE WE GO AGAIN! HANG ON! THAT'S FIVE QUAKES THIS MORNING!
QUICK! SHELTER UNDER HERE! ROCKS FALL FROM THE ROOF!

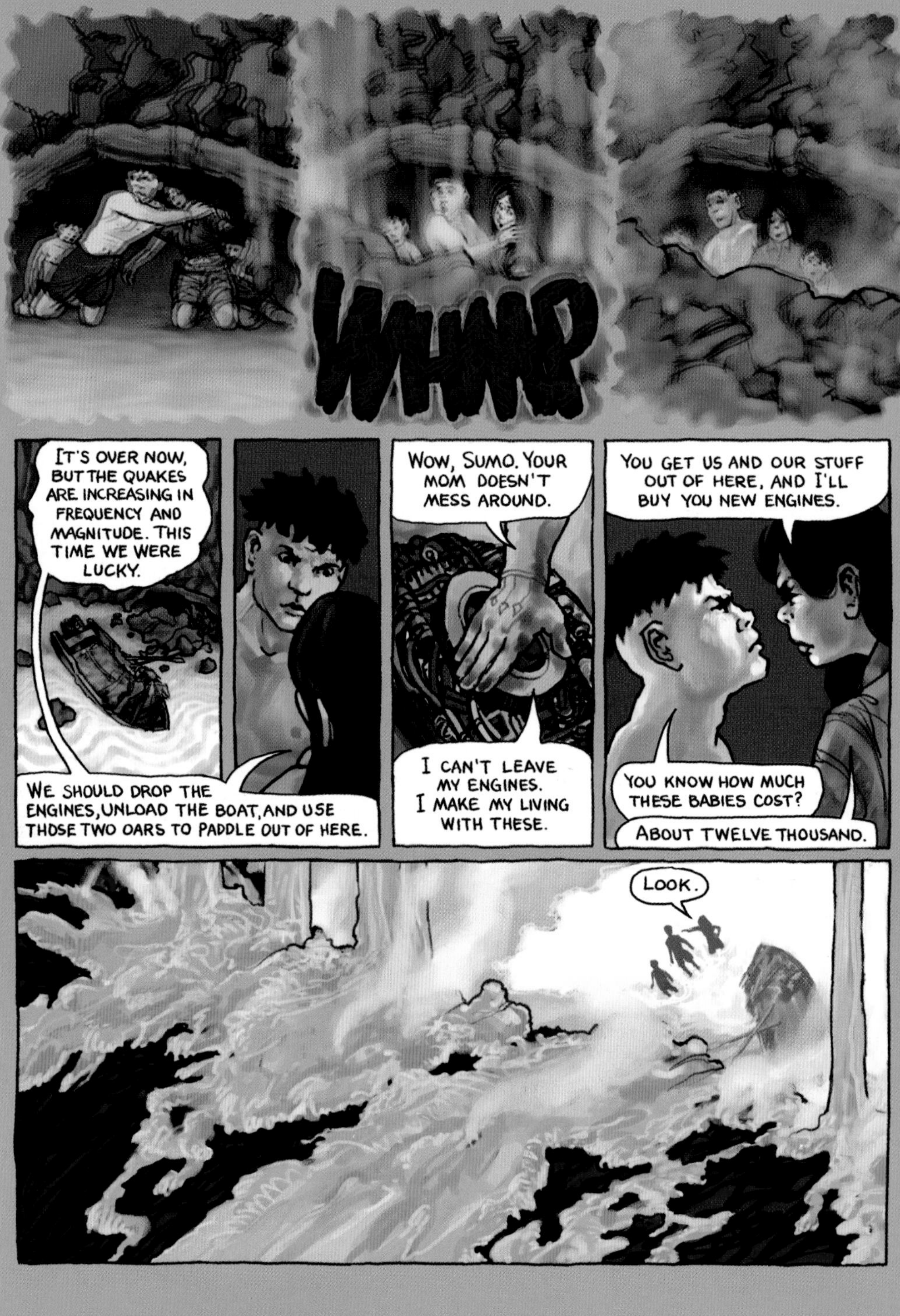
WHMP
IT'S OVER NOW, BUT THE QUAKES ARE INCREASING IN FREQUENCY AND MAGNITUDE. THIS TIME WE WERE LUCKY.
WE SHOULD DROP THE ENGINES, UNLOAD THE BOAT, AND USE THOSE TWO OARS TO PADDLE OUT OF HERE.
WOW, SUMO. YOUR MOM DOESN'T MESS AROUND.
I CAN'T LEAVE MY ENGINES. I MAKE MY LIVING WITH THESE.
YOU GET US AND OUR STUFF OUT OF HERE, AND I'LL BUY YOU NEW ENGINES.
YOU KNOW HOW MUCH THESE BABIES COST?
ABOUT TWELVE THOUSAND.
LOOK.

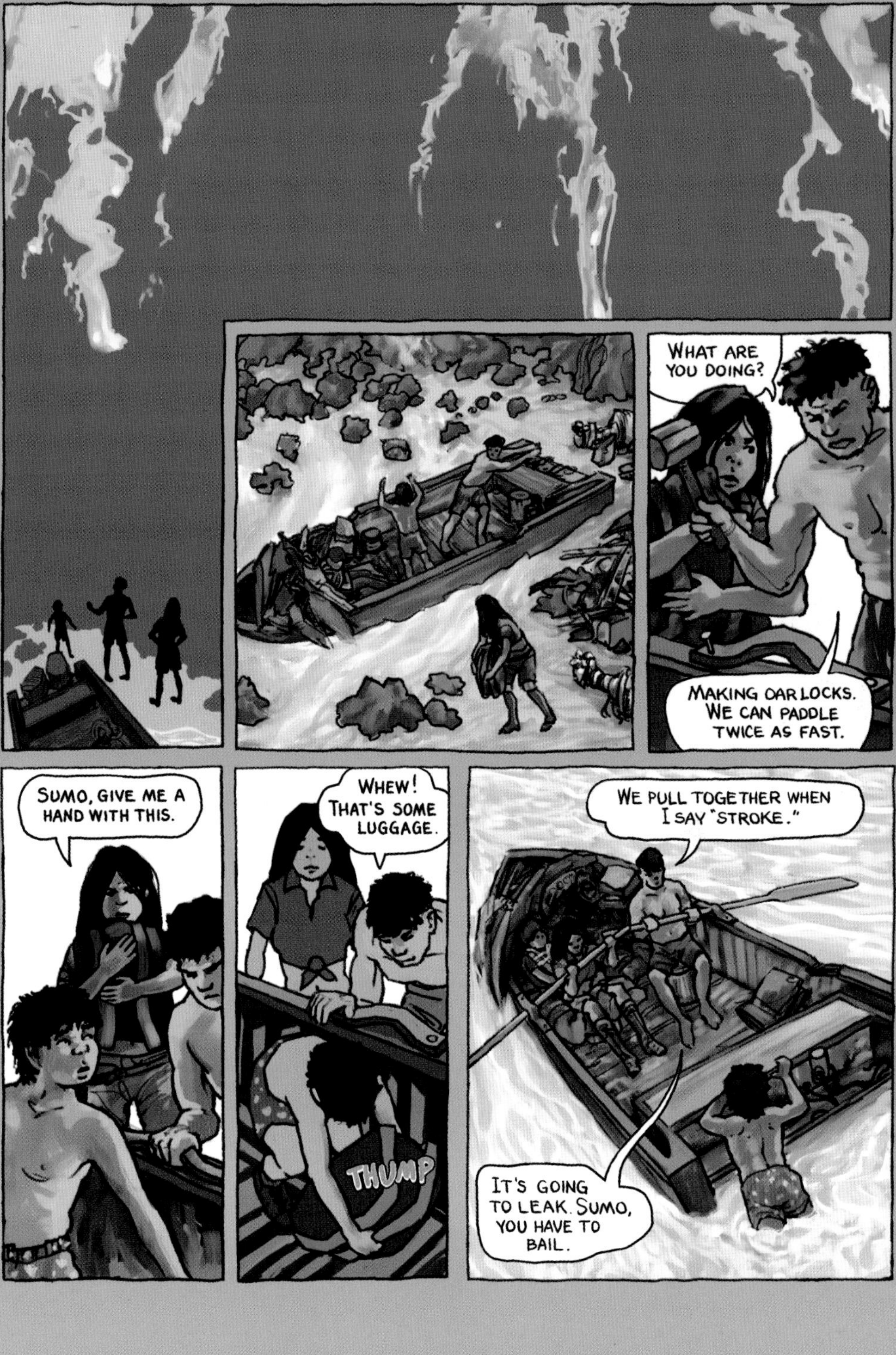
WHAT ARE YOU DOING?
MAKING OAR LOCKS. WE CAN PADDLE TWICE AS FAST.
SUMO, GIVE ME A HAND WITH THIS.
WHEW! THAT'S SOME LUGGAGE.
THUMP
WE PULL TOGETHER WHEN I SAY "STROKE."
IT'S GOING TO LEAK. SUMO, YOU HAVE TO BAIL.

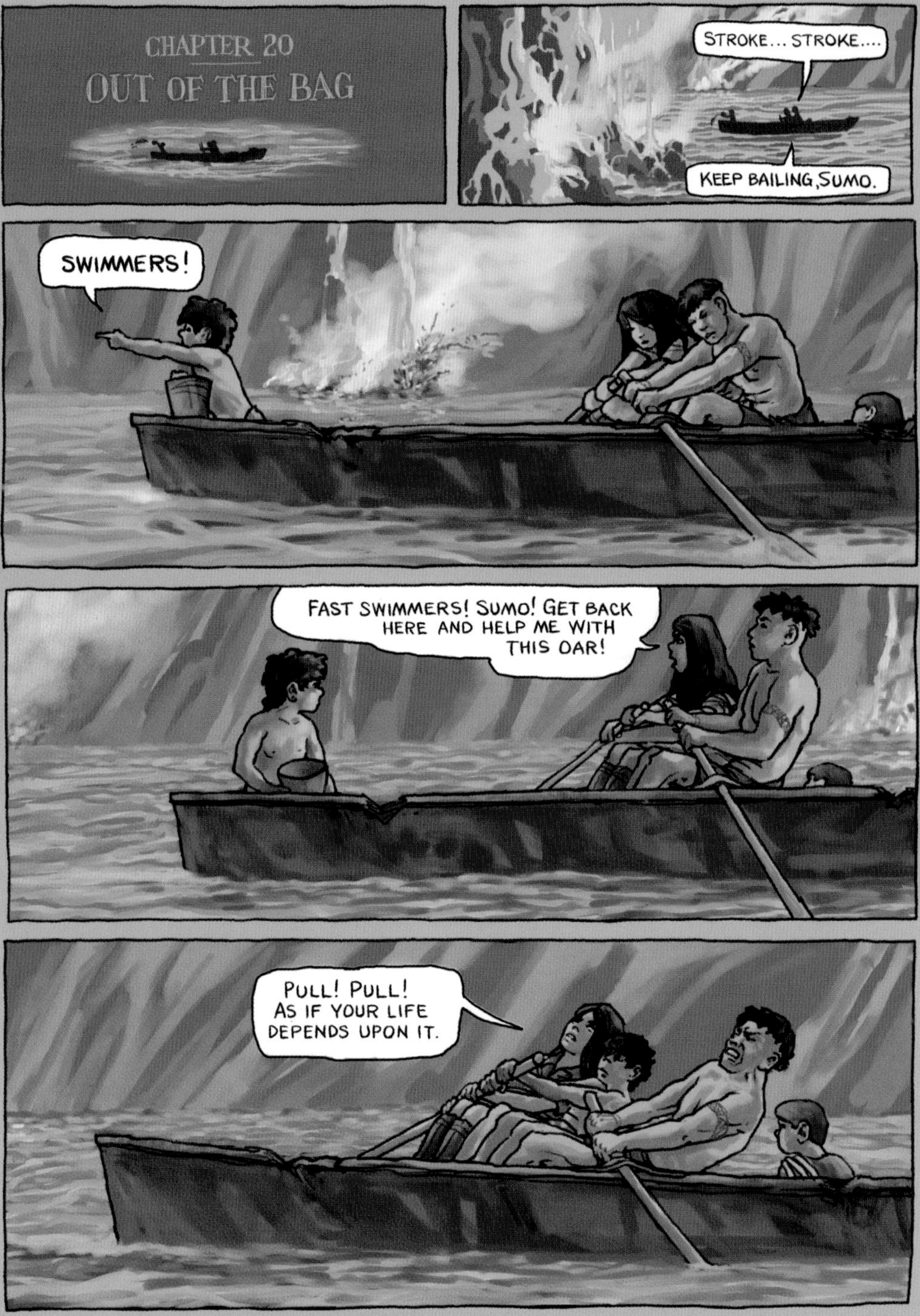
CHAPTER 20
OUT OF THE BAG
STROKE... STROKE....
KEEP BAILING, SUMO.
SWIMMERS!
FAST SWIMMERS! SUMO! GET BACK HERE AND HELP ME WITH THIS OAR!
PULL! PULL! AS IF YOUR LIFE DEPENDS UPON IT.

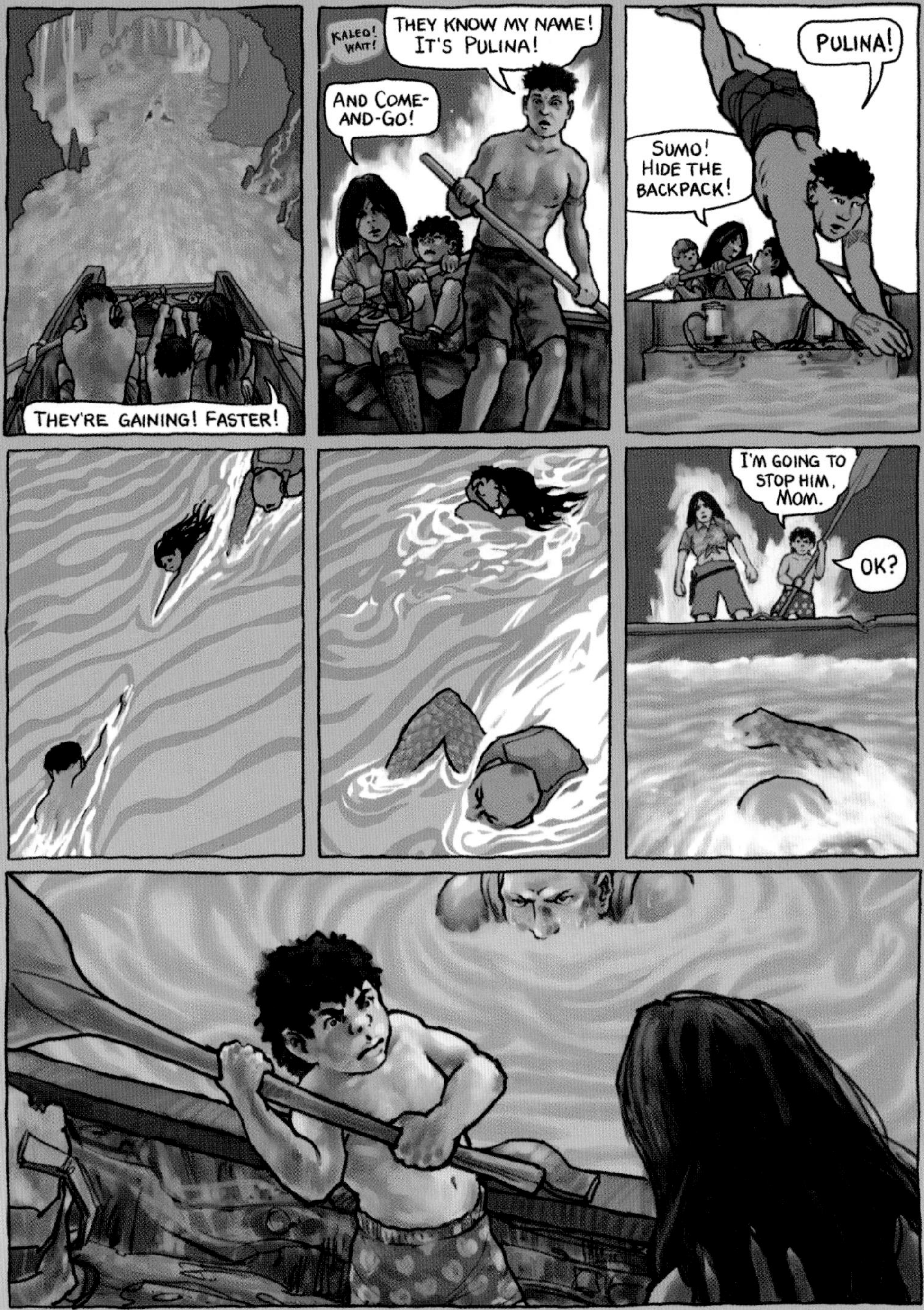
THEY'RE GAINING! FASTER!
KALEO! WAIT!
THEY KNOW MY NAME! IT'S PULINA!
AND COME-AND-GO!
PULINA!
SUMO! HIDE THE BACKPACK!
I'M GOING TO STOP HIM, MOM.
OK?

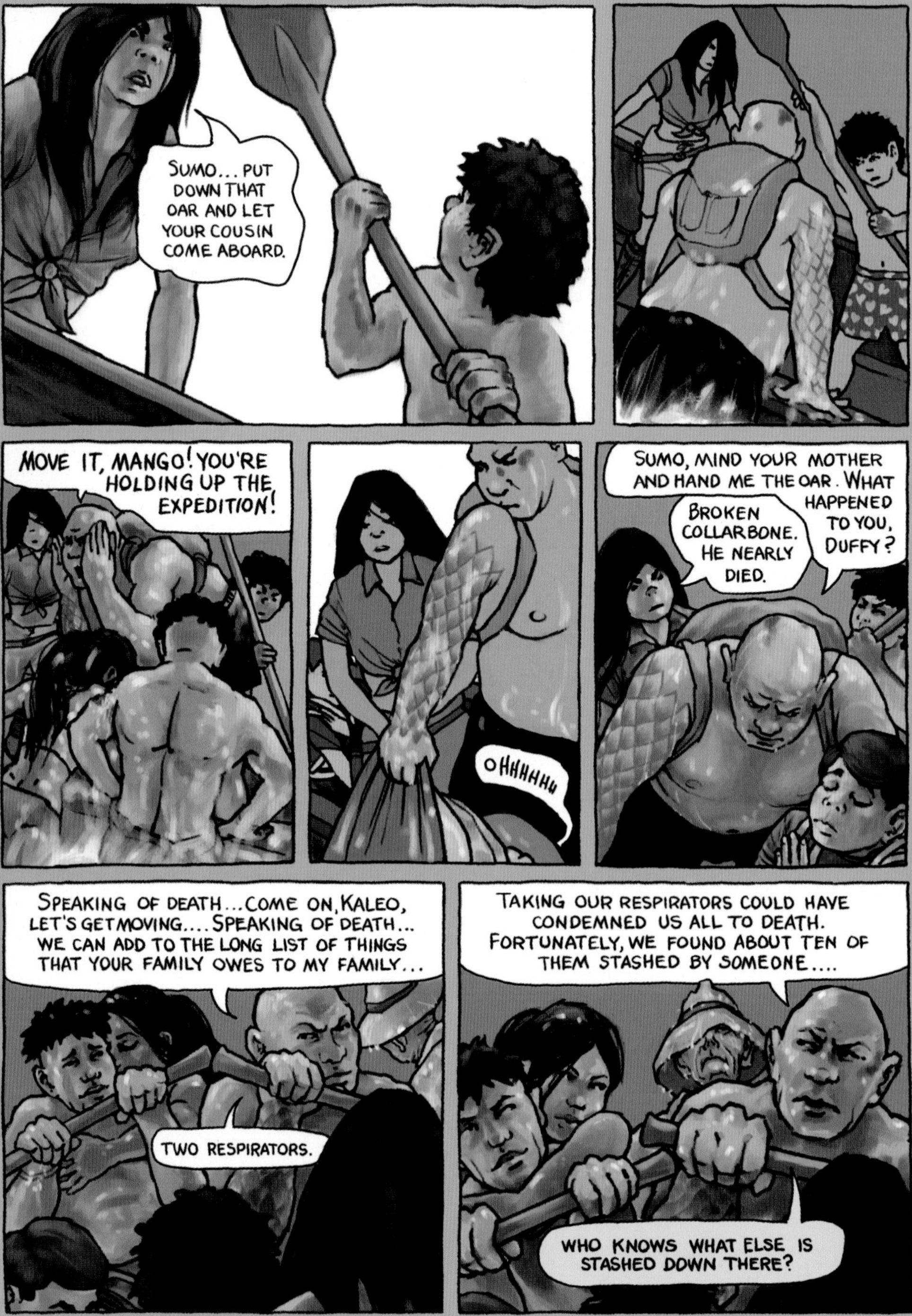
SUMO... PUT DOWN THAT OAR AND LET YOUR COUSIN COME ABOARD.
MOVE IT, MANGO! YOU'RE HOLDING UP THE EXPEDITION!
OHHHHHH
SUMO, MIND YOUR MOTHER AND HAND ME THE OAR. WHAT HAPPENED TO YOU, DUFFY?
BROKEN COLLARBONE. HE NEARLY DIED.
SPEAKING OF DEATH... COME ON, KALEO, LET'S GET MOVING.... SPEAKING OF DEATH... WE CAN ADD TO THE LONG LIST OF THINGS THAT YOUR FAMILY OWES TO MY FAMILY...
TWO RESPIRATORS.
TAKING OUR RESPIRATORS COULD HAVE CONDEMNED US ALL TO DEATH. FORTUNATELY, WE FOUND ABOUT TEN OF THEM STASHED BY SOMEONE....
WHO KNOWS WHAT ELSE IS STASHED DOWN THERE?

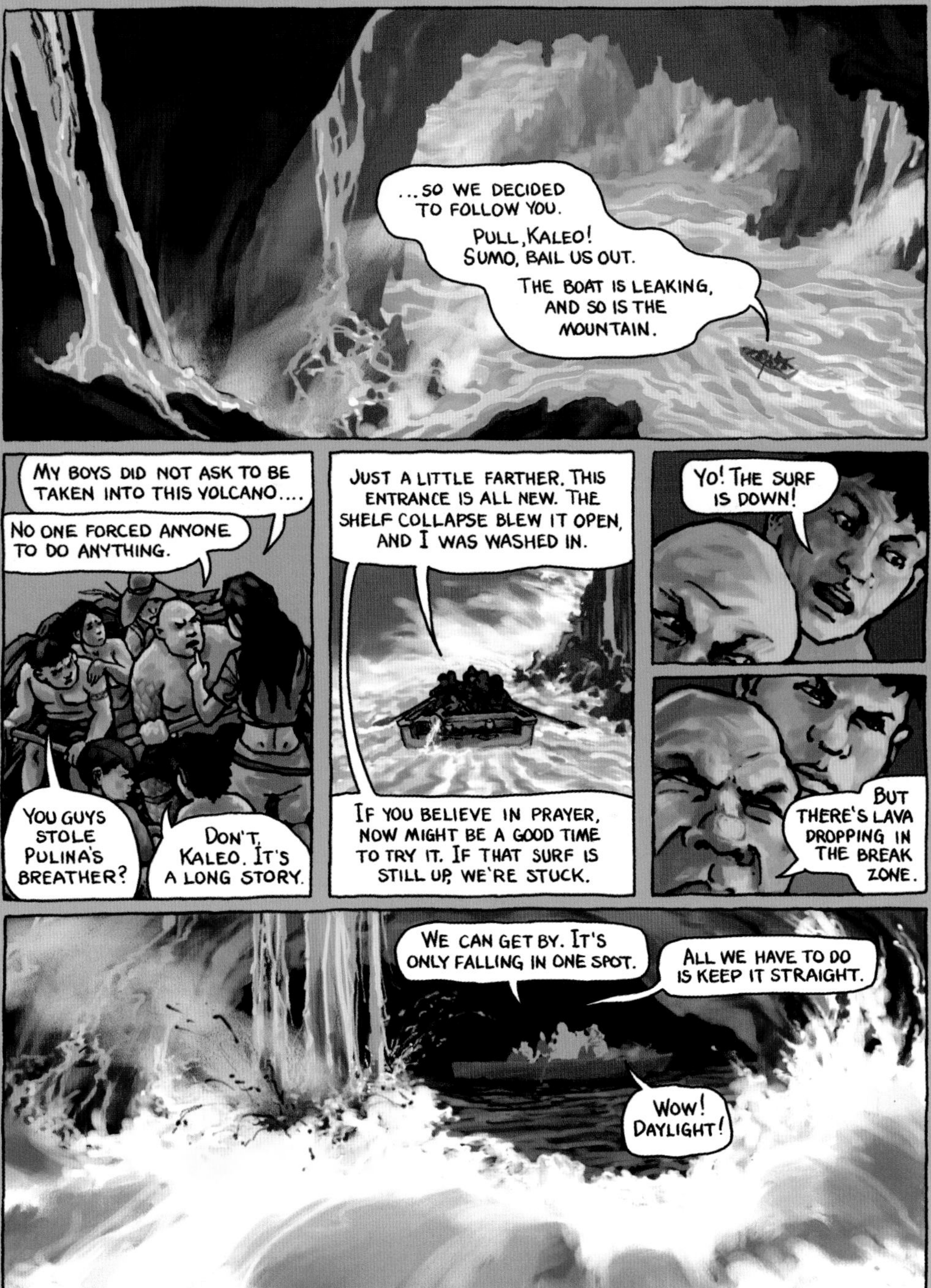
...SO WE DECIDED TO FOLLOW YOU.
PULL, KALEO! SUMO, BAIL US OUT.
THE BOAT IS LEAKING, AND SO IS THE MOUNTAIN.
MY BOYS DID NOT ASK TO BE TAKEN INTO THIS VOLCANO....
NO ONE FORCED ANYONE TO DO ANYTHING.
YOU GUYS STOLE PULINA'S BREATHER?
DON'T, KALEO. IT'S A LONG STORY.
JUST A LITTLE FARTHER. THIS ENTRANCE IS ALL NEW. THE SHELF COLLAPSE BLEW IT OPEN, AND I WAS WASHED IN.
IF YOU BELIEVE IN PRAYER, NOW MIGHT BE A GOOD TIME TO TRY IT. IF THAT SURF IS STILL UP, WE'RE STUCK.
YO! THE SURF IS DOWN!
BUT THERE'S LAVA DROPPING IN THE BREAK ZONE.
WE CAN GET BY. IT'S ONLY FALLING IN ONE SPOT.
ALL WE HAVE TO DO IS KEEP IT STRAIGHT.
WOW! DAYLIGHT!

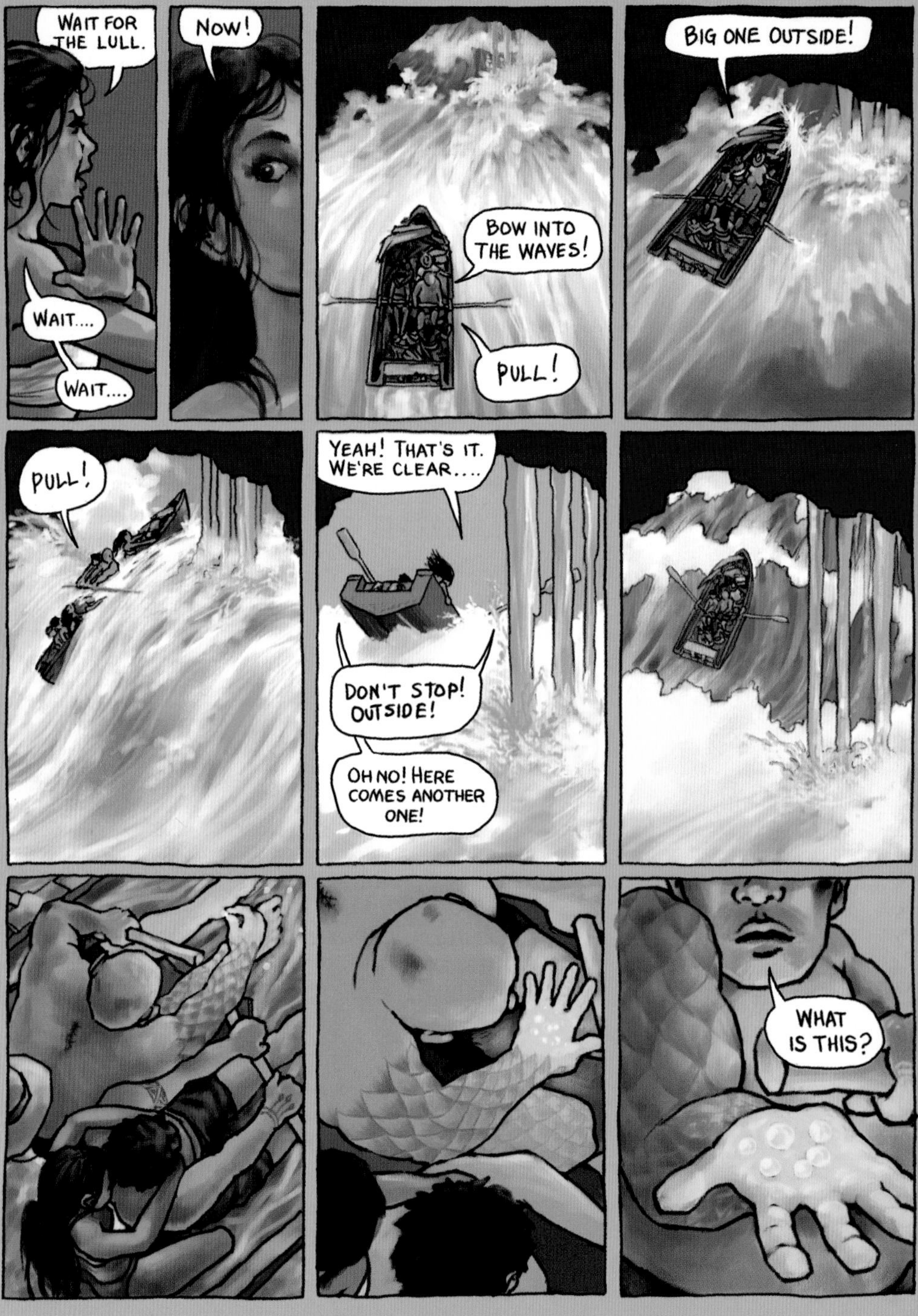
WAIT FOR THE LULL.
WAIT....
WAIT....
NOW!
BOW INTO THE WAVES!
PULL!
BIG ONE OUTSIDE!
PULL!
YEAH! THAT'S IT. WE'RE CLEAR....
DON'T STOP! OUTSIDE!
OH NO! HERE COMES ANOTHER ONE!
WHAT IS THIS?

COULD THESE BE THE FABLED GREEN-DIAMOND PEARLS OF THE VOLCANO? FUNNY, I'VE NEVER SEEN ONE.

THREE YEARS OF MY LIFE SPENT PERFECTING A METHOD TO EXTRACT THESE LITTLE BEAUTIES FROM TERMINAL GREEN MAGMA...

VERY NICE.

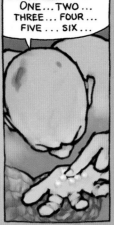

ONE... TWO... THREE... FOUR... FIVE... SIX...

LET'S SEE... ACCORDING TO OUR DEAL... THREE OF THESE ARE MINE.

THOSE WERE NOT EXTRACTED WITH YOUR METHOD!

YOUR METHOD DIDN'T WORK. I DEVELOPED MY OWN, MUCH BETTER, EXTRACTION PROCEDURE.

BASED UPON OUR RESEARCH, NO DOUBT.

HEY, COME-AND-GO!

WE WILL DISCUSS THIS LATER.

THEY'RE SPILLING OUT OF THAT BACKPACK. MANGO! GO AFT AND GET IT.

COME-AND-GO!

MANGO! GO GET THAT BACK-PACK.

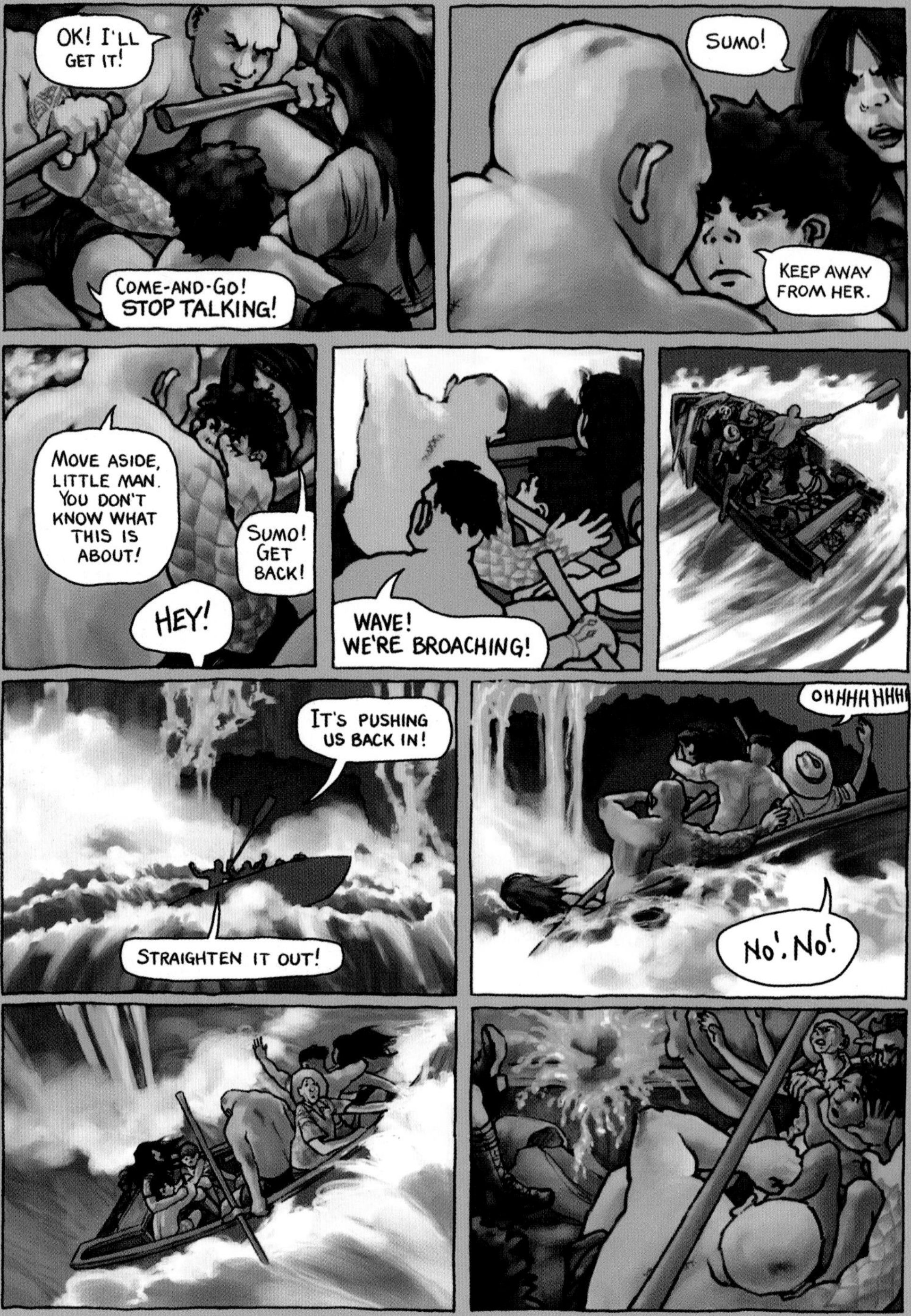
OK! I'LL GET IT!
COME-AND-GO! STOP TALKING!
SUMO!
KEEP AWAY FROM HER.
MOVE ASIDE, LITTLE MAN. YOU DON'T KNOW WHAT THIS IS ABOUT!
SUMO! GET BACK!
HEY!
WAVE! WE'RE BROACHING!
IT'S PUSHING US BACK IN!
STRAIGHTEN IT OUT!
OHHHHHHH
NO! NO!

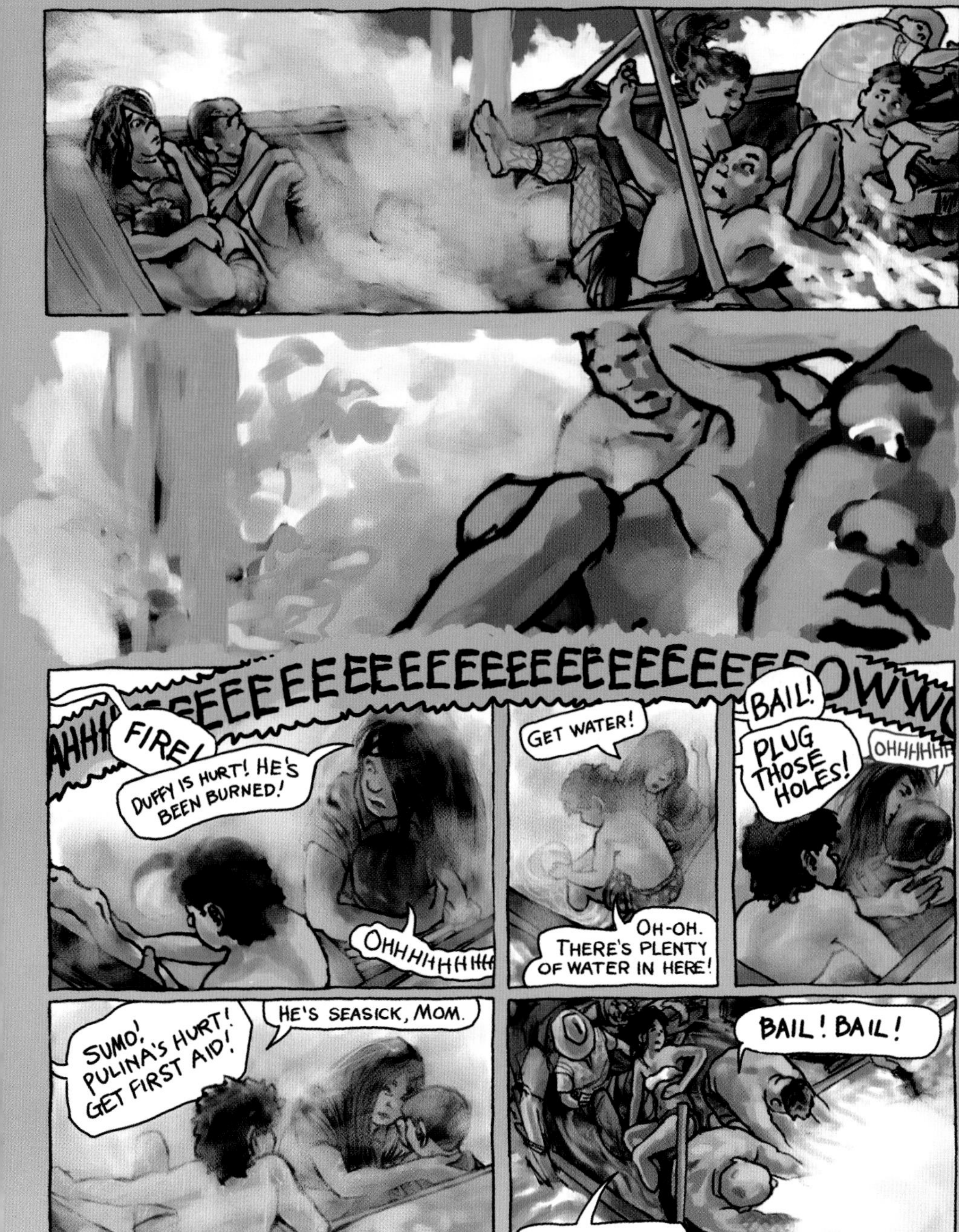
AHHH EEEEEEEEEEEEEEEEEEEEEEEEEEEEOWWO
FIRE!
DUFFY IS HURT! HE'S BEEN BURNED!
OHHHHHHHHH
GET WATER!
OH-OH. THERE'S PLENTY OF WATER IN HERE!
BAIL!
PLUG THOSE HOLES!
OHHHHHH
SUMO! PULINA'S HURT! GET FIRST AID!
HE'S SEASICK, MOM.
BAIL! BAIL!
NO, KALEO! YOU HELP ME.... OWWW....

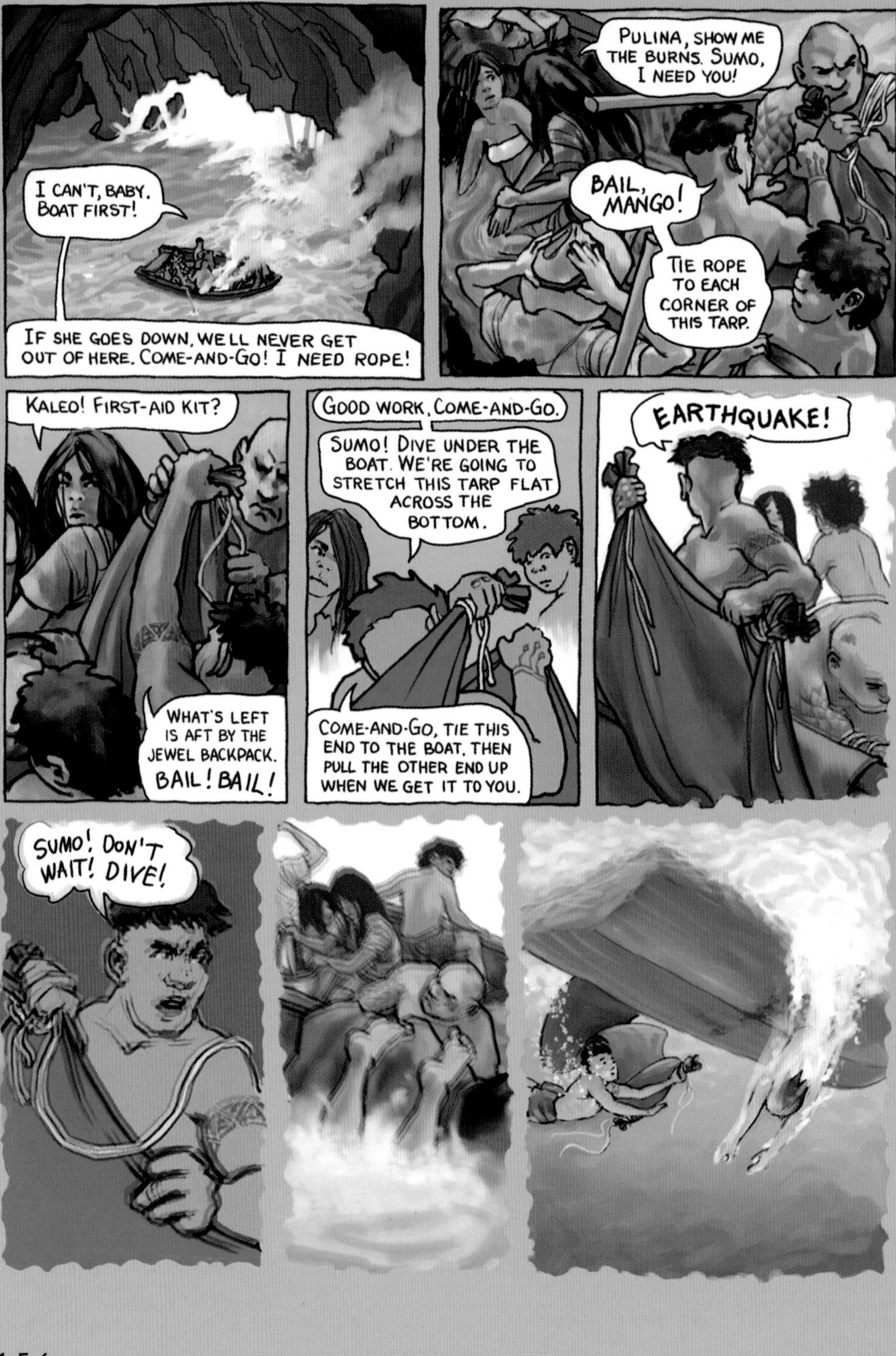
I CAN'T, BABY. BOAT FIRST!
IF SHE GOES DOWN, WE'LL NEVER GET OUT OF HERE. COME-AND-GO! I NEED ROPE!
PULINA, SHOW ME THE BURNS. SUMO, I NEED YOU!
BAIL, MANGO!
TIE ROPE TO EACH CORNER OF THIS TARP.
KALEO! FIRST-AID KIT?
WHAT'S LEFT IS AFT BY THE JEWEL BACKPACK. BAIL! BAIL!
GOOD WORK, COME-AND-GO.
SUMO! DIVE UNDER THE BOAT. WE'RE GOING TO STRETCH THIS TARP FLAT ACROSS THE BOTTOM.
COME-AND-GO, TIE THIS END TO THE BOAT, THEN PULL THE OTHER END UP WHEN WE GET IT TO YOU.
EARTHQUAKE!
SUMO! DON'T WAIT! DIVE!

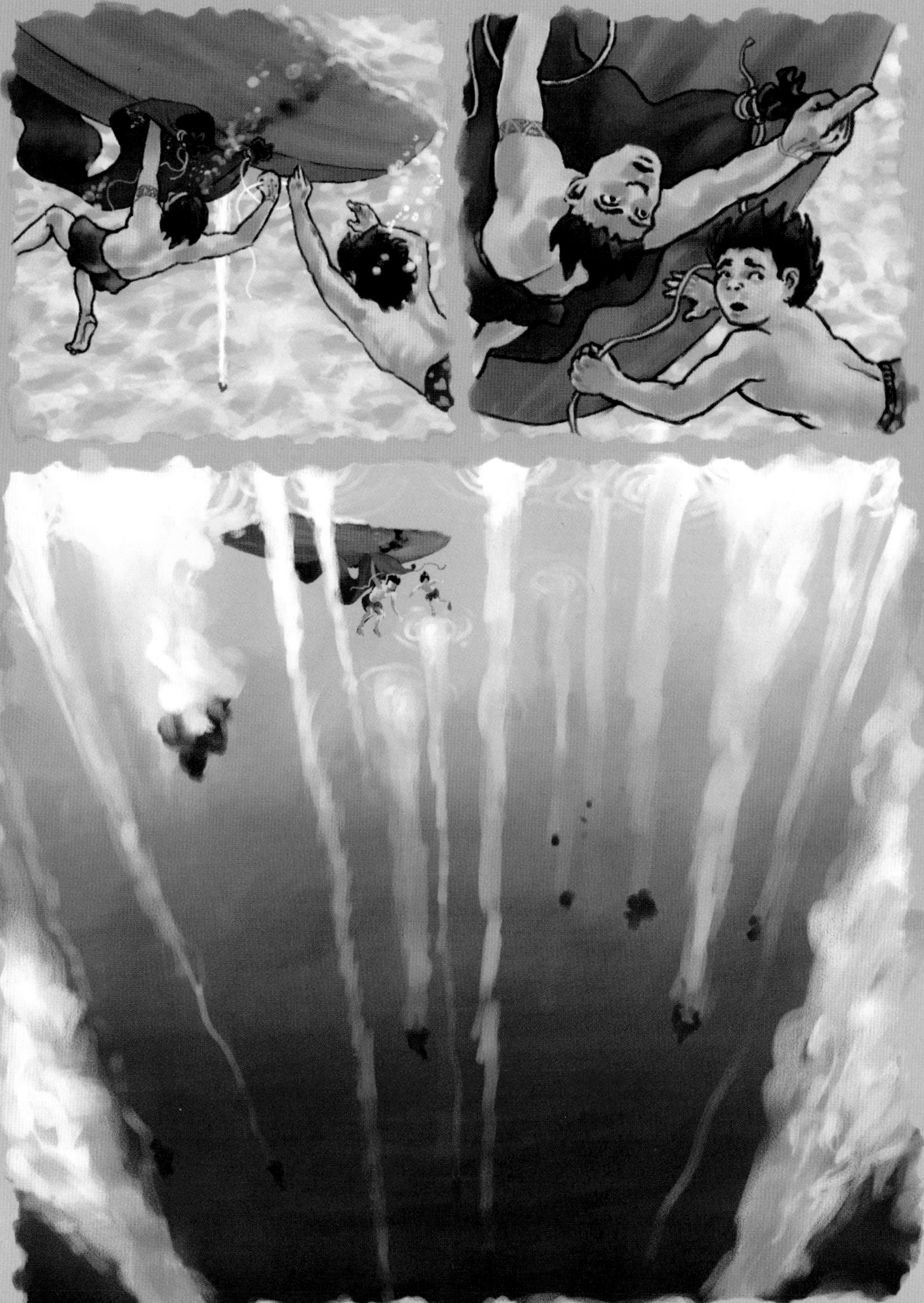

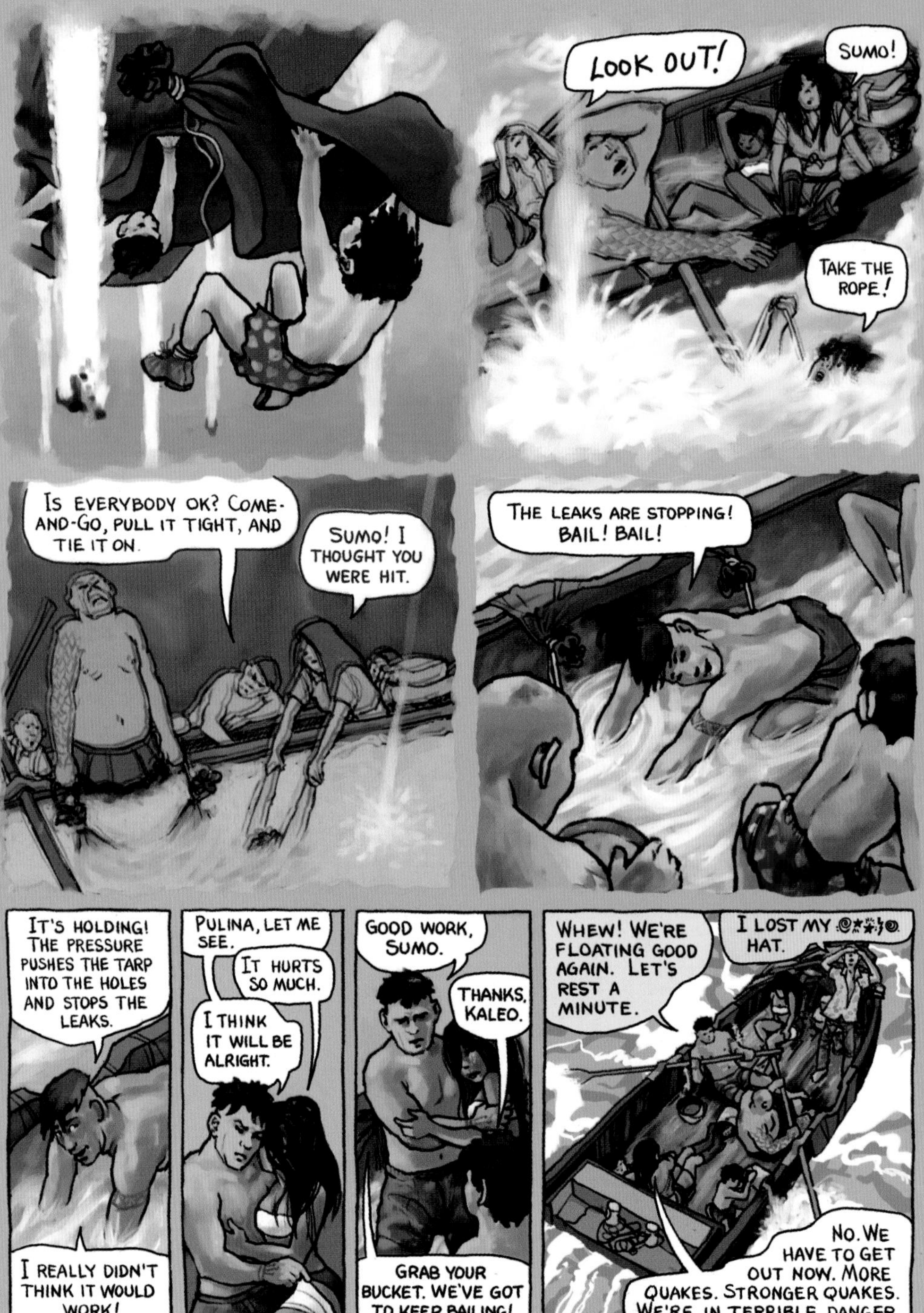
LOOK OUT!
SUMO!
TAKE THE ROPE!
IS EVERYBODY OK? COME-AND-GO, PULL IT TIGHT, AND TIE IT ON.
SUMO! I THOUGHT YOU WERE HIT.
THE LEAKS ARE STOPPING! BAIL! BAIL!
IT'S HOLDING! THE PRESSURE PUSHES THE TARP INTO THE HOLES AND STOPS THE LEAKS.
I REALLY DIDN'T THINK IT WOULD WORK!
PULINA, LET ME SEE.
IT HURTS SO MUCH.
I THINK IT WILL BE ALRIGHT.
GOOD WORK, SUMO.
THANKS, KALEO.
GRAB YOUR BUCKET. WE'VE GOT TO KEEP BAILING!
WHEW! WE'RE FLOATING GOOD AGAIN. LET'S REST A MINUTE.
I LOST MY HAT.
NO. WE HAVE TO GET OUT NOW. MORE QUAKES. STRONGER QUAKES. WE'RE IN TERRIBLE DANGER.

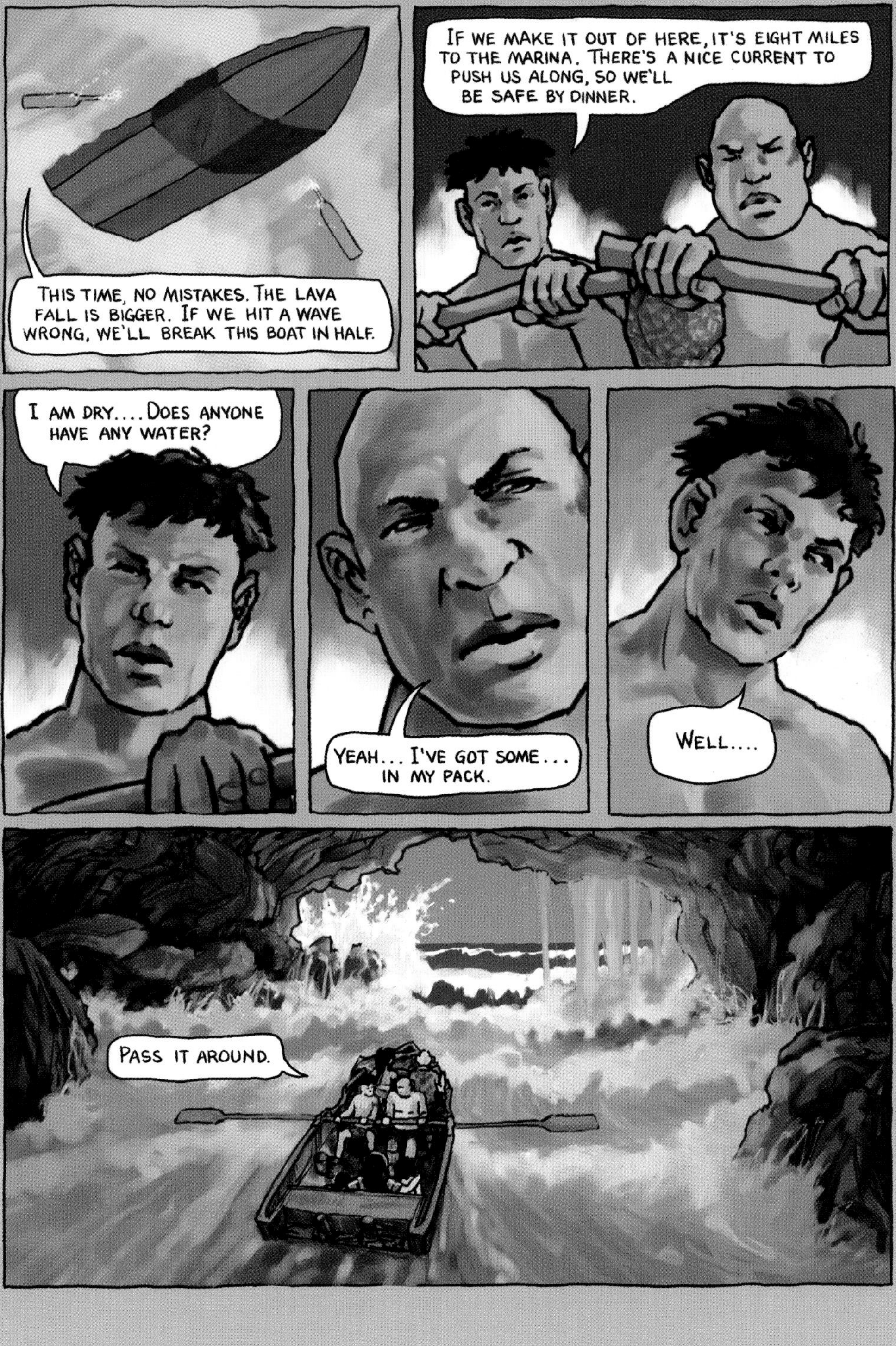
THIS TIME, NO MISTAKES. THE LAVA FALL IS BIGGER. IF WE HIT A WAVE WRONG, WE'LL BREAK THIS BOAT IN HALF.
IF WE MAKE IT OUT OF HERE, IT'S EIGHT MILES TO THE MARINA. THERE'S A NICE CURRENT TO PUSH US ALONG, SO WE'LL BE SAFE BY DINNER.
I AM DRY.... DOES ANYONE HAVE ANY WATER?
YEAH... I'VE GOT SOME... IN MY PACK.
WELL....
PASS IT AROUND.

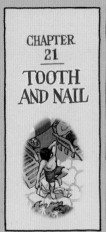

CHAPTER
21

TOOTH
AND NAIL

NO... RIGHT NOW I FEEL PRETTY GOOD.... THEY SAID IT WAS A GOOD, CLEAN BREAK, BUT IT WAS ....

WHAT DID THEY SAY, MOM?

"BADLY ABUSED."

IT WAS "BADLY ABUSED"! HAH!

I'LL BE FINE, BUT WE CAN'T COME HOME FOR A WEEK. DAD, YOU WOULDN'T BELIEVE THE PAIN, AND SUMO...

SUMO SAVED MY LIFE OVER AND OVER. HE'S A HERO!

YES! YOUR SUMO.

KNOCK KNOCK

YOO HOO... LATA LATA..

OUT! OUT!!!

UH-OH...

SIS...WE JUST WANTED TO....

HOW DARE YOU SHOW UP HERE! YOU ALMOST KILLED MY BOYS! GET OUT!

WE JUST WENT DOWN THERE TO FIND YOU. WE WERE WORRIED.

GET AWAY FROM MY BOYS!

ALRIGHT, PEOPLE. YOU'RE DISTURBING MY PATIENT. CLEAR THE ROOM.

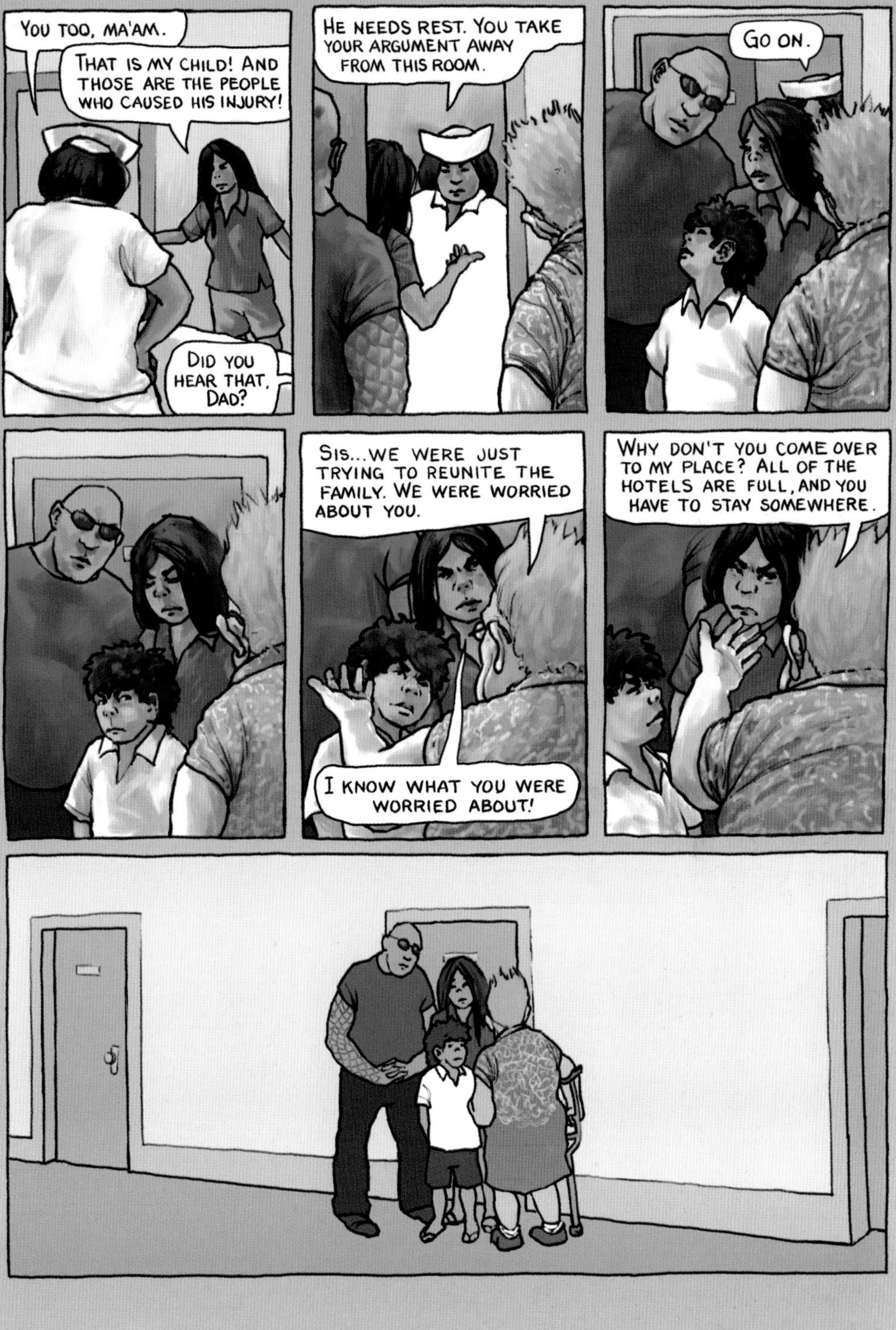
YOU TOO, MA'AM.
THAT IS MY CHILD! AND THOSE ARE THE PEOPLE WHO CAUSED HIS INJURY!
DID YOU HEAR THAT, DAD?
HE NEEDS REST. YOU TAKE YOUR ARGUMENT AWAY FROM THIS ROOM.
GO ON.
SIS...WE WERE JUST TRYING TO REUNITE THE FAMILY. WE WERE WORRIED ABOUT YOU.
I KNOW WHAT YOU WERE WORRIED ABOUT!
WHY DON'T YOU COME OVER TO MY PLACE? ALL OF THE HOTELS ARE FULL, AND YOU HAVE TO STAY SOMEWHERE.

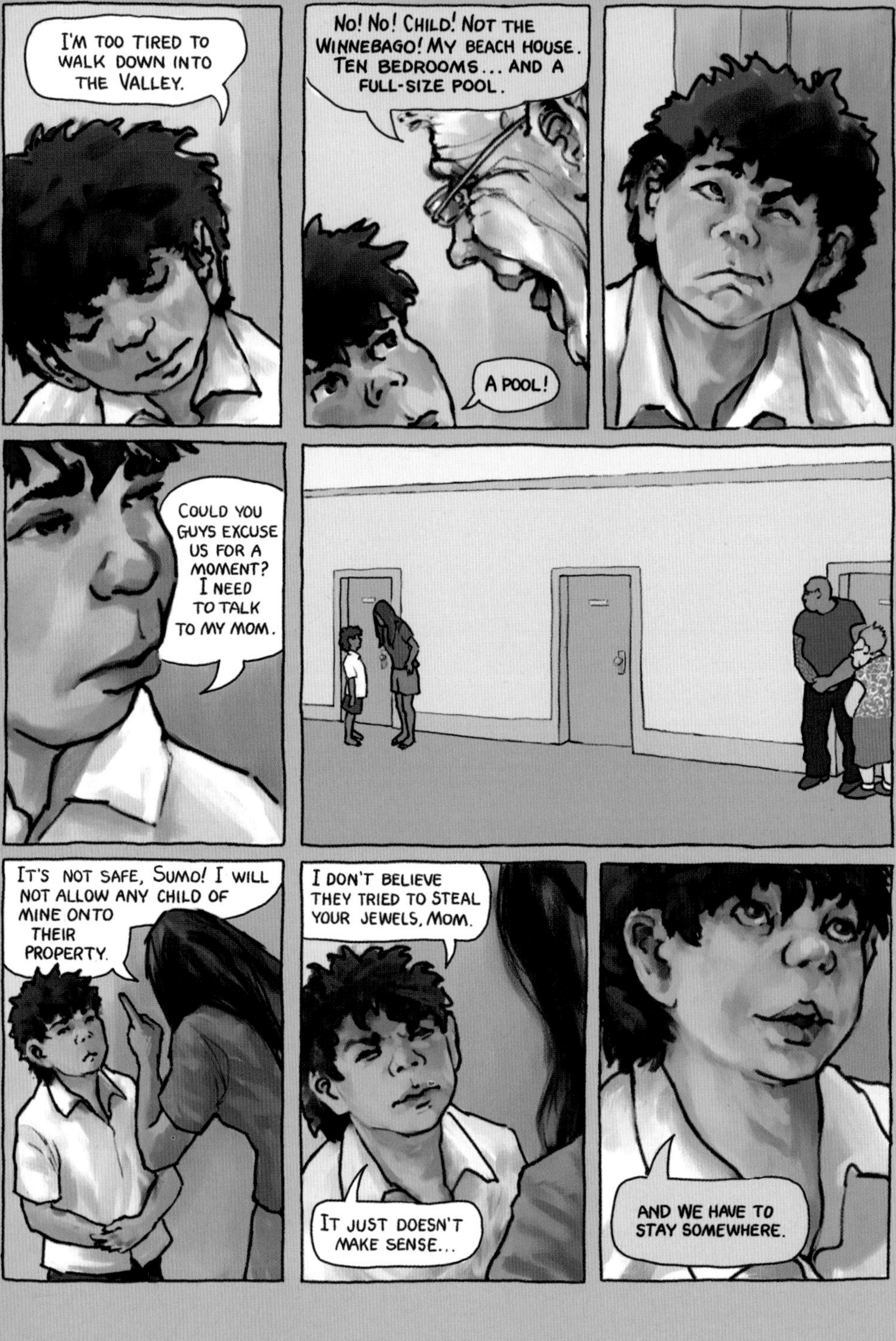
I'M TOO TIRED TO WALK DOWN INTO THE VALLEY.
NO! NO! CHILD! NOT THE WINNEBAGO! MY BEACH HOUSE. TEN BEDROOMS... AND A FULL-SIZE POOL.
A POOL!
COULD YOU GUYS EXCUSE US FOR A MOMENT? I NEED TO TALK TO MY MOM.
IT'S NOT SAFE, SUMO! I WILL NOT ALLOW ANY CHILD OF MINE ONTO THEIR PROPERTY.
I DON'T BELIEVE THEY TRIED TO STEAL YOUR JEWELS, MOM.
IT JUST DOESN'T MAKE SENSE...
AND WE HAVE TO STAY SOMEWHERE.

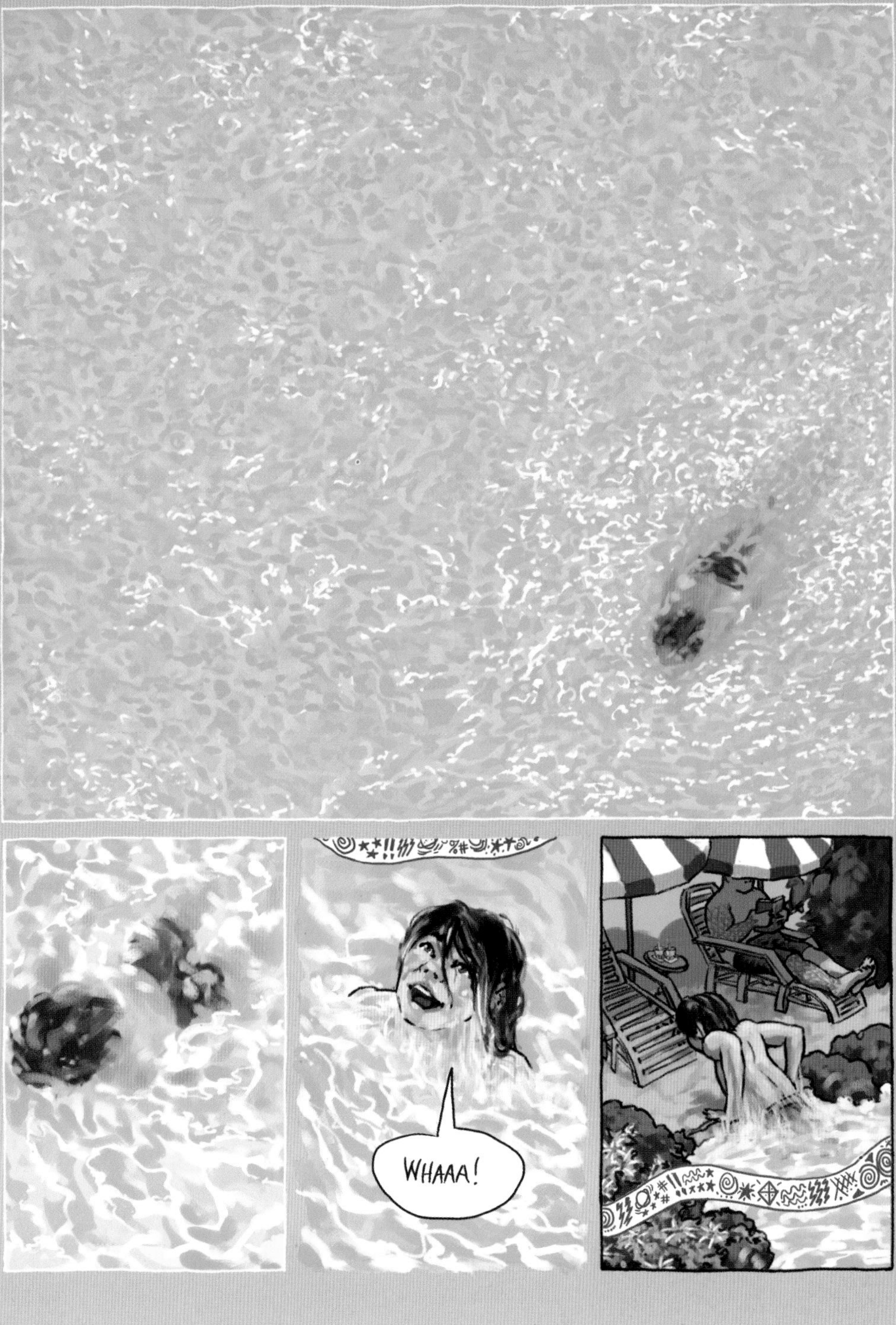
WHAAA!

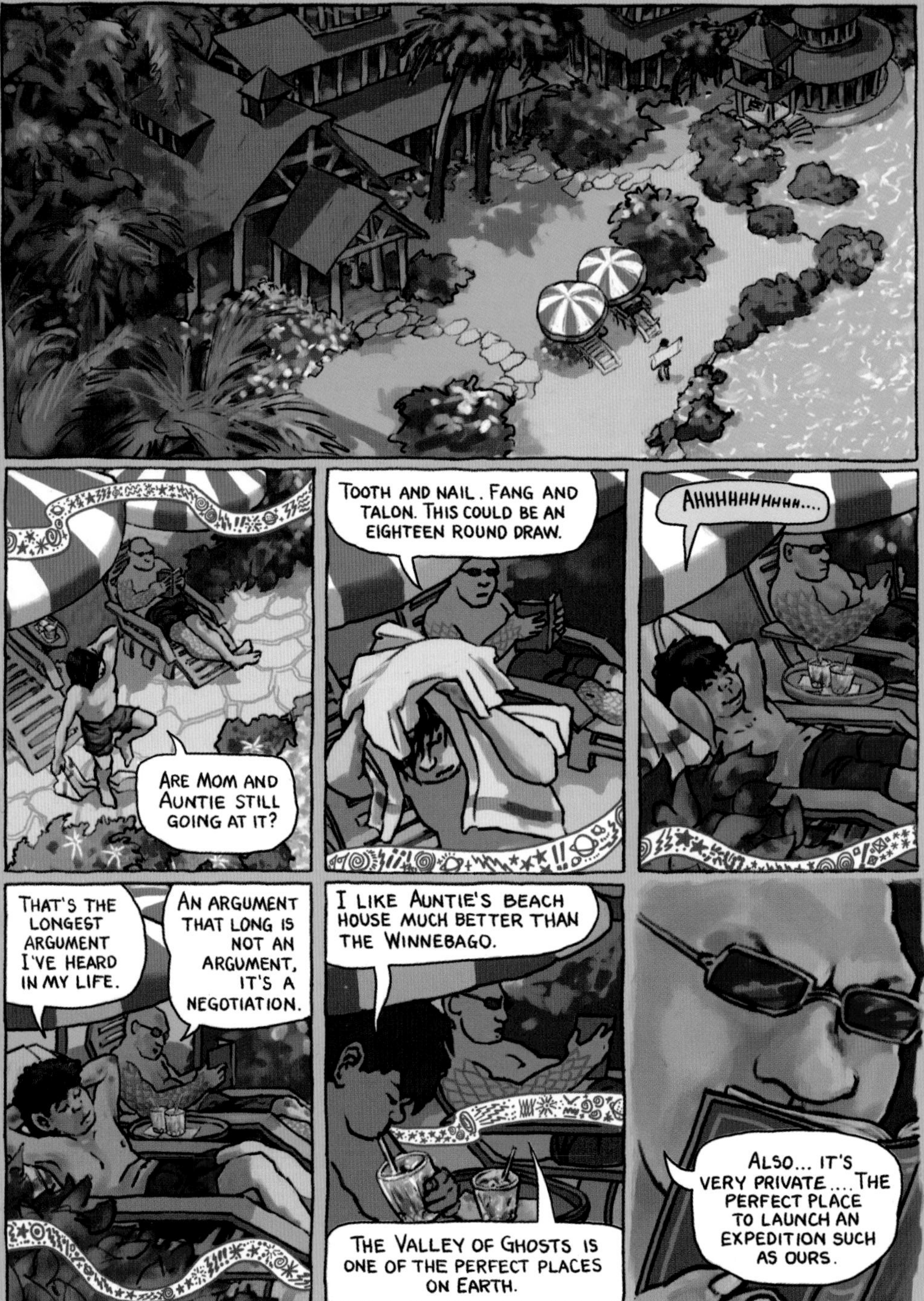
ARE MOM AND AUNTIE STILL GOING AT IT?
TOOTH AND NAIL. FANG AND TALON. THIS COULD BE AN EIGHTEEN ROUND DRAW.
AHHHHHHHHHH....
THAT'S THE LONGEST ARGUMENT I'VE HEARD IN MY LIFE.
AN ARGUMENT THAT LONG IS NOT AN ARGUMENT, IT'S A NEGOTIATION.
I LIKE AUNTIE'S BEACH HOUSE MUCH BETTER THAN THE WINNEBAGO.
THE VALLEY OF GHOSTS IS ONE OF THE PERFECT PLACES ON EARTH.
ALSO... IT'S VERY PRIVATE.... THE PERFECT PLACE TO LAUNCH AN EXPEDITION SUCH AS OURS.

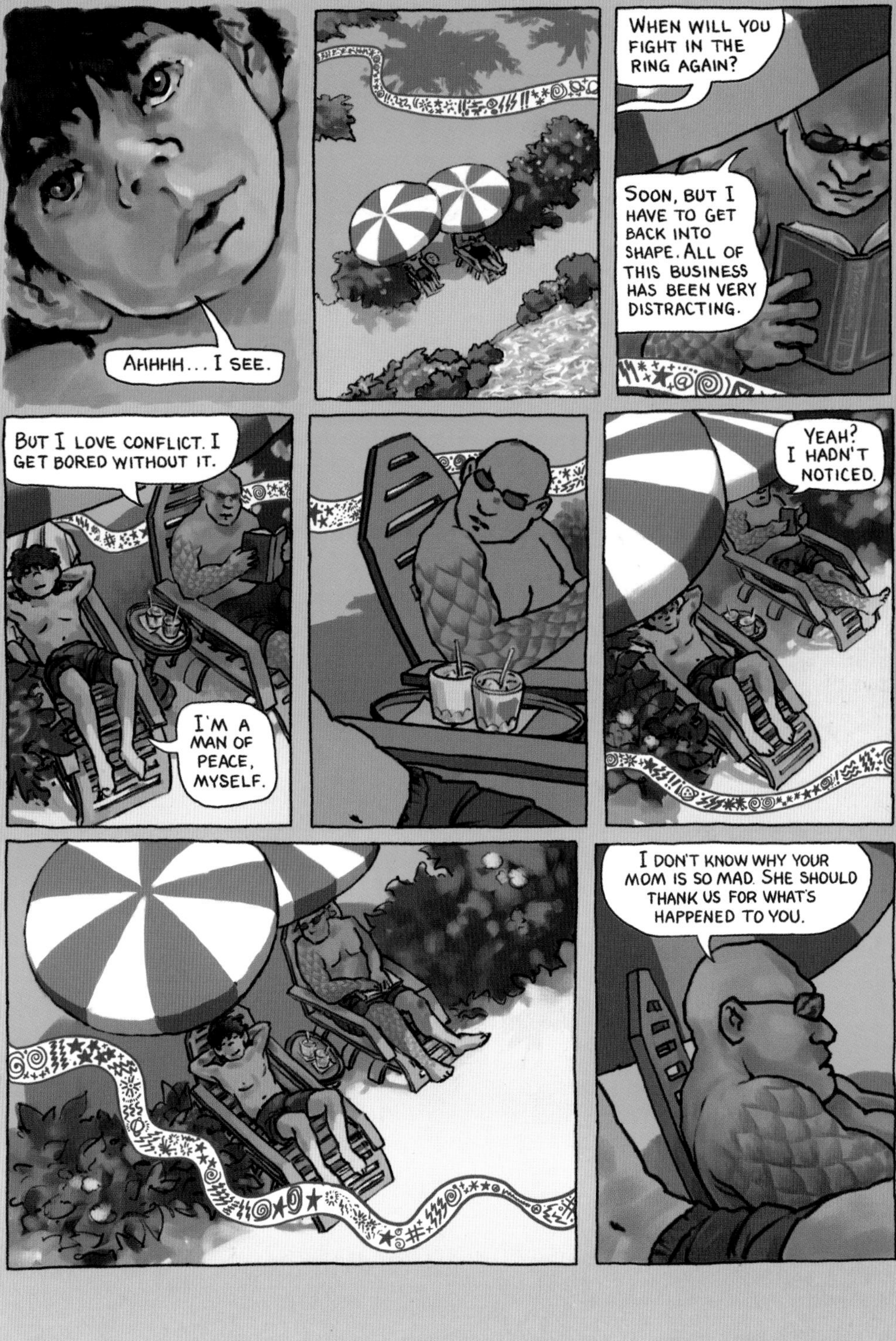
AHHHH... I SEE.
WHEN WILL YOU FIGHT IN THE RING AGAIN?
SOON, BUT I HAVE TO GET BACK INTO SHAPE. ALL OF THIS BUSINESS HAS BEEN VERY DISTRACTING.
BUT I LOVE CONFLICT. I GET BORED WITHOUT IT.
I'M A MAN OF PEACE, MYSELF.
YEAH? I HADN'T NOTICED.
I DON'T KNOW WHY YOUR MOM IS SO MAD. SHE SHOULD THANK US FOR WHAT'S HAPPENED TO YOU.

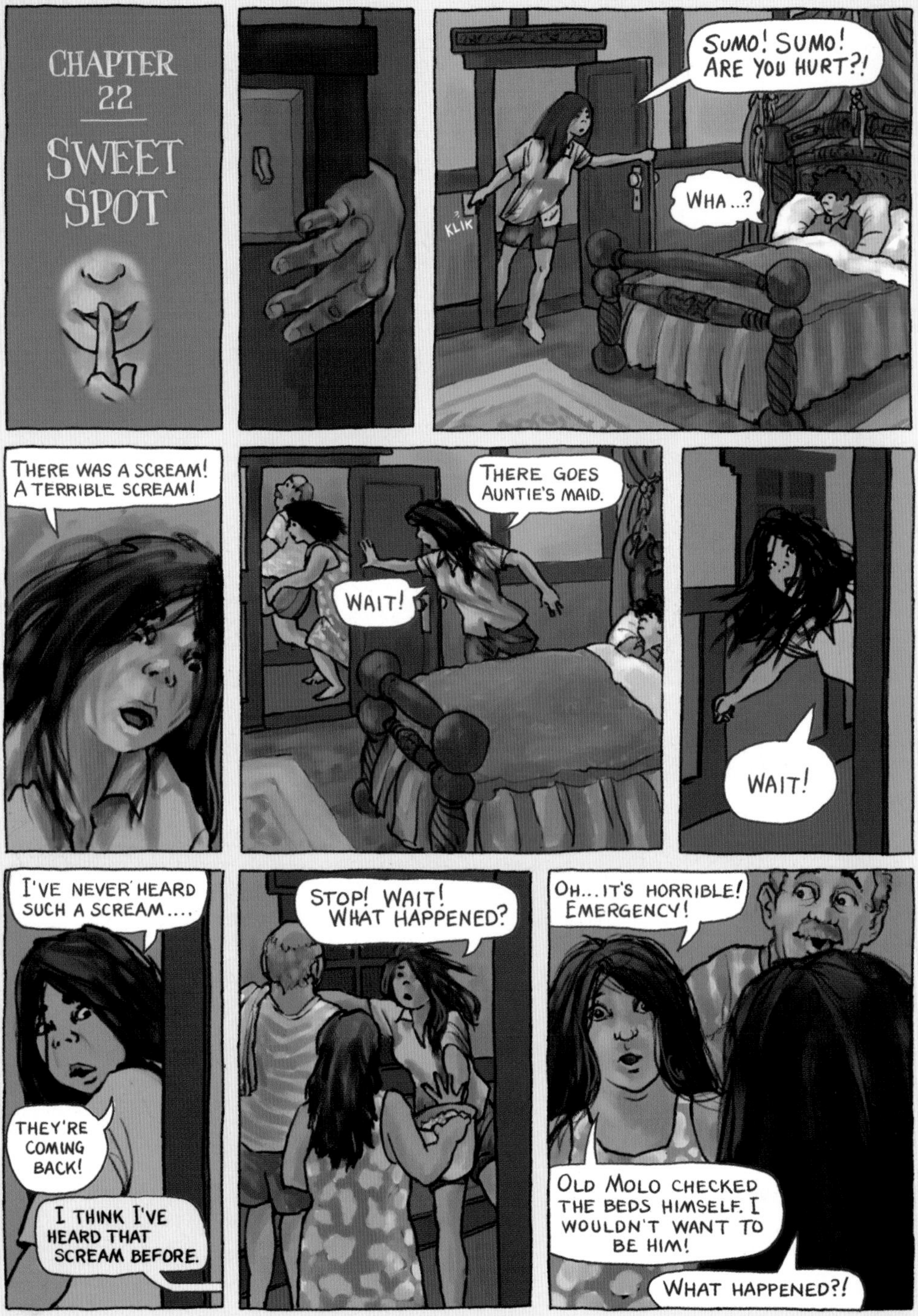
CHAPTER 22
SWEET SPOT
SUMO! SUMO! ARE YOU HURT?!
KLIK
WHA...?
THERE WAS A SCREAM! A TERRIBLE SCREAM!
THERE GOES AUNTIE'S MAID.
WAIT!
WAIT!
I'VE NEVER HEARD SUCH A SCREAM....
THEY'RE COMING BACK!
I THINK I'VE HEARD THAT SCREAM BEFORE.
STOP! WAIT! WHAT HAPPENED?
OH...IT'S HORRIBLE! EMERGENCY!
OLD MOLO CHECKED THE BEDS HIMSELF. I WOULDN'T WANT TO BE HIM!
WHAT HAPPENED?!

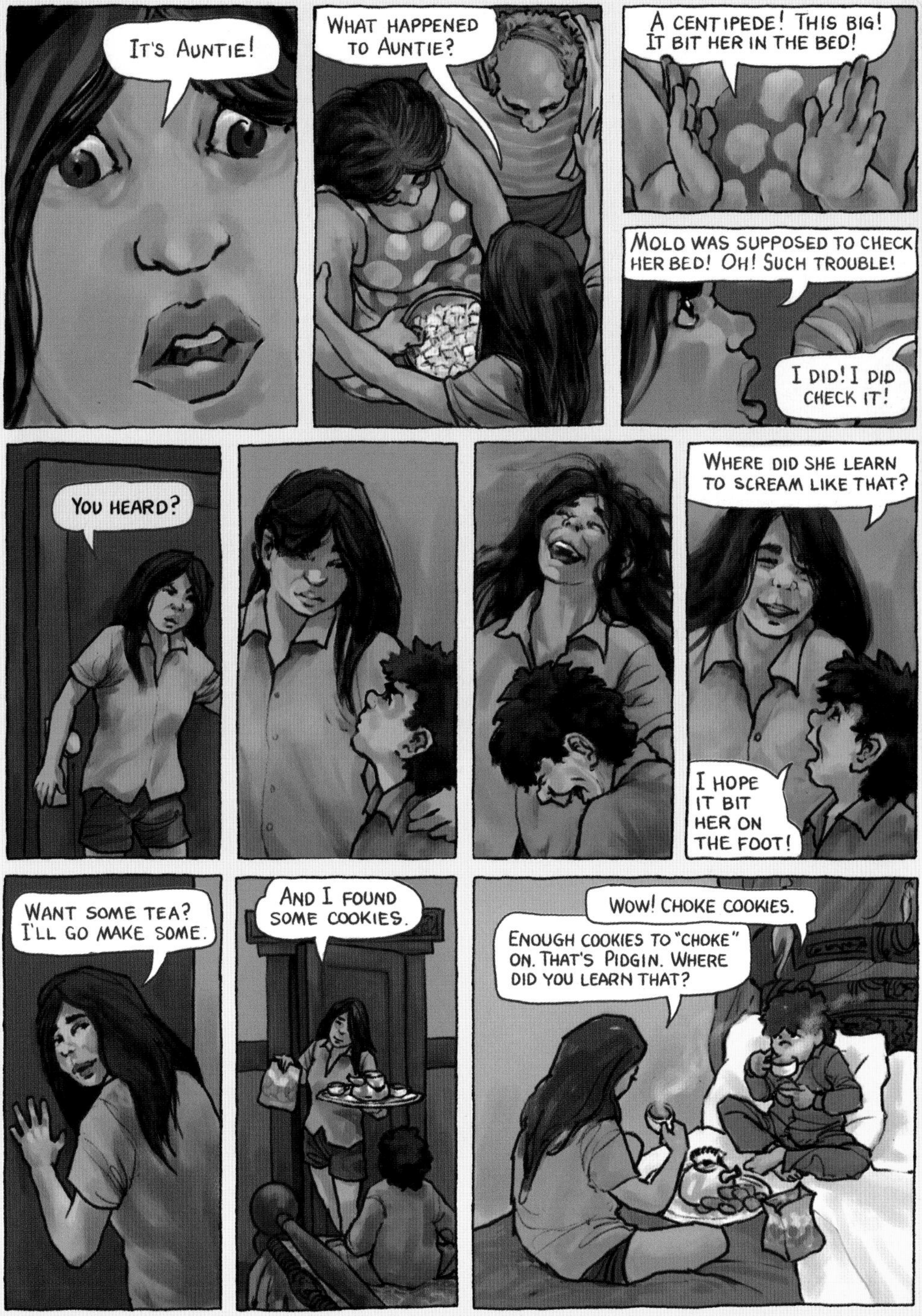

IT'S AUNTIE!
WHAT HAPPENED TO AUNTIE?
A CENTIPEDE! THIS BIG! IT BIT HER IN THE BED!
MOLD WAS SUPPOSED TO CHECK HER BED! OH! SUCH TROUBLE!
I DID! I DID CHECK IT!
YOU HEARD?
WHERE DID SHE LEARN TO SCREAM LIKE THAT?
I HOPE IT BIT HER ON THE FOOT!
WANT SOME TEA? I'LL GO MAKE SOME.
AND I FOUND SOME COOKIES.
WOW! CHOKE COOKIES.
ENOUGH COOKIES TO "CHOKE" ON. THAT'S PIDGIN. WHERE DID YOU LEARN THAT?

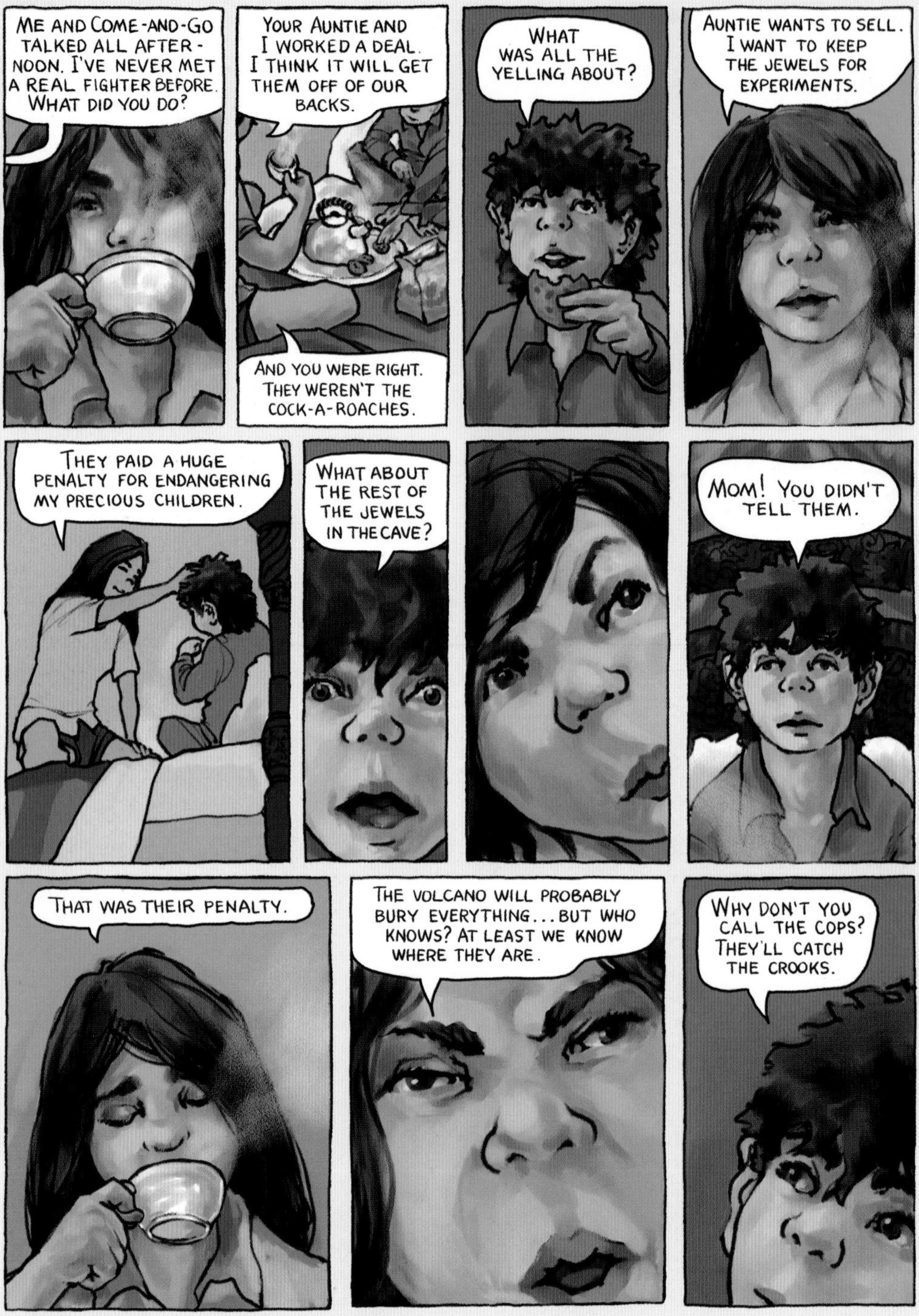
ME AND COME-AND-GO TALKED ALL AFTER-NOON. I'VE NEVER MET A REAL FIGHTER BEFORE. WHAT DID YOU DO?
YOUR AUNTIE AND I WORKED A DEAL. I THINK IT WILL GET THEM OFF OF OUR BACKS.
AND YOU WERE RIGHT. THEY WEREN'T THE COCK-A-ROACHES.
WHAT WAS ALL THE YELLING ABOUT?
AUNTIE WANTS TO SELL. I WANT TO KEEP THE JEWELS FOR EXPERIMENTS.
THEY PAID A HUGE PENALTY FOR ENDANGERING MY PRECIOUS CHILDREN.
WHAT ABOUT THE REST OF THE JEWELS IN THE CAVE?
MOM! YOU DIDN'T TELL THEM.
THAT WAS THEIR PENALTY.
THE VOLCANO WILL PROBABLY BURY EVERYTHING... BUT WHO KNOWS? AT LEAST WE KNOW WHERE THEY ARE.
WHY DON'T YOU CALL THE COPS? THEY'LL CATCH THE CROOKS.

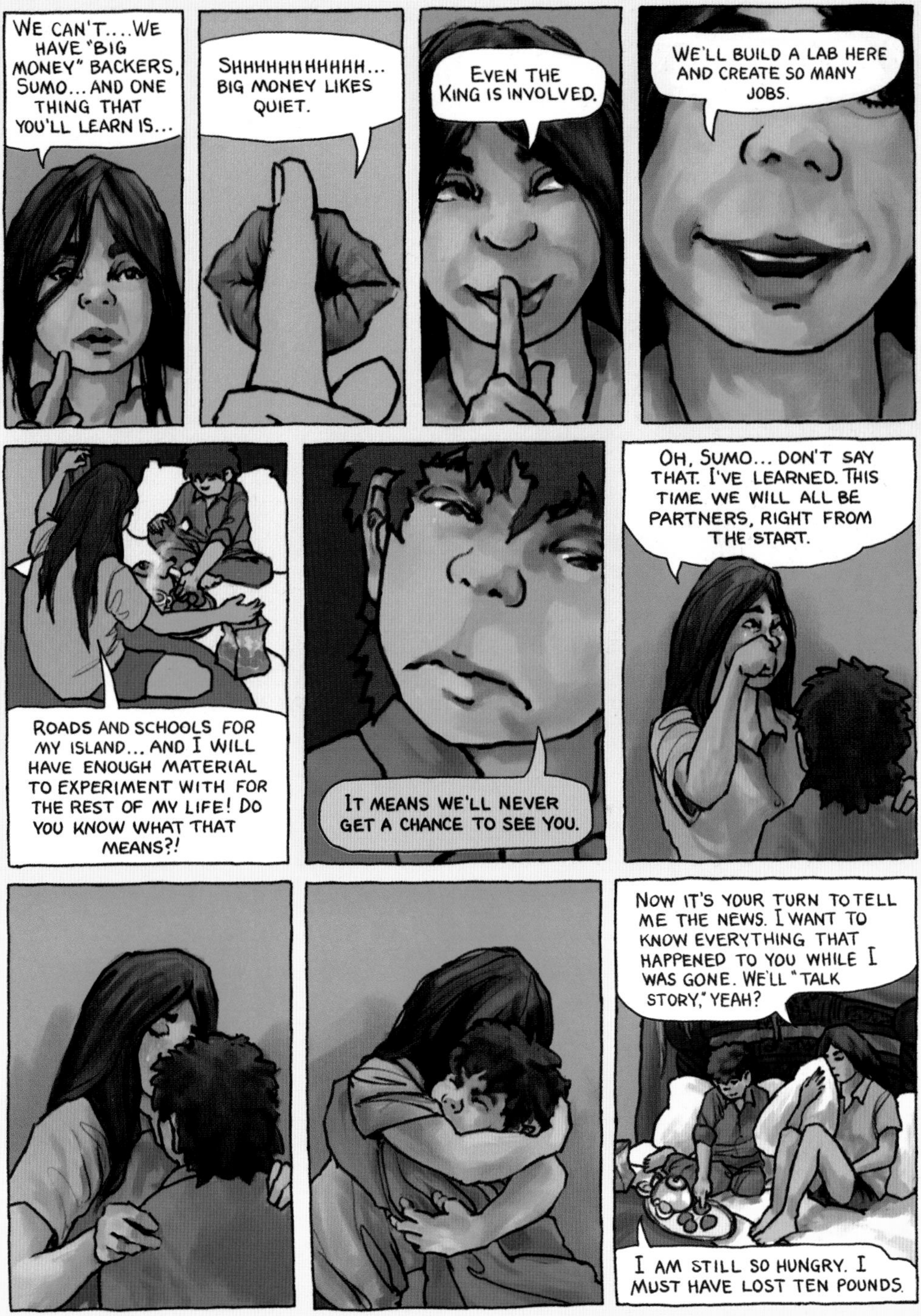
WE CAN'T.... WE HAVE "BIG MONEY" BACKERS, SUMO... AND ONE THING THAT YOU'LL LEARN IS...
SHHHHHHHHHHH... BIG MONEY LIKES QUIET.
EVEN THE KING IS INVOLVED.
WE'LL BUILD A LAB HERE AND CREATE SO MANY JOBS.
ROADS AND SCHOOLS FOR MY ISLAND... AND I WILL HAVE ENOUGH MATERIAL TO EXPERIMENT WITH FOR THE REST OF MY LIFE! DO YOU KNOW WHAT THAT MEANS?!
IT MEANS WE'LL NEVER GET A CHANCE TO SEE YOU.
OH, SUMO... DON'T SAY THAT. I'VE LEARNED. THIS TIME WE WILL ALL BE PARTNERS, RIGHT FROM THE START.
NOW IT'S YOUR TURN TO TELL ME THE NEWS. I WANT TO KNOW EVERYTHING THAT HAPPENED TO YOU WHILE I WAS GONE. WE'LL "TALK STORY," YEAH?
I AM STILL SO HUNGRY. I MUST HAVE LOST TEN POUNDS.

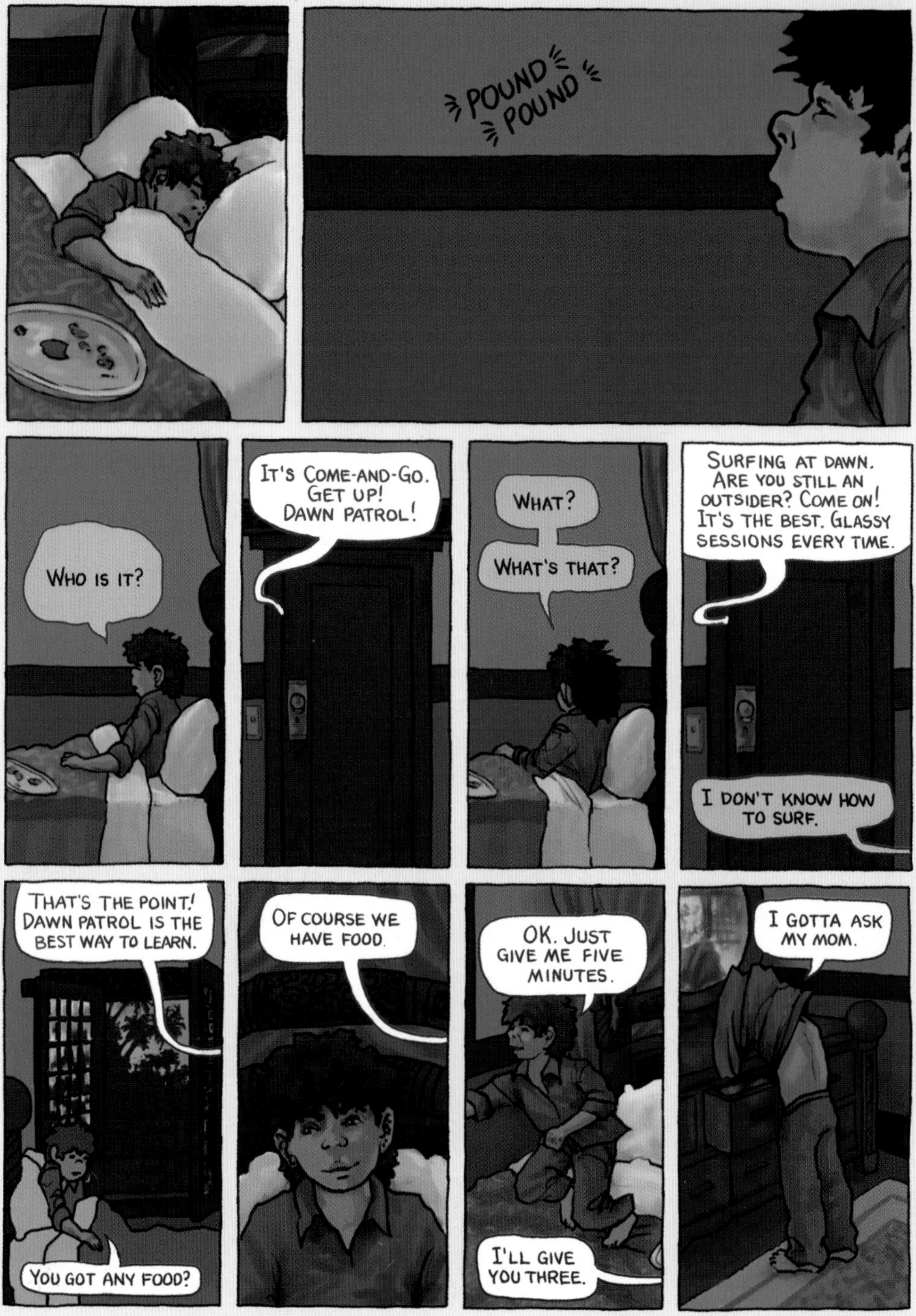
POUND
POUND
WHO IS IT?
IT'S COME-AND-GO. GET UP! DAWN PATROL!
WHAT?
WHAT'S THAT?
SURFING AT DAWN. ARE YOU STILL AN OUTSIDER? COME ON! IT'S THE BEST. GLASSY SESSIONS EVERY TIME.
I DON'T KNOW HOW TO SURF.
THAT'S THE POINT! DAWN PATROL IS THE BEST WAY TO LEARN.
YOU GOT ANY FOOD?
OF COURSE WE HAVE FOOD.
OK. JUST GIVE ME FIVE MINUTES.
I'LL GIVE YOU THREE.
I GOTTA ASK MY MOM.

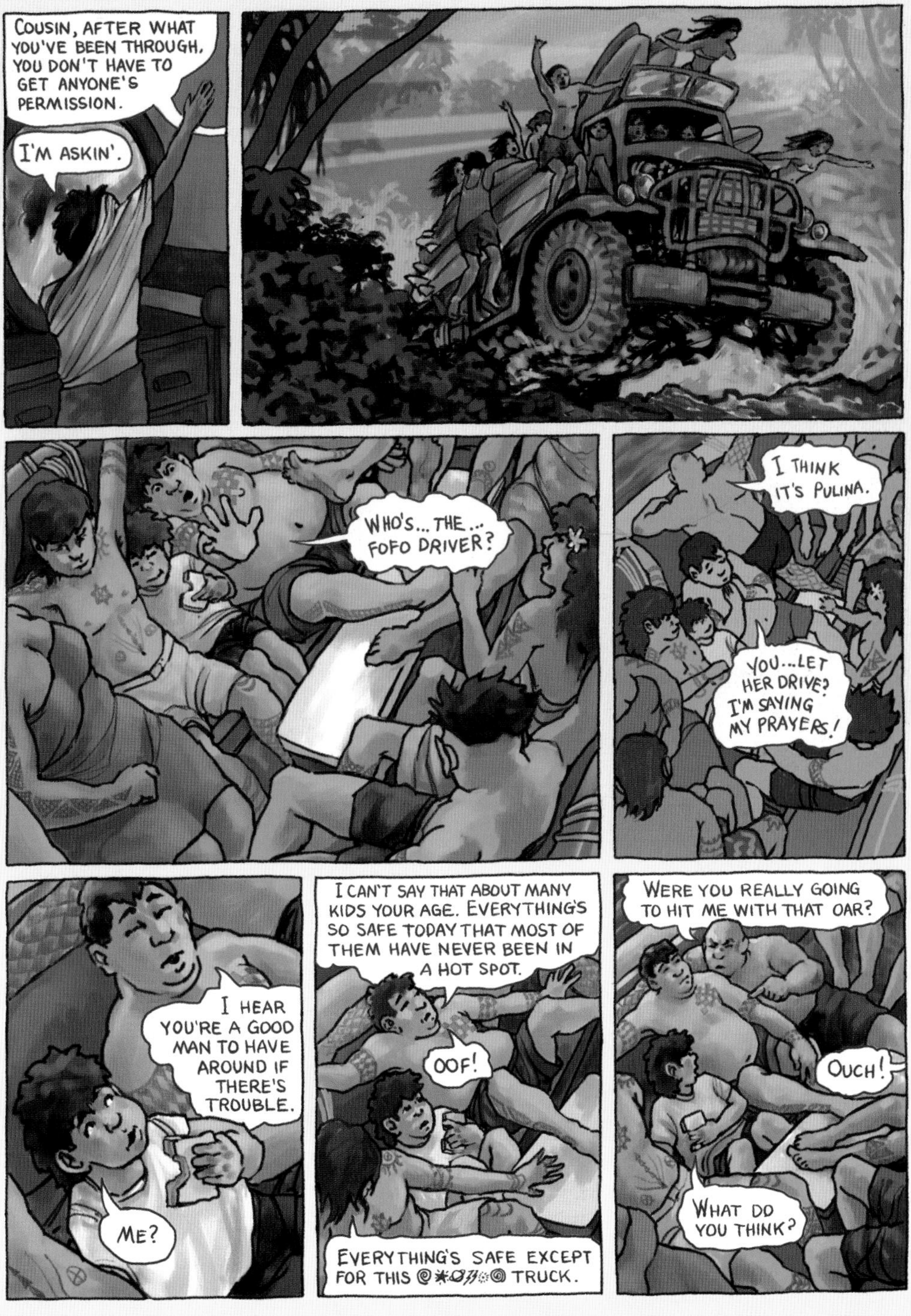
COUSIN, AFTER WHAT YOU'VE BEEN THROUGH, YOU DON'T HAVE TO GET ANYONE'S PERMISSION.
I'M ASKIN'.
WHO'S... THE... FOFO DRIVER?
I THINK IT'S PULINA.
YOU...LET HER DRIVE? I'M SAYING MY PRAYERS!
I HEAR YOU'RE A GOOD MAN TO HAVE AROUND IF THERE'S TROUBLE.
ME?
I CAN'T SAY THAT ABOUT MANY KIDS YOUR AGE. EVERYTHING'S SO SAFE TODAY THAT MOST OF THEM HAVE NEVER BEEN IN A HOT SPOT.
OOF!
EVERYTHING'S SAFE EXCEPT FOR THIS @*@!!@ TRUCK.
WERE YOU REALLY GOING TO HIT ME WITH THAT OAR?
OUCH!
WHAT DO YOU THINK?

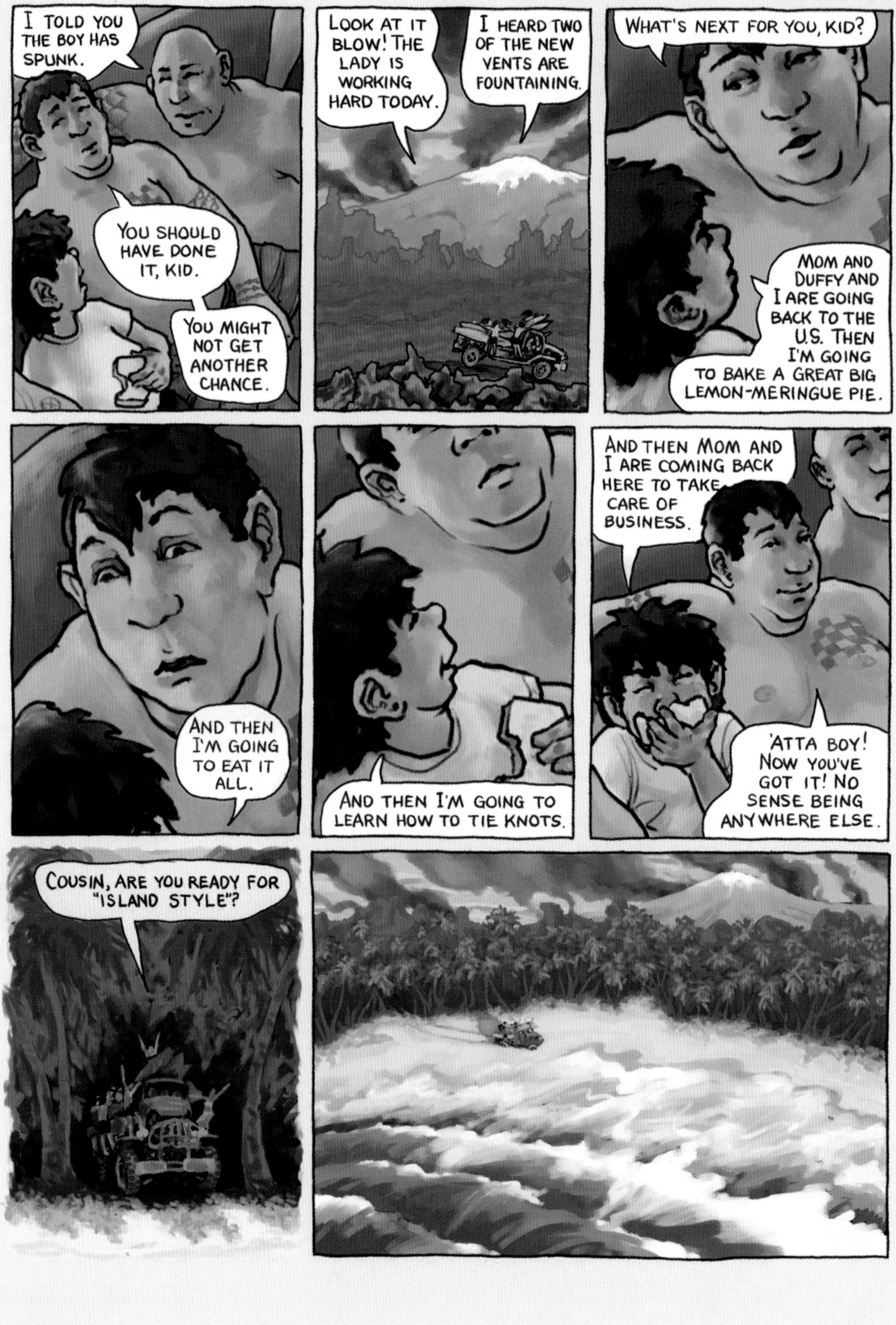
I TOLD YOU THE BOY HAS SPUNK.
YOU SHOULD HAVE DONE IT, KID.
YOU MIGHT NOT GET ANOTHER CHANCE.
LOOK AT IT BLOW! THE LADY IS WORKING HARD TODAY.
I HEARD TWO OF THE NEW VENTS ARE FOUNTAINING.
WHAT'S NEXT FOR YOU, KID?
MOM AND DUFFY AND I ARE GOING BACK TO THE U.S. THEN I'M GOING TO BAKE A GREAT BIG LEMON-MERINGUE PIE.
AND THEN I'M GOING TO EAT IT ALL.
AND THEN I'M GOING TO LEARN HOW TO TIE KNOTS.
AND THEN MOM AND I ARE COMING BACK HERE TO TAKE CARE OF BUSINESS.
'ATTA BOY! NOW YOU'VE GOT IT! NO SENSE BEING ANYWHERE ELSE.
COUSIN, ARE YOU READY FOR "ISLAND STYLE"?

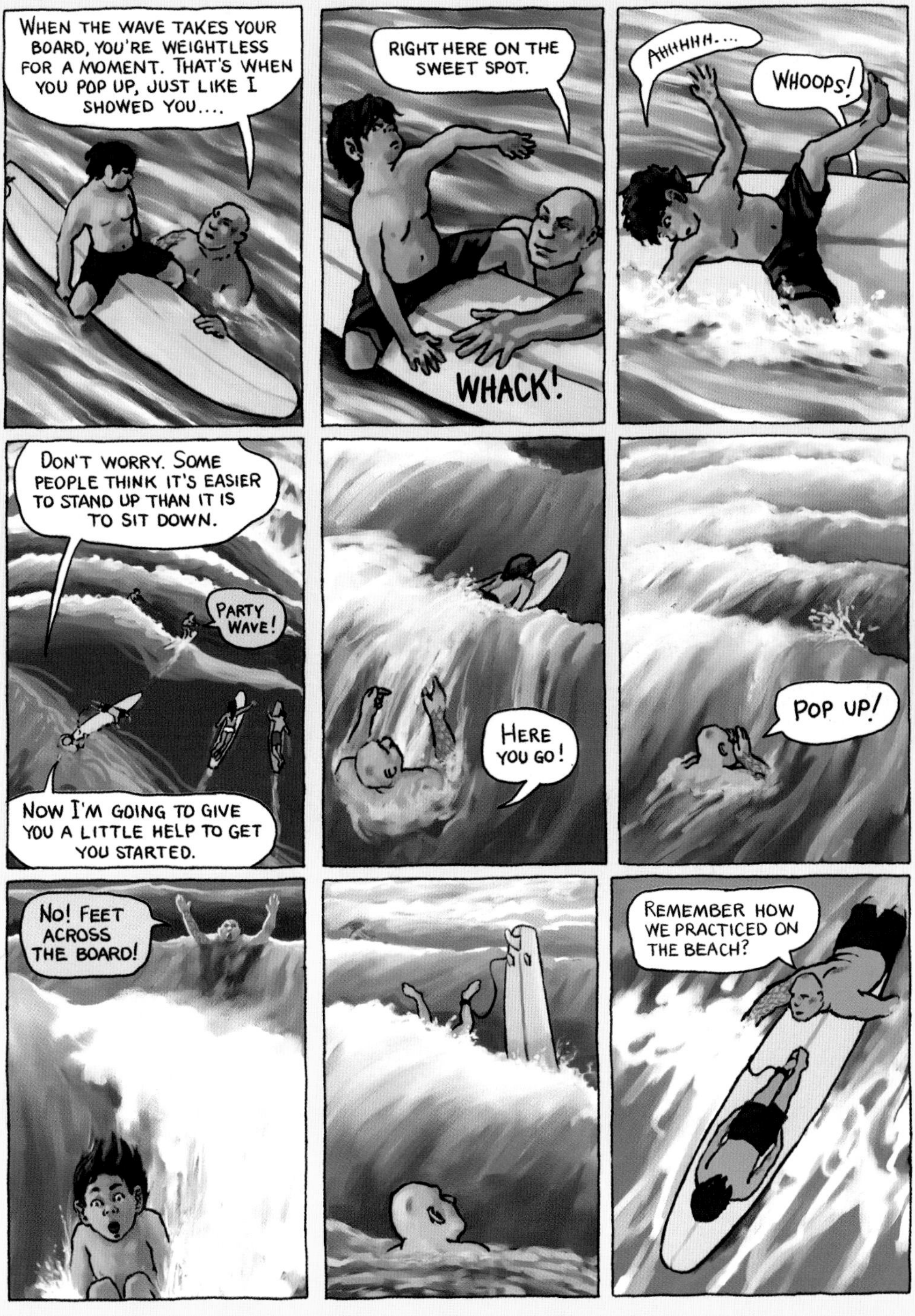
WHEN THE WAVE TAKES YOUR BOARD, YOU'RE WEIGHTLESS FOR A MOMENT. THAT'S WHEN YOU POP UP, JUST LIKE I SHOWED YOU....
RIGHT HERE ON THE SWEET SPOT.
WHACK!
AHHHHH....
WHOOPS!
DON'T WORRY. SOME PEOPLE THINK IT'S EASIER TO STAND UP THAN IT IS TO SIT DOWN.
PARTY WAVE!
NOW I'M GOING TO GIVE YOU A LITTLE HELP TO GET YOU STARTED.
HERE YOU GO!
POP UP!
NO! FEET ACROSS THE BOARD!
REMEMBER HOW WE PRACTICED ON THE BEACH?

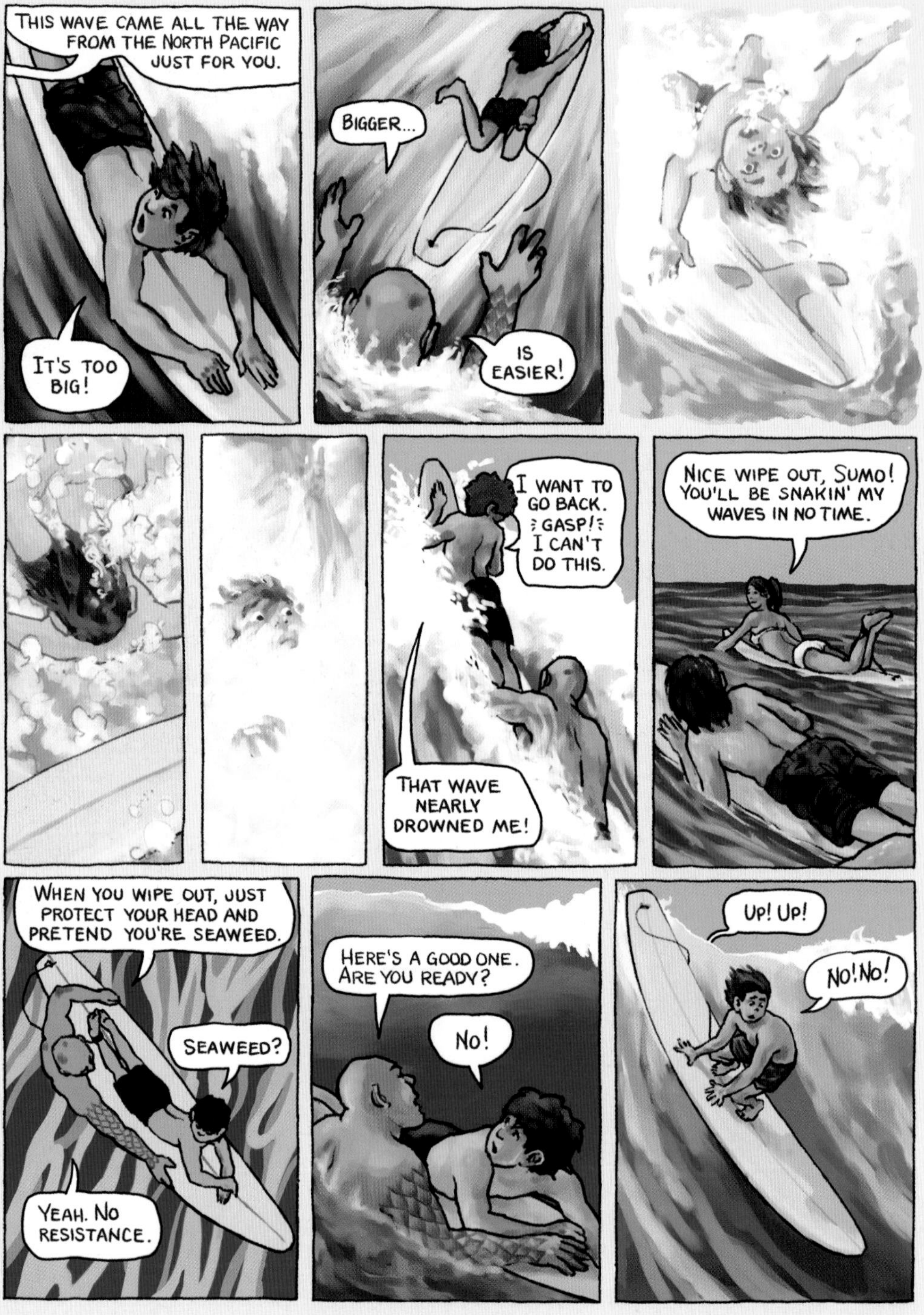
THIS WAVE CAME ALL THE WAY FROM THE NORTH PACIFIC JUST FOR YOU.
IT'S TOO BIG!
BIGGER...
IS EASIER!
I WANT TO GO BACK. GASP! I CAN'T DO THIS.
THAT WAVE NEARLY DROWNED ME!
NICE WIPE OUT, SUMO! YOU'LL BE SNAKIN' MY WAVES IN NO TIME.
WHEN YOU WIPE OUT, JUST PROTECT YOUR HEAD AND PRETEND YOU'RE SEAWEED.
SEAWEED?
YEAH. NO RESISTANCE.
HERE'S A GOOD ONE. ARE YOU READY?
NO!
UP! UP!
NO! NO!

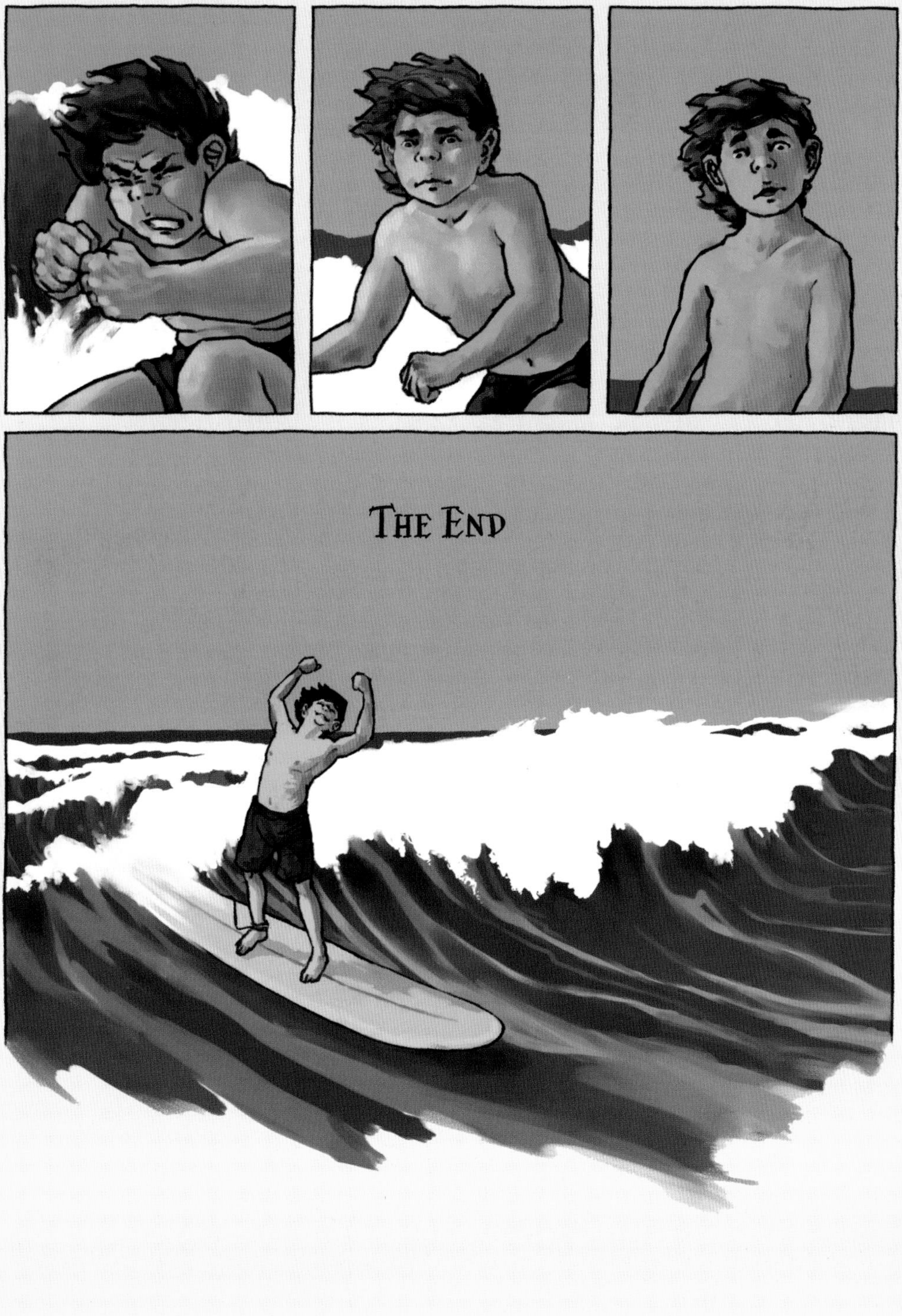
THE END

THIS BOOK IS DEDICATED TO AUDREY WOOD.

This book was originally published in hardcover by the Blue Sky Press in 2008.

ISBN 978-0-439-72674-0

10 9 8 7 6 5 4 3 2 1   12 13 14 15 16

Printed in China   38
First Scholastic paperback printing, June 2012